Praise for

ICE SONG

by Kirsten Imani Kasai

**SELECTED FOR *SCHOOL LIBRARY JOURNAL*'S
2009 BEST ADULT BOOKS FOR HIGH SCHOOL STUDENTS**

Winner San Diego Book Award for Best Science Fiction & Fantasy

"I'm loving it—it's like furry sexy biopunk arctic witchery."
—ANNALEE NEWITZ, i09.com

"Kasai's debut is a boldly adventurous tale depicting a richly detailed world." —*Booklist*

"Reminiscent of Ursula Le Guin's paradigm-shattering *The Left Hand of Darkness*, this piercingly moving story belongs in most fantasy collections." —*Library Journal*

"*Ice Song* is a near-perfect combination of fantasy, great storytelling and social commentary." —*Philadelphia Gay News*

"Those looking for a powerful and provocative female voice in their fantasy reading fare should definitely pick up this stellar debut . . . A deeply lyrical and sublimely haunting narrative powers this intriguing fusion of science fiction, fantasy and subtle social commentary." —PAUL GOAT ALLEN

"A debut notable for its vivid intensity." —*Kirkus*

BY KIRSTEN IMANI KASAI

Ice Song

Tattoo

TATTOO

TATTOO

KIRSTEN IMANI KASAI

BALLANTINE BOOKS

NEW YORK

A Del Rey Trade Paperback Original

Copyright © 2011 by Kirsten Imani Kasai

Published in the United States by Del Rey, an imprint of The Random House Publishing Group, a division of Random House, Inc., New York.

DEL REY is a registered trademark and the Del Rey colophon is a trademark of Random House, Inc.

LIBRARY OF CONGRESS CATALOGING-IN-PUBLICATION DATA

Kasai, Kirsten Imani.
Tattoo / Kirsten Imani Kasai.
p. cm.
ISBN 978-0-345-50882-9 (pbk.)
ISBN 978-0-345-52636-6 (ebook)
I. Title.
PS3611.A7849T38 2011
813'.6—dc22   2010049241

Printed in the United States of America

www.delreybooks.com

9 8 7 6 5 4 3 2 1

Book design by Christopher M. Zucker

For my mother

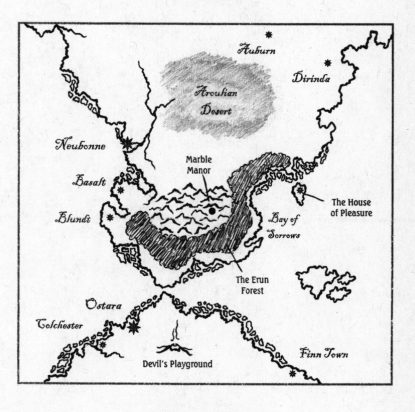

MORIGI FAMILY TREE

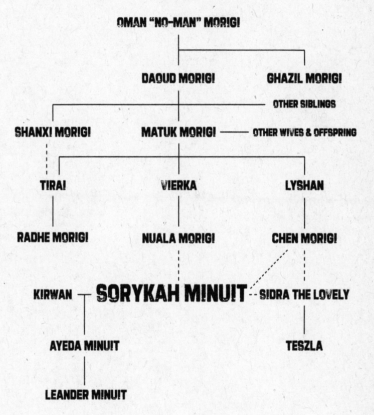

OMAN "NO-MAN" MORIGI

DAOUD MORIGI   GHAZIL MORIGI

OTHER SIBLINGS

SHANXI MORIGI   MATUK MORIGI —— OTHER WIVES & OFFSPRING

TIRAI   VIERKA   LYSHAN

RADHE MORIGI   NUALA MORIGI   CHEN MORIGI

KIRWAN — SORYKAH MINUIT -- SIDRA THE LOVELY

AYEDA MINUIT   TESZLA

LEANDER MINUIT

Characters

Ayeda	(Eye-ada)	*Sorykah's daughter, a Trader*
Barret Scot/		
Butterscotch		*scholarship boy and Chen's hired thug*
Bodkin		*company finance administrator*
Carac	(Care-ak)	*a par-wolf, Sidra's second-in-command*
Chen		*son of Matuk Morigi, heir to Tirai Industries*
Diabolo		*a demon*
Dunya	(Dun-ya)	*the dog-faced girl, Matuk's former housemaid*
Egil	(Egg-il)	*an octameroon, Rava's cousin*
Farouj	(Fa-rooj)	*a rebel of the tribe Qa'a'nesh*
Gowyr	(Gow-er)	*Yetive's son*
Hans my		
Hedgehog		*Erun resident, Sidra's friend*
Jandi	(Jan-dee)	*a tattoo artist*
Jerusha	(Jer-oo-sha)	*holy mother, protectress of women and children*
Kirwan	(Ker-win)	*father of Sorykah's children*
Leander	(Lee-ann-der)	*Sorykah's son, a Trader*
Matuk	(Ma-took)	*Head of Tirai Industries, Chen's father*
Mehemija	(Meh-heh-me-ya)	*Farouj's daughter*
Nels		*Sorykah's nanny, a devotee of Jerusha*
Nuala	(New-ah-la)	*daughter of Matuk the Collector*
Nunn		*bursar aboard the Nimbus*
Oona	(Ooh-na)	*an elderly Siguelandic washerwoman*

Pertana	(Per-tahn-a)	*a somatic bombmaker*
Qa'a'nesh	(Ka-ah-nesh)	*a tribe in the Aroulian desert*
Rava	(Rah-va)	*an octameroon*
Reginald		
Woolley-Wallace/		
The Plaid Lad		*Chen's hired thug*
Sidra the Lovely		*Queen of the Erun Forest, guardian of somatics*
Soryk	(Sor-ik)	*male alter of Sorykah*
Sorykah	(Sor-ik-ah)	*a Trader, female primary of Soryk*
Tarumi	(Ta-room-ee)	*son of the sun, a god*
Teszla	(Tez-la)	*Sidra's child*
Tjaler	(Taller)	*a somatic bombmaker*
Töti	(Toe-tee)	*an octameroon, Rava's cousin*
Udor	(Oo-dor)	*a somatic bombmaker*
Ur	(Oo-rrr)	*daughter of the sky, a goddess*
Vierka	(Vee-air-kah)	*Nuala's mother, Matuk's second wife*
Yetive	(Yeh-teev)	*a midwife in the Erun forest city*
Zarina	(Za-ree-na)	*Chen's girlfriend, Sorykah's mortal enemy*
oenathe	(oh-nath-ee)	*a restorative herb*
somatic		*human genetic variant with animal characteristics*
t'naq	(t' nok)	*energy-spirit*

Every desire, however innocent, grows dangerous
as by long indulgence it becomes ascendant in the mind.

— SAMUEL JOHNSON

TO DINE ON THE
FLESH OF THE DEAD

TARUMI AND UR WERE BORN to mothers in the same household. There, the kings and queens of heaven and earth, and of the planets and elements, lived in divine harmony for millennia ruling the seasons, plants, and all beasts that swam, flew, wiggled, and walked. When the gods intermarried, it was according to celestial decree as ordered by Asta, the universal mother. Because the gods were wise, gentle, and obedient, they accepted Asta's will and kept to it and were peaceful.

The mothers of Tarumi and Ur were cousins and companions of childhood and the heart. So close, the gods said, they were as womb sisters or two branches from the same strong tree.

Everyone knew that Tarumi's mother had a sunspot in her eye. This tiny speck of gold marked her as the sun's chosen consort, next in line to receive his seed and birth the son who would succeed him. They did not know that Ur's mother also had a sunspot hidden behind her pupil where its light filled her vision and blinded her. With one good eye, she could read and play, and sew fine, close stitches, so none had ever suspected and the poor girl, through no fault of her own, knew no differently and so could not complain.

When these maidens reached womanhood and marriageable age, the crone of Asta's temple augured a hand-fasting between the sun and mother of Tarumi. She was marked—it was clear to see who was to be her intended, but the fate of Ur's mother was less certain. Asta remained silent despite prayers, entreaties, and spinning dancers who flung droplets of blood into the ceremonial fire to summon her and seek her aid.

The mother of Tarumi was married in a splendid ceremony. Dressed in gold, her long hair plaited and stitched to her head so that it should not catch fire when the heat of her new husband inflamed her, she walked the sacred path. That night, the sun came to her and gave her a son.

Certain that Asta would soon announce her betrothal, Ur's mother waited patiently, for she was ripe and comely, and eager for the marriage bed. Yet Asta remained silent, despite another whirling circle of dancers, despite the blood shed into the fire and a young girl's pleas.

The gods began to talk. They suggested, politely, that Asta had chosen her to play the venerated role of crone, for at all times the holy triumvirate dwelled in a sacred house—a maiden, who must serve the goddess for one year; a mother, who must serve for twenty; and a crone, whose entire adult life was designed to serve Asta and, who like the maiden, would remain intact during her service, sealed like a tomb. The present crone was ancient and withered, her eyes veiled by time, her joints gnarled, her skin drawn like a fig left for weeks in the sun.

There would be no marriage bed, no ceremony, and no child swelling this girl's womb. This did not suit.

Blind in one eye, likewise blinded by the bleakness of her fate, Ur's mother fled the house of her birth. She scaled the highest mountain—a craggy, windswept peak slick with ice, glaring and white in the sunlight—raised her arms to the sky, and begged intercession.

Sky—capricious, inconstant, and given to whimsy—saw the golden sunspot in this girl's eye. He knew that she was marked as the sun's property, but knew also that Asta would only permit the sun a single human consort once every thousand years. He also knew that the sun, fearing the early death of his consort to childbirth and the loss of his heir (as had happened the previous cycle, when his new wife succumbed to the sugar crystallizing her blood and died with his child unborn), had marked this girl in secret.

Sky cloaked himself in sunlight and came down to join Ur's mother on the mountaintop.

"I am the sun," said he, grinning at the success of his deceit. "Though Asta decreed your womb sister my chosen bride, it is you who I choose for myself. You whom I have watched, you who enslaves my heart."

Thinking him the sun, she laid down for him, hungry to taste the sweet pleasures of the marriage bed. He possessed her and filled her belly with Sky, not Sun. Filled her with his moodiness, trickster ways, and fickleness. When she opened her eyes, he was gone, flown away laughing and delighting in his cleverness.

Nine months later, Tarumi's mother and Ur's mother gave birth on the same day, at the same hour, in the same household.

Tarumi, the sun's true heir, was red-skinned, golden-haired, and bright-eyed. Ur, the sky's child, had gray skin, wispy white hair, and blue eyes.

Furious that mortals had maligned her divine order, Asta banished Ur's mother and her child to the Sigue, a frozen pole at the end of the world. There they dwelt together until the mother passed into the ground. Ur became a woman and vowed revenge on the goddess who banished them to that lonely island of ice and snow, inhabited only by the demon Diabolo, slumbering deep within a smoking cleft in the earth.

Ur's rage was too great to be contained within the gods' world. It was a terrible fury, a storm that blew and whipped the sea to a frenzy and roused the dormant demon from his fiery lair.

Diabolo had slept through eons of earth change. When he woke, shaking off centuries of ash and magma, he found the surface and the woman who had summoned him, a gray-skinned creature with hair the color of new-fallen snow and eyes like chips of sea ice. His demon heart, long dormant like the volcano in which he slept, awakened.

Ur wanted revenge. She promised to wed Diabolo after he had flown to the site of her conception and punished Sky, ripped open his guts with lightning, seared him with smoke, and burned him with hot lava. Left to smolder like hot coals banked by embers during the endless winter of her banishment, Ur's rage ignited.

"Tear down Sky," she commanded. "Strip away his airy blue garments and reveal the sun to me so that I might spit in the coward's face who marked us as his failsafe, for whom my mother was no more than a dish to catch what overflowed the bowl."

Smitten, Diabolo did as asked. He flew to the mountaintop, rent the sky, and tore the color from the roof of the world. Believing that he also captured Ur's affections, Diabolo captured Sun and imprisoned him in a barren and lightless cave tucked deep within a mountain crevasse.

Without the sun, the Sigue grew darker and colder still, became a wintry haven for snowdrifts and pillars of ice. The winds ceased to blow; the sea froze into fields of sharp peaks and treacherous valleys. Ice crept thieflike into the houses of the gods, making them shiver and shake and fret themselves in circles.

Grown into his beauty, Tarumi struck out to find his father the sun and restore order to the world, but Tarumi was pampered and kind. He did not know his way and wandered in the perpetual twilight, seeking a glimmer of his father's light and warmth but finding none.

Lost and alone, Tarumi struggled across the far reaches of the world. When he found the Sigue, he was shriveled and dull-witted from cold. Ice rimmed his eyes and mouth; his red skin was pale and his golden hair lank and lusterless.

Ur saw the stranger and her heart quickened with fear, for she was innocent of men and fearful of Diabolo's reproach. Tarumi flung himself at Ur's feet, and when they looked into each other's eyes, the sunspots embedded therein flared and blinded them to everything but each other.

Tarumi regained his brightness. Love and desire transformed Ur. She glowed and became translucent as wind and her father Sky. Tarumi's love coursed through his body and poured into his limbs. It seeped from his feet, dripping from his fingers and chin like rain-drops of light to saturate the Sigue's frozen ground. Green leaves sprang up from the hard earth, softened by Tarumi's warmth. The frost-sharpened sea thawed and flowed in great shushing waves. Creatures stirred and buzzed. Flowers budded and popped open in showy displays of pink, crimson, and orange. The volcano sighed and quieted, sunk into deeper dreams. Ur and Tarumi took each other's hands, tasted each other's mouths, and together, their light was dazzling.

Soon, Ur grew fat with child. Just as the clouds swell with rain, grow gray and ponderous and burst within a single afternoon, so did Ur give birth to Tarumi's children: seven red-skinned charmers with bright laughing eyes and white curls, like a cap of snowflakes, upon their tiny heads.

When Diabolo, keeping vigilant watch upon the sun as he waited for Ur to extract her revenge, heard the first child's cry, he flew down from the mountaintop to find Ur and Tarumi making more babies.

Devastated by Ur's treachery, the furious Diabolo strangled gentle Tarumi with his wicked demon's hands and heaped curses upon Ur's children. His words grew spidery legs and hooked barbs, scuttled over to Ur's seven babies, crawled into their throats, and lodged there.

Eight appendages burst forth and rolled out, flapping and puck-ering white suckers. Their human legs shrank and vanished, and

Ur's children flopped helplessly on the sand, gasping for breath as their octopus arms scrabbled on the frosty rime, searching for the sea. Ur fell to the stony beach. She tore her hair, beat her breast, and mourned Tarumi's death with deep breathy wails.

Diabolo covered his ears and spat. The clump of his smoldering mucus divided itself into seven drops as it hit the stones and splashed into the eyes of Ur's cursed children, snuffing out the fading spark of sun nestled within their summer-sky irises. Diabolo's spit was as black as ink and tar-thick. It burrowed deep inside those children, shrouding itself within a tough, keratinous membrane, thrusting and breeding, a foul packet of demon seed.

Ur's children clung to the rocky shore with dimpled human hands even as their tentacles snaked toward the Southern Sea, yearning for the water's touch on their skins, desperate for cold ocean to soothe the curse hung like a burning lantern in their throats.

Ur did scream and thrash, plait her long white hair into a strong, glassy cord to lash Diabolo, but this did not revive Tarumi or cease her children's progress into the sea. When the water closed over her children's heads, Ur—who could not swim nor set toe into the water for fear of drowning—ran along the shoreline, calling their names.

"By force or by will, I shall have you," Diabolo pledged as his iron-nailed fingers closed around Ur's wrist and fleeing ankle.

Did she beg intervention from the skies? Plead with her true father Sky or her false father Sun, to welcome her into the house of the gods and spare her the demon's wrath? No, she cried out to her departed lover Tarumi, summoning him back from the shades.

Rising from its mortal tomb, Tarumi's soul brushed but one of Ur's cloud-thread hairs and filled her with his light. Tarumi's sun-warm caress drew Ur from her fleshy shell, flensed away all skin, bone, and hair to free the sky inside her.

Tarumi, sun, and Ur, sky. She watched him evaporate like mist upon the water, assaulted by morning heat. She saw Diabolo stomp back to his volcano and clamber down inside it, wounded and bitter.

Ur watched the seas shift and stop as Tarumi's blessing faded. The volcano vomited steam and fire and Ur could not arise to join Tarumi, a seam of white and gold lacing together heaven and earth like a broad satin ribbon. Ur could only circle the beach of the Sigue, mournfully roaming the shores and staring out to sea to await the return of her seven lost babes.

Now, it is told that the song of the Sigue is Ur calling home her children. The wind sighs and moans, the ice buckles and groans, rocks clamor and click, and the snow croons a sad lullaby as it blows restless over the stones.

"Come back to me," chants Ur. "Tarumi, my love. Come back to me, my children, my heart. Come back."

Ur sings and her song goads the sleeping demon to recall his misdeed. She disturbs his sleep and ruins his rest. Sigue song does not leave men peaceful. Even the noisy calving bergs rebuke them with Ur's voice and chide Diabolo for his faults.

And the seven children of Tarumi and Ur, sun and sky, both blessed and blighted? They swim in dark waters where no sun shines. Half human, half octopus with eight swarming tentacles and sacs bursting with Diabolo's poisonous mucus, they have become children of the night: ancient, eternal, and silent. They cluster together for comfort, seeking the shelter of ice caves and rocky hollows. Had Diabolo not quenched the light in their eyes, they could find their way to the surface where the water is the same cool gray as Ur's skin. They would hear her song, a funeral dirge played with symphonic precision by Sigue ice sheets, pealing and tinging in concert.

Diabolo lingers within his nocturne, and his curse, forged with links of rage and vengeance, remains strong. Ur keens with the voice of the wind. Diabolo's spit is a hook in her children's guts, tugging them away from the sun toward Hell. The children of Ur have no peace.

TATTOO

1

AN ECONOMY OF WORDS

WHEN SHE FIRST REALIZED she was pregnant, Queen Sidra the Lovely decided that her child would never be safe in a world with the Morigi family in it. Oman No-Man's many descendants had been harmless—except for one. Bad seed Matuk the Collector had been an anomaly, but it was his genetic line that concerned her. He had selected one child from each of his wives to bear the brunt of his will and uphold family law. Radhe was first but she had come to a sad end, stricken with a somatic blight and transformed into a monster. Abandoned by the father who'd murdered her mother, Radhe haunted the Erun Forest for years, prowling the perimeter of Matuk's grounds as the dreaded Wood Beast. He'd killed her eventually, her death the result of some foul "cure" administered on the tips of poisoned arrows. Poor Radhe now rotted on the loam, a feast for beetles and the enormous sooty ravens that descended in spiraling hordes to peck at her carcass, their whirring wings blotting out the milky spring sunshine.

Next in line was Nuala, who had disappeared years ago. There was some history of her at the university in Dirinda, but she'd withdrawn during her third year and no one had seen her since. Cream-cheeked Chen rose to the top, basking in his father's attention for a year or two before Matuk became trapped in his white marble mansion and his affection was damned like a river choked with stones.

Chen Morigi was the favored son whose name would open doors and coffers. He'd made such a show of his failed romance with Sidra! He wore his rejection like a hairshirt—a public suffering designed to elicit pity from gullible women who wanted only to salve his tender heart. Like his father, Chen did not care about restoring the rights of the country's indigent somatics. A desire to make money and to indulge in any available sin smothered whatever genuine feeling he had. Sidra's appeals to him had failed. She'd watched him sink deeper into a morass of corruption and knew his snubs to be deliberate. Chen's debauchery fueled her rage. Like a glib worm in a barrel of apples, he spoiled everything he touched.

If only Soryk would come back! Then she was certain everything would be all right, but days slipped by and he did not appear. She'd not believe him safe until she held him in her arms. What a glorious and triumphant return it would be! Soryk had changed the world by dispatching a most loathed enemy. She could double her strength by crowning him king of the Erun Forest. His antler coronet would be shorter, naturally, and his rulings subject to her prior approval—at least until he'd demonstrated his capability with the scepter. Beside him, she could better face the reports of grisly dismemberments increasing in frequency and absurdity and a growing drug trade that claimed her best agents. Together they would become a fist to smash all resistance and crush Tirai Industries in its grip.

Sidra stopped walking and crouched to catch her breath. Her swollen womb bore down on her hips and she was certain that she could hear her pelvic cradle fracturing. The doctors had warned her that she must handle herself as if blown from glass, quite blunt in their assertion that her retrofitted skeleton was not built for childbearing.

Hers had been an experimental surgery and the synthetic marrow in her bones could never heal a break. Giving birth would almost certainly cause her a mortal injury.

She had always been co careful—seeds were not planted; cells did not divide. Call it fate, destiny, or simply bad luck, Soryk's arrow had hit its mark. The uterus elongated its neck during orgasm, straining downward like the beak of a honey-sipping bird to draw in seminal fluid—how her little pink pear had flexed and quivered inside her, thrilled by the oddity of sex with her very own Trader, a human man, if only temporarily. The pregnancy was a grim gift—this child the product of a chemically induced eroticism—Sidra taking Sorykah's tart tongue into her mouth and beckoning Soryk with poetry and kisses like sweet, silver-bloomed damsons. She'd whispered Rossetti in Soryk's ear after his change: "Did you miss me? Come and kiss me. Never mind my bruises, hug me, kiss me, suck my juices. Squeezed from goblin fruits for you, goblin pulp and goblin dew. Eat me, drink me, love me . . . make much of me."

Sidra had indicated the carousal in the great hall and said, "For your sake I have braved the glen and had to do with goblin merchant men."

Thoughts of goblins, even those as attractive as Chen, made her shiver now. It had been a mistake to come out here alone. The twilight forest loomed around her. Once-sweet pines and cedars waved threatening branches, and clouds gulped down the sun. Moment by moment, the specter of death drew closed its cloak until safety and joy were naught more than the echoes of dead stars. Sidra feared for her life and the bloody dénouement creeping ever closer.

"Carac!" Her voice was reedy and insubstantial. She hadn't seen him for hours, but his habit of trailing her ensured that he would be near. She called again but only the pines responded. That noise again—surely it was the sound of her skeleton splitting inside her skin, or far bracken snapping beneath a careless tread. Sidra fished a wooden whistle from her pocket. Carac hated its call, a piercing and urgent thing that only he could hear. It stung his ears and filled his head with the drone of bumblebees, but she needed him. She blew and Carac appeared, wild-eyed with panic and pain.

"What have you been doing?" Sidra was aghast at the sight of him, bare-chested, foamy with sweat, smears of fur and what she presumed to be blood caking his forearms and chin. She'd never seen him thus, so careful had he been to hide the signs of his occasional slaughters.

"You summoned me, my lovely." He rubbed his hands against his pant legs, as if wiping away his startlingly human expression of guilt.

"I did." Sidra hesitated, reluctant to admit her panic to the bloodied par-wolf before her. "I was frightened. It was nothing. A silly daydream, that's all."

Carac's lolling tongue dripped a viscous dirty slime and Sidra remembered all the long winter nights when that agile red muscle had lapped over the hills and dales of her body. She shivered beneath Carac's feral gaze. She had never doubted him before, but today the forest was the gloomy hunting ground of ghosts and every certainty was in question.

"What do you hear from the cities?" she asked. "Any news of Soryk?"

Carac shook his head. "Nothing yet, but the infestation is spreading, my queen. I suggest we repel it by sealing our borders and barring all travel."

"That would mean we could no longer offer refuge to somatics fleeing the north. No, I cannot do that," Sidra said. "Our Neubonne agent says poison soaks the streets, blue and toxic beneath an odor of flowers. Every little pleasure house and bar is a tap for the stuff. Bluing is hard to resist and easy to buy, and the ink trade intensifies along with it. You know how vulnerable we are to substances not of our blood."

Opium had swept though the Sigue some years earlier, leaving many somatics addicted and ill. Sidra had been unable to treat them herself, and she knew the damage done by it. Matuk's doing—this trafficking of drugs and somatic bodies.

Carac said, "I saw Jodhi and Monarch heading for the trading markets in Basalt."

"Did you ask about Soryk?"

"Jodhi couldn't spare a kind word for him, but Monarch told me that the Collector's marble manor has burned to the ground. He and Jodhi took some of the piked heads to sell. Not to worry, my lovely, the heads are safe at home. You may dispense them as you like."

"Good lad, Carac. You always know what to do."

"My lovely, there is one other thing." Carac hated to arouse her ire, but her anger would be greater if she discovered he'd kept information from her. "Digi-reels in the Neubonne pleasure houses show a Trader's change . . . Sorykah's change."

Sidra halted, her eyes blazing. "There's only one place where she could've been filmed, and he gains by it! Chen's depravity is boundless!" Sidra ground her fist into her open palm. "So, he profits fourfold. Why is he so gluttonous? Can he not be satisfied with his father's empire?"

"There are rumors of internal fractures within the Company. If Tirai Industries is divided equally among all the Morigis, Chen shall inherit but a fraction of it. He will lose his funds."

"Then he'll have to work and make his own way for the first time ever. Ha!" Sidra barked. "That improves my mood a bit." Sidra's attention dispersed, hopes of Soryk's return dancing in her head. They reached the hidden entrance to one of the lesser tunnels. Carac hoisted a creaking, well-concealed door and held aside hanging roots as she entered. Shadowy and cool, the tunnel smelled faintly of damp earth and vegetation.

Sidra shed her cloak and rubbed her hands in anticipation. She would derive even more pleasure from ruining Chen now that she knew the extent of his betrayal. Sidra's agents would plant the bombs and light the fuses. Mechanical spiders would descend on synthetic silk, and Tirai Industries' fossil water plant would explode in a blast of sand and smoke. She would leave him with nothing, and then he would understand what it meant to depend on the mercy of others for his survival. Perhaps he would even come to the Erun city, his fortunes spoilt, to apologize for his earlier and ongoing stupidities. She cackled with glee and savored his forthcoming fall.

DAY ONE

LONG SILENCED, THE ERUN FOREST awoke from decades of slumber to rejoice in its liberation. Wood spirits crawled, dug, and tunneled from piney cemetery plots to emerge squinting and trembling in a new dawn. Insects erupted from egg sacs, cocoons, and the damp crevices that housed them to stretch their wings and flash their colors. Massive moths blundered through the wood on feathery wings. Cedars spontaneously generated songbirds among their boughs, chirping riots of electric blue, crimson, and yellow. Ravens besieged the trees and at dusk, horned owls swooped overhead with wiggling grubbits pinched in their beaks.

Gleeful in their triumph, Sorykah and her retinue—her nine-month-old twins Ayeda and Leander, their nanny Nels, Kika the sled dog, and Matuk the Collector's former housemaid, Dunya the dog-faced girl—had with every step grown lighter and more carefree. For two days, heat from the burning manor warmed their backs as they fled its conflagration. Sooty plumes climbed the sky as the inferno billowed, announcing the obliteration of the tyrant Matuk the Collector. Fire had quickly eviscerated the manor, heaping marble slag and charred beams on the salt-crusted spring meadow, verdant after recent rains. The greasy remains of somatics whom Dunya had abandoned in their dungeon cells bubbled beneath the still-warm earth, roasting in their own fat.

Each considering only her luck, her fate, and her weariness, the women pressed on. The path to the Erun city eluded them. The forest was a vast tract of towering trees, dense underbrush, and confusing twists and turns. It was easy to wander in circles, to turn and turn again, thinking oneself found but becoming even more lost. The travel was worst for Sorykah, who nursed two children and suffered constant headaches from thirst and hunger. A week after she'd thrust her Magar blade into the chest of the man who'd taken her children, the feel of it still lingered in her hands: the crunch of brittle bone and the slight vibration that traveled along the length of her blade from his beating heart to her fingers—frantic, then still. Righteous retribution was hers; she ought to tuck it in her cheek like a sweet-and-sour ball to enjoy at leisure. *It should feel better,* she mused, *shouldn't it?* But worries twitched in the back of her mind, and a sense of incompletion sapped the pleasure of her revenge.

As the landscape became more familiar, Sorykah relied on her alter's wisdom for the first time. Soryk had traversed these woods alongside Sidra. He would recognize the well-camouflaged marks that distinguished signposts from ordinary lumps of stone. *You've been here before. Tell me what I'm seeing.*

Initiated by Sidra to unite Soryk/ah's fractured personas, establish awareness between male alter and female primary, and strengthen their communication, the treatment was fledgling and untried. She stumbled between the trees, unsure how much longer she could walk before fainting. Desperation picked at her with sharp claws, pulling apart the threads of her composure. *Talk to me, please! You know what to look for. Show me what I need to see.*

She'd hoped to hear Soryk's voice in her head. Instead it sounded from her throat, rasping and dry, the voice of a re-animant crawling from the grave. "Left between the thickets to find the evergreen glade and the pit."

Nels's and Dunya's stares bored into Sorykah's back as she fumbled toward a stand of trees whose dancing leaves urged silence—*shh, shh*—with each gust of wind.

Born of nightmares and premonitions, her alter's voice was solemn and terrible. It slithered from her mouth to coil in her ears, as cozy as a snake in a rabbit burrow. "Under the trees. Into the pit. Nine times knock to be received."

Sorykah was first to drop into the camouflaged tiger trap and call a warning to the others. Nels lay on her belly to hand down the babies before she slid clumsily over the edge, staining the side of her gown—a taffeta monstrosity Matuk had forced her to wear while she played piano to lull him to sleep—with mud and water made amber by fallen leaves.

Nels called to Dunya. "It's safe! Jump down!"

Dunya circled the pit, snarling. Her tongue dangled from her mouth like a wet pink rag.

"Come on, Dunya!" Nels could not help it. She patted her thighs. "Come on, girl. Jump!"

Dunya leapt like one pushed from behind to nip the meaty strip on Nels's hand between pinkie and wrist, leaving a welt but no blood. "Ye needn't call me like a dog, save I look like one," Dunya cried.

Nels's apology was lost in the flurry of the opening door. Light spilled into the pit. A large and dreadful beast loomed, stiff silver-black hackles tufting across his wolfish neck. A sneer played across his lips and a growl rose in his throat.

"Nice to see you, too." Sorykah swallowed her fear and pushed him aside. "Carac," she said, by way of introduction. To quell Nels's and Dunya's evident panic she added, "It's all right. He looks fierce, but he's very loyal to Sidra and would only harm us at her command. Isn't that right, Carac?"

Corded muscles bunched and quivered beneath his jersey as Carac reluctantly deferred to the guests and let them enter. "She's been waiting for you."

They followed him past a series of doors, each adorned with bric-a-brac scavenged from the surface world. It disconcerted Sorykah to see some bit of junk and hear bells of recognition, however muted, sound in her head or to experience a redundant horror at the sight of a door apparently knitted from human hair. Carac admitted them into a massive, hollowed cedar so big it could comfortably house a herd of elephants. Carved from the pith of the living tree, a circular stairwell rose along the inside wall, widening to create railed platforms for sleeping, eating, and storage. Woodpecker holes in hand-planed walls buffed and oiled to a honeyed shine provided access to light and fresh air.

Carac bellowed up into the swaying height of the tree. An undignified summons for a queen, but one that worked. A woman's head appeared over the edge of a high platform. She squinted at them and waved delightedly. Queen Sidra the Lovely, who seemed naked without her crown of red deer antlers, flew down the stairs with winged feet.

"You're home! You did it!" She launched her body at Sorykah, crushing her in a fierce hug.

Sorykah peeled her off and made introductions. Much praise and exclamation followed as Sorykah, Nels, and Dunya reenacted the story of Matuk's slaughter, their escape, and the fire. Sidra smeared ointment over the stump of Sorykah's severed pinky finger and offered Dunya a permanent place among the Erun's somatic residents, the prospect of which thrilled the poor girl so much that she had to excuse herself from the festivities. Nels wisely followed, taking the children from their mother and leaving Sorykah alone with Sidra, impatient and brimming with voluble concern.

"My heart's been in my throat since you left. Saint Catherine kept watch over you and brought you safely home, just as I requested. It is so good to have you back. Both of you." Sidra's eyes gleamed with desire. She parted her lips and squeezed Sorykah's hand. "I would not ask but I must see him. Please," Sidra begged, anxious for the sight of her lover's face, his touch. "Please change for me."

As if it were a parlor trick Sorykah could perform on command! She squirmed inside her skin. It was too weird, looking Sidra in the eyes after everything they had done together. It had been all right in the House of Pleasure when everyone pranced naked and drooling, and that devil Chen prodded them with his pitchfork, eliciting their compliance and depravity. Sorykah had been high then, didn't Sidra know that? She wormed from Sidra's grasp seeking coolness, restraint.

"Pretty please," Sidra wheedled.

"How can you ask this of me?" Sorykah feigned betrayal. Part of her, Soryk probably, perked up and began to salivate. She ached to say, "No part of me wants you," but it wasn't her that wanted, was it? Woken from sleep, her male alter hungered for life.

Sidra gathered Sorykah's black hair in her hands and pressed her smaller body close. "Didn't I rescue you? Assemble your broken parts? Aren't you better now?"

"Better? You mean speaking in tongues and possessed by devils? That's my recovery?" It was nice to be held, even as Sorykah rebelled against it.

Sidra squeezed her, grinning. "Yes, you speak now. Two-way communication. An improvement over your ignorant silence."

Sorykah grimaced.

"Come on, darling! Admit it! You weren't happy before; you couldn't be."

"Happiness is overrated." Tired, hungry, and very grumpy, Sorykah announced, "I am absolutely wrecked and now you're pestering me for sex and doubting my capacity for joy. Honestly!"

"Pestering you for sex." Sidra smirked, breaking into giggles.

"Not funny! You haven't seen me for ages and the first thing you want to do is get into my alter's trousers." Sorykah was annoyed to be the source of Sidra's mirth.

"Only if he bathes first." Sidra poked Sorykah's arm. "You're very gloomy."

"Wouldn't you be?"

"Yes, I'm being very insensitive. I am terribly grateful to see you here alive and mostly intact, to meet your precious babes and know that this whole ordeal is finished. Now, let us fill your belly with hot food and hear your tale from beginning to end." Sidra called to Carac, "Fetch Hans my Hedgehog and we shall enjoy a feast and good stories."

Hans soon arrived, a short, barrel-shaped bundle of quivering quills, his human face misshaped by beady black eyes and a furred and pointed snout. His little girl's voice trilled nervously in the presence of strangers. Dunya especially seemed to terrify him. His quills bristled and clattered when she neared, nose twitching.

Sidra pushed them together, dog and hedgehog, two natural enemies. "I've been looking for a lady friend for Hans for the longest time, and here she is. *Fait accompli!*" She beamed.

"Is matchmaking one of your duties?" asked Sorykah.

"Naturally! The Erun's residents have charged me with their welfare. That entails caring for the whole person—I attend to matters of the body, mind, and heart. I nurture the political health of this small empire and preserve our democratic process."

"Have you considered that your intense attention might better resemble a dictatorship than a democracy?"

"Absolutely not!" Sidra sniffed at the insult. "We are all free here, whether born so or liberated from the Others' tyranny by our changes."

"You consider the change a form of liberation?" Sorykah was incredulous.

"The change frees us from the strictures of society. Once you have changed, you are no longer restrained by the rules that govern the Others. Their rejection severs the binding cord that kept you muffled and compliant. Living in the surface world is to suffer a smothering embrace, to move like a phantom through a hollow existence, a creature of pretense and fantasy. Sorykah." Sidra leaned in, her expression grave. "Are you certain that Matuk is dead?"

"There's no chance that he could have survived." She wished that she could transmit by telepathy the image of Matuk's body shriveled around the clotted fatal wound to his heart. "Had he managed to live, he surely would have perished in the fire. We were quite thorough in our execution." Sorykah grinned as if relishing the taste of his blood on her teeth. A surge of anxiety swept through her. "You suspect otherwise?"

"There is evidence of a growing threat in the north. Reports of murder and many missing somatics. Disappearances in numbers greater than usual. Some dastardly machinery is stalking and dispatching us, in answer to, or despite the Collector's command." Suspicion was an unanticipated side effect of pregnancy. It warped Sidra's sunny nature, a hormonal rain dance summoning storm clouds of dread and envy.

Sorykah shivered. Would Matuk's family retaliate against her?

As if reading her mind, Sidra said, "They're a villainous lot, but the Morigi clan won't seek revenge. Chen's probably already celebrating his father's demise. This is something much more insidious than a family quarrel."

"Chen doesn't share his father's hatred of somatics," Carac said, inserting himself into the conversation. "He's only interested in putting drugs in his mouth and putting his—"

"Carac! Don't be crude," Sidra snapped.

The par-wolf hunched his shoulders in an attempt to disappear.

At the mention of Chen's name, Sorykah blushed deeply. She'd surrendered to him at the House of Pleasure on the high bed that towered like a wedding cake, his body coiled around hers in some dissolute entanglement. That vision had pasted itself on her mind, a sticky découpage of images that could not be peeled away, no matter how she picked at them.

Soryk's last words to Sidra lingered in the queen's head: "All that I am is nothing without you." Now she presaged Sorykah's departure and the banishment of her male alter. She wouldn't allow Sorykah to leave forever without at least the chance to say goodbye to Soryk.

Sidra stood, a hand clamped to her mouth. "I don't feel well. Please excuse me." She reached the latrine just in time. Sick splashed the basin and Sidra paled, her eyes filling with tears. Her first emotion upon seeing Sorykah had been disappointment; it was all she could do to withhold her sobs. The appearance of Sorykah's beardless face at her door had spoiled Sidra's fantasies of a happy reunion. She forced herself to maintain a carefree charade while her uterus cramped and her breasts ached. The pregnancy was already wearing on her. She had considered asking Sorykah to take the child should she not live. No, she could not think that way. There was too much yet to do. Matuk was dead, but Tirai Industries still ruled. Its contemptible grasp stretched down the continent to drain the Sigue's wealth. TI stole land by rule of eminent domain and campaigned to barter, buy, or coerce somatic children from their homes and families, farming them out to work like beasts of burden in factories, sweatshops, and dockyards.

Sidra's womb contracted in sympathetic anger as if the child inside clenched its fists in rage. This baby might kill her yet, but before succumbing to an early death, she would dismantle TI brick by brick and smile as the monolith crumbled.

DAY TWO

SIDRA THE LOVELY PROPPED HERSELF up on an elbow and leaned over Soryk, her eyes crinkled with mirth. It had taken just a kiss and a slip of the tongue to get her lover back last night. How easily her touch subdued the woman and brought the man to the fore!

She trailed a waving lock of hair under Soryk's nose, making it wrinkle and twitch. He groaned and shooed her away, scrunching deeper into the warm bedclothes. A shaft of green light pierced the dimness as the sun warmed the room uppermost in the queen's tree house. Last night the massive cedar had swayed in a stormy wind, but now it was still and solid.

"A new day dawns." Sidra flicked the tip of her tongue along the whorl of Soryk's ear and blew softly on his closed eyelids.

Soryk's lips curved into a grin as she bent to kiss his mouth, familiar again after the hours they had lain together in mutual enchantment, all defeated dangers far behind them. The edges of his broken teeth scraped her lip, souvenirs of his battle with Matuk.

"Your breath smells odd," Soryk murmured. "Are you getting sick?" He opened dark eyes to gaze at her with concern. Soryk's expression shifted and for a second, Sidra was convinced that she saw

Sorykah there, reflected in a glimmer of suspicion, and then she was gone.

It was true. Sidra's mouth tasted of schoolroom paste. Sweets were sharply sugary; salt shrunk her tongue. Nothing felt right.

"I think it best that you stay abed today." Soryk kissed Sidra's cheek. "I'll inform Carac that the queen is ill, and he is to reign in your stead for one day."

"Goodness, no! Don't tell him that! We'll be overrun with problems. Angry somatics will beat down my door, wanting to know why singing in the tunnels is forbidden."

Carac had grumbled about Dunya the Dog-Faced Girl's habit of singing to herself. He complained that her noise occluded his aural view. How could he accurately listen for danger above- and below-ground when Dunya was forever caterwauling through the Erun city's tunnels?

Soryk patted Sidra's rump and slid into a pair of trousers, a castoff Sidra had brought for him in anticipation of the change. He smiled, stretching his arms wide to encompass the wooden walls, the rumpled bed, and their homey happiness. "It's nice, isn't it?"

"Yes," she smiled. "It's very nice."

"Ah!" Soryk rubbed a flat belly dusted with fine black hair. "Potatoes, you said last night. Potatoes and eggs."

"Of all the things one could request!" Sidra wiggled her toes beneath the blankets, filling Soryk's empty space.

"An onion! I forgot the onion," he said.

"No matter, there are those that grow wild. I can point you in the right direction."

Soryk debated the long journey from Sidra's tree to the nearest exit from the Erun city, and his fruitless search as he rummaged among tree roots and strands of green things that all looked the same to him. "I'll make do." Soryk grinned and disappeared down the stairs; soon the clatter of dishes and pop of hot oil drifted up, filling the tree house with domestic sounds. Soryk's precious eggs smelled of sulfur. Sidra's stomach rebelled and turned.

"It's nothing," she whispered. "It will go away." *Go away*, she commanded, *go away. We don't want you.* Keeping this child meant losing herself. She sometimes thought it would be better to empty her womb and keep the time left to her. Better that it had never been conceived. She closed her eyes and pressed her hands to her ears, blocking out the world as if to bury herself alive and silence that second minuscule heart beating within her belly. *I am queen and my word is law. I shall not have you here.*

LEANDER RUBBED HIS FACE ON Dunya's shoulder as she carried him down to the kitchen.

"What's wrong with ye, laddie? Yer all in a fit."

"His gums hurt," answered a man's tenor, sonorous with the early morning peace of a day yet undisturbed. The knowledge came quickly to him, and he grimaced at this.

Unease traveled through Dunya's body but she shook it off. The sight of Sorykah's male alter was still strangely shocking. Dunya couldn't quite get her head round the fact that this man—"Stinking of rutting," Carac snorted, entering the room—was really a woman. Or was the woman really a man?

Queen Sidra had explained it to them all over supper, much to Sorykah's dismay. Traders were subject to raging hormonal storms. They lacked a genetic fix on gender; while their skeletons remained intact and unblemished, all organs, musculature, and soft tissues were susceptible to fluctuation.

Sorykah had turned a bright cherry red and excused herself from the table. Sidra followed and soon the sounds of arguing, and later, something that sounded like arguing—but wasn't—issued from Sidra's room, uppermost in the tree house. The following morning, this man was in her place.

"Why don't you find nanny Nels and tell her that breakfast is ready," said Soryk. "I'm sure she's famished." He watched Dunya scurry from the room, then turned his attention to his potatoes, frying up brown and delicious in a pool of grease.

Carac shifted about the tiny kitchen, his wiry hair standing on end, his fierce eyes narrow and mean as he slapped an assortment of comestibles on a platter, making it clear he would not deign to eat Soryk's food. Resentment radiated from his skin like heat from the sun, singeing everyone in close contact. Carac loomed over Soryk's shoulder, lips parted to reveal daggerlike teeth.

Soryk's fingers tightened around the paring knife. A part of him panicked but after its initial flush, exhilaration swelled. They would fight, and Soryk found he liked the taste of it.

Carac panted with suppressed rage. The par-wolf could imagine his teeth in the smaller man's throat as it folded, yielding and liquid, around his ripping jaws. He could also imagine, with sharp clarity, the shame of banishment when Queen Sidra found him guilty of succumbing to base instinct. She would view Soryk's death as a murder and Carac would be forced from her bed, permanently this time, ejected from her life, their world and his role in it. With great reluctance, Carac forced himself to turn away.

Soryk relaxed his grip on the knife. This was his first day in the tree house with Sidra. It was all too new to destroy with childish squabbles. He'd barely had time to think about what was happening. His last clear memory was of Dunya and Nels bandaging his severed finger in the marble manor tower. There were scraps of memories after that—a painful and bloody fight with swords and grim instruments, and massive grizzled dogs with foaming muzzles and eyes the orange of hot coals. A woman's voice had slithered inside his mind, goading him to battle and a selfless surrender so that she could rise and take command.

Sidra explained everything as many times as he needed to hear it, but it was still too strange, too fantastic for him to accept as truth. Sidra said he braved both Wood Beast and Gatekeeper to yank the twins back from the lip of their open grave, so when the baby boy that Dunya carried reached for him, Soryk was compelled to take him in his arms and gingerly commence to rocking, shifting Leander like a sack of turnips over his hard forearms. The baby rooted in the open placket of his shirt, then thrust his head back and screamed when he located Soryk's flat male nipples. Dunya watched Soryk struggle with the distressed baby, her mouth hitched up in laughter. Alerted by Leander's wounded howl, Nels came in, Ayeda captive in her firm embrace.

"Your child," Nels reminded Soryk, then smiled mischievously. "She wants her mam. Can't you pop out a tit to please this one?"

Soryk fumed. Hot with humiliation, he pushed Leander onto Dunya as the boy's cries accelerated in pitch and frequency.

He's just tired. The woman's voice was back, just as sure and precise in Soryk's head as his own thoughts. *He needs a cuddle, a song, a bit of cold rag to suck on. Take care of my little boy, please.*

Soryk did not like his female primary manipulating him as though he were a marionette made to dance with just a flick of the strings. Heat bubbled inside him and he was suddenly drowsy. The changing sleep. He was livid, terrified. Once the change began, Sorykah would absorb him into a fuzzy limbo-land of powerlessness, every aspect of him subsumed and devoured, leaving him trapped like smoke in a glass vial until the change uncorked it and he rose, freed again.

Maybe I'm a djinn, he thought, *and Sidra is my magic-lamp rubber.* He grinned, flushed with a private memory. It pleased him greatly to look at her conducting her queenly tasks and know what sounds she uttered in the pitch of ecstasy. He thought of her often, found himself tumbling head over toes into some swirling cosmos of enfolding velvet and creamy red bliss. He knew the scent of the warm space beneath her hair at the back of her neck, the feel of her, small and sturdy, in his hands. He knew the vague slope of her belly pot and the lilt of her laughter when he pleased her in the dark of night. These memories anchored him in the present. He would cling to Sidra like a talisman and use his feelings for her to keep his primary at bay. That meant that he would also have to care for Sorykah's children, though Nels and Dunya did a fine job of that. Why muddy the pond?

Carrying up the breakfast he'd prepared, his stomach growled. It felt like he hadn't eaten in years. There was much making up to do: food and drink to enjoy, a forest realm of somatic fugitives to explore, a coronation to consider, and, as he entered Sidra's room and spied her asleep on the bed, much pleasure to savor.

He flopped down beside her and let the steam from the food waft toward her. She lurched upright, a look of panic in her eyes, and leapt from the bed to retch into a chamber pot.

"My dove." Soryk offered Sidra a glass of cool water. "I knew you were sick. Your city will have to run without you for one day."

She nodded, as gray and clammy as an oyster. *This is no virus, 'tis your beloved's child. Tell him,* Sidra's conscience nagged. *Tell him and let him judge the outcome. It's me or the babe, he can't have both.* Women feared pregnancy and motherhood but men feared the infants themselves, as though betrayal and patricide coiled in wait within their budding tragedian's hearts, poised to spring and stab. *He will urge a return to yesterday. He would want you unencumbered.* She would make him the foil and then, through the right tincture and no fault of her own, she would be herself again, washing bloodied sheets in the stream. She envisioned herself reaching for the powders and vials, taking in hand her mortar and pestle to grind the herbs and make the expelling draft.

Tansy—effective but potentially toxic. Should it fail, there would be maternal liver and organ disruption and irreparable damage to a fetus that survived the herb's action. Perhaps tempered with pennyroyal and boiled in a tea with blue cohosh and parsley, it would nudge the blood and make it flow. She had no cotton root bark but rose hips and orange peel might suffice. She wasn't that far gone. There was still time. She must also consider the danger of disaster when working with herbs' unknown quantities and strengths, and the likelihood of injuring herself and needing surgical intervention unattainable in the Erun.

Sorykah would be devastated to learn that Sidra did not crave this child. Sorykah had leapt and swung among the stars to string her wishes to recover her children alive. She had cut off her own finger to quench the thirsting blood-lock in the marble manor's lone work-

ing door and turn it with a severed bone, still dripping, from her left
hand. What sacrifice would she make to save another of her offspring?

Perhaps neither of them need know about the pregnancy. No
admission of guilt. No words. Sidra would seal her mouth. Words
summoned spirits and flesh from the other side; words called them
home. She'd not confess only to drive him away or rope him into
staying.

"My lovely." His kiss was tender, touching, his breath honey-
sweet. "I'll never leave you again," Soryk insisted, knowing it false.

"You have a proper life in Ostara. Would you give it up for me?"

"*Her* life," he said tonelessly. "I could make my own here with
you."

"It belongs to both of you. I've explained this before," she insisted.

Soryk groaned. "But it's not my choice. I get so little time! If only
I could see myself when I'm her. If I could feel it . . ." *No*, he
thought. *I don't want to feel it. Don't want to recognize myself as a
sub-personality of the woman, Sorykah. I am my own man.*

He existed outside of time and reality in Sidra's realm. The Erun
city had absorbed him but would soon cough him up and spit him
back into the world. Male or female, primary or alter, there were the
children to consider—Soryk's by blood if not by birth.

It was a vile deceit. Soryk's brief life had been rapturous with sensation and excitement before he woke to find himself a father to not
one, but two demanding, relentless leeches.

No, not leeches, he admonished. *Ticks? Lice?* He could summon
no compliments for those two. They had the foreign odors of
strangers and their odious baby perfume of spoilt milk, slobber-
soaked wool, and pissy diapers repulsed him.

"Shh," Sidra soothed, sliding her hands down his ribs and over
his hips. "Enjoy what you have. This moment." She pushed her
hands between his thighs. "This kiss." She smiled, descending, and
it was good, like a summer vine studded with bright berries, ripe and
sweet.

Free of the brambles, leaves, and snarls that usually decorated it,

Sidra's wild hair hid her face. He'd not yet had the nerve to touch the scabbed knobs of flesh lurking beneath it. Soryk knew enough about their queen's history to recognize the sawed-off horns that sparked an uprising in Neubonne some years ago. While Sidra lay in hospital, the protuberant bones of her scalp smoking from recent cauterization, somatics had rioted in the streets demanding her release. Sidra and her anarchic posse of somatics sought asylum in the Erun city. Back then, it was just a collection of hovels and tree houses loosely connected by a few sagging tunnels. Under Sidra's rule, the city had been transformed into the well-protected haven they all called home.

"You grow fat and fine," he said, by which he meant "you are as delicious as fresh-churned butter, new-made cheese, and sugar icing—things sweet and good that I would spread upon soft breads and devour."

"So eat me." She offered her arm, which he lavished with kisses.

Soryk's hand strayed over the crown of her head, brushing the dual knobs of bone, gruesome with scars, thrusting up from her skull like deadly mushrooms. She did not object; he did not flinch. True love, at last.

2

FLIGHT

DAY THREE

AROUSED BY SOME CHANGE in the atmosphere, Sidra stirred in her sleep. A scent was in her nose: sickness, fever sweat. Beside her, Soryk's breathing was deep and labored. She woke mindful of a hovering nausea that unsettled her stomach. The kitchen and bread were far off, down many levels of circular stairs. She would not wake the others with her descent. There was candied ginger in a wooden box beside the bed; it would suffice. She fumbled in the dark, found the ginger, and chewed it slowly, focusing on its spicy sweetness, a zesty lemon-pepper flavor that eased her nausea for a moment.

Beside her, Soryk moaned and thrashed his arms as if in reaction to being held down.

"My love," Sidra whispered, remembering. "*My lark, my dove, my pretty queen,*" he had said when she moved atop him at the House of Pleasure, coaxing truth from his lips—from Sorykah's lips. Sidra grew cold with a sudden chill. Her hand floated in the darkness and felt heat rise from her lover's frame as she let it fall to meet his skin. Her fingers traveled the doughy depression of belly, vaguely puckered and tracked by stretch marks. She found the fleshy rise of a breast and moved through a dripping line of liquid, pulling fingers to her nose to draw in the sweet aroma of Sorykah's breast milk.

Sidra withdrew to the edge of the mattress. It was wrong to feel betrayed but she could not embrace this body in her bed as she had once before, searching for Soryk inside another's skin. She was fecund with Soryk's baby, conceived during Chen's vicious bacchanal. She wanted only him. Could she climb aboard this vessel and steer that ship of bone and muscle into the twilight of the change? Could her touch again enliven the man sleeping within Sorykah's body?

Sorykah would wake full of purpose and intention, and pack herself, her children, and her nanny off to frosty southern climes, returned to the Sigue's singing sea and the subarctic desert of ice and snow. There would be silence in the tree house then until Sidra's birthing cries broke the mournful quiet.

Sorykah moaned, spewed a few nonsense words, then descended again into struggle and strife. Longing for a fugitive, Sidra cried herself to sleep, the taste of ginger warm in her mouth.

SORYK TASTED GINGER when he kissed Sidra, tugged from sleep by some vague awareness of her unhappiness. Still spicy, the white buds of her teeth were cool cubes to break the heat as his tongue curled into her mouth. He swam among the bedclothes. He dove into her as one might plunge from a great height to sink beneath the sea. Its divine skin musky and intoxicating, the body beneath his was a magic-making wish-granter. The full life Sidra promised him eased his animal wanting, assuaged that altogether too unpleasant sense of being a dog beneath the table, waiting for scraps to fall.

"You feel like home," he murmured, enraptured. "My place is beside you, forever. But it's not easy, like fighting a rising tide. All the sandbags in the world can't hold her back." Soryk pushed himself deeper inside, closer to Sidra's soul. "I would never hurt you."

Sidra froze beneath Soryk as the change churned inside him.

"Not on purpose," Sorykah added, as if telephoning from another dimension. "Not if you let me go. If you cling too tightly, I will flee." A whisper of protest arose within Soryk's suppressed consciousness; Sorykah was glad to be the stronger of the two so she could quash his objections and silence him.

Soryk/ah's body was hot and slick against Sidra's—slippery changing flesh that ran through Sidra's fingers like seawater. She knew not with whom she lay, but she tightened her embrace as Sorykah confessed, "Chen offered me his kingdom, his own tiny and insignificant realm. He asked that I remain on the Isle of Mourning and become his chatelaine or something."

"His duchess," Sidra whispered, dully stung. "Mistress of his petit duchy."

"Yes, that's it." Sorykah sounded as though she smiled. "And you as well, then?"

"Yes," Sidra moaned. "Me as well."

"Bugger 'im." Sorykah laughed. "Not to worry, my lovely. Pride before the fall, you know? He'll get his." Sorykah shifted, sighed, and was gone. Soryk resumed his motion and Sidra's heart beat so fast that she could not catch her breath and fell into the void of space where suns were born and died, and she could no longer hear the voice of her traitorous Trader lover. She heard only the rapid thumpity-thump of a miniature heart, the child, no bigger than a field mouse, who would be the cause of her destruction.

DAY FOUR

IN THE MORNING, SIDRA brushed a fine silt of Soryk's expelled body hairs from the bed. They formed a shadowy scrim on the white linen, a reverse outline proving his existence. Sidra lay curled on her side, her back to Soryk. He slid an arm around her middle, tucked her breast into his hand, and pushed a thigh between hers. In another room, the twins screamed, their cries spiraling upward like New Year's rockets trapped inside a tube.

"Don't you want to see to the babies?" Sidra said, her voice thick with sleep.

He grunted. "Nels or Dunya can handle it."

"Their cries set my teeth on edge. Doesn't it bother you?"

"Should it?"

Sidra faced him, her long, brown hair like skeins of tangled silk. Soryk did not like her expression. He groaned. She would allow him no access; the game had ended.

A pink stain crept over Sidra's skin, rimmed her eyes, and set her cheeks ablaze. "Sorykah would never ignore them. Why would you leave them to a nanny when you only need to hold them, let them hear your voice?"

"I'm not their mother. I can't give them anything they can't get from Nels, can I?"

Sidra crumpled. His placidity was maddening. Changing hormones left her horribly unbalanced. Her emotions were wily, rolling things slippery in her grasp, eager to elude or confound her. She'd been too long without the touch of a human man. Her want weakened her. It was why she'd chosen Carac, driven to accept his unspoken invitation from nothing but a simple hunger for release and the yearning to be wrapped up in another's arms. Carac was so unpredictable, so wild and terrifying! Yet she held sway over him as one breaks a fierce dog—without showing fear or compromising her authority—and by Jerusha, he was tamed. He would lick her hand when they were alone together. She quivered when she offered herself to him, but there was little true tenderness. Carac could not, or would not, kiss her. He did not take his time. He did not lay with her, mouthing sweet secrets throughout the small hours, though he might stretch beside her, limpid and panting, his gaze grateful and conflicted.

She could feel Soryk's eyes upon her and wished that he would change, just this once, so she could confide her loneliness to a friend. When Sorykah left, she would take with her warmth and humanity. Like Sidra, Sorykah was a woman pushed to the far limits of society, a wary and precocious neighbor to tradition risen above the petty distinctions imposed by her gender and background.

Sidra was the queen. Of loyal subjects, trustworthy advisors, lovers, and workmates, she had plenty. What she did not have was a friend on equal footing, a partner to whom she could entrust her confidences. Soryk would leave her here with this child who had dug into her very organs, wormed into the wall of her womb expecting board with its room, a most demanding and unsatisfied lodger. She must make plans to carry on without him.

Sidra could not think for his presence, his breathing so disturbed her. If she confessed to carrying his child, would he stay?

DAY FIVE

SORYKAH WAS IN THE KITCHEN with Nels and Dunya. Their conversation halted when Sidra appeared, breaking into a conspiratorial circle of women's talk from which she sensed herself purposefully excluded. Sidra ran a light hand the length of Sorykah's arm. Her touch roused the sleeping beast, just as Ur's presence had once charmed the demon Diabolo from his subterranean lair. *We mimic the gods*, Sidra mused.

Sorykah's eyelids began to droop, and the panic that signaled the change showed itself. Ever more readily, the heat came on and the change percolated inside her, poison in a pot.

"Come upstairs, my love," Sidra said, smiling. "Let me make much of you."

Hating her body's ready response and Soryk's lusting want, Sorykah stumbled mutely after her. Nels watched, frowning as they climbed the stairs—Sorykah moving like an automaton, Sidra already pulling off her cloak in giddy anticipation. They would all have to block their ears to sleep that night.

THE QUEEN SLEPT SOUNDLY and did not stir when Sorykah woke beside her. Sorykah's calm certainty was a solid and watchful thing, assured of its own intent.

Say goodbye now, she thought, speaking to Soryk as though he too were awake and planning her demise. *You must end it. I'll take my children and go home and you will sink into the depths from which you came. You shall drown and vanish inside me, pull the waters over your head, and let the dark come to claim you. Sleep now and forever, and let me rise from my grave to walk among the living. Sleep now.* She closed her eyes. A veil passed over them. Her body effervesced as her blood drained and was replaced with sparkling soda pop. Sorykah dug in with her nails, clinging to her selfhood like a life raft. The tide of the coming change sucked at her, hung on her legs, dragged her from awareness into an oblivion of shadows, mumbled voices, and muffled sensation.

Soryk strained to reach out and pull Sidra to him, taste her mouth, smother her beneath his body. Sorykah lay like one comatose, feeling blindly for some recognizable sound or an identifiable touch but Soryk's hunger was too great, and it snuffed out her light.

DAY SIX

THE TIME HAD COME. Sorykah rose from the bed where Sidra still slept, flushed with the exertion of her dreams. She could not pause to stroke Sidra's bare skin. Dared not press a kiss to her brow lest she wake the sleeper and be confronted with her rebuke. Now was the time—while the sun shone green and unripe through emerald leaves. Now—while the household was silent and her departure less tragic and clamorous than it would be later, somatics lined up at

Sidra's door to offer well wishes and gawk at the queen's two-sexed lover and her changeling children. Sorykah hesitated, doubting again her decision to leave without saying goodbye. She scanned the room, drawing in its rich, woodsy warmth, the spice of herbs, the scent of their recent lovemaking.

Unrepentant, Sorykah thought, heading downstairs to wake her nanny. *That's what I am.* She was surprised to note that she didn't feel especially guilty about her deceptive departure. There was no other way. She would not let Soryk claim her days. He was to remain suppressed, stuffed down like a jack-in-the-box passively waiting release.

The change had crept over her during sleep and she'd risen, her clothes—Soryk's clothes—damp with sweat, to flee, a thief of hearts exiting a tragic romance. She'd grown tired of her exploits and longed to return to orderly civilization—hot running water, a proper stove and oven, trains and shops and prepackaged food that did not taste of the gamy wilderness.

Nels's eyes lit up when she saw Sorykah. "Oh! You did it! I was afraid that you wouldn't be able to leave her." She shimmied from the pallet and crawled to her mistress's side, pressing a welcoming hand to Sorykah's shoulder, something she'd not have done to her alter. She liked Soryk and trusted him, but was well aware of the fragility of his bond with her. Though some inner compulsion urged him to kindness for the children's sake, an electric current warned her away.

"It's not easy. Her presence, the nearness of her . . ." Sorykah's eyes narrowed and she flicked a tongue over her lips. ". . . it binds me. She is truly extraordinary, but what would we do here? *He* shall not make me his alter."

Sidra might have opened the channels between gender-selves, but there were too many unknown factors to allow them to settle into a life that suited them both. Sorykah was the boss, and Soryk would just have to deal with it. Sorykah's departure would occur to him as a dreary, drawn-out nightmare that would fill his eyes with stinging tears and cause him to next waken with the stench of betrayal thick upon his skin.

"Pack up the children. Carac can escort us to the train depot at Fair Fallows. We'll leave Kika here. She'll be happier in the forest than my house."

"Carac?" Nels had developed a fear of somatics since her theft by Matuk's half-walrus henchman, Meertham. Because of this, she avoided contact with Carac and Sidra's visitors. Only Dunya was easy with her—Dunya, small, hairy, and endlessly helpful—yet even she had turned on Nels in the pit, sensing her momentary fear, aroused by Nels's slur (calling to her as if she were no more than a pampered house pet).

Sorykah brushed aside her nanny's fears. "He won't hurt you, I promise. He must behave or risk Sidra's rebuke. Carac will be more than happy to oblige the request. He wants nothing more than to see me gone."

"But won't he tell? You plot to deceive her."

"There are no politics in play here. I'm not going to overthrow her!"

"Just break her heart," Nels added softly.

Sorykah sighed. Too true, that. "She's my friend. She'll understand."

"But to sneak off without even saying goodbye!" Nels's whisper was overloud, vigorous.

"She will not take it well. As it is, she barely speaks to me, so great is her anticipation of the coming end. Should I be so callous as to smash her heart without softening the blow?"

Sorykah would never admit that the longer she stayed with Sidra, the more porous became the division between her selves. Sorykah spent all her time in a state of half sleep; voices came in tinny and thin. Brief sensations roused her skin as if someone manipulated her limbs while she slept. Once, she'd pulled up from the blackness to feel the flexing muscle of Sidra's tongue against Soryk's, as finely grained as a strawberry. There were other sensations, too, lingering like brown sugar in her mouth—the slickery tumble of long hair, the determined lust of a man, so different from her own diffuse arousal—sense memories in her organs and hands.

Sorykah shook herself, muttered "Unnecessary complications," and turned to Nels. "We have to go now. I'm afraid that I won't be able to come out of it if I wait any longer. Sidra must understand that this is temporary, no matter how strong their love." Sorykah wrapped a length of cloth round her torso and tied it at one shoulder. Both she and Nels would carry the children in these homemade slings. "I'll get the babies ready. You find Carac and tell him we're ready to leave."

Nels nodded and did as told. Sorykah was her mistress; she would take orders from no other lest she find herself out of a job.

Carac was waiting in the front room when Sorykah came downstairs carrying her sleeping children. His face was grizzled, and his eyes were red and exhausted. Sorykah shuddered at the prospect of entrusting her family to the par-wolf's toothy care. Could they be certain he'd not lead them to a ravine, snap their necks, and shove them in? Abandon them in the wilderness, or worse? She hoped he was a wolf of honor. The faster and further she left behind this absurd and dreadful escapade, the better.

Carac led them through the city's underground maze, offering nothing more than a gruff "This way" or "Watch your head" as they moved through the close, chill tunnels, morbid with the smell of vegetative rot, stagnant water, and a mineral odor that seemed to leach from the rocky veins lining the walls.

They stopped once to feed the babies, and walked another six miles until Nels pleaded exhaustion. Carac's breath was hot and labored. The wiry hairs on his neck and ears twisted like antennae to collect and transmit subtle atmospheric signals. Did he suffer on his queen's behalf, Sorykah wondered, or was he simply worn out by the exhaustive preparations of the torture he'd devised for them? Nels followed Sorykah's example and pretended that the par-wolf did not stand panting over them, that they did not mind the sound of his saliva plinking from pointed canines to slick the floor.

Sorykah swallowed her fear and tucked her hand into her pocket to feel for the small knife she carried. Expecting the scrape of teeth and snap of bones, she closed her eyes. When she opened them, Carac had gone far ahead, as if unable to bear the nearness of babies' succulent, milk-fed flesh.

Light filled the tunnel's end atop a flight of crude stairs composed of interlocking tree roots. Carac gestured them up and out into air fresh and sweet with the scent of dew-wet pines. A meadow bordered by the Glass Mountains' jagged peaks was visible beyond the trees. Confronting that sun-splashed open space, Sorykah realized that this was the very valley where she'd been swept by the flood. Here, two poachers in camouflage and vivid hunter's orange had savaged her, releasing the fear that changed her, after years of steady sameness, into a man. She still wore one poacher's knife-print on her belly like a shiny mauve birthmark.

Carac was now a liability. Which was more enticing? Women, slowed down by children and unable to outpace poachers intent on rape, or the lively-haired skin of a par-wolf, one of perhaps a dozen in the entire world? Panic surged like an electric current, setting her nerves on fire. Heavy on Sorykah's back, Ayeda fidgeted and kicked in her sling. Sorykah had a sudden, intense inclination to turn and run to the cool and sheltering wood—back to the shadows and safety, and the close, creaking tree house where Sidra's authority would open itself like an umbrella to shelter her.

"Sorykah!" Nels's voice was faint outside the ringing in her head. Sorykah's ears had rung like this in the House of Pleasure, her auditory senses buzzing in a hiss of static, but now she did not turn in a warm bed to face a smiling lover. She crouched, her ears filled with the sound of train whistles and rattling rails.

"The train! I have to light the lamp." Carac lit from the bracken, his face dour. Sparks flew as he waved a flint fire starter and shimmied up the far lamppost stuck in the middle of a meadow like a radio tower on a city rooftop. A will-o'-the-wisp danced between the lampshade's glass panes, as black as the surrounding night yet alive with its own fickle brilliance. He ran toward them, mouth canted sideways into something that resembled a grin. "Now we wait." Carac slipped beneath the branches of a tangled copse of trees. "Better to remain with our mother than let the empty space take us."

Squirming and restless, the babies fussed and fidgeted. Sorykah's legs cramped and tingled. Her bottom ached from sitting on the hard ground. She was growing annoyed and was just about to make a snide remark when Carac raised his hand.

"Watch." Slowly, the trees around them began to bleed. Great fat droplets of dun and ancient gray oozed like sap from a broken stem, pushing out from the Erun's dark and secret places to pool upon the meadow, picked out in rose and violet by the fading sun.

People, or what looked to Sorykah like bodies attempting to pass as human, slunk across the grass, bundles of ragged cloth and dowdy satchels strapped to bent backs. The skittering rustle of their footsteps sounded like a waterfall in Sorykah's ears. She began to rise.

Carac gripped her arm, tugged her down. "Not yet. Wait. Watch. We must be sure."

Sorykah's eyes strained in the gloom. A train slowed, a sleek steel centipede a half mile long. The signal lamp emitted no light and the train was black but for the yellow pulse of the conductor's car windows.

Dragging their meager gear, the forest dwellers pushed forward.

Shots pierced the night. A creature of dread and death, the train snaked along the valley floor picking off somatics like wooden ducks in a shooting gallery. Carac crouched unfazed, his face immobile as he watched the slaughter unfold, a red blanket spreading itself across the chilly meadow.

Sorykah knew that sound. The pneumatic hiss of an air gun firing and its sky-streaking missile floated to the top of her memory like a hair rising to mar the surface of fresh cream. She'd been shot down from the sky as she fled the Isle of Mourning in her beautiful hot air balloon with her lover Elu by her side. Elu was crippled, his hand blown apart before the balloon burst into flame and exploded on the rocky beach. Sorykah recalled the cairn she'd constructed for Elu's body, left to decompose inside her homemade mausoleum, and wondered how the three of them now would be able to find enough stones to cover all of these bodies.

Sorykah scrambled to her feet and Carac jerked her down again, making Ayeda cry. Silent and lightless, the train slithered into the night. The smell of death lifted from the corpses on the field, a grisly, choking thing, to sidle ghostlike into the clearings between trees, a cloying odor of spilled human waste, blood, and the sweet, dusty fragrance of splattered brain and shattered bone.

Nels pressed her hands to her mouth, biting back her horror.

Carac did not gag like the women beside him. He opened his mouth, inhaled deeply to accustom himself to the taste of genocide, and spit into the tall grass.

"Now." He stood, gesturing in the dark. "Our train comes."

Sorykah and Nels could not speak. Squelching their cries and the hysteria that would surely ensue given the opportunity, they trailed Carac across the cadaver-strewn field.

A high mournful whistle sang in the distance, tardily followed by the clackety-clack rhythm of the overland train puttering through the lonely evening. Carac waved them forward.

Nels jerked Carac's sleeve. "How do you know?" Her voice trembled. "How can you be sure?"

Carac's face was invisible; the whites of his eyes flashed like semaphore flags. "The lamp burns with a black flame. See?" A second specter led the iron train, an optical illusion of light, the antithesis of light, flickering within its collar. "Only an emissary of the queen may light the signal lantern. They will slow. Board the last car for passage to the coast. Here." Carac thrust a packet into Sorykah's hand. "From Sidra."

Sorykah's heart seized, remembering. *And I have braved the glen and made to do with goblin men for you.* She had not even said goodbye.

"Thank her," Sorykah spoke to the night wind. Carac was gone.

Sorykah and Nels huddled beneath the signal lamp. At each point in this terrible odyssey, Sorykah had wondered how much longer it could drag along, how much more strife she could bear—still she muddled forward through sorrow, longing for a lasting measure of ease and calm.

Distinctive shuffling issued from the brush close by, followed by a squeal and whine, the sound of lapping tongues and the crack of marrowbones. Nels grabbed Sorykah's hand and began to pray aloud. Sorykah wondered if Jerusha would guard them. Did the mother goddess care enough to spread her cloak over them and guarantee their safety? Sorykah felt that she must be the grown-up here, murmur reassurances and step firmly onto the open platform appearing before her, as if she had no cares or woes to distress her.

The train did not stop. The final car chugged past as they stood watching their only transport to reality glide away.

Sorykah pushed Nels toward the moving train and shoved her onto a narrow step before grabbing the rails and hauling herself up, her back straining under Ayeda's weight. Inside the passenger car, somatics clustered in quiet sympathy, watching their approach as they sought empty seats and lifted the babies from their backs.

"I'm so tired," Sorykah whimpered, her face hot under the threat of tears. Home had been foremost in her mind for so long she could scarcely believe it near. Soon they would reach the tiny seaport at the end of the line, use the money that Carac had pressed upon them (Sidra's dosh, carefully hoarded, some of the bills so outdated as to no longer be in circulation) to purchase passage to the Sigue.

Sigue song, the discordant wolf wail of the living ice, already played in her head. She would not believe herself home and her children safe until it filled her ears and blocked the transmission of sorrows broadcast by a restless memory. Only on Ostara's now longed-for harbor could she abandon the cloying fear of some vicious retribution, some secret cult of Matuk's that meant to do her harm. Sorykah closed her eyes but the image of Sidra's face appeared, reproachful and forlorn, and she could not sleep.

3

THE MOST NAUGHTY FELLOW

THE JOURNEY HOME WAS ARDUOUS. She'd been holding herself together rather badly, and the last of her composure was unraveling. Sigue song filled Sorykah's ears as the supply ship pulled slowly into Ostara's harbor. Anxiety gripped her gut. Sorykah scanned the pier for Company men and saw none. The *Nimbus* must be out to sea; she could delay unveiling the outlandish fabrication she'd concocted to explain her absence, delay the groveling that would surely follow as she begged for her job.

Naturally, she would lie. There was no impulse toward truth-telling. Admission of her deliberate disappearance would lead to questions about the whys and wheres of her travel. No friend to somatics, the Company would find her culpable in conspiracy with them. Any mention of the children's abduction would surely spark an inquiry. Sorykah had killed Plein Eïre's wealthiest and most influential citizen, no matter that he was asylum-bait and a criminal. Matuk's death had altered every fiber of her being. She was a killer just like him, but her low status would merit a stiffer punishment, and Neubonne's gaols were notoriously cruel.

Cautiously, Sorykah led Nels through spring-warmed avenues, wet with slush. Restless Siguelanders thronged the streets as if their daily duties had no claim on them. Joyful dogs cantered freely over wooden walkways, but most startling of all, Sorykah saw people's faces. Ostara's bitter cold and frigid sea winds normally forced everyone to cover everything but their eyes, and those were often barricaded by goggles. Now she saw exposed foreheads, red cheeks, noses, mouths, and even hair where hoods had been pushed back. Instead of lashing winds, the air roamed lazily through the village. Even the Sigue's whine was muffled and less piercing than she remembered.

Fortunately, Sorykah's key still opened the door of the Quonset hut assigned to her by the Company. Nels volunteered to get supplies and a hot lunch from town. Sorykah stripped the babies and they all settled in a marvelous-feeling tub of lukewarm water, courtesy of the small water heater that after weeks of deprivation seemed a great luxury.

Nels and Sorykah had grown comfortable with each other; all formality was gone. They were friends now, after Matuk. "After . . . you know," they said, reluctant to speak his name as if voicing it would summon the ghoul from his afterworld.

"Poisons must be named, shan't they?" Nels said, thinking of that barren white tower, the hunger and cold that had nibbled her fingers while Matuk kept her captive. "Lest the innocent take them unknowing. You'd not swallow the rhubarb leaf with its toxic bitter milk, though the innocent pink weedies look ever so pretty in the salad, you see."

Sorykah nodded. She did see. They must force themselves to dilute Matuk's powerful memory. The forest, the yearning for salvation and importance of rescue had to be sugared in order to melt, and so Nels and Sorykah made themselves into companions, kindhearted ladies in love with two babes freshly rescued from hard times.

SORYKAH GATHERED THE SLACK threads of her life and wove herself into existence. The days filled themselves up and drained away, made sour by a profound guilt resolutely ignored. Sidra, the Erun, the marble manor, and the House of Pleasure lost color, just as a photograph fades with time until only the faintest of images remain. She waited for the ax to fall, expecting a knock on the door and angry Company admins demanding that she vacate the Quonset. She had to muscle her way back into the job that had been hers, or they would not survive.

Each morning, Sorykah went into town to look for the *Nimbus*. The sun shone with unvarying intensity and water puddled in once-frozen streets. Strange green stems uncurled from the soil and stretched into the air. This elicited much astonishment from Siguelanders who had never seen anything grow from the ground. A slick of moss, perhaps, or the orange and gray lichen that stained the rocks in summer but never an actual plant. Sorykah snipped a few specimens but none of the people she asked could identify them. She was certain these were some species of oenathe, a restorative healing herb, for what else could survive the climate?

Though she typically kept to a routine path—home, harbor, and store—Sorykah's interest in the plants led her to roam. She followed their trail, noting how some grew particularly dense in areas where the ice had melted away revealing strange soil beneath, black as volcanic rock. The plants vanished, trampled beneath the planks of the wooden walkways. She stopped and looked up for the first time. Wandering with her eyes to the ground, Sorykah did not realize that she had retraced her steps to the Stuck Tongue, where months ago, she had encountered her first somatic. That same pockmarked sign still swung overhead, depicting a disembodied tongue frozen to a pole.

Compelled to enter, she reached for the door. Crowds of locals drank and conversed loudly, excited by the relative heat. They wore shirtsleeves and took particular delight in rolling them up for arm-wrestling matches. A Siguelander stood behind the counter in place of Pavel, the somatic bartender, but the hookah pipe still burbled in the back room beneath a haze of expelled smoke.

Though common sense urged her to leave, something else propelled her toward the pipe, its surround of cushions, clustering bodies, and the tart, burnt-sugar odor of opioids. Sorykah's heart fluttered as she searched the faces of the people around the pipe, looking for Rava, the terrifying octameroon Sorykah had ferried through the wasteland, but she was not among the smokers. Someone offered her a seat. She hesitated, remembering the feel of that white smoke in her lungs and the peaceful dreaminess it imparted. Regretfully declining, she asked in her rudimentary Siguelandic if anyone had seen a red-haired woman in a wheelchair. One hand pointed to a shadowy corner. A body lay on the floor, clumsily barricaded beneath a white fur rug. A tendril of mauve hair snaked across the pillows.

Dismayed, Sorykah crouched to pull back the fur. Despite a lingering revulsion for the touch of cold tentacles, she prodded the body. Rava was jelly-limbed, and a violet stain masked her eyes. Rava had been conscious the first time and able to lead Sorykah to her cave and the water tank in which she must submerge herself, but alone, Sorykah could not lift Rava's heavy body, the legs Pavel had said dragged like anchors. Where was he? Perhaps Pavel's absence had so upset Rava that she could only numb her pain with the pipe.

Sorykah turned to the men. "Brothers, where is the man Pavel who works this bar?"

They rolled bleary eyes and laughed, coughing up smoke. From the ensuing loud conversation, Sorykah ascertained that Pavel had disappeared two months prior, shortly after Sorykah's departure. Rumor was he'd gone into the waste to find some missing relative or his wife—one beloved, anyway. None had seen him since. Poor Pavel! Certainly, he had died on the journey. Sorykah would've perished herself if superhuman determination to find her children had not driven her so fiercely.

Rava groaned and Sorykah sprang into action, requesting fossil water from the bar and siphoning it into Rava's mouth with a straw. When that failed to rouse her, Sorykah poured it along gill flaps and tentacles, watching Rava's white suckers for movement. Sorykah pulled out the oenathe leaves she'd collected earlier, tore them into tiny pieces, and swished them around in a bit of fossil water. She opened Rava's mouth and packed the leaves inside, poured the remaining water into her mouth, and massaged her cheeks. Sorykah had almost resigned herself to failure when Rava opened her eyes. Those cold amber orbs striped by vertical pupils lit Sorykah with irrational fleeting terror.

Rava's small mouth curved into an approximation of a smile. "Sor-i-kah . . ."

"You remember! I'm so glad," and she was.

Rava pushed herself up on her elbows, gasped, and fell back.

"What is it?"

"My back." Rava twisted to look, her tentacles reaching up like extra hands to prod her flesh.

"Let me see," Sorykah said, but the sticky puddle of ink beneath Rava spoke eloquently—a clumsy incision stitched with thick thread marred her hip. "Your wound has reopened."

Pearl-tears fell from Rava's eyes. "It does not matter. Pavel is gone. My kin stolen by the boomer. The sea is empty. What is left for me?"

But the pipe, Sorykah concluded.

"Since you took me from here"—Rava's keyhole pupils contracted, the only indication of emotion in her subhuman face—"the world died. You took me, though I did not wish to go. You left me in the waste, then a man with tusks took me from the witch's place and put me in the sea and I was alone."

Sorykah met Rava's unfeeling stare, fearing the brutal musculature of livid orange tentacles thumping the floor, suckers popping open and closed. "Pavel"—she amended *blackmailed me*—"begged me to take you. He thought you were going to die. He only wanted to save you."

"Save me he did not. Fool man! I am the only one who can see, so, it is my duty to watch. Pavel called me a cuckoo's egg. I was not there to warn them and the claw plucked my brothers and sisters from the water." Rava's stare pierced Sorykah.

"What do you mean? Whose claw? I don't understand."

"The boomer! The ice eater." The violet stain deepened across Rava's cheeks as she depleted her blood oxygen levels trying to express herself adequately. "There is fire in the water. The volcano spills into the sea. Diabolo wakes." Rava's tentacles thrashed in annoyance. "Bodies cover the seafloor."

Rava spoke as if the ancient stories were true. As if there really were a demon, big enough and strong enough to survive centuries of hibernation within a dormant volcano, sleeping on a lava bed beneath blankets of smoke and ash. One such as he would rise from slumber, mean-tempered and destructive, with a taste for human blood, she imagined. Diabolo or not, a breach in the volcano's thick crust would threaten the entire pole. Hovering at a near-constant temperature of 26°F, the Southern Sea ice would melt with a rise of a few degrees. Rava's understanding of the phenomenon was precarious. In place of the scientific dialogue she craved, Sorykah must maneuver through garbled speculation and story to excavate a small nugget of truth.

She wasn't eager to make amends to the octameroon for taking her away from her precious opium. She'd do the same again—Rava's life for that of her babes—but her fate had inexplicably woven itself among Sigue and somatic warp and weft, and could not be unpicked. "What can I do for you?"

"Take me to the sea. The demon will climb from his bed. He will wreak vengeance on us and glut himself on our sufferings. I must stop him."

"You're not afraid?" Sorykah asked, half in jest.

Rava spit oenathe remains into her delicate human hand. "One who is already cursed does not fear the devil." Rava hauled herself into her wheelchair, scattering the saltwater iridescence of her sorrow across the floorboards. Sorykah pushed her from the bar as she had those many weeks ago, when she first met Rava and left behind the world of human privilege. This time, however, the almost-summer sun shone high in a blue sky. A disorienting arousal had settled over the town, sprigged by spring growth, and Ostara's streets rang with the din of human chatter.

Rava told Sorykah to take a narrow-planked walkway to Land's End, a glacial promontory rife with treacherous caverns where icicles spilled from the cave roofs to stab the sea. Wind buffeted the desolate point and snatched at their clothes and hair. Rava pointed to a blue glacier with steep, flaking sides. "I go there." She stripped off her clothing and heaped it on the rocks beside her chair. The mottled skin of her tentacles was a network of mauve veins textured in deep orange. Rava's human upper body was as shiny as a plastic doll's, and the dull points of her vestigial breasts belied her mammalian genetic coding. She thrust herself from her chair, tentacles sucking and sliding over slimy wet rocks as she moved to a low cliff jutting over the ocean—then she was gone.

Sorykah ran to look but there was no swirl of rust red hair or thrashing tentacles, just a vortex of sea foam. The Sigue beat and churned. Its once-solid pack ice was now a chunky stew of gray floes and debris-strewn slush. A far glacier groaned and calved, birthing a jagged berg. Sorykah picked her way down to the cave, suddenly aware of her idiocy when she slipped and skidded across lichen-splotched crags, tumbling into a crack in the rock. Shaking, she clambered out, her legs bruised by the fall. The glacier loomed ahead, a pyramid of ethereal blue ice lit by the sun. Inside the cavernous berg, Sorykah found a flimsy strip of ice-coated rock circling a subglacial lake and crawled its length, searching for Rava. She heard strange cries but dismissed them as echoes of Sigue song. Clinging to available handholds, she stared into the bright aquamarine water and its midnight heart, envisioning a fall into that frigid vacuum, her face receding into darkness as the bubbles left her lips.

Sorykah heard a high-frequency, almost electronic call that gave her chills. Rava appeared in the pool as though viewed through the wide end of a microscope before finally surfacing. Tentacles made gentle S-curves below the water. "I have called them. We wait now, and see who answers."

Shadows blanketed the glacier and dimmed the light. The water frothed. Rava circled and dived, surfacing in a ring of foam to call, "They come!"

Two octameroons materialized from the depths, bearing a rapidly melting block of ice gored by a puddle of molten lava. Like Rava, their mauve-and-apricot-colored skin was dotted with blistery liver spots, but their long hair was nearly translucent. They gaped in her direction, swiveling clouded marbles in the puckered pouches of their blind eyes. With slits in place of nostrils, fleshy lumps for ears, and bulbous domed foreheads, Rava's kin had a more tenuous grasp on humanity. Sorykah shuddered, glad that they could not see her revulsion.

"You see? The demon bleeds into the sea." Delighted, Rava displayed a tight smile. "But we will lock up the gates. My cousins Töti and Egil come to repair the cracks." Tentacles swarmed together, stroking, writhing—a nest of vipers.

Sorykah strained to see in the failing light. "I don't understand."

"Holes." Rava said. "Like worms digging." A tentacle demonstrated the wiggle of a worm tunneling through dirt. "Töti will fetch ice from the floes. Egil will push ice into the holes to block the demon's escape. He is much braver than Töti."

Sorykah puzzled over this. None of it made sense, nor could she discern why Rava wanted to share it with her. The sun had dipped below the horizon and the glacier emitted weak gray light. Soon she would have to leave or it would be too dark and too cold to find her way back. Though the days were balmy, Sigue nights could be fatally frigid.

"The sun is setting, I have to go." Sorykah raised her hands. "I'm sorry."

"We are dying! If Diabolo escapes, there will be only fire here. No more Ostara. No more you, no more me. You must stop the boomer and find the taken." Exasperated, Rava clenched human fists and dipped below the water to communicate with her cousins. Moiling tentacles disturbed the sea and Sorykah turned away, repulsed by the octameroons' obscene congress. Rava popped up again. Her yellow eyes held the last of the fading light. "We can make you see. Come closer."

Shadows obscured the slippery ledge. A precipitous fatal fall awaited the turning of clumsy ankles. Sorykah slid and skittered, doubting her sanity, cursing the intrigue that lured her away from the cavern's open mouth and deeper into its cold throat.

"Here I am!" She knelt on a sliver of ice. Frost bit through her gloves. The still water was so clear that she felt a strong flashlight shined into its depths would reveal the sandy floor miles below.

"Give me your hands." Rava squeezed Sorykah's fingers, her own as frigid and hard as metal. Rava had so little body heat that she didn't even steam. Panic burbled in Sorykah's belly as Rava dragged her closer to that fathomless pool rimmed in ice that thickened before her eyes.

"Watch," Rava commanded. Töti and Egil swam closer until their submerged faces broke the surface. Lipless mouths opened, showing needle-fine teeth tipped in barbs: scavenger's teeth, designed to rip skin from bone and shred decayed flesh. Biochromatic cells in their skin contracted and released, flaunting bloodred, amber, and brown pigments. Dermal chromatophores reflected blue, green, and pink iridescence. Faster and faster, the light rings rippled along the octameroons tentacles. Bulbous foreheads strained and throbbed. An aura of hazy stars and blinking traffic lights illuminated the pool. Grown dizzy, Sorykah tried to look away but Rava would not release her.

The octameroons captivated Sorykah with their light show, just as the clever cuttlefish dazzles and stuns its victim, its only intention to devour and swallow. Sorykah ceased breathing. Her eyes were pegged open, a ghostly host of images capering before them. Even the change did not enthrall her so. *The change.* The sleep hovered, powerless to disrupt the octameroons' mesmerism. Tears gathered and ran over her lashes, dropping into the sea. Subaquatic sonar distortions of color pulsed in radiated arcs, a sensory onslaught of octameroon experience. She shut her mind against the bludgeoning broadcast; Rava's will hammered it open again. Oblivious to everything but the rhythm of light, ignoring her body's urgent cry for air or movement that would break the spell, Sorykah slid headfirst and silent into the water.

LIKE HER GENEROUS FIGURE, Nels had ample capacity for love, passion, pleasure. She was girlish and romantic, though she tried to disguise this behind a screen of holy devotion to the Blessed Mother. Nels's fidelity was a product of her amorous nature. That broad and free-flowing channel of adoration required damming to avoid overflow and her potential drowning. She'd struggled with her appetites since childhood. Hunger for cakes and sugary treats was replaced by a hunger for affection and physical satiety. She tempered her lusts—running her tongue over her lips and her hands over her hips—with prayer and invocation. Certainly, many others before her had done the same thing, for what good was religion if not to smother and douse? Though Nels devoted herself to studying the liturgies of the holy mother, she could not resist the pretty boys who came to call.

The mother goddess had no steady consort and her children, the pantheon of saints who called themselves her daughters and sons, were routinely fatherless. Jerusha did not prescribe specific behaviors; rather, she advised her followers to adhere to a moral order determined by their own innate understanding of empathy and higher good. Jerushian philosophy had no restrictions against intimate relations conducted with mutual honor. Nels was left to assign value to her wanting, to suppress or express as desire dictated. She aligned herself with faith, took to rigorous examination of holy texts, and wore her devotion like a cloaking, blinding veil. Though her gentleman callers treated Nels with tender respect, her frequent trysts proved too intense a distraction from her liturgical study. Poring over sacred illuminated manuscripts at the College of the Compassionate Heart in Auburn, Nels sought an even greater elevation. *Lift me above the distractions of my body*, she prayed. *Absolve me of profanity*, Nels pleaded. *Shine the light in my eyes and keep my feet steady on the true path.*

Ready to test the application of her faith in the wider world, Nels responded to a posting for a nanny in the job placement office. There were few professional positions open for scripture historians. Only the college had use for her but its departments were already full of professors and graduate students. The employment officer said that the woman who'd placed the ad was relocating to the Sigue, a frozen pole at the southernmost end of Plein Eïre. In spite of its cold and manifold dangers of lonely men and boredom, it struck Nels as an exotic assignment, and as no other applicants came forward, the position was hers by default. She interviewed with Sorykah Minuit, the mother of two-month-old twins. Reserved and unsmiling, the woman quizzed Nels on her experience with children, her personal and professional background, and her beliefs. A twinge marred Sorykah's mouth when Nels waxed on overlong about her sacred education but she came across polite and charming, bright and eager for an escape. The job was hers.

After Nels had been in Sorykah's household for a few weeks, Sorykah confided, albeit in vague terms, her children's mutation and by proxy her own. Weeks passed before one of the children changed, and months before Nels finally met her employer's alter, Soryk, when he ambushed Matuk's manor and she sewed on his severed finger.

Before then, Nels had been sufficiently occupied by her duties to dwell on nothing more than dirty diapers, feedings, and the housekeeping tasks assigned her. Nels touched Soryk for the first time after his tumble down the manor's slick stairs, her exultation at being rescued overcoming any shyness. She knew her mistress right away despite her male guise, for alter and primary were nearly identical.

In the Erun tree house, the sounds of ecstasy accompanying Sidra and Soryk's remove to its uppermost room inflamed Nels's imagination. She prayed for Jerusha to shield her from the vision of slender Soryk curling his arms around Sidra, his glinting gaze and the single dimple revealed on his cheek during a private moment of laughter. But Sidra had a firm grip on her devotee, and he was too besotted to notice anyone but her.

At home in the Quonset, the image of a love-dazzled and starry-eyed Soryk haunted the nanny's brain. Nels savored the enticement. Although there were no theology students to lead astray in Ostara, there was an abundance of dangerous and wily men: regimental, thermosuited Company men, miners with rustic beards and temperaments and Siguelanders with crinkling dark eyes and sensuous mouths.

Like most intelligent young women, Nels was curious and bored easily. She had few entertainments in Sorykah's household, and no one to comfort her when she writhed between the bedclothes at night, entangled by nightmares of icy piano keys, the contraction of her starving belly, or the alarm call of rustling, mildewed taffeta. Longing for attention, Nels was vulnerable to the advances of a man above her station. She much enjoyed her torments and would bait the trap of Soryk's masculine simplicity with a plump and willing lure.

Nels bit her fingernails and dithered. Sorykah had been gone for hours. The sun was setting when she finally decided to venture out. It would have to be a short trip. The children were sleeping in their beds and Nels could spare only the few minutes it would take to reach the harbor and make inquiries. Oona, the Siguelandic woman who ran the washhouse at the end of the street, was a grandmother, and Nels asked her to stay with the babies while she ran her errand.

Though Nels exhaled frosty clouds, it did not feel that her fingers would snap off or some dreadful urge to sleep would lure her to her death. Oenathe plants glimmered everywhere, breaking through crusts of ice. Drunk on moonshine, Siguelanders sang in the streets. Slowly the night emerged, a shabby imitation of its former self. There was no killing frost. Death could gain no foothold on this strange, mild evening.

Half a mile from Ostara, a huge black body floated in the sea beneath a ring of blue lights. Nels thought it a whale until she drew closer, saw its conning tower, and recognized Company men in thermosuits and long-coats streaming along Port Street. The *Nimbus* had returned. It sidled into port, slush foaming across its nose. Company workers ran the length of the harbor, trying to signal the captain through the tiny lens of his periscope to anchor at bay. They darted over the boards, shouting orders to underlings to pitch rowboats into the brine. Soon they cast out lines of bristly rope, launched a fleet, and bounced over the waves toward the *Nimbus*. It was too dark to see what they discovered at sea, but an emergency flare skimmed skyward. The Company medical team soon appeared, carrying portable oxygen tanks and a stretcher bearing a deflated warming tent.

One boat turned its lantern filter to red and motored back to shore while the others continued to the submarine. Four men heaved a motionless body from the boat's belly. The medical team advanced, administering oxygen and inflating the warming tent. Nels moved closer, suddenly cognizant of the sour taste in her throat and a permeating dread.

The rescued body was slender, its wet black hair frozen into meringue peaks of ice. Closed eyes and the cadaverous pallor of bloodless skin did not disguise Sorykah. Nels screamed.

THE ACCIDENT SERVED SORYKAH well. When the captain of the *Nimbus* spied Sorykah adrift on a floe, bedraggled and unresponsive, it was easy to pretend herself the victim of some terrible accident. None of the men remembered seeing Sorykah dock in Ostara those months ago. She could've been washed from the deck into the sea.

A depraved seaman might have abducted her or else a polar illness had weakened her, made her vulnerable to forgetfulness and wandering.

The medical team whisked her to the Company's head office on Port Street, equipped with a single infirmary bed and a two-man brig. They pumped her full of stimulants and heated fossil water, jump-started her failing, erratic heart, and cut her clothes from her. Sorykah woke naked beneath a sheet in an overheated room. Sensing the fortuitous nature of her situation, she merely shook her head when the Company doctor, a pudgy, gray-haired man of indeterminate age, inquired about her history and the cause of her accident. She could not remember. The round marks stippling her skin, like coffee rings or the imprints of burst bubbles, suggested a painful torture. He did not press her. A notation in her file insisted that she be allowed to resume her duties without questions. Sent by Chen Morigi, the unusual order was tantamount to a presidential pardon. Two administrators shoved paperwork beneath her signature, sent her home on a dogsled, and that was that.

Except that it wasn't—Nels hovered and pried, assuming the role of nurse and endlessly shoving mugs of hot ale and ox blood soup Sorykah's way, insisting that she warm up inside. She perched on the edge of Sorykah's bed, gawking at the fading imprints of octameroon tentacles on her mistress's skin. Distracted by caregiving, she began to forget the reedy man with the quirked mouth who lurked within Sorykah, restless and brimming with masculine need.

The octameroons' mesmerism left Sorykah vulnerable to flashbacks and hallucinations. Blurry pinpoint images would surface and recede, bringing with them intimations of brutal, cold darkness and the gaseous, sweet taste of decayed flesh. Rava's longing for the red glass hookah vibrated within Sorykah's head. She did not understand what she was meant to see in these visions. There were moments of stabbing pain, asphyxiation, or panicked swimming below the icy Sigue. If she looked too closely, tried to focus and wring some clarity from the sensory jumble in her head, the change would percolate inside her. She resisted it fiercely. Soryk would initiate a quest to gain the Erun and revisit Sidra. She could keep a grip on herself as long as she pushed away the visions. She could return to work when the week was out and the *Nimbus* set to sea again. Whatever Rava meant for Sorykah to discover would have to wait.

The days leading up to Sorykah's departure were dreary. She wanted only to be busy, to forget and keep moving forward without rest, sharklike. Soryk squirmed and wrestled inside her, a parasite within her gut. The change came at night, flipping her over, turning her facedown among the pillows to suffocate while Soryk crawled out, crowing in liberation. She tried to speak to him but he refused to listen. As much as Sidra insisted that Soryk/ah was one being with a common mind, she could not perceive her alter as herself. His maleness was alien. His engrossing lusts, a source of shame. Sorykah quarantined herself in her room, avoiding Nels and taking solace in her children and their bubble-dripping smiles.

She could not risk becoming Soryk aboard the *Nimbus*. The miners would not be kind. She would be a freak to them. Fathoms below sea, without benefit of royal advocates, par-wolves, or rich-dandy protectors, she would be vulnerable to everything from social ostracism to assassination.

Brawny and determined, clamoring for a life of his own, Soryk forced the change. Sorykah could not always resist. What happened next was inevitable.

NELS NO LONGER BOTHERED to knock at her mistress's door before entering. Long had they shared a home and they were well used to the routine joining their days.

"Sorykah, have you seen the paper today?" Nels threw open the bedroom door without so much as a cleared throat to announce her presence. She froze, flushed a hot, chili-pepper red, and stammered a faint apology. Her knees went liquid and she sagged against the doorjamb, her forehead creased in astonishment.

Soryk lay atop the bed, his face flushed with effort and excitement. His hair had been pushed, sweat-slicked, from his forehead and the air hummed with electricity. He turned away from her, drawing the sheet round his hips. Soryk flexed and hunched, and shuddered quietly. A ripple ran beneath his skin, traveling from his core to his extremities.

Nels could hear the newspaper fluttering in her hand, her shallow breath washing in and out. Tiny storms rose and gathered between her legs; heat built and spread.

Flustered, she took two deliberate steps backward and closed the door to lean against it, panting. It was such a shock to see him again, the familiar face barely altered but now sketched with definitively thicker strokes.

In their crib, Leander and Ayeda squabbled over a trinket but their complaints, which would have ordinarily sent Nels flying to soothe them, carried on as she lingered outside Soryk's door. She replayed the scene, searching for the source of her pique and sudden desire. The repetitive motion, his cheeks pink with exertion. Had he? Was that the first thing that sprang to mind (and to hand, she snorted) after the change? Nels pressed her ear to the door. Silence. Quickly she retreated down the stairs. Certainly, Sorykah would be perturbed at the interruption—Nels catching her alter in such a compromised state. She busied herself with dishwashing and baby-play, praying that he would soon retreat.

SORYK THREW CLOTHES ONTO his body. He hated that Sorykah kept but a couple of pairs of trousers and a few jerseys in the bottom drawer of her dresser for him. He had not even proper socks or underwear. She clothed him like an orphan! He rifled through her nightstand, fished her wallet from her rucksack, and tucked it into his pocket. He could wear her boots but he didn't want to. He wanted his *own* boots, his own gear, his own life!

Ransacking the bathroom, pitching Sorykah's few toiletries into a drawer, and clean-sweeping the shelves, he grieved for the existence denied him, the love stolen from him—Sidra.

"I could be king without you." He spoke only to his reflection, that lost-looking man who woke from slumber already bearing the world's weight on his slim shoulders. His primary was too present. He smelled her breast milk on his skin and disliked the exhumed-corpse odor of Sorykah's menstrual blood, stronger to him than it would ever be to another, so sensitive was he to the hormonal dregs that washed from her body each moon.

Soryk paced the room, irritated and shaking from the speed of the most recent change. Each time, he seemed to surge through more easily and with less physical distress than before. He wasn't used to it yet, couldn't court it without still fearing the submersion of some aspect of self. Still, the need to claim a bit of livelihood was overpowering.

Shiny gold embroidery scissors lay in a tray on the dresser. They seemed familiar, though he couldn't place them. They were small in his hands and sharp. He flipped them open, the bird's beak parting to snip whatever he placed between the blades. He examined himself in Sorykah's mirror. His hair was too feminine. It hung past his shoulders, a glossy black curtain. He grabbed a chunk, sawed through it, and discarded it on the dresser. The pile of shorn hair mounted along with Soryk's pleasure. *There.* Jagged and short but manly and much better. Armed with a new look, he decided to go into town to purchase clothing for himself. The location of shops was a mystery to him but Sorykah knew the way, didn't she?

A voice from below gave him pause. He vacillated, knowing himself caught in flagrante delicto. Perhaps the girl had seen nothing but his bare skin, had not guessed what he got up to when missing Sidra was too much to bear. Cautiously, he tiptoed through the house intending to sneak out the door. Nels spotted him and the blush that colored her cheeks betrayed her.

She bid him come. With her eyes: sly she-devils bright as bluebells. With her lips: pink and plump, and moist. With her soft hands and cushiony breasts. *Come,* she said wordlessly. Soryk sensed her desire and it clouded his mind, tamped out the cautious female voice of his primary that urged him to resist for the sake of their arrangement, good help being so hard to find. *If not for me, then for the sake of the babes — for they love her,* the voice whispered, *you must know, you will break their hearts if you drive her away.*

He heard none of it. He thought of Nels alone in her bed at night. Nels, whose juicy sweetness overran her like the sap of a fruit left to spoil on a warm counter.

Soryk slipped out the door, leaving Nels to worry about him getting lost in Ostara. After a few hours, he returned clutching his shopping bags. Nels stood wringing her hands in prayer. He pulled off his hat and said, "I was careful. No one bothered me."

"Yes, mistress. I mean . . ." She licked her lips and reddened. "Soryk."

He turned his back on the tension that vibrated the air between them and retreated upstairs. The children were bathed and tucked in their shared crib. He smiled at their songs and soft murmuring in the language they spoke when they thought themselves alone — not baby talk, English, or Siguelandic. He left them to wander through their made-up words and pulled fast the door. The house hummed, a sleeping beast with a generator heart and furnace lungs blasting on and off intermittently. Soryk smelled its evening smells: Nels's coffee nightcap brewing in the kitchen, the fading odor of dirty diapers, washing powder, and the lingering fermentation of spilled juice.

She would be at the kitchen table with her coffee now, spreading out the evening paper, poring over Ostara's six pages of news, opinions, and obituaries. Then she would tidy up, tucking away toys, books, stray socks, and cups. Retire to her room to change into her robe, let down her hair, and proceed to the bathroom to commence her bedtime routine.

Soryk's primary knew to wait until Nels came to say good night before addressing the day's tiny troubles, or commenting on the business of the household. Sorykah always allowed her nanny this solitude and left her in peace, untroubled by lurking hungers or the energy between a man and woman cooped in a Quonset on some frozen pole where warm bodies, shower-fresh and still damp, were rarely, if ever, encountered. Sorykah knew Nels well enough, but Soryk did not. He was a jackal, clever and lean, and Nels was a plump hen bursting with eggs. Soryk prowled the upstairs hall. He heard Nels refold the paper and set her mug in the sink. She swept through the common room and dumped a handful of toys in the bin. He met her at the top of the stairs. She jumped to see him waiting there, but there was no surprise in her eyes.

"Did you think I wouldn't say anything?" Soryk said.

Nels raised an eyebrow. "About your haircut?"

Soryk pursed his lips in imitation of his primary. "About your birthday. You'll find a small token of my appreciation for all your hard work on your nightstand."

Soryk followed Nels into her bedroom. She squealed when she saw the small, gift-wrapped box. Practical, unsentimental Sorykah would have simply handed her an envelope with money inside.

"Oh la! It's lovely!" She grinned, holding up the pendant so that she could admire his gift, a heavy glass droplet rich with gold veining and a hot streak of alizarin fire at its center.

Soryk stepped forward and took the chain from Nels's hands. "It's a dragon's eye. The eye of knowledge, a seer of fates. Do you like it?"

"Very much." Nels smiled, showing him her back and lifting her hair as he draped the chain across her collarbone.

"Happy birthday, dear Nels," Soryk said, silently thanking his primary for her date book's meticulous notations. The pale hair on Nels's nape was fine and wavy. He moved closer, pressed himself against her backside, testing. Holding her breath, she made not a sound. He wrapped his arms around her and squeezed. She placed her hands on his and turned to face him.

Her lips parted unconsciously and Soryk felt himself to be a hawk alighting on a pigeon when he kissed her. Her mouth opened to him. Their tongues met and a liquid sizzle traveled through his core—not love, he coolly noted, but want.

Nels kissed him back, deliberately silencing her inner objections.

"Surely Sorykah would frown upon my recklessness," Soryk teased, feeling cocky. "She'd be aggrieved by the impropriety of her alter taking advantage of her sweet, kind nanny on her birthday."

"I am neither sweet nor kind," replied Nels, pulling him deeper into her kiss. *And I'm not kissing my boss, I'm not. I'm kissing a lovely man who just happens to be renting out her body.*

Soryk's mouth traveled. He sprung Nels from her clothes. He ran his hands over her skin and fell beside her onto the bed, reaching beneath her tunic to tug off her knickers.

There was a moment when Nels saw Sorykah in his face, the way he half closed his eyes as if tired or a bit drunk. Would Sorykah come through to put an end to their shenanigans? Was she inside there, banging to get out? Then it was gone and Nels was relieved, though she turned away from him.

Soryk tucked one slender arm between her breasts to hold her tight against him and Nels parted her legs, wondering, as he slid inside, if he was fertile.

"Can Trader alters make babies?" Nels asked. "I think she would be very unhappy if you made me pregnant."

Soryk moaned, remembering his hands pressed against a window of cold glass. *No, not right,* he shook his head but the sensations lingered. Odors of smoky plum and vanilla tobacco were in his nose and a man's smooth voice was in his ear, in Sorykah's ear, calling her his duchess as he closed a strong hand around her throat and emptied himself inside her.

Soryk imagined Sidra there beneath his hands, giggling and sleek as a trout. A sharp pang of longing gouged his heart and a short sigh escaped. It was home he wanted. Leafy green, the swaying tree house and his own beloved, small and dear. Sorykah bound her alter with visions, first of the twins, lost and drowned in the Sigue Sea and now Rava's unending nightmare of black water and slashing scalpels. He had nothing to claim for himself. Nels was full of youthful abandon and naïveté. She should understand that this moment was devoid of meaning, that he used her like a rag to wipe away the images crowding his brain. He regretted his callousness. He should stop, *right now*, but he didn't, thrusting and panting like one possessed.

Closing his eyes, he could summon Sidra's shade. Could pretend himself with her, if he just avoided looking at Nels or touching her overmuch. However, Nels would not stop talking and it spoiled the illusion. He quickly finished and fled the room, the chastising voice in his head sneering, *Shame on you, you wicked, dirty dog*.

4

CORE ROOM CORPSES

FEAR RICOCHETED INSIDE SORYKAH. The *Nimbus*'s hatch
clanged shut behind her with the resolute clang of a prison cell door.
Waterlocks hissed and spit. The Inflatex seal plumped up, plugging
gaps around the door and converting the submarine into an airtight,
seagoing coffin.

Not a coffin, Sorykah reminded herself. She'd been down this
road before, and it was never good. Just when one terror was con-
quered, another erupted fully formed to take its place. Words became worries that became a heart-stopping spectacle of panic. Too
often, dread ambushed her, left her heart thumping and the world
reeling. Clamping down on her fears, she filed down the narrow corridors toward her cell, already imagining that the diminishing air
grew stale. Wistfully, she recalled the Erun's stratospheric ever-
greens and the endless snowy vistas of the Sigue's white wastelands,
its broad rocky shores and the sky that stretched forever overhead, silver with snow flurries or an astonishing, blinding blue.

Back aboard the *Nimbus* after a three-month absence, Sorykah existed within a dream. She had pulled it off. Rava had done her a favor by leaving her afloat in Ostara bay. After rescuing her, the Employee Resource Manager had meticulously transcribed that implausible, ridiculous story into her file. He'd wished her well, his impervious manner fronting a cool superiority that all Company representatives seemed to hone by night on keen whetstones. Here she was again in a thermosuit and magnet boots, preparing for another coring mission as if she had never left, and the whole, terrible experience was just some gruesome fairy tale or clinging nightmare.

Anxiety meant avoidance. It manifested itself as an urge to hide from people or situations that might prove dangerous and anyone who might express a sexual interest in her. Filled with miners who, through her untimely change, could discover Sorykah's secret, the *Nimbus* had become a vessel of terror. Within corridors cluttered with exposed pipes, gears, and gauges, the *Nimbus*'s crew was sweaty and consumptive, sucking down the recycled air, pressing too closely against her, the heat from their oily bodies like a suffocating blanket. The miners, foremen, cooks, and crew moved like stick puppets and their voices inched sluggishly over the panes of her awareness. Sorykah's crew would work, dine, and recreate together for a fortnight. Rather, eleven men would work and eat alongside Sorykah but would not invite her to join in their card games or banter. She was too aloof. Although they trusted her to do her job, her social reticence alienated those who might befriend her. The loneliness had not been so bad before; she'd grown used to it. Now, the thought of two weeks of near solitude left her weary. She missed her babies. It was a travesty to leave them so soon, but they had to eat, didn't they? She could not sustain her family without this job and the comforts it provided.

She missed Sidra, Nels, and even dour Carac with his dripping jaws and surly demeanor. They were her kind—somatics, aliens, outlaws. Not so the miners or the uniformly shipshape Company men with their slick-shiny hair, crisp suits, and gleaming insignias. They couldn't help it—they gawked. Sorykah was the fly in the milk. Returned from death's woolly wilds leaner and meaner, and missing a digit, her somber face shadowed by lingering sorrows as if she'd suffered dreadful things and lived. She'd picked up her tools and jumped right back into the hollow she'd left behind, and this frightened them.

The *Nimbus* began its descent. The floor pitched but magnet boots kept the crew from sliding forward and losing their balance on the inclines. Quick and nimble, the *Nimbus* shot through the ocean, heading for the core ice farm at the base of the pole. During the minutes en route to the midnight zone, some ten thousand feet below the surface, the crews would endure cooperative-work lectures orchestrated by the Company's newest import and resident cheerleader. Farouj dal Tajeet was a natty corporate flunky whose double-breasted suit and wingtips bespoke his inadequate preparation and ignorant surface-world surety. Affably beaming, his brown eyes latched on to each miner, forcing a personal connection. When his gaze alighted on Sorykah, its warmth cooled for a brief second, then enlivened again with new heat.

Sorykah squirmed beneath it, certain that some avaricious burrowing thing connected them. Maybe she was just paranoid. He looked at her too long, as if he wanted to speak but decided at the last minute to refrain. His cultured voice held traces of an Aroulian accent sanded down by training and arduously polished.

The presentation dragged on. Mr. Tajeet's enthusiasm for ice coring strategies and fossil water consumption statistics was unflagging. He braced himself against a row of pipes as the sub hurtled into blackness. The engines thundered in their ears but he merely raised his voice and plowed ahead. When the lecture ended, the miners rose yawning to shuffle to their bunks and await dinner service. Reluctant to push through the crowd, Sorykah was the last one out. Tajeet cornered her, thrusting his hand forward and lancing her with his smile.

"Have we met before?" He had the lacquered, liquid eyes of a silent film star, rimmed with coarse black lashes. He forced his hand into hers.

Sorykah shook her head, shrinking inwardly.

"I'm quite sure of it," Farouj said. "Aboard the *Celestia*? The *Solaria*?"

Again, she declined, leaning toward the door. He refused to release her, smiling insistently and waiting for her to speak.

"No, I think not." She slipped from his grasp—soft, manicured fingers the color of gingerbread. The heat from his hand lingered on hers like a glove.

"I'm certain of it. You seem so familiar."

"You're wrong," she said. "I don't know you."

"If you say so," he conceded, gesturing her toward the door. "Pardon me."

Sorykah slunk away, tremors jostling her legs. She wanted to bristle with dislike but he was an agreeable fellow. She couldn't decide why the encounter was so unnerving.

Sorykah's small cell was cold. She'd been unable to rid it of a persistent odor of dirty socks and was dismayed to think that someone else had been using her room in her absence. All the miners bunked double but as the *Nimbus*'s only female worker, Sorykah was granted a cell to herself. Though nothing more than a converted storage unit with a manual lock, the solo space was highly coveted. Crawling into the frigid, narrow bunk, she was again acutely aware of her solitariness. Shaken free of the old austerity, Sorykah's newly awakened senses throbbed, seeking something to feast upon. Sidra's voice trailed through the nights like a spectral winding sheet, unspooling from the corpse of Soryk's thwarted affection.

Soryk's memories of Sidra had begun to invade her own, arriving as a sudden sensory invasion of the queen's intoxicating fragrance of herbs, earth, and woman. Or the way she had looked at Soryk, her mirthful eyes shiny with want. These jumbled desires were a scattering of peas beneath her mattress. Sorykah's efforts to suppress those dreams that elicited the most yearning resulted in waking to the sound of Soryk's voice calling Sidra's name. Most uncomfortable was the intensity with which Soryk craved Sidra, as if he were a dying man and she were an oasis of spring water shimmering on the Aroulian desert horizon. Sorykah yearned for rest but was afraid she'd dream of Sidra's naked flesh and wake the beast in her, Soryk.

At first, she thought that leaving the sub would help but the inky polar ocean squeezed her like a fist. Though her days were strenuous—blasting and coring ice for eight straight hours, two more spent preparing to brave the ocean's intense pressure, decompressing, suiting up, suiting down, checking equipment, and logging her take—she fell into bed exhausted but wide awake. Sleep deprivation left her wired, frantic, and strung-out. She welcomed the occasional company of Pip and Squeak, the *Nimbus*'s resident mousers, who visited for an hour or two, hoping that she would reward their affections with a dish of breast milk squeezed out fresh and frothy. The babies were getting older; because of her lengthy coring missions, Sorykah had reluctantly decided to wean them. Her breasts ached, and milk still flowed, but less and less. She'd struggled to maintain her supply in their absence, filled with images of her nourishing breast milk healing her reclaimed babes. Milk as sweet as honey flowed in their veins, but they'd grown up too much in the interim and were no longer bound to her with infancy's strong belly cords. She had but a few drops to offer the cats on the tips of her fingers. The sudden interruption of the bosun's disembodied voice crackling from the loudspeakers startled Pip so much he inadvertently nipped her finger with a sharp canine.

"Code black, code black! Prepare for impact. Five hundred feet."

Warning sirens blared, rattling the coolant pipes. Acid orange signal lights flashed, illuminating empty walkways. Both cats hissed and scurried beneath the bed.

Instantly alert, Sorykah toppled from her bunk, magnet boots smacking the corrugated steel. The *Nimbus* pitched to port. A helmet slid from the narrow shelf, whacking Sorykah's shoulder before bouncing off the opposite wall and hitting the floor. Sorykah clutched the bunk pole as the sub lurched and righted itself.

"Two hundred feet," blared the loudspeakers.

Sorykah placed a hand on the wall, taking the engine's pulse. Subtle vibrations from the engine room traveled through the inner hull, telegraphing a record of the sub's efforts to break leads through pack ice and the slushy berg halos. Adept at judging the vibrations' intensity and speed, Sorykah could read the ocean environment as capably as the controllers with their sonic and radar equipment. A deep, rolling shudder followed by a coarse, grating noise broke the engine's steady cadence.

"One hundred feet. Prepare for impact." The bosun's brisk voice anchored the miners and kept them sensible in the face of impending danger. Every man aboard the sub would measure it for any hint of alarm, calibrating his own response against these impartial announcements.

"Fifty feet. Impact is imminent! Remain in your cells. Do not leave your cells."

There was a slight probability that the sub would be smashed between massive shifting ice plates, crumpled into a mangled ball of metal and death, miners, engineers, and Company overseers suffocated by miles of ocean pressing down, squeezing the breath and life from them.

Sorykah had done the math before accepting her position with the Company, using published data on shipping and submarine incidents, compiled with a slew of numbers culled from the marine administration's safety and engineering reports to arrive at her figure. The chance of dying in an accident was minimal; fewer than one in a thousand expeditions would end in catastrophe. Reasonable odds, she believed, and so she had taken the job.

"Twenty feet to impact!"

Numbers provided small comfort at times like these. She wondered at the size of the berg. A skilled helmsman could avoid it by diving into deeper waters if it tapered below the surface but Sorykah had little faith in theirs. Once, he had abruptly dived, plunging the sub nearly vertical in an attempt to circumvent a head-on collision with a five-thousand-year-old glacier. They had been knocked sideways in an explosion of sheared ice as the *Nimbus* grazed the berg. An obscene metallic crunch had reverberated through the ship, temporarily deafening the miners working in the core preservation room. Slush had accumulated around the viewing portals, effectively blinding the miners but not before they got a glimpse of the berg's underside, flaring out into the sea like a dancer's flowing skirt. That accident had added an extra week to the expedition as the huge dent was pounded out and repaired, leaving an uneasy crew trapped in a damaged submarine.

A muted "boom" throbbed inside Sorykah's head and the *Nimbus* seemed to contract in a momentary impulse of self-protection. Sorykah listened intently, her hand to the wall. The engine had quieted. They were running ancillary propellers—low-noise thrusters used when the motion of the main propeller might damage fragile ice formations or aggravate cracks in the bergs, causing sudden splits. Sorykah imagined the submarine entombed in the ocean floor's everlasting darkness. She waited to hear the wet, granular thud and scrape of the *Nimbus* coming to rest on the undersea permafrost and the hiss of compressed air leaking through split seams as the hull crumpled and caved in. She eyed the room's welded joints for faults and dripping water and found nothing but an eerie, unnerving quiet.

Sorykah cranked the hatch and stepping into the deserted passageway. Although the miners weren't forbidden from exploring the vessel in their free time, it was frowned upon. The Company expected them to confine themselves to the dining hall, their workstations, or crew cells unless otherwise directed. The others heeded the bosun's warning to remain in their cells but Sorykah convinced herself that her years of diligent schooling were required to avert a crisis. She would go to the core room and offer her services. A pep talk scrolled through her head, a series of cheerful assurances that should have made her feel better but didn't. Sorykah feigned confidence and strode briskly to the chutes leading to the core preservation room. Blue reserve lights illuminated the walkway. Amber beacons swirled round the passage, alighting on the ladder to the control rooms and the chutes to the drilling deck one floor below.

She heard only the soft susurration of the heating vents circulating warmed oxygen and the sporadic buzz of the bulbs spluttering in their sockets. Pale bands of light revolved across the open end of the chute creating the illusion of sunlight playing upon the water. It was a little sensory feint the Company used to make the miners think the surface was within kicking distance should they choose to pop up for a breath of fresh air. The dining hall had a similar trompe l'oeil—a scrolling picture window of summer pastures and stone fences penning in the occasional grazing, walleyed cow—which gave the miners the impression that they coasted through rural lushness in a steaming locomotive, free to step from the train into beds of flowering clover.

Sorykah descended, boots ringing against the ladder's steel rungs. The core room was deserted. Round vacuum-lock doors eighteen feet in circumference studded the core preservation chamber's walls. Each one had a tear-away seal of Inflatex foam that sprayed from jets around the rim of the door to harden into a semipermanent seal. Once the miners loaded their quota into the deep-freeze chambers and locked the vacuum doors, there was no need for a watchman. Controlled by an independent computer system, the self-monitoring chambers corrected fluctuations in temperature and pressure. If there were additional problems, the system would notify the mainframe and the ship's mechanic would make manual adjustments. Upon arriving at the processing station to deliver their haul, a team of cargo inspectors would invade the core room to test the seals' fastness. Damaged or broken seals meant that the cargo would be rejected. Hundreds of potentially tainted ice cores would be dumped into the sea and the miners' bonuses reduced by a commensurate percentage, a "Cores for Cash" policy meant to make them protective of their investment.

Sorykah crept through the room, running her fingers over the vacuum locks. All were intact but for a few empty chambers at the end of the row. Shining metal pallets inside the core slots grimly resembled autopsy tables. She punched in the code to launch the undersea imager used to track core extractions. The mapping system crackled to life, its holographic generator glowing. Lasers webbed the air over the imaging table and a 3-D map materialized—a grid of glowing blue and white lines detailing the interior of the massive berg. Tunnels spiraled toward convergence within its icy heart, an ant colony of furrows and chambers that followed a mysterious logic of their own.

Stars winked in one of the tunnels, moving into the open sea— possibly a pod of rogue whales on a fishing expedition, but mammals wouldn't be able to come so far below and make it back to the surface before running out of oxygen. Ships, perhaps, or submarines?

Something broke away from the ball of light that represented the *Nimbus*. Sorykah heard the distinctive clanging whoosh of exploratory orbital pods detaching from the rear hatch. Blips of light flared from the imaged sub and fanned beneath the berg, like spores released. Two orbitals closed ranks, heading straight up the tunnel. Realizing that she watched a hunt in progress, Sorykah's curiosity turned to horror. The orbitals split up. One continued toward the stars while the other diverged into a side tunnel, speeding toward a breach in the ice that would put it behind its target. Zigzagging wildly, the trapped stars attempted escape. An orbital mimicked their maneuvers, running them down and exhausting them while the other blocked the exit.

One by one, the pods consumed the stars. Bellies full, the orbitals headed for the *Nimbus* to dock and discharge their cargo in the preservation room. The faint sound of engaging orbitals rang through the *ship*. Sorykah envisioned the core room's floor wet with seawater and perhaps blood, thermosuited drivers—hunters—gloating over their triumph and the final, fatal hiss of expanding Inflatex seals. Quickly she shut down the imager, returned to her cell, and locked the door, putting her hands to the wall to steady her shaking legs.

After morning bells, the speakers crackled with life. The bosun's voice radiated a strained and conscripted glee. "Last night, we experienced a slight malfunction with the ship's security function. The glitch has been repaired and your doors should be unlocked. If any crew member cannot exit his cell, sit tight and someone will get around. Again, nothing to worry about."

Lockdown would explain the previous night's disturbing quiet and the curious absence of crew. She hadn't realized that the *Nimbus*'s computer could manipulate the door locks but naturally, it would exert that last sinister measure of control over its workers. *Penning us up like goats*, Sorykah thought, and shuddered. *What do they not want seen? What extinguished stars lie frozen in the cargo hold?*

Voices filled the corridor as the men headed for the dining hall and breakfast. Normalcy returned by degrees. The *Nimbus* burbled upward as the ballast tanks shed their weight, leaving behind the complex tunneling inside the berg. Sorykah had little appetite but felt that she ought to maintain the appearance of ignorance. As lunatic as it sounded, she feared that she had stumbled into a conspiracy. The surface seemed very far away indeed.

THE FOLLOWING NIGHT, SORYKAH lay awake long past the call for lights-out, graphing notebooks and organic chemistry books strewn across her lap. The wee hours were a fertile ground for abstractions and mulling over her inventions, such as a waterless wash pad, enzyme tablets to kill the stench of night soil buckets, or more vexingly, a method to clean dishes with only a modicum of effort, detergent, and water. Beneath her, the *Nimbus* gently rolled. There were no currents at this depth so this swaying, occurring now for the third successive night, was aberrant. Certain that she could hear the gurgle of waterlocks and the occasional clang of metal upon metal, she listened, ears straining. The ship remained

quiet but for the occasional close-quarters quarrel, bursts of laughter from a closed cell, or very occasionally, muted thumps and
moans that everyone pretended not to hear. The miners were supposed to remain in their cells from 23:00 to 06:00. The Company enforced this policy to save energy, just as toilets were not flushed and
the taps turned off to conserve water. Consequently, the stench of
night soil was strongest in the morning, before the cleanup crew
flushed the previous evening's excretions through waste portals into
the sea.

The dim light from her reading lamp's single bulb strained her
eyes. Her cell was damp and stuffy. She had to get out. The dining
hall would be empty. She could stand in front of the air vents and
pretend that she was on the Sigue's shore, buffeted by subarctic
winds.

Sorykah was twenty minutes into a novel when a man touched
her. She jumped, slamming her book closed on her thumb and
sending a chair careening across the dining room. It was only the
harmless Company man.

He smiled at her, his teeth glowing blue beneath the emergency
lights. "Did I frighten you?"

She noted that Mr. Tajeet wore a thermosuit and magnet boots
and congratulated him on his more sensible dress.

"Loafers are slippery, as you can imagine. This is much more
practical. Please, call me Farouj." His face swam into view in the circle of lamplight. "May I sit?" Farouj settled himself across from her.
"Your hair is different."

"I hate it." Sorykah fingered the choppy cut.

"It suits you." Farouj took her hands in his. One thumb stroked
Sorykah's wrist and she felt that she should object, but she did not.

"Where did you say we met?"

"Not long ago, I attended a very grand party, given by a man with
much money. He's devoted to pleasure and the sensual arts, music,
food, and women, yet he's not satisfied. Corruption breeds within
him like a disease."

A tremor traveled from Sorykah's chest down into her thighs, quivering beneath the table.

"This man," Farouj continued, "buys and sells dreams, favors, people—even hymens. He fancies himself a filmmaker. He takes advantage of desperate people who seek his help and forces them to perform for him."

"And you? Are you a buyer or a seller?"

"I'm a guardian, a watcher. I gather information but I am no pleasure-seeker. I'm not one of them."

"You speak of Chen Morigi."

Farouj nodded. Sorykah wanted to leap from the table and barricade herself in her room.

"I was the leopard who declared you female," he said. "Do you remember?"

Yes, she remembered. Farouj had been one of the party guests at the House of Pleasure when Chen had bartered the secret of the unpickable lock for her ritual defilement. Half naked and costumed in black spots and gold body paint, he had kissed her hand. Even now, his broad thumb stroked her skin as if rubbing in the traces of that long-ago kiss.

"Why are you here?" It was an extortion plot, she was certain.

"I wanted to warn you. Your face is displayed on every digi-reel screen in Neubonne."

"What do you mean, you've seen my face in town?"

Farouj had the decency to look ashamed. "Your films. Your body," Farouj hesitated. "Changing."

Then she understood. The images of her coerced copulations and the forced transformation into her male primary had been captured on digi-reel. She thought that Chen merely broadcast the experience on silk screens for his audience. Instead he'd preserved her change on film and had either sold or distributed the reels himself. Her careful illusion of safety, the self-preserving of modesty and invisibility she'd woven around herself, had been pulled away, exposing her deepest and most painful secret.

She paled. "Why are you telling me this?"

"People are talking. Some of the miners have already seen the reels."

"And you? You've seen them and now you stalk and solicit me?" She vibrated with rage. How foolish to think Chen would not profit at her expense. "Are you here to watch me?" Sorykah railed. "To spy on me? Report back to the Company and have me fired?" She tumbled in a maelstrom of paranoia and fear, worried for her financial future, her career. "I had to do it," she sagged toward the table. "For my children's sake. What would you have done?"

"The same, I suppose."

"What do you want from me?"

"Sorykah, your name is pasted on every somatic tongue in Plein Eïre. You killed the Collector. A woman who can take down the enemy of an entire nation, one who will do whatever is necessary to meet her goal—you're a hero." Farouj was a flatterer, but a sincere one.

She felt ill. How could Farouj know about Matuk's murder? The only witnesses to the destruction of the manor were Nels and Dunya. Nels had little opportunity to talk and no one to talk to, aside from the children. Dunya then, or Sidra, Carac, Hans, or any of the somatics who had passed through Sidra's tree house after their return from the Erun. It would only take an offhand mention, a moment of pride, or a confession of guilt to let slip the truth of her role in Matuk's murder. The somatics would never keep such a thing quiet, nor had Sorykah asked Nels or Dunya to refrain from discussing it. She assumed that like her, they were glad just to be done with it and to leave that white palace of death.

"Who told you?"

"Somatics talk. Dog-faced girls, anyway. When they heard the marble manor burned down, two Erunites looted what was left of the spoils. They carried their story back to the trading posts and it spread as far as the Aroulian desert, my homeland. My heart sang for you. Brave, beautiful Sorykah! I felt then that I understood you, that you were kind and honest. That you would help us."

"How can I possibly help you?"

Farouj inhaled deeply; it was his turn to trust now. "There is a processing station for fossil water on the Aroulian Qa'a'nesh reserve."

"I know it. A bit of a far trek just to bottle water."

"But the labor is free. Corpocratic law prevents the Five Nations from intervening. As long as the Qa'a'nesh live on Company land, they work in exchange for room and board, nothing else. It's slavery."

Sorykah shook her head. She knew all about TI's subjugation of Plein Eïre's indigenous populations. Tirai Industries owned two-thirds of the continental landmass stretching from the eastern shores to the northern desert and down the coast to Blundt, where TI manufactured chemicals and smelted steel, all the way to the frozen Sigue. When it purchased the northern territories, TI evicted the Qa'a'nesh from their ancestral lands and installed them on a reserve in the Aroulian desert. The Qa'a'nesh did not take to their forcible confinement. Tirai Industries staked out the reserve's perimeters with border patrol stations, razor wire, and electrified mesh. Cut off from their food supply—roving herds of desert deer, seasonal flowering cacti and succulents—and dependent on the rations available at TI's commissary, the tribe languished. When TI opened its fossil water plant on the reserve and offered to pay its workers in commissary credit, the tribe eagerly accepted the yoke of their submission, for the Qa'a'nesh love children and prize their well-being above all else. Watching their babies starve was incentive enough to ensure their obedience. Within months, TI made an entire people dependent on its provisions.

Steering the conversation to topics slightly less depressing than the systematic annihilation of the Qa'a'nesh, Farouj said, "The People need freedom. Help me convince them to leave the reserve. Security is minimal. No one travels the desert but the nomads, and they avoid the plant as much as possible . . ."

Footfalls echoed in the corridor. The dining hall door slid open and in came Nunn, the bursar.

Farouj dropped Sorykah's hands and, for Nunn's benefit, demanded of her, "Why aren't you in your cell? You should not roam the ship after lights out. The captain will be most unhappy to discover his orders flouted."

Nunn's gaze landed on Sorykah and Farouj, alone in the abandoned canteen. His plain-as-pudding face shifted slightly.

"As I was explaining, the mess is closed." Farouj stood and waved Sorykah up from the table. "I'm sure there is sufficient light in your cell to study there. You were just leaving," he insisted.

Sorykah rose, books pressed close like paperbound armor. Nunn sucked his teeth as Sorykah squeezed past him, exhaling against his moist aura of moldy woolens.

He flashed a gingival grin. "Back to bed now. Scurry on." Nunn leered at Sorykah's back and turned to Farouj, scanning him with a shifty gaze. "Hadn't pegged you for a freak. Crumb-catchers don't usually start sniffing round 'til at least a week at sea. You work fast, I'll give you that."

"Just looking for a coffee. Thought I might find the cook in."

Nunn harrumphed. "You're a man of peculiar tastes. That swill they pass off as coffee doesn't have a drop of the real thing in it. But maybe that's the way your type likes it."

"My type?" Farouj bristled. He really didn't want to start something but he wasn't going to take abuse from a clerical hack like Nunn.

"Sand fleas. Your type." Nunn sucked his teeth again. "Get a taste for it at your fancy college? I suspect they don't even know what coffee is up on that reserve of yours. Camel's milk might suit you better." Nunn brayed in deranged imitation of a dromedary.

Farouj quickly rejected his first three impulses: fist strike to the solar plexus, heel of hand driven up into Nunn's nose, shattering its bridge and forcing bone shards into his prefrontal cortex, or elbow in the gut followed by a swift uppercut. He was left with little recourse but to ignore Nunn's bait and walk away. The brutality that leapt so readily to his defense was nothing more than an old reflex, a mindless muscle twitching in response to a physical trigger. He had given his oath before the goddess and cast his blood into the flames to seal their pact. No violence without mercy. No punishment without forgiveness, so sayeth the warrior code. *Blast it.* He wanted to feel virtuous, but he didn't. All he wanted was to wring that little toad's neck. Now he'd have to find Sorykah and start over from scratch.

5

WE VANISH

FAROUJ CONSIDERED HIMSELF a good guy, a nice guy, even though his intentions were sometimes less than admirable. For example, his carefully considered and deliberate ascension within Tirai Industries. From minor admin to Worker Relations Liaison with travel credits and security clearance, Farouj could justify his every choice, emotion, and action. The lies he told were necessary and the conceits he perpetrated vital to his mission. He was beholden to ideals much grander and more important than his own petty ones. The future of his people was at stake. Should he, a true son of the Qa'a'nesh, abdicate duty like the tribal elders, stuffed with cheap commissary food and liquor, bloated with sloth and captivity?

His parents' tawdry death had ridiculed the tribe and watered Farouj's voice within the elder gatherings. They thought him a half-blood half-wit, good for nothing but emulating his father's indulgences. He wouldn't sacrifice his cousins and sisters to the elders' apathy. They must throw off their chains! But they laughed him out of every prayer circle and humiliated him so intensely that at last, he threw a dog against the electrified fence, cut the shorted wires around the burning carcass, and fled the compound.

He might be tempted to abandon them and let the Qa'a'nesh malinger, grow fat and soft on Company pap, but he could not. He'd made a promise. Raised by his grandmother, Farouj owed everything to her. She'd protected him when his grandfather and the tribal elders, angered by the loss of their daughters, wanted to cast him out. Aziza dal Tajeet drew a circle of blood around him and summoned Asta to guard him in her sight. Chastened by her power, the elders obeyed. Aziza died just one year after the Qa'a'nesh lost their land, not ill, but heartbroken. Farouj watched her wither, refusing to eat commissary rations, longing for the fierce desert wind and heat. It was too damp and dark underground. She shivered perpetually, coughing against the drafts blowing up from the lowest levels. Aziza had predicted everything—long years of subtle dissolution as their ways eroded and new generations came into the world far from the sun and shackled by corporate ownership.

"Save the People," Aziza whispered, skeletal hand clenching his. Her skin was as dry as papyrus. "You will find a way. If not you, One Foot Outside, then who?"

FAROUJ TAPPED AT SORYKAH'S cell door.

She rose, still groggy, to admit him. "You again. What do you want? I already told you that I can't help you." She smoothed her hair, self-conscious before this striking, well-groomed man.

"I want to show you something. It might change your mind."

Sorykah peered out her tiny porthole into the sea's unvarying blackness. "I don't see anything."

"You wouldn't. Haven't you noticed that the port side always faces away from the berg at night?"

True. Sorykah had never once had an evening view of the berg, though she gazed at it all day long, but she'd never considered this unusual design.

"Go away. You've already caused me too much trouble."

"Look, Nunn's all bark and no bite. You don't have to worry about him. When this is over, he'll lack a pissing pot, and we'll be the ones in control. Now, come with me." Sorykah trailed him through the *Nimbus*'s bowels, a maze of tight corridors crowded with pipes, control panels, and valves. Farouj unlocked a double-reinforced door and they entered another corridor, its corrugated floor slick with brine. Thrumming generators made her teeth vibrate as pumps hissed and bellowed; ahead sounded murmuring voices and the muffled ring and clatter of metal instruments.

Sorykah crept behind Farouj into an empty workroom. Two cages of steel bars were soldered to the ship's interior wall beside shelves of equipment such as one might see in a surgery from an earlier age: strange hooks, thin, curved knives, and a long pole with an electrified collar and manacles attached to one end. Farouj opened a cabinet to show Sorykah boxes of thick-barreled syringes with eight-inch needles and boxes of plastic envelopes used for storing blood and body fluids. Steel tanks of etherine sulfate, an anesthetic, lined the floor. A huge spindle of waxed black thread sat in a scum puddle.

Something flashed outside the porthole, briefly illuminating the room and filling the pane with a blast of light. The submarine seemed to buckle and belched strange gunfire that made Sorykah's head ache. *The boomer.*

"Sonar pulse." Farouj clung to the porthole, staring into the sea. "Watch."

A glaring spotlight scoped the side of the berg, stark white against the black ocean. Clumps of leafy, rust red kelp floated into view. A primitive fish darted by, Ping-Pong ball eyes glowing within ghostly scales. A drifting carcass buffeted the windowpane, its unconscious humanoid face a slack and purple smear, its limbs and tentacles motionless. The octameroon drifted toward the berg and the light followed it, illuminating thousands of hollowed black core tubes in the ice.

"Oh," Sorykah breathed, absorbing the wreckage of the mighty berg. "I hadn't realized we'd taken so much. It's awful."

Farouj grimaced. "It looks like lace."

Together they watched the *Nimbus* extend its claw to pluck the body of the stunned octameroon from the water and draw it into its mouth. The core room door whooshed, and the sea relapsed into darkness.

"Not much longer now," Farouj said.

Lithe and twisting, a deep despair convulsed within Sorykah. When the *Nimbus* spat out another octameroon, the ensuing flash of light framed the body awash on the deep ocean currents and made her stomach tighten. "Why do you show me these things?"

"Because you should know the whole story, else I would not expect you to care," Farouj answered mildly. "TI transports octameroons by ship and train from the Sigue to the fossil water plant and puts them in a drug-induced coma. They *milk* them. If the ink's taken slowly, it regenerates at the rate of removal. A single octameroon produces about six ounces daily. Sorykah, you have slain the worst enemy of our time. Like it or not, you are a part of history. Perhaps Jerusha intends more for you."

Sorykah balked. "I don't follow Jerusha and I'm no one's savior."

He beamed. "Ah, you're Astarian! An adherent of the old religion. Then you know that when the souls of a man and woman join within a single body, Asta is reborn to again drive the shadow gods from the bright world, wielding her sword of flame."

"This is your purpose? To elicit my sympathies and employ my sword against a new enemy? You are mistaken, Farouj. I am not she."

"Sometimes we do not want to read our own stories, but you cannot prevent the world from continuing to write for you. Sorykah, you were born a Trader for a reason."

"There are other Traders. You don't need me."

"But they didn't kill Matuk." He touched her again, as he always seemed to do. It wasn't intrusive or handsy. His palms were warm on her thin shoulders, firm and steady.

Sorykah closed her eyes, remembering Rava's pleas for aid. Suppressed guilt surged forward. She could not help thinking like a mother. Rava was someone's child, just as Radhe, trapped within the shell of the dreaded Wood Beast, had been a child in need of help. *Even when we are grown, we are still just children,* she thought. Dunya had cared for Sorykah's babies despite her fear because it was the right thing to do. Nels said that Jerusha counseled living according to one's highest moral order. Sorykah could not pretend that her ethical ceiling was lower, simply to avoid a challenge.

"I can't do it. I've only just come back to my normal life. I won't leave my children to chase wild geese."

"Even to punish Chen? To satisfy your hunger to see the Morigis destroyed?"

"What do you know about Chen?" Sorykah was livid at the mention of his name. She stamped with vicious feet at the memory of pleasure that heated her belly and sent tremors through her skin, remembering the smoky plum scent of him, the fever heat of his skin and the tug of his lips against hers. "Ergh," she groaned, forcing herself away from that irksome arousal to Chen's betrayal by digi-reel.

Farouj smiled, amused by the sudden color in her cheeks. "He makes and sells the reels. He profits from the sale of fossil water and ink. The Company's just an arm of Tirai Industries, and now that his father is gone, Chen reaps the spoils."

Sorykah was aghast. She'd been so intent at putting the entire escapade out of her mind that she hadn't considered the natural chain of progression, that Chen would inherit his father's vast empire at Matuk's death.

"Tirai Industries will end the bloodline of Ur's children, and with it, our last connection to the old gods. We'll be left without a history. You have ties to the Morigis," Farouj whispered, "ties to the Sigue. Our world will disintegrate if this theft continues. Deep cracks vent the glacier, disharmonies play in the Sigue Song. The harbor recedes as the ice thins and breaks. The octameroons are vital to the health of the pole. Their slaughter threatens the safety of all somatics and humans."

"What do you care?"

"Siguelanders are cousins to the Qa'a'nesh. We've both been betrayed and must protect each other from further decimation." Farouj's eyes held a faraway look. "It is the end of an era." Farouj came back to her and said, "I fear these changes. None of us will survive if Chen retains control of TI. He's a lout, consumed by his need to scratch that most primitive of itches, as you well know."

There were sudden shouts down the hall and Farouj grabbed Sorykah's hand. "Quickly now, let's go."

They slipped silently through the corridors and returned to Sorykah's cell. Farouj followed her inside. His presence made the tiny cell seem impossibly confining and short of air. His breath was warm against her neck as he pressed his palms to her chest, decorously avoiding the swell of her breasts. "I feel your heart beating . . . it gallops like a horse." He smiled and closed his eyes, murmuring a short prayer in his native tongue.

"What did you say?" Sorykah was a bit awestruck by his proximity. She could see the black pepper sprinkle of his beard just below the skin, and a single strand of gray hair at his temple.

"It's a summons. Everything we do, every interaction we have with others is like a coal or water droplet upon a fire—feeding or dousing our *t'naq*: spirit. Just like we warm our hands and cook food to nourish our bodies over a fire, our *t'naq* is a radiant energy. Taking Matuk's life fueled yours. It burns brightly inside you—a light to guide the People." He cupped his hands over his face as if inhaling her essence. "The *t'naq* travels through touch—flows through my hands into my heart." He smiled. "You've shared your courage with me. Now share it with the Qa'a'nesh."

"You took it from me," she countered weakly. Sorykah felt the press of Farouj's masculinity upon her female senses, or was it the heat of his *t'naq* that lit a fire in her belly? The thought of capsizing the Morigi empire was almost too tantalizing to pass up, a final stroke of revenge against the Collector. Farouj coaxed with glib words but it was not enough. Asta may have been reborn, but not in her.

"You ask too much. I can't do it." She shook her head, resolutely crossing her arms.

"What's your enticement then? Money? Enough to leave this place for good?"

Sorykah's gaze flickered as she considered.

"People are like safes requiring only the correct combination to pop right open," he murmured, pressing his cheek to hers. "If not money, then glory and righteousness, or food, or home and creature comforts. The necessary pleasures of bed and body."

Thoughts of Nels swam unbidden into Sorykah's mind. Her dear nanny, that pious girl. *That naughty girl.* Sensation bloomed in her fingertips, lips, and nethers. Would she always be prey to changing upon the voicing of certain words, the releasing of specific scents, captive to the caprices of her body and enslaved by the whims of her genetic code? She craved a return to her battened-down days, sexless and silent, her body like an unfeeling board instead of a hot pot that boiled over at a whisper or the lightest of feather strokes.

Sorykah suspected that if she took Farouj's full bottom lip between her teeth, she'd feel the thin pulse of a blood vessel. *Shit, shit, shit.*

"You have to leave now!" Sorykah pushed him out the door as the change bubbled in her fingers and toes. "Get out!"

"I won't give up, Sorykah." Farouj melted into the shadows of the empty corridor.

Sorykah tumbled to her thin mattress, vision dimming as she tried to assert her will and fend off another change. This was the wrong time, the wrong place. She'd so skillfully managed her body's treacherous nature, she could not quite believe control would so easily slip from her grasp. There were too many others inside her mind, all vying for her attention. She forced herself to think of her bonny babies, but her breasts did not respond with the customary burn of milk-making. Instead her skin tingled with hormonal excess; storms of testosterone and androgen surged. Soryk would claim her life. As the darkness gathered and the change raged, she tried desperately to imbue Soryk's burgeoning awareness with a sense of duty and caution. *Be temperate, keep to yourself, and for Jerusha's sake, shave!* And then, she was gone.

THOUGH HIS CALM DEMEANOR had barely changed, the glimmer in Farouj's eyes revealed his elation. He slipped into Sorykah's cell before morning bells.

"Good morning! I have news for you." He hovered over the bunk, prodding the body wrapped tightly in blankets.

"Go away!" Sorykah's voice was throaty.

"I thought you might have changed your mind, having slept on the problem. Thought that night or dreams convinced you, where I failed," said Farouj.

Soryk clutched the covers around his head, his heart hammering. He'd not yet reconciled himself to this strange place, engine vibration thrumming beneath his feet, shaking the walls around him. The stench of night soil buckets permeated the cells. Distant pings and clicks indicated the *Nimbus*'s activity level as the submarine warmed its propellers, defrosting its nighttime accumulation of ice. The recycled air was sticky against Soryk's skin. He was tired of waking up in strange places. Soryk prodded his memory, searching for some sliver of information about the owner of the voice in his room. Sorykah's sleeping awareness was as murky as mud, and wading into it in search of submerged gems, images from recent life, was an arduous task. Snapshots of events surfaced, blurred and water-warped. Voices distorted themselves, manipulated by the forgetfulness of the Perilous Curse, Soryk/ah's dread disease. Sudden guilt plagued him upon remembering what he'd done to Nels, *with* Nels and *for* Nels, her vivacious excess, Soryk wearing the scent of her tuberose perfume like a second skin when he fled the bedroom. He groaned. What had he done? He'd never be able to look her in the eye again. What a mess he'd made of things.

Morning bells chimed, startling them both.

"I took the liberty of having you reassigned to the eastern slope crew to cut cores within the vent." Farouj knew that Sorykah rarely drilled inside the berg. She took most of her quota from its surface, else she scouted for veins of fossil ice and prepared explosive charges to sever them from the glacial pack. The reassignment required a bit of finagling and well-worded wheedling, but he'd gotten his way, just as he knew he would. Using the berg to guide them upward, their ascent would be quicker, shielded on one side by the mountain of ice. Thousands of feet above them, a fishing trawler circumnavigated Ostara bay, awaiting Farouj's radio signal and his appearance, breaking the water with another in tow, anxious to be hauled up and under way.

"Why?" Soryk was intrigued. He figured that keeping his answers brief might disguise him long enough for the other party to say his piece and leave, giving Soryk some much-needed solitude.

"Again, I plead my people's case. Sorykah, the Qa'a'nesh are becoming completely assimilated. We're forgetting our ways. Our children are born into slavery knowing nothing of the desert. Our traditions will die. What will those children do when they can no longer suckle the corporate teat? They're already becoming sugar-heads used to spoon-feeding and ease."

"Sugar-heads?" Soryk couldn't resist asking.

"Head full of sugar means no meat, no blood. No imagination."

Soryk grunted. He liked it. It was getting hot under the covers and it was clear from the resolute way his body had settled into maleness that the change was not coming. "Wait, change my mind about what?"

"Are you joking? If so, I find your humor too dry for my taste." For the first time, an edge of irritation crept into Farouj's voice.

"Sorry. Just tell me once again what you asked me to do."

Finally, suspicion stirred. Farouj said, "Fine. But I prefer to speak to you face-to-face. Unless you're hiding something." He stepped forward, peering at the single lock of black hair poking from beneath the blanket. "Sorykah? Have you changed?"

Soryk threw back the covers and stared at Farouj with gratitude and alarm, waiting for one emotion to outweigh the other. "You know me? You know about the change?"

Nonplussed, Farouj nodded. "I told Sorykah the whole story. I was at the House of Pleasure when you—when she—performed for Chen." Farouj explained the rest of their communal history, from Chen's to the previous night, when they'd snuck through the *Nimbus*'s lower decks, spying on the octameroon hunt. "The Qa'a'nesh await the rebirth of Asta. Even though TI forced our conversion to the House of Jerusha, the elders still believe that Asta will remake her body and return to drive away the shadow gods. Matuk's death was a sign that Asta is here, at last. Now, the People need only to see her, see Asta's split repaired and her body whole. If they witnessed the transformation of a body, from male to female, they would be delivered of their bonds. Don't you see?" Farouj's brown eyes burned with a fierce light. "Come with me. Your *t'naq* is strong. Show the People that you are real and help them shake off their stupor!"

Soryk considered this. Here was the chance to forge his own destiny. Inspiration flared like a white-hot magnesium fire. "Sorykah stole me away from my queen, but she can't keep me from fulfilling Sidra's wishes. She'll be furious if I do this thing. I'll not be second best, chained to another's will," Soryk said. He grinned broadly. "What do you propose?"

Sorykah's protests cut through the murk, a far and muted fury. Her fists beat upon the closed doors of his conscience, demanding attention. The prospect of a glorious adventure as a righteous knight fighting for his queen, along with an escape from the shame of facing Nels again and the chore of caring for Sorykah's babies, proved too tantalizing a lure.

Farouj's conviction mixed with Soryk's desire to define his life through actions of his own design. Together they could achieve what could not be done alone: combine two immiscible goals, parallel yet complementary, each with its own purpose. Farouj was asking the impossible. Soryk must change on command and risk his disappearance. Could he do it? He'd never tried before, but suddenly, he began to see that if he could learn to master the change, he would no longer be its slave.

"What if I can't change at the right time? What if they don't believe me? Or you?"

"There are Traders who support themselves by changing. It's their job. Surely, if they can learn how to do it, you can too. Come with me to Neubonne. We'll find someone to teach you."

Filled with the queasy, sick joy of one plotting a murder, Soryk licked his lips and swallowed the bile that filled his throat. If he could achieve this, he would be the primary. *Sidra.* For her, anything. "All right. I'll do it. And you'll get me back to the Erun when it's over."

"Agreed." Farouj shook Soryk's hand but could not meet the other man's eyes. "Look, it's getting late. You should already be in the dining hall by now. If you don't show up for your shift, someone will come to find you. You have a better chance of eluding discovery if you act normal. Best to hide in plain sight."

"They'll know. Look at me!" Soryk dropped the blanket, revealing a flat chest inside a plain white T-shirt. He gestured to his body in frustration.

"The short hair doesn't help. Your gear is bulky, though. It will disguise what's missing. Just keep your speech to a minimum. Go along with what everyone else is doing and I'll handle the rest. Most important," Farouj said, stroking his chin, "get rid of that beard."

STRAINING THROUGH THICK SLUSH, the *Nimbus* nosed into a tapering channel beneath the berg to drill cores for transport to the processing station on the mainland. During this foray, they would cull six hundred pounds of core ice from the berg to meet their quota. Otherwise they would be forced to remain at sea, roving the subarctic circle in search of another mine with ice porous enough to drill. There was just enough time before the shift bell rang to slip into the computer room and send a message to Nels on the ship-to-shore communication terminal.

Soryk's words reeked of folly. He knew he was foolish and gullible, a man abdicating responsibility.

> Nels,
> I *have business dealings in Neubonne, something I cannot leave undone. I may be gone an extra week or two. Keep the holy mother's eyes upon me and bless me in her stead.*
>
> Sorykah

He'd hesitated, adding those last two letters to his name. Odd that a single vowel and consonant could speak so eloquently, that a lone syllable held a world of meaning and disguised the existence of an entire person. He logged off and joined the eastern slope crew strapping on tanks and masks in the kit room. A few eyes flickered his way and his appearance teased grins from two miners who examined Soryk with rude curiosity. Though his temper flared, he recalled Farouj's advice and feigned disinterest, just as he imagined Sorykah would have done. Farouj was not among the crew. This was madness. He'd only said to watch for his signal and be prepared to swim. Soryk was nervous when greeted by the foreman, whose cool stare revealed nothing but distaste for his newest crew member. Mimicking the others as they manipulated fasteners and hoses, Soryk donned a deep-sea diving suit constructed with a fiberglass lattice between its neoprene lining and external cast-aluminum segments. The suit boasted a complicated circulatory network of vessels similar to the human body, which transported warmed oxygen to its occupant while diverting exhaled carbon dioxide to the external layers to serve as insulation. The foreman ran through the ranks, double-checking gear. He tightened a loose strap, tapped a glass gauge, and gave the thumbs-up. Soryk filed in behind the others packing into the waterlock, his coring drill pointed at the floor. Its sharp cyndrilical nose would soon sniff out ribbons of fossil water, leaving behind a twenty-foot-long core tube. A poster on the wall explained the colors of the signal lamps: White meant "go" or "deploy," yellow "slow" or "possible danger," and blue "withdraw to the ship." Red, the color that best cut through the gloom, meant "clear for blasting."

The crewmen were relative strangers. Sorykah hadn't trained with them, and neither their faces nor mannerisms were friendly. No doubt they were equally suspicious of Soryk, whose breath came in shallow gasps as the interior waterlock sealed itself, the sluice opened, and frigid seawater poured in, contracting the glass on the pressure gauges and filling the air with a dozen muffled snaps. He had no clue what he was doing. It ought to feel familiar, some rote memory of repeated gestures and actions should direct him, but he stood with a throbbing heart, seconds away from total immersion. He pleaded with his primary to waken and serve him, speak and soothe him, but she was uncharacteristically and grudgingly silent.

Submerged inside the waterlock, the team leader flashed the white beacon on his helmet. Soryk and the crew floated into the open ocean. Water trapped him in its smothering, pythonlike embrace, and he panicked. Soryk's heart danced erratically and his limbs began to shake. Farouj had warned him that if he sucked too hard on his oxygen, his yellow beacon would flash and he'd be excused from duty and forced to spend the day's remainder in the infirmary. His getaway, and Farouj's careful planning and hopes, both crushed.

He held his breath, forcing himself through the motions while he calmed himself. The ocean was an oppressive night more infinite than outer space. At least there, stars glimmered and winked and distant suns gave scant light. Beneath the Sigue, enrobed in salty ink that slowed his movements as if binding him in webbing, the only stars were the ludicrously faint gleams of miners' beacons. Glowing tethers roped the miners together, providing only the slightest suggestion of safety and connection. Looking up, down, behind him, Soryk encountered only impenetrable darkness.

The crew maneuvered toward the glacier, a ghostly expanse of moon glow straining toward the sun. Soryk followed the team leader's signal, moving into position alongside three other miners. He watched them lift their core drills into place and did the same. Quickly they embedded clamps in the ice, and aimed drill tips at the center of a target picked out in blue LED spikes hammered into the glacier. Vibrations churned the water and shook Soryk's arms. Hot blades sliced a finger of fossil water from the body of the berg. Soryk's crew clipped the tube and carefully extracted the ice core. Two miners broke formation to carry the core back to the *Nimbus* and lay it in the empty racks protruding from the sub's underside. When the racks were full, the *Nimbus* would retract them; a second crew inside the submarine would sort and slot the tubes into freezer-storage compartments for transportation.

Soryk scanned the ocean. Aside from two other four-man crews drilling ice farther down the slope, they were alone. What was the signal? How long would he drill before Farouj arrived?

Drilling recommenced and Soryk became lost in the novelty of his task, which helped to distract him from his fear, pulling out five more cores before the team leader flashed his red beacon. Another miner tapped the shell of Soryk's suit. The man's face was barely visible through a frost-coated faceplate. Was it Farouj? Soryk could not tell. The team leader hammered blast points into the glacier and flashed his beacon, red-blue-red-blue. Imminent explosion. They had but minutes to clear the blast zone. Bubbles filled their wake as they jetted to safely, the charges embedded in the ice flashing a countdown.

The man beside Soryk tapped his suit again, motioned "cut the lights," and pointed upward. An explosion rocked the *Nimbus*, flattening the miners against its side as the blast radiated through the ocean. Even in the pressure suit, shock waves forced the breath from him. Chunks of ice tumbled from the glacier and spilled into the sea. All the miners were riveted by the spectacle. Soryk clicked off the safety lights on his helmet, his heart pounding as he watched the man slash the nylon tether connecting Soryk to the *Nimbus*. The man clicked a lead through the G-link on Soryk's suit and clicked off his own lights. Together they watched blinking beacons fade and go dark.

The man tugged and Soryk followed, conscious only of the whirring burble of his propulsion unit and the sound of his own breathing. He clenched the coring drill like a life preserver, but it created too much drag and slowed them down. Opening his fingers, the drill floated away. Black-cloaked and invisible, the *Nimbus* diminished behind him, a safe haven of light, people, air, and warmth. He saw nothing, felt only the buzzing of toes already growing cold and the tug of the new tether. Should it come loose, he would drift aimlessly. A weak sun glowed far above the surface, too distant to summon him homeward to land. Without light, Soryk could not tell whether he faced up or down. He jerked the tether, but Farouj swam no closer. There was only a tedious constant movement, but forward or back, toward the surface or seabed, he could not tell. His yellow beacon popped on and flashed a warning as his breathing grew erratic. He coiled the tether around his wrist, but the line seemed to spool on forever. As many times as he wound it around his hand and groped in the sea for the comfort of another body, he was alone.

The tingling in his limbs amplified to a full-body pins-and-needles burn. Deprived of light, Soryk's strained eyes pulsed with blobs of orange and green. Consciousness wavered. Images of the recent past streamed by, a blurred montage of faces and sensations, and the sea invaded his reverie. *Sleep*, it crooned, the abductor's hand over his mouth, its breath in his ear. *Fall into me, and sleep.*

He closed his eyes against the rushing storm beneath his skin, the change wakening and stretching, Sorykah pushing herself up from the murky depths of his Trader's body, staking her claim. He slept, sinking like a discarded corpse to the seafloor.

SORYKAH PANICKED WHEN SHE opened her eyes. She thought she'd gone blind, but a bank of white lights flickered, illuminating the body of a person in a metallic suit floating toward her. A helmet pressed itself to hers, but Sorykah saw little through her ice-caked visor. She scratched at it with gloved hands until the other forced her arm away and waggled a finger.

"Where am I? Shit, shit, shit," she whispered, reassured by the sound of her own voice, however tinny and warped within the helmet.

Confused and disoriented, she presumed herself in space. Weightless and floating, she hovered in a starless void. Were they not dressed like cosmonauts with oxygen tanks and whirring jet packs in an atmosphere whose unending and invariable dark pressed in around her, buoying them without gravity? But space travel was still only experimental; its few far-flung missions were already the stuff of history. A gradual sensation of light, so thin and diffuse as to be only a suggestion of itself, filtered down from above. She was drawn steadily toward it—a spirit flying into the eternal light—and wondered if she was dead. Perhaps the person in the other suit was an angel, then, or one of the old gods, come to usher her into heaven.

Nothing so grand, she decided as the atmosphere lightened. A large fish with a hooked, toothy jaw thwacked its tail against her faceplate. *Undersea.* Everything fell into place. She knew the pressure suit, and was comforted by its familiar bulk and clumsy apparatus. Soon the sea was a bright translucent gray, and bobbing ice floes sailed overhead like clouds in the sky. When the current grew rough, the other diver reeled in the tether and hoisted her bodily through the currents, motioning for her to begin swimming. Movement was difficult in the heavy suit, but Sorykah pushed herself to the surface, following her companion's commands. They broke apart the shell of a winter-white world. Slush heaved and tossed, knocking together huge blocks of ice.

A trawler bobbed on the waves. Men, their mahogany complexions pallid in the weak sunshine, lowered a skiff. Her companion gestured for her to get in and she did so, straining beneath the hard weight of the pressure suit, its metal plates and stiff joints making it almost impossible to maneuver. The other diver pushed Sorykah over the lip of the boat and she lay wiggling on her back like an inverted insect, unable to rise until he rolled her onto her hands and knees.

The interior of Sorykah's faceplate was beaded by moisture. Someone twisted the helmet and lifted it off, dumping ice shards into her collar. Subarctic air stung her damp cheeks. Her lungs ached in the fresh air.

"You're back!" Farouj sat across from her, smiling as the skiff was raised and anchored to the fishing trawler. "You were frightened down there, yes?"

"Farouj! Where are we?" Sorykah searched the horizon, recognizing the distant outlines of Colchester's clustered Quonset huts. People were tiny black dots crawling along the harbor. "Colchester? No, this isn't right. I don't want to be here." Sorykah climbed from the skiff onto the trawler. Despite her confusion, she sensed that she was safe enough for the moment. She groped the edges of this new jagged gap in her consciousness, and trusted that her alter had not led them too far astray. Would she ever grow used to waking up to find herself living someone else's life, thrust into the center of another character's story as if pushed onstage mid-performance? The stage lights blazed, the audience waited, and she must pick up the gist and regain the lines to carry on the show.

"It's right. You're right—for inspiration and the job." Farouj efficiently aborted Sorykah's next question, introducing her to four men who spoke in a tongue she did not recognize.

"These are Bokharan tribesmen from the North. Like Siguelanders, we share a common bloodline."

Many years earlier, a tidal wave had wiped out the Bokharan reserve on an isolated string of islands along the Yashim border. Perhaps a few still survived there, holding fast to a remnant of the old ways, but most had died of disease bred in the compounds or fled for workaday jobs in the cities.

"Come inside. There's hot food and tea waiting." Farouj easily dismantled and shed his bulky gear. Even after hours in it, his insulating thermosuit was crisp and his dark hair lay smooth against his head. Sorykah, by contrast, wrestled futilely with her gear, her cold, sleepy fingers stiff. Farouj deftly unpacked her, tossing both suits overboard with a grunt.

"That takes care of that. You and I are now officially missing and presumed dead."

6

HYPODERMIA

NUALA MORIGI'S DISPLEASURE with her family intensified to the point that it spoiled her enjoyment in coffee and left her stomach sour. She'd never cared much for it anyway, but to have the mild and occasional pleasure she took in a really good cup ruined by her own disgust, well, that would not do.

Although she'd comfortably managed to maintain Tirai Industries' network of Intelligent Energy Receptors from her flat in Neubonne's Botanica district, exigent circumstances had recently forced her from her highly secured lair in search of her brother. Nuala knew little of Chen. They had not been raised together and met but once at a Tirai Industries banquet, a gathering carelessly engineered by a man who only acknowledged his spawn by seating them together at the Morigi family table.

Matuk took little interest in young Nuala. He hadn't even spoken to her until her twelfth birthday, when Nuala's mother brought her to Matuk's wedding, perhaps the fourth or fifth.

"Too many daughters," he griped as he wrote the check and signed the papers to dispense with yet another wife. Nuala's mother, Vierka, had been cleverer than her predecessor, the infantile and treacherous Tirai. Once her own marriage to Matuk dissolved, Vierka smuggled Nuala from Neubonne on the evening train and took her far north to Dirinda, a quiet city of small proportions and bookish academics. She was determined to raise her daughter in a better environment, one of learned scholars who worked to solve the country's many troubles, rooted for its history among legends and myths, and diligently restored and preserved Plein Eïre's treasures and artworks.

Nuala came to maturity ignorant of her lineage. Vierka grew taciturn when inevitable discussions turned to Nuala's bloodline and her history. Being a rational, coolheaded girl, Nuala resolved to investigate on her own. In the interim, she would allow Vierka the illusion of believing her daughter satisfied with her mother's meager explanations.

Nuala left for university at sixteen. Vierka wiped her eyes and squeezed her hard, depositing her daughter at the doors of the State University of Story Arts and Language Sciences. Two days later, Vierka boarded a ship and sailed for her home country, some 1,300 miles distant.

Nuala settled easily into university life and was elected prefect. In her third year, she earned a much-coveted all-access pass to the Mythology Library. A small, climate-controlled room, it housed the country's most extensive collection of ancient documents and artifacts: pottery shards striped with rudimentary symbols depicting the creation of the universe, the birth of the gods, and later, carved into wood tablets and eventually inked on linen paper, the stories of the gods themselves.

The library was Nuala's heart. Its stories fanned the fire of her imagination. The focus of her final year's thesis was proving that genesis myths were not fanciful fairy stories created to entertain primitive tribes or explain natural phenomena, but were based on actual people and events. Since the rise of the House of Jerusha, the old gods had been tossed aside and forgotten. Nearly everyone adhered to the new religion, one free of bloodshed, grotesqueries, and dehumanizing deformity. All was blessedly peaceful until Oman No-Man's deviance. The raven feathers sprouting from his skin and the collapse of his human world sent him running. He fled to the Erun forest to wait out the ensuing terrifying epidemic of somatic change, and there remarried and began the tainted Morigi family line. Some of the more fanatical Jerushians called this plague of sin just punishment (despite knowing that Jerusha did not advocate violence, forced conversion, coercion, or persecution) and sought to isolate and punish somatics, to corral, silence, or stamp them out.

A direct descendant of the first somatic, for her father Matuk was Oman's grandson, Nuala feared the coding of her own genetics. If Oman had changed, so could she. Yet she would not be persecuted as a mindless demon, a heedless beast. If Nuala could show the world that the old gods were the first somatics, she could erase the blame sullying the Morigi name. She could confirm that they had existed long before Jerusha, and no longer have to endure the rabid hatred of an increasingly vocal splinter group intent on debasing them, and worse.

The truth was swaddled in stories. The ancient myths were rife with red- and blue-skinned deities, demons whose caustic bellies carried bubbling tar pits, winged familiars with the power of human speech, and messengers crafted of cobbled together spare parts from Asta's own body shop. Nuala needed but a bone, an image, or a specimen to prove her theory and throw the fanatics into chaos. She would pull apart the stories layer by layer and find the gleaming treasure hidden within their hearts.

Only Nuala's promise that she would fund her investigation with monies from her personal trust garnered her authorization to pursue the theory from her presiding professor, the dean of mythology studies, and the Theological Research Approval Committee.

Naturally, Morigi family money, already rank with corruption, financed the project that would later cause the destruction of an environment and a deadly aphrodisiacal addiction. Nuala knew nothing of this then—her head was full of ideas disconnected from reality and anything that might repercuss upon the mythical pantheon whose existence she'd made it her mission to prove. Deep in study, she combed the stacks and archives, examining documents from the past two thousand years in search of evidence to verify her theory. One story in particular captivated her imagination and upon this, she fixated. Brutal and terribly tragic, it was the sorrowful story of the octameroons of the Singing Sea. It was the best place to start, for the Southern Ocean, swirling with fury around the subarctic pole, did actually sing. The squeak of boots on crisp new snow, the chime of wind-rattled icicles, the thunderous crack and drone of shifting behemoths of ice—it was music distinct from any other in the world. Logic followed that if the Singing Sea was real, likely the chimeras rumored to stalk its depths might be real, too.

A glance at a current atlas verified the location of the Sigue, a volcanic landmass thickly rimmed in glacial ice. The Sigue was barren and terribly remote, host to three tiny villages established within the last century under the auspices of an intrepid clutch of explorers and the straggling remnants of an indigenous people. Traveling through the subarctic desert to the volcano at its center—the demon Diabolo's mythical lair—was a suicidal exercise. A stormy, smashing wreck of glacial fallout, slush, enormous floes, and sudden, deathly temperature shifts, the Southern Ocean repelled undersea exploration. No one had yet returned bearing tales of mysterious creatures with lashing tentacles or pockets of livid demon spit nestled within their skins. *Not yet*, she thought, *but soon*.

Nuala's research shifted to the present. Paging though shipping registers and military documents, she discovered a submarine prototype. Crafted to withstand environmental extremes, the *Nimbus* was designed for deep-sea stealth, trolling the ocean floor out of range of radar and sonic detection. Perfect for diving below the surface, navigating berg shards and ice caves.

Nuala's efforts to obtain the sub met with little and laughable success. Frustrated by her failure and determined to prove her point, Nuala defied Vierka's years of careful oversight. She contacted the solicitor in charge of her trust and demanded a meeting with her father.

Nuala took the train to Neubonne, growing more dazzled with every inch of progress into Matuk's city. Unlike Dirinda, a relatively new city sprung up around the university to support and house its students and scholars, Neubonne's buildings were centuries old, heavily decorated with looping whorls and flowery embellishments in weather-ravaged marble and soot-stained stone. Jutting between the cracked and crumbling remnants of the past, sleek new towers and shops burst and spread, lording modernity over ancient neighbors.

Matuk sent a town car to the train station to collect Nuala. The courteous driver spoke little. He was used to visits from Matuk's cast-off children, come home periodically to beg a slice of the family fortune; he knew not to become embroiled in heated discussions with delinquent offspring and their grasping mothers.

When she arrived at the black Onyx Tower, her father's assistant, Mr. Bodkin, an inscrutable man with a face like a brick, escorted her to Matuk's office high above Neubonne. The opulent suite was sparsely decorated. Two suited Company administrators sat at opposite ends of the lobby, poised like guardians at the gates. Bodkin strolled past them, one firm hand on Nuala's elbow as he steered her through winding corridors of glinting moonstone-pale marble. Matuk's vast office encompassed half the floor. Discreet panels lined the walls, hiding shelves packed with bound volumes of financial records, and behind them, hidden in a cavernous safe room, a second set of account books. Matuk's desk was an island in a sea of light pouring from the wide windows. He seemed tiny amid the grand-scale splendor surrounding him.

"Daughter," he said, coming from behind his desk to embrace her. They were the same height; Matuk's compact frame was wiry with muscle. Black hair edged with silver lay slick against his head, and his eyes were keenly assessing beneath heavy brows already creased and drooping with age. Nuala wondered if he'd forgotten her name. "Such a pleasure to see you again. It's been too long."

"Yes, and you, too." Nuala hesitated. Should she entertain his niceties or just get down to business? Nuala had few memories of the man she called father. Vierka spoke little of him, preferring that Nuala develop her own opinion of Matuk rather than acquire a prejudiced hand-me-down. She hoped he'd be kind to her but he had a short temper and a reputation for brutality.

"Please, seat yourself. Tell me of your studies."

Nuala did so.

"And your mother, is she well?"

"Departed for her home country three years ago, but yes, she's well, thank you."

Matuk searched Nuala's face, examining her for some shared likeness, she imagined. "Bodkin tells me that you excel in your studies. You've already made prefect."

Nuala nodded, gripping her hands tightly together in her lap.

"Yet you are unsatisfied. Your trust was more than adequate, but you see fit to visit me after many years of silence to ask for more."

Nuala shook her head vigorously. "You've been exceedingly kind to me, more than generous. I don't need money. I need a ship. The submarine *Nimbus* belongs to Plein Eïre's national oceanic research trust, but it's not for rent, obviously. TI has contacts within the marine administration. I was hoping you might be able to convince them to let me use it for a mission."

"An exploratory deep-sea servant is not a toy, girl. What do you know of sailing and diving? Nothing, I think." Matuk's cold eyes glittered.

"True, but I would need to make only a single voyage. She's the only one capable of reaching the depths around the Sigue. I'd just need a few days to patrol the berg and find evidence to support my claim—that the stories of the old gods are founded in physical reality. It's the focus of my final paper." Nuala sat forward in her chair, her eagerness apparent.

Matuk chewed on this. "It's an expensive venture. Each trip would require a full crew, propellants to power the sub, much equipment and supplies. I'm flattered that you think me so powerful. If I could obtain it for you, how would I benefit should I choose to partner with you in the search?"

Partner? Nuala gulped. She'd not presaged that her father would have any interest in her expedition. She was unsure of his motivations, but she wanted the *Nimbus* very badly and her desire for it overshadowed everything else. "You'd be privy to my findings. As long I make the first public claim, I don't foresee any conflict."

Years later, Nuala would replay this conversation in her mind, berating herself for her ignorance. If only she could travel back in time and circumvent the entire voyage! The Sigue would not now be breaking apart beneath her fingers like wet chalk. She'd not carry the burden of so many deaths upon her shoulders. Dismembered octameroons would not wash up on Sigue beaches, their slashed-open hips scored with stitches. Neubonne would not suffer infestations of ink and fossil water, her brother would not pad his coffers with the bodies of deceased ink rats and somatics, and Nuala would not feel the eyes of the old gods upon her, resurrected ghosts reluctantly yanked from centuries of slumber to mourn afresh their own demise. But in the moment, the glow of possibility was blindingly bright, a tantalizing globe luring her to a lunatic end like the full moon summoning madness in a maiden. She knew nothing then of octameroon ink, its caustic, smoking flare, her skin alight with sensation and desire, gray ghosts waltzing on demon-spit feet.

That journey was the point of no return. She tore the tapestry created by the old gods, and invited, however innocently, the shadow gods to swarm through the rend.

———————————

NUALA'S FIRST AND ONLY MISSION aboard the *Nimbus* was freakishly successful. She was fearless, pushing the crew to deeper dives,
silent and wide-eyed as she listened to the submarine's hull crack
and compress. She didn't exactly know what they were looking for as
she sat in the captain's office, sliding the spotlight's beam over icy
slopes and fissures. There was little life at that depth, so the flash of
tentacles, just at the edge of her spotlight, set her heightened senses to
"kill." Maybe it was the Morigi blood in her, excited by conquest, that
led her to mount a one-woman mutiny and take control of the ship,
sending it careening wildly through the lightless sea, her beam
trained on that elusive tantalizing undulation. She forced the captain from the wheel and grabbed it. Nuala, who had never even ridden a bicycle, delighted in the *Nimbus*'s agility as she forced it
farther down into a black and empty sea. The sub creaked and shuddered all around her, making the gunner shriek and beg.

She smacked him away, clamped her hands to the handles of the
sonic blaster, and yelled "Fire!" as the flailing tentacles of some
enormous thing shot before the beam.

Sonic blasts rocked the ship. Pressure compacted the noise bomb
and great bursts of juddering sound waves imploded inside their
heads, popping capillaries in their eyeballs and causing their hearts
to skip a beat. Then it was over and the thing floated stunned and
nearly lifeless. Nuala jumped up and down and whooped, thinking
only of her university triumph, her name in all the journals, the long
and distinguished academic career that would surely follow.

When the deploy team returned, the unconscious octameroon
wrapped tightly in neon netting, Nuala found she could not breathe.
They dumped it onto the floor, cut away the netting, and stood gaping at this creature that had never seen sunlight. Rubbery, finely
grained skin the color of apricots covered a human torso, blunted by
mutation and adaptation. Fingers tapered like carrots, terminating
long and oddly jointed arms. With a lump of nose and puckered
pouches housing bulging eyes, the face was a gross approximation of
human. Trailing colorless hair lay like bundled fiber optic threads,

but worst of all was the flared, heavily muscled skirt of sucker-splotched tentacles. Six sprawled like empty garden hoses but two still thrashed, longer than the others and tipped with spatulate paddles rimmed in sharp hairs and curved cat's-claw hooks.

Backed against the wall, the stunned gunner trembled, pee running down his leg. Nuala ordered him to fetch the doctor, who burst into the room looking slightly nauseous, surgical kit in hand.

Chaos ensued. The first cut startled the beast; hooked arms thrashed and knocked the doctor from his feet but did not deter him. Nuala could think of nothing to do, so shocked was she by the knowledge that she had been right. The mythology of the old gods, a religion now two thousand years dead, was rooted in fact. The Sigue's wailing maternal grievances, Ur's lamentation echoing through the eons, permeated the very fabric of the pole. Generations of Ur's children skived in the frozen muck, eating and mating their own, a terrible oceanic virus.

Together Nuala and the crew doctor investigated the oxygen-deprived octameroon, mindless of its desperate thrashing. Skin grew over the slitted nostrils, thin gill flaps rippled and jerked along its neck, and the eyes rolled wildly.

Nuala had not thought this far. She had no preparation to preserve the beast's life. It lay dying, its mouth cycling through a series of silent syllables. Nuala jittered with the thrill of discovery. By the time the doctor pointed out the octameroon's expiration, the scalpel tips were already embedded within the rubbery flesh, gashing, splitting, and spilling. She gave the order and pried the thing apart, her head filled with sick, swarming delirium that left her drunk with satisfaction. She had been *right*. Was there any better feeling?

Remnant lungs took up little space within the chest cavity. Crafted of cartilage, its spine and the long bones of the octameroon's arms were as yellow as gristle. Blood the color of seawater on a sunny day congealed beneath Nuala's boots.

"Find the ink sac," Nuala urged, leaning on the doctor's shoulder, her weight forcing his blade even deeper into the soft tissues.

The ship's doctor, a balding, skinny-chinned man, pushed his fingers between the cold organs. "What am I looking for?"

"You know the story," Nuala said. "Diabolo's spit is lodged within them. Find it."

Having been so long at sea, he knew something of the anatomy of marine creatures. A mixture of octopus, squid, and human, the octameroons defied logic. Therefore, it would be illogical to continue the pursuit in a methodical fashion.

He sat back on his heels, eyeing the monster. "What do you want to do with this? Keep it?" He waved a hand in front of his face. "It's already starting to stink."

"Just find the black stain." Nuala crouched low, running her hands along the limp tentacles. She rummaged behind the intestinal packet, shoving her fingers between liver and spleen. "What's this? Kidney?" She jerked it a bit and showed him a lengthy vessel spread across her palm. "Urethra?" The tough vein slipped between the pads of her fingers, a single firm spaghetti. "Where does it go?"

"Here," said the green-gilled doctor, brandishing a scalpel. "Let me."

She gripped the tube and followed it to its origin, a membranous bag streaked with bands of hard polished keratin and emerald veins. "You've found it! Take it out."

Panicked by his collusion in what he now viewed as a murder, he jabbed with a wanton blade, gashing Nuala's wrist. Nuala gasped and pinched her skin together as crimson blood dripped into the octameroon's open carcass.

Sweat dripped from the doctor's brow. How could he have known what he would unleash upon the Sigue with the removal of that organ? He might have refused, bludgeoned Nuala unconscious, and rolled the corpse into the waterlock for a quick disposal at sea, had his conscience been more keen. But he did not, and again the blade—its handle slick with sweat, octameroon slime, and Nuala's blood—slipped, puncturing the bag. A bead of tarry substance swelled before their eyes. As stiff and glossy as glass, it wobbled under its own weight and tipped sideways, spilling, pushing, and widening the gash. Its sulfurous odor made them cough. Nuala reached to rub it between her fingers, slippery and gelatinous. When it seeped into her open cut as if drawn to the scent of her human blood, she leapt back and cried out.

The burn of raw ink, like smoking volcanic lava, made white stars of burning phosphorous flare inside her eyes. She staggered back, octameroon ink diluting her own blood and turning it momentarily black. Her pupils dilated and contracted to pinpoints. The ink traveled through her system like a suicide bomber launching fiery grenades and projectiles, burning the place down. Nuala turned on the doctor, her expression manic and glazed. The scalpel clattered from his hand as Nuala advanced red-cheeked and panting, tearing at the zipper on her thermosuit. "I'm on fire inside," she cried. "Put it out! Put it out!"

She scrambled for the waterlock door, determined to quench herself in the Sigue Sea. The doctor blocked her way, his narrow chin determined, his watery eyes frightened. He drew her arm close to examine the injury, an angry purple scab clotted high with blood.

She moaned and twitched as his fingers skimmed her flesh, rubbing away the clot and reopening the wound. "Touch me," Nuala begged. "Not there." She relocated his hand and saw understanding bloom in his eyes. "Here."

WHEN IT WAS OVER—Nuala lying bruised and heaving, the raw ink in her bloodstream still blurring her vision—she stared helplessly at the octameroon's ruined body. Already its limbs had begun to dry and tighten, the tentacles shrinking and stiffening. The mouth gaped in a face contorted by suffering.

Nuala burst into tears. The doctor zipped up his pants and hastily departed. Lying dead on the floor was proof of the old gods' existence. Nuala crawled to the corpse, examining the octameroon's sharklike skin. She traced its features with her fingers, twisted its

spun-glass hair and pressed its suckers against her palm. A fog of confusion filled her brain. What would she do? She spied a collecting
jar in the specimen kit the doctor had left behind. Fluid seeped from
the octameroon's punctured ink sac. Nuala pressed the lip of her
jar to the wound, massaging the organ to encourage the flow. Anticipation flickered in her eyes as demon spit oozed into her jar. It
seemed to speak to her. A voice filled her mind, urging her to indulge again in unimaginable pleasures. Was it the voice of Diabolo?
Nuala put her hands to her ears and squeezed her eyes shut. The
voice grew silent. Only when she looked at the slain octameroon,
dark fluid pooling in the crevices around its organs, did the voice resume. It came and went, a soft background hum. Nuala shook off
her shock and photographed the body, collected tissue samples, and
finally, as the octameroon withered and disintegrated into jelly, consigned it to the sea. Now she possessed a box of drawings, photo-
graphs, and dozens of sealed vials containing suckers, fingers, hair,
gills, teeth, and eyes—anything that she might cut off and save. Her
wrist ached and burned. She rubbed it, launching waves of hot need
throughout her body. She would later learn to avoid touching it and
activating the demon spit after she'd made short work of the ship's
cook, the terrified gunner, and a machinist. Because she was Matuk's
daughter, none refused her. Nuala's strange new scent of resin, salt,
and volcanic ash overwhelmed their senses and made them hers, if
only for a few contorted moments.

The *Nimbus* burbled back to the surface and Nuala staggered
from the submarine, her eyes smarting in the sunlight. Her body was
raw, its delicate membranes rubbed pink and bloody. Ink was her
only concern; she forgot all about her paper. She lay in her single
dormitory bed gripping that black vial and willing herself to forget
the ecstasies that robbed her of breath and will, the peaks and
troughs she'd ridden in her quest for an even greater pleasure. Ink
filled her head with seawater and muffled reason.

Matuk summoned her but she refused to answer his call. He was
displeased, but it mattered little. Nuala's head was a swarm of emotion: lust, regret, greed, and obsession.

"Ask the gunner," she wrote to Matuk. "Ask the machinist or the ship's doctor what they found, but leave me alone. I was wrong. There is nothing of value in the Sigue, nothing but grief."

Nuala soon realized that publishing her paper would mean death for the octameroons. Fanatics, trophy hunters, antisomatic activists, Jerushian extremists, and sensation seekers would all descend on the Sigue to fish out the octameroons and put them to terrible purpose. Except that ink-lust was an infection she could neither resist nor treat. The bottle of extruded demon sputum whispered to her constantly. How difficult it was to concentrate! How arduous were her efforts to fight the urges that consumed her! Nuala lived in fear of being cut again or accidentally splotched and took to wearing only white to better spy any dark drop of blood or ink. Flag-white to proclaim her innocence and surrender, white as a winter ptarmigan camouflaged by Sigue snows. She painted all of her furnishings and belongings white. When she began tearing the covers from the books in the library, the university dismissed her from duty.

"Just until you're well," the school psychiatrist told Nuala, though both knew she would never be well again.

Where else could she go, her mother having fled the country, their house let to strangers? Matuk, though he did not welcome her with open arms and a smile, nevertheless gave her a suite in the Onyx Tower. As if Matuk had anticipated the entire escapade and forecast the expression of his daughter's madness, its every interior surface was wonderfully white. While Nuala devoted herself to the installation and maintenance of Tirai Industries' spy network, Matuk quietly commissioned the *Nimbus* to capture and bleed octameroons of their ink. Bodkin and Nunn, the *Nimbus*'s bursar, took charge of the operation and developed the fossil water ploy to divert attention from TI's presence in the Sigue. Dual income streams flowed from the Sigue Sea into the *Nimbus*'s hold. Poor Nuala had believed Matuk's assurances that he'd cover up her discovery and leave the octameroons in peace. Uttering false promises, he stroked her hair, admiring the gold curls so like the brass coins he dispensed to the Siguelanders and the Qa'a'nesh when promising them a fair share of his wealth in exchange for surrendering their land, their seas, and their future. Though Diabolo's ink still beckoned Nuala, Matuk's voice was louder and stronger. He was her father. Despot or no, he'd not lie to her, would he?

7

CHILD OF UR

A BODY FLOATED THROUGH the inky Sigue Sea, its ten limbs adrift in the current. Others like it flickered and swarmed, touching hands to the lifeless body, drawing it deeper into the watery night. Sensitive fingers quickly located and traced the most recent sutures atop the ridges of older wounds clustered along the hip, site of multiple ink extractions. Its blue-ice irises encircled by snow, the creature's pupils were blank and clouded. Brittle white hairs, like strands of spun glass with a tinsel shine, disengaged from their follicles to snare the sea in webbing. Small fish entangled themselves there, taking momentary refuge from the bleak ocean's crushing cold and the large chompers that swam and skived, snapping up the littler things.

This is what they endured—a rain of decimated bodies, slain brethren choking the waters after an age of quiet, their existence long forgotten by those on land.

First come the blackouts. A sleek metal capsule invaded their realm and blasted sonar pulses into the sea, deafening and nearly fatal. Stunned octameroons slipped from the rock crevices and ice caves to clutter the water, making easy the collection of their bodies. The capsule extended flexible arms, scooping the bodies into metal cages and shaking them into its mouth. Later, at the conclusion of their nightmare, the stars woke dazed and in pain, respiration made sluggish by sleeping gas. Fire incinerated their guts. Black ink leaked from holes cut into their flesh. Sometimes, they failed to rouse. Too much etherine or a cutter pressed for time, making incisions too deeply, his furtive laboring rushed and sloppy. Life did not resume. The spoiled body was quickly discarded into the sea of its birth. It was soon recognized and towed farther down, where the abysmal murk stifled flashing bioluminescence and the cursed were truly comfortable. Certain of privacy, nimble fingers shredded and dismantled gelatinous tentacles, casting the fleshy detritus upon the waters. This was their supper; they ground serrated jaws back and forth to saw bits of meat into bellies clear as plastic sacks. The human torso, less easily destroyed, required tucking under a rock until small nibblers and those with bigger teeth came to share the feast.

Insubstantial and weightless, the bones settled on the subarctic seafloor, a frail scattering of pins.

Did they eat their dead? Legend says so.

Did they love each other? Were their remnant-human brains capable of sustained affection? Did the god-bits circulating within their blood leave them dolorous when a family member fell from the raping submarine into the sea? Did they mourn a death as their mother Ur once bemoaned their loss, wailing and walking the rocky shore, brokenhearted and destroyed?

Untouched by time, the octameroons had not changed until the birth of one with sighted eyes and colored hair. The mother of the sole aberrant realized that her child had shed the curse, and her chameleonic skin, shifting from pearly white to ruddy red and liverish mauve, could not endure the cold. The mother brought her child into the light to let her revel in the shifting shades of blue and green that characterize the epipelagic sea, and smacks of jostling jellies, diving leopard seals, schools of fish, and pudgy flightless birds, Rava can break the ocean's surface and sip the air like a land-walker, and watch the white bergs crash icy cymbals.

The sounds from shore enticed her. The water where her kin dwelled was too deep, too black and formidable. She frequented sunnier realms, peering into the watery chasm below her tentacles as she pondered her family's fate. Her parents rarely ventured to the surface to see their daughter. Sigue song torments them; they prefer silence.

Pushing her body through an obstacle course of slushy sea and flotillas of ice calves, the child trained herself to open the tight seams of her sealed nostrils and take in the air, rich with scents of human activity: burning gasoline and oil; fish netted in five-hundred-pound catches and eviscerated on the rough quay stones, their bloody guts kicked into the sea; a gustatory enticement she'd later learn to savor—pan-fried flatbread coated with crumbling yellow rock salt; bodies ripe with human stink and allure, mammal sweat and the grease that seeps from scalps, skin, and glands; animals fighting and mating, exuding territorial musk and signpost urine. She listened to the dockyard calls of coopers, drapers, fullers, and riggers, and bar-gaining shoppers clinking their coins—the sound track of commerce. Frightened by the leather skiffs that the Siguelanders pilot through the slush in search of flotsam, the child slipped soundlessly away, vanishing into the oceanic abyss as if behind a cloud of ink.

She could not yet identify the odor of what would become her downfall, her jeweled delight: opium. It would enslave her, leave her obsessed with her own intoxication and suffering—she would sacri-fice much to court that pleasing pain.

MISFIT RAVA WAS A MUTANT in a plethora of strange mutations. Her naïveté was her undoing. She wasn't cautious when she should have been; thinking the sleek metal capsule that followed her just another playful fancy like the cavorting orcas who sometimes swam beside her, their soft eyes fixed upon her and never straying. When she was finally caught, the thieves kept her from the water overlong, marveling at the alien beauty of her slender lady arms with fingers that tapered like spring carrots. Layered with an unnerving ceramic glaze, Rava's nacreous eyes lent her an illusion of blindness. Bundled in tight plaits, her beetroot hair streamed past a delicate waist unmarked by an umbilical scar. Below wide hips, her pleated skirt of white suckered tentacles flicked lazy tips.

Men had jerked her from the sea like a fish on a line, closed her eyes with numbing injections to force an early, unnatural sleep, pushed her onto a canvas sling, and hauled her onto a metal slab. They rooted with precise strokes and stabs, seeking and finding the ink sac, a shimmering bladder of red-oak slime. They pierced its lining, inserted needled straws, and watched as small suction engines jiggled and whooshed, drawing up the ink as one might prime a water pump and watch its contents splash into a bucket.

The sac was stapled closed and taped with the epithelial membrane of a fetal pig, lab-grown for just this purpose, and tucked back inside its cavity. The intestines, muscles, fat, and skin were pressed into place in the exact manner that one wraps a gift for an unpopular coworker, his name drawn from a hat.

These thieves were uninspired by aesthetics. They did not care that the coarse black stitches were ugly against Rava's sensitive skin, didn't mind slotting her into a core tube for later investigation (for they all wanted to know if she harbored a second mouth under all those tentacles). True octopus or true woman? They'd never seen her kind before. She was a miracle. A unique specimen destined for examination and later exhumation.

Their faulty miscalculations left her vulnerable to early waking, submerged in a tenuous half-sleep and not the sleep of corpses. When next they cranked the core tube seal and opened the door, she exploded from the narrow chamber. Used to small spaces and with a skeleton formed from cartilage, not bone, she could maneuver enough to propel herself into the room, landing with a dry thunk on the core room floor. Her tentacles whipped wildly, seeking targets to destroy. Rava smacked one man across the face, the force of her attack great enough to pop his eyeball from the socket where it hung warm and oozy on his cheek, dangling from a ribbon of gore. Another man was run through—Rava's two front tentacles wore pointed caps of keratin. She was strong enough to jab these horns into a belly, to pierce unprotected organs and lacerate a liver.

There was much screaming. They hit her with aluminum trays, hoses, and the steel extraction poles used to core icebergs. They flushed her toward the door, arguing over which of them would enter the containment room, punch in the safety code to decompress the air, and release the seal that would allow the sea to penetrate the waterlock. They muscled a smaller fellow into the room and yelled while he performed the necessary actions with trembling fingers as his comrades beat back the livid octameroon, which hissed and flailed like a knot of angry serpents.

The boy began to panic. Other hands wrenched open the door, pushing the angry half-girl into the gap. Her lips parted to reveal tiny, terrible teeth, each one pointed and jagged—a baby shark, a broken saw. Three tentacles wrapped around the boy's neck and squeezed. They curled around his body, popped the sack of his skin, probed his innards. Strangled him. Tentacles affixed themselves to his ears, lips, eyelids and *pulled*. An octopus is strong enough to open pickle jars, to prise apart stiff mollusks and clam shells, to tug the meat from a bone—Rava's human hands flailed, reaching to pull her own tentacles from the neck of the boy dancing her macabre waltz.

She had never before looked into a human face, and the close proximity of a youthful male startled her into a newer and deeper awareness. As she juiced the life from that pink-cheeked boy, she admired him—the lashes that brushed the line of his eyebrows, the fineness of his features, the brown hairs that frosted his jaw similar to the fur of the seals with whom she swam. Even as Rava killed him, she was falling in love. Even as the Southern Sea flooded the containment room and drowned him, she wanted him for herself, as girls want pretty babies in dresses and crinolines or little porcelain-headed dolls wearing starched sailor suits.

When the submarine's hatch opened and sucked them into the sea, Rava's human hands sought to save him, opposing the octopus tentacles that quartered him. The rest of the crew watched from behind the glass door, sweat thick on their faces. The sea opened its mouth and swallowed.

"Donal," one man mouthed, pressing his fingers to the glass. "My son."

When Rava released him, he fell in parts of three and five. His body broke apart like cake in the water. She followed him down until the light ended and the abyss began, the realm of her people. They would dismember him joint by joint, making fish food of her beloved to fertilize beds of glass tulips, five-foot-tall tunicates that rose in flowering fields from the ocean floor, their worm mouths straining detritus from a cloudy sea. At least he would be cared for. Haunted by that final image of Donal's father, guilt pushed Rava ashore.

Thrusting her suckers onto the gray-pebbled beach, she dragged her body from the surf. She saw much but not enough to tell her to beware and retreat into the sea. Rava crawled onto the sand and taught herself to walk, an eerie locomotion of undulating tentacles that left whirlwinds of S-patterns in the snow. Venturing close to town, she recognized a submarine fin above the water and watched men stream from its snout like marauder beetles who picked clean fields of lichen during the short subarctic summers, but she did not see Donal's father.

Pavel, a short barrel of a man with thick white fur layering his olive skin, lured her from the water with bits of fish, saucers of cream, shiny shells, and snips of silver strewn across the stones. Day after day, he wove his net with infinite patience and care, gentling that wild child of Ur. He caught the pearls that dripped from her eyes and pocketed them to sell in town. Pavel scoured the stones to collect the fallen white beads of Rava's tears. When he'd earned enough money, he bought a shuttered bar, installed beer taps and a hookah pipe, and kept Rava, his golden goose, there. He nursed her habit and taught her how to load the pipe, fill the hookah's bowl with water, inhale, and hold until her lungs, still in their infancy, rebelled and coughed up strings of fishy green slime.

Pavel clothed Rava. He enticed her to cry and used the pearl-tears to purchase a wheelchair so that she might move more freely within the boundaries of the bar. Although she was to remain hidden during serving hours, he could not bear the separation and brought her into the darkest corner, draped her in furs and blankets where he could stare at her as he pulled pints, mixed herbs for tea, and served those of his kind unwelcome in other ports.

"Do you love me, little doll?" he asked, combing her hair, spoon feeding her herring soup and soothing her tentacles with a cloth and bucket of Sigue seawater drawn fresh from the coast, ice still clinking in the pail.

She might nod or mumble some strange thing, wiggling her fingers to draw the pipe closer still. Pavel taught her to speak. She was a fast learner and eager to occupy her mind with some task other than worrying after Donal's father.

Worry made Pavel's white hair grow yellow and coarsen. For all that he did for her, he was certain that she would leave him. As he rubbed salt into her skin, dressed her, and entertained her with shadow puppets and crude displays of strength, jealousy swam through his belly and churned sour there as if to curdle his gut into hard cheese. She was demanding. Sometimes surly and a bit mean-spirited. She took to tripping him, whipping a tentacle under his feet to send him sprawling onto the floor. Rava next refused to cry. Her first phrase in English? "I shall not spill a tear."

Pavel was helpless, bewitched. Rava's strange exoticism was more fascinating and otherworldly than the somatics who roamed Ostara's streets and docks, their collars pulled high to hide the abundance of hair and fur, or twisted, whiskery features. Rava came from the ocean like a spirit materializes from the fog. Popping and puckering, her suckers were a hundred small mouths begging kisses. Pavel could hear that wet sucking noise in his sleep, the disruptions that traveled her octopus legs, six-foot-long ribbons of tiny barnacles or oysters, opening, closing, and shucking themselves into the air.

His attraction sickened and enthralled him. He fed her cuts of decayed flesh. A seal steak left too long on the sideboard had already begun to spoil by the time he prepared it for her. Myth proclaimed her a cannibal, a devourer of the dead. *Consider it a test*, he thought, slicing meat already foul with its rancid off-odors of spoilage.

Rava did not complain. She ate her food in silence, sent the platter careening across the floor with a flick and a ting of her horned tentacle. Her eyes tracked him. The pupils, he noticed, did not change.

"You are a child of Ur," Pavel breathed, groveling before her on his knees, pressing his white-furred hands to her fishy skin, smooth as underwater silk or the rubber belly of an inflated balloon.

"Child of Ur!" he cried, his mind reeling. Rava's existence meant that the old gods were *real*, that they lived, walked, and breathed in their heavenly house. Sky and Sun still fought, blaming each other for Ur's death and the banishment of her spawn. That's why the sky clouded, why night and day knew no equality—those mortal enemies had sworn a feudal oath and drawn swords against each other.

Pavel knew Rava's fetter was too short and constricting, so he cut the cord. Having not yet located Donal's father, the man to whom she must make amends, she did not leave. She had no words to explain this nebulous sense of justice, the compulsion to trade her grief for his.

In a cave furnished with rough spoils coughed up by the sea, a working toilet and serviceable camp kitchen, Pavel spent the last of Rava's pearls to hire a welder to construct an enormous metal tank in which she could submerge herself. Hidden from the world, Rava chewed on her remorse just as a baby gnaws any rubbery thing that feels good against its gums. Rava was delighted with her tank of Sigue sea. She slicked her octopus arms up and down Pavel's body, her suckers softly crackling like cereal in milk.

Pavel was a kind and loving jailer. Rava thought confinement due penance for killing Donal and discarding his body in the ocean like a sprinkle of tinned fish food. Sometimes she allowed Pavel to recline in the wickerwork of her braided tentacles while she absentmindedly twirled his fur with a human hand. This earned her a bit of freedom, release from her gentle bondage. Pavel kept her the way a dog might keep a cat for a pet or a witch her enchanted, magical songbird. Perhaps he believed she would grant him wishes or protection from the old gods when they arose.

She could come and go quite freely by the time Sorykah met her. Rava was warped by her isolation, yet so desperate for companionship that she made an effort to befriend the lost Trader, whose face was a shimmering mask of panic. Her aromatic deviation wafted from her pores like incense smoke. Did no one see it, smell it? Such a strange, uncertain scent, unlike anything Rava could catalog in her brief experience on land. She feared Pavel's discovery of the woman's talent—that he might claim and keep her, too. She'd have a companion then, a cellmate. There'd been no time to decide what to do because poachers stormed the bar, making Pavel call the guards, gigantic somatic men with the swinging protuberant noses of elephant seals and the same abusive temperament.

Rava ran and Sorykah followed. It was what Rava wanted, what she loathed. When smoke filled her lungs she could not think in the logic circuits and leapfrog abstractions typical of her kind. Weeping bright pearls, she thought only of her servitude.

It had been a year since she first glimpsed the black submarine, and many months since she had abandoned her search, using the hookah to help her forget the bulge of young Donal's eyes, the purpling of his lips as she choked the life out of him.

Penance—that was a word Pavel sometimes used when he drank, called her goddess, and wept into his moonshine. His salt-tears excited Rava's tentacles, which crept as quiet as kittens to swirl around his homely face and drink the ocean draining from his eyes. *Pop pop.* The suckers transferred tiny droplets to Rava's hidden nether mouth, some monstrous primordial remnant of beak tucked inside the nest of her eight legs like the buried head of an absorbed fetal twin, and she delighted in their taste.

This is my penance, Rava echoed, and shed a few spontaneous tears. She left the pearls on the floor when she fled the bar with Sorykah, named the Stuck Tongue for her earlier unwillingness to speak to Pavel and reveal her origins.

There was little glamour in her story; it was better for Pavel to believe her a lost and singular spirit than a malicious somatic with small magicks and little pity, save her mourning of Donal. She could have remained lashed to that wheel, circling over the same ground, suffering Pavel's prayers but for the whisper gathering inside her head, the growing storm and dreary rains that further muddled her thinking. More than the threat of capture and the ensuing ink extraction, she feared for her family, her brothers and sisters, aunts and uncles, the children of Ur who swam among the bones of their carefully tended gardens, pruning glass tulips with their teeth. Though catatonic with opioids, Rava could not ignore the slow and certain decimation of her people.

She curled into herself, a statue still and cold, watching. Her ceramic gaze neither reflected light nor absorbed emotion. She suppressed her breath, calmed the movement of her tentacles, changed the color of her skin as much as she was able, to become a shadow and disappear. She listened. She watched the Company men come into Pavel's bar, ask after the location of the best fishing spots in the Sigue, and fluff and preen before him, flaunting rolls of paper money. Pavel panted at the enticement, but his lockbox burst with pearls and gave him the strength to resist the Company men's lure. They waved a bottle of ink under his nose, and Rava's skin contracted in horror. Essence of Tindor, her cousin, in a bottle.

Piled upon the wooden bar, the money danced for the Company men, did their talking and kept their hands clean. It sang and others were lulled. Others came forward to betray Ur's children yet again, took money in claw or paw or hand and pointed to the western rim, where the sea shelf dropped into oblivion and the ocean seethed, as viscid and black as oil.

They were off, diving in their wicked machine, hunting Rava's kin.

Mummified in furs and space blankets, Rava mused on this as Sorykah dragged her across the barren interior toward salvation at the witch's hands. Rava felt ink dribble from wounds that had never healed and were still as fresh and raw as at the hour of first cutting. Mad for the taste of her drug and semiconscious in the brutal, bone-cracking cold, she was lulled by the motion of the sled shushing across crystallized snow. She considered Donal's father and the finding of him as she endured the fossil water drip inserted into her arm by the witch, Shanxi. Oenathe, the richly oxygenated plants that Shanxi cultivated, rattled their leaves and whispered among themselves, discussing her care with the witch, who murmured and rattled along with them. Panting in synchronicity, oenathe leaves clattered like translucent green scales.

Shanxi pumped Rava full of oenathe sap and fossil water extracted from the melted ice cores drilled in the Sigue's berg, the ice of her homeland. It was not a permanent cure but it brought her thinking into line and order so that she could endure the journey to the Southern Sea without dying, sick with need. Rava returned home after much time away to find her glacier vandalized and vermiculate with disease. Submariner parasites, Donal's kind, stole ice and carved pathways to the volcano's hot heart.

Rava flashed through the ocean, the feel of the water upon her dry, thirsting skin better than any balm or drug. The ice songs were magic. She thought she could understand them now, could hear Ur's ancestral voice in the creaking bergs, the smash and clatter of slush and rocks. Ur, summoning her children up from the murdering-grounds. They must be protected from the invaders who stole and ravaged their bodies to extract Diabolo's inky spit.

Hadn't the ocean been frostier before? She could still feel her limbs; the constant and welcome numbness had yet to set in. Strange fish foreign to the Southern Sea darted and flashed. Tiny feeders clogged Rava's mouth, fingernail-sized jellies that clouded the water and attracted round moon jellies come to feast upon their kin.

Rava batted the feeders away, but they stuck to her skin and lashes, snared by her hair. She swam faster, seeking freedom from their stings. A crevice in the rock offered a reprieve and she darted toward it, ready to curl into its cavity. Her tentacles felt the lip of the crevice, rolled themselves inside, and Rava's suckers latched on to the rock face. She pushed herself into the gap, then recoiled, flailing. Hot seawater bubbled deep within the vent and spilled outward, raising the temperature and creating a breeding zone for feeders. Rava used her lady fingers to pull the clinging jellies from her lashes. Lava boiled at the bottom of the crevice. Where was the ice? The Sigue landmass was swathed in it, but here the rock was peppered with craters from blasting, and what ice remained hung like ragged lace.

Donal's folk had done this. Implanting sonar bombs and blast points to weaken the ice before gouging it with corers and sucking out tubes of frozen Sigue sea. The awakened volcano rumbled and shook. Diabolo would crawl from his long sleep, intent on vengeance. Without the glacier to imprison the demon's rage, lava would pour into the ocean, heating it enough to melt the entire pole. Nothing would be left but the volcano's smoking nose, jutting above a blue and iceless sea. She was astonished at the speed with which her world was being destroyed.

Rava darted downward, searching for her kin. She found her cousins packing core tubes with broken blocks of ice dragged from the crumbling bergs. They spoke wordlessly, pulsing tentacles slid-ing back and forth, suckers opening and closing like mouths in speech. Octameroon communication was based on touch and scent, the interpretation of chemical emissions, the language of human hands and puckering suckers.

Egil and Töti confirmed her suspicions. Too many of them had been captured in her absence, even more thrown back dead, the gaping wounds of their ripped-open ink sacs not even stitched closed. The tribe was imperiled by this new and ruthless threat. Their population was small and they could not afford to lose many more members without suffering terribly. The octameroons had no experience in handling humans, defending themselves against anything more dangerous than a whale or a frigid winter. Rava would be their emissary, sent to plead clemency from those bad men with their knives and needles. She alone breathed air and walked on land; she alone could speak for her brethren. Only Rava could lead her small army's charge, once more into the fray.

Pavel could help her. Pavel, her kind and loving jailer. The Stuck Tongue felt like a house abandoned when she returned. Pavel was gone but the pipe was there, gleaming red and gold, its sinuous white smoke rising like charmed serpents from a basket.

Come to me, my darling, my only love, spoke the smoke. *We belong together. Come to me, be one with me, lose yourself in me, and I shall fill you and shoulder all your woes and burdens. Breathe me in and let me carry you.*

That was Rava's lure, a song more beautiful than any other, promising forgiveness, salving her solitude, and soothing her sorrows. The white dragon flapped its wings and sailed down from the sky, snorting and steaming. His gleaming golden eyes afire with ancient wisdom, he unfolded himself inside her, stripping off scales and thorns to dissolve like snow into the plasma of her blue-green blood.

8

THERE IS A LIGHT

There is a light in this place
A red spark beneath the hill
A hummingbird's heartbeat
Divinity
A change, feeding like a fire
Amidst a mound of ashes
A change to break the coming world
And paste it back together

QUEEN SIDRA THE LOVELY nibbled her lower lip, forcing the words to surface through her trivial thoughts. There was a deeper yearning for expression, something much more meaningful to reveal if only she could grasp it. She tapped her quill against her forehead and rubbed the belly now large enough to rest atop her folded legs. Turning tiny somersaults, the baby shifted inside Sidra's womb, restless to be in the world. She, for Sidra knew that this child would be a girl. Had she not prophesied it in her dreams? Seen the girl—a tiny thing with melancholy eyes and milk teeth as sharp as her tongue—making pronouncements with her miniature mouth, rousing the rabble and tempting the fates?

As much as she tried to emulate her heroine the poetess Saint Catherine, words did not flow easily from Sidra's pen or leap like spring hares from tall grasses to flash through sunlight and spark wonder. She must tell Soryk about the baby. Still, she could not approach him with simple language when she had silenced herself, and their common tongue was the speech of bodies in movement. Dreams had too often foretold her demise; each tiny fracture of her bones resonated through her consciousness, another step in her march toward death.

Duty, as much as desire, pushed her to write. If she did not live to see her child reach adulthood or take her first steps, she must imbue the girl's father with a sense of obligation. Sidra feared the demise of the Erun city at her passing. Its residents were too chaotic and wild to survive without strong leadership. Carac's thinking was limited by his wolf brain; his animal drives often suppressed the pull toward rational analysis and politics. She had no successor. Rather, her successor was yet unborn and could not benefit from her mother's guidance.

Sidra's mind went blank. She listened to the soft thump of her own heart, and the rapid echo of the smaller one beneath it. Rereading the note—whose convoluted words meant "Our child grows within me now. This daughter will take my place and fill the hole I leave behind. Keep her, and groom her to tend the wilds. One day, she will wear the crown I abandoned."—Sidra was satisfied that Soryk would understand it and soon reappear on her doorstep. She kept this image fixed firmly in mind, Soryk's dark eyes kind and slightly worried, his arms outstretched to take the baby from her failing grip.

Sorykah had left an address, however remote the possibility that a messenger could actually travel to the Sigue and navigate Ostara's den of thieves to locate "S. Minuit, Parcel 4, Station 29, Section 7-H:TI." What a vague and confusing address! Sometimes Sidra convinced herself that it was false, invented only to distance Soryk/ah from the likeliest threat to her dominance.

A young man waited in Sidra's parlor, solid enough to warn away attackers but ruddy-faced with good cheer and the excitement of having been selected for a royal task. Gowyr bowed when Sidra approached and she smiled. Perhaps when he returned, she would find a better use for him than messenger. Carac had grown so surly of late.

"Greetings, friend." Sidra smiled and was pleased to see that he was courteous enough not to hold out his hand like some demanding child.

"My queen." A nervous flush colored Gowyr's cheeks. "Hans my Hedgehog sent me."

"I have a message for a close friend in Ostara. Do you know it?"

"Aye. My da' trades oil in Colchester. Me mum's Yetive the midwife. I'm just here visiting her for the season."

"Good lad. You know what the Sigue is like. You won't be tempted by devious sweeties, then."

"Pardon?"

"Just be careful what you put into your mouth, that's all."

Carac reported an infestation of Chen's drug in the Sigue's cities. Miners picked it up in Blundt and Neubonne, and the tradesmen and dockworkers ferried it south to Ostara, where any form of entertainment was welcome to enliven the dreary winter nights and temporarily dispel the stinging cold. Sidra decided not to risk Gowyr's intrigue by mentioning it.

"Just go to the address marked and deliver it straight into her hands." It was addressed to Sorykah, but meant for Soryk. Sidra hadn't quite perfected her delivery system; hopefully, each would get the message intended. "Hans will give you everything you need to get there and back. You are in my hire until you return to me, mind." Sidra glared at Gowyr, imparting her will, and he nearly bent from the force of it.

"Yes, my lovely. Deliver the letter and come right back," Gowyr said. Meeting the queen in person, he did see how someone who appeared plain from a distance could shine like a diamond in the right light. "Miss, can I pop in on me da' just for a night or two?"

"I suppose that would be all right. But no longer. I shall expect your return by month's end." The missive slid from her fingers into his. "Travel well."

He bowed again and departed. As the door latched shut behind him, a prescient chill passed over Sidra. She dismissed it, confident that Soryk would soon be en route to the Erun city. She stopped by Hans my Hedgehog's to inquire after Dunya's well-being. Hans betrayed his happiness at the mention of Dunya's name, and Sidra was pleased. She'd turned two magnets to opposite ends. Where once they repelled, they now attracted. That was an item to tick off her list.

Sidra left Hans too deeply rooted in his newfound joy to remark on her short visit. In the tunnels, she sagged against the wall, breathing through her pain. Her bones ached. They creaked and groaned from the strain of that small baby distending her womb, as the synthetic marrow within granulated and grew powdery. Her bones would soon be as thin and brittle as sugar wafers.

A couple neared, the man bowing and the hobbled old woman curtsying awkwardly as they passed. Sidra assumed her royal expression—one part haughty remove, two parts magnanimous concern. Lately, summoning this mask was her only defense against being completely overwhelmed and falling to pieces. Soryk/ah's departure left her perforate with grief. It poured right through her. Regret filled her up and overflowed. How silly she'd been to withhold speech, to deny confessing to the one thing that might keep him with her just a little bit longer. Even Sorykah would understand Sidra's need for her man, and perhaps would have been more inclined to share her body with him. Now Sidra couldn't recall the reason for her silence, some snit or bloody-minded conviction that must've seemed deeply meaningful at the time.

She always walked as if balancing a pitcher of water upon her head, for her topsy-turvy antler crown had a way of snagging on roots jutting through the tunnel ceilings or sliding off to one side. Heat that started in her pelvis and radiated through her legs and belly further impeded her progress. It crawled along her spine, invaded her jaw, and lit her scalp on fire.

Gowyr's mum, Yetive the midwife, was home. When she was out on a call, she tied the figurine of a small brass bird to the handle of her woven ox-hair door to indicate that she'd flown but would soon return. Today there was no bird. The door, too similar to human hair to allow any but Yetive to touch it without revulsion, yielded to Sidra's presence, gaping a bit to allow her to call inside.

Yetive arrived puffing and reddened, her gray-streaked brown hair curling in the muggy steam that filled her home. Gowyr had not returned to Yetive's house after Hans my Hedgehog summoned him to see Queen Sidra. Her charming boy was the apple of many a girl's eye, somatic or human, and Sidra had a reputation for picking and eating those apples, seeds and all. One did not flout the good queen's wishes but Yetive worried to think her son inducted too soon into adult realms. She longed to ask after him but doing so would be an admission of distrust and put the midwife in a poor light, so she bit her tongue.

"Come in, come in, mistress. I'm just making dumplings." Yetive waved Sidra into her tree house, one of the smaller cedars in the Erun. The fragrance of rosemary, marjoram, and savory broth enlivened the atmosphere. "Have a sit, mistress," Yetive pushed her pet, a surly eighteen-pound rabbit, from the sofa. He moved with reluctance, nose twitching in irritation as he loped beneath a rocking chair. "Henry!" Yetive scolded. "I was told rabbits were sweet and easygoing."

Sidra smiled, glad for the distraction. "Whoever told you that was putting one over on you. Just look at him sulk!"

Henry barricaded himself behind fatty folds of skin, his fur bunching up around his neck like a lace ruff. Yetive kept a close watch on him. Rabbit meat was a much-desired delicacy among the somatics. He would disappear in an instant without the midwife's constant vigil.

"Feeling poorly, are we?" Yetive set a kettle on the fire ring. "The pain getting worse?"

Sidra nodded.

"Let's have a listen." Opening her medical bag, Yetive grabbed a battered stethoscope and placed it on Sidra's belly. The midwife cocked her head and listened. "All seems well enough. Lie back." Her firm hands palpated Sidra's abdomen, feeling for the placement of the baby's head, discerning the lump of a protruding elbow from the bump of a bony knee. She whipped out a measuring tape and sized up the height of the fundus. "She's growing. Be pleased, mum."

Sidra nodded, tears welling.

"Now, tell me about the pain."

Sidra knew that Yetive could little assuage the pain that came in waves, but her kindness helped to placate Sidra's mounting misery. "Worse during the day. It seems best when I stay in bed, but obviously, I cannot do that."

Yetive filled her ceramic teapot, bringing cups and pot to the small table. Years of midwifery had taught her to let mums speak when the spirit called, not when pressed.

"There's too much to do, too many plans under way." Sidra's rank and the need to observe rules of etiquette too often prevailed over her need for a confidante. She could not comfortably speak of the blue disease infiltrating the cities above- and below-ground. Yetive had her own sources and wisdom; Sidra would not compromise her by making her privy to more information than she ought to have.

"You know that there's little we can do for you here. If you went to Neubonne you could go to a proper hospital. Get quality care." *They might even be able to save you*, Yetive thought.

"Not possible. They wouldn't have any better idea how to care for my health than you. There's no precedent, no model. I'm the only person who's had the transplant. I doubt anyone expected me to live this long."

When she first left the Father's Charity Hospital after the experimental surgery, pills and mania numbed both mind and body. She felt immortal, unbreakable, and although her condition made her fatalistic, delight in a second chance chased away the death so often lingering in her shadow. It had been a good run. She'd transformed herself from a nurse to a queen, guardian of hundreds across the country of Plein Eïre, organized the somatics into a loosely unified body, initiated countrywide communications and messaging systems, and ensured their safety in the secret underground Erun city. But her time as queen was coming to an end. "I won't last forever."

Yetive patted Sidra's belly. "Nor will she if you don't slow down."

"I simply can't do it. Not yet. I'll trust in your herbs and my instincts for now."

Yetive pursed disapproving lips. "Yes, my lovely. But one day soon, I'll prevail." Her stern features softened. "I'll see you kept in bed even if I have to tie you to it."

Sidra laughed, a glimmer of her old self. "That I would pay to see! Now, I have a new girl who needs a livelihood and I suspect you are in need of an assistant."

9

STAINED

KIRWAN STAGGERED FROM JANDI'S tattoo parlor, his pulse rapid and inconstant. The feeling wasn't coming, dammit, the rush was too slow and thick as molasses. Kirwan rubbed his tattooed crotch and worked in the ink, begging sweet Jerusha to kick it into high gear and loose that blessed chain of delicious release.

Crowded by couples careless in their synchronous high, a long line snaked up the alley to the entrance of the Hanging Garden, a once-extravagant nightclub flanked by peeling gold-painted sphinxes and graffiti-covered columns. Kirwan shuffled into line. He scanned the crowd, sliding a cold slippery gaze over the women, the sensation one of ice cubes gliding along sweat-warmed skin. One or two shifted their eyes his way. Taking in the wasted, skinny body haunted by the gray ghosts of faded tats, they dismissed him for the junkie he was. Rejected by pretty girls who kept their habits under control and hadn't yet let ink-lust warp their looks, Kirwan shivered and sniffled, mentally berating Jandi for dosing him with diluted ink.

A girl sidled up to him, rubbing her arm into her breast. Kirwan recognized the gesture. She was a kindred spirit, as habitual in her indulgence as he was in his, thirsting for sensation but not finding it. He nodded. She fastened herself to his arm. The club doorman would admit a pair more readily than singletons. The girl jiggled her forearm, nudging her breast. Kirwan squeezed her hard, whispering, "Be still."

Shaking his head, the bouncer thumbed them aside to await inspection. His muscles flexed powerfully beneath his tight tank top. The tattooed raven's wings sprawling across his pecs in honor of his namesake, Oman No-Man, the first somatic and founder of the Erun Forest's underground city, rippled and stretched, beating as if in flight. Kirwan and the girl waited in silence, knowing that need would distort their voices with telltale urgency. Oman waved in the robust and the beautiful, plucking out the ink addicts and discarding them behind the red ropes to await the terse approval he parceled out like some irritable and judgmental god.

Kirwan's weak tattoo was already losing what little potency it had. His decoy nodded off and drooled on his jersey. It felt like hours before Oman grimaced with disgust and waved them into the nearly empty club. They slunk through the doorway, wild-eyed and suddenly alert, the girl more eager than he, jerking his arm as she dragged Kirwan into a corner and down onto a stained pallet, her clothes falling away from her body as she opened herself beneath him.

"Hurry, hurry," she urged, flicking a blue-dyed tongue. She ripped open his trousers, stuffing him into her half erect. She pumped her hips to arouse him but for Kirwan, it was too late. He thrust into her lamely, without interest. There would be only the dull throb, a muted and tepid climax entirely without the pleasure he could feel only when ink pooled viscous beneath his skin. He crawled off the girl. Without even closing her dress, she was up and searching. Another man, still high and not yet sated, took her. Kirwan watched from the corner of his eye as they fell against each other, as frenzied as rabid animals.

In the toilets, the fluorescent light was hospital-bright and blue-white. Limp and lavender, Kirwan's inked penis flopped into his hand. Jandi's tats were mere smudges, and he hadn't even gotten high. The bathroom's intense stink of body fluids, sweat, and disinfectant turned his belly. Kirwan retched into the sink, coughing up foam and yellow slime. He hadn't eaten for days, having saved up his dosh to buy the latest design. Now he realized that he'd waited too long. Blackness hovered and his eyes rolled back in his head. Kirwan worried for his safety, waking up in the men's room as a woman in an environment like this, where his female body would be subject to violence and abuse. The change was coming. Already his testes shriveled inside his fist as he clutched them, willing his body to hold steady and stay male. If he were lucky, he'd find cash in hand when he woke, compensation for a sore crotch and mechanical sex with a faceless stranger.

Kirwan's head glanced against the sink as he fell but the pain was nothing compared to the need to return to Jandi as quickly as possible. He envisioned the artwork, concentric spirals hypnotizing his breasts and the feathers that would curl from the crack of his female ass. Minutely plumped by the change, his lips curved into a smile.

He lay in a puddle of sewage seeping from a rusted toilet line, his skinny rear cushioned by the hips swelling there. The world was lacy with shadows and the outlines of new tats danced beneath his lids. He had not been a woman for a long time. He didn't like being his alter, Kirwana; hated that he had to be weepy and vulnerable, and walk the rough streets with that juice box dripping between his legs when he'd rather be a cigarette of a man, tall and thin, burning with urgent, smoking desire.

"Eh, fer feck's sake." A boot inserted itself between Kirwan's buttocks, its metal toe nosing between his ropey, slack thighs. "Damned ink rat! Get her out of here. Oman! Bugger, I told him not to let any more of these stinkin' geezers in the door."

Fingers clasped Kirwan's upper arms and dragged him across the wet floor. He was conscious but couldn't open his eyes, speak, or rise to defend himself. *I am not an ink rat!* His indignity was voiceless.

The cursing, spitting owner of the manacle hands tugged him across carpeting damp with spilled lager. Where were they taking him? Kirwan remembered. There was a back room in this club. Pay for play, except that the pay would swim into the club king's hands and not his own. He could not wake yet; the change had him sleep-drugged. His tongue was a block of wood in his mouth.

Someone hoisted him onto a sagging, squeaking sofa and propped him into a sitting position.

"Merc, please close the door." A new voice. Cultured, rich, and sensual. Confident within its velveteen range and arrogant with pride of ownership. The man neared Kirwan amid masculine smells of leather and smoky plum, his breath sweet with vanilla tobacco.

"What's her fecking problem?" inquired Merc.

"Oh it's no problem, lad. No problem at all." The man laughed— a sound of gravel thrown into a well or the hissing serpent opening its jaws to strike, venom beading and dripping from needled fangs.

Kirwan struggled to rouse from his fog and speak but he could not. *Sweet Jerusha,* he fretted. *What have I gotten myself into?*

A woman's voice resounded in Kirwan's ear as she bent to inspect him. Parchment skin crinkled at the corners of her slitted yellow eyes. Red hair hung limp against the smooth cylinder of her throat as she loomed above him, her thin, cruel lips nibbled by her boredom.

"Another Trader," she yawned, but even in his fog, Kirwan sensed her agitation. Her anger was a red flare against the gloom.

"Yes." The man crouched beside him, wiping violet saliva from his mouth with a black handkerchief. "He's a poor specimen. Just look." The man poked Kirwan's concave belly, shadowed with fading gray stains. "No meat to him. No curves. You can hardly tell that he is a she." He laughed and lifted Kirwan's shirt. "See?" He flicked Kirwan's nipple with the tip of his long finger. "Barely a mouthful."

"How dull!" She sneered, narrowing foxy eyes. Her temper rose as it always did at the mention of Traders. She calmed herself with the memory of her finger sliding along the trigger of her beloved air gun as it released its dart and sent that bitch Sorykah plummeting to her death. Elu, too; that had been a loss. Still, she was not sorry for it.

"Why waste the opportunity?" he chided, displaying a money clip jammed with dosh. The woman extracted a few bills, muttered an epithet, and stalked from the room, leaving the wealthy man to close the door. He cracked open a traveling case and removed a small silver camera.

Still drugged from the changing sleep, Kirwan was powerless to move as the man forced two blue sugar cubes between his slack lips and held his jaws closed with silk-gloved hands.

Kirwan's eyes began to cloud as the room, and everything in it, turned blue. Danger was all around him, a palpable stink in the smoky air. Again, he cursed his untimely change and the dreadful vulnerability of womanhood.

A stark, hot light glared against his face. The blue in Kirwan's eyes deepened to indigo and then to black. Hands clasped his arms and legs and lifted him from the ground. Mercifully, the black soaked into his ears, throat, and head, until there was nothing left to see or hear or feel.

Kirwan woke much later, gathered his splayed limbs, and pulled himself up from the street where he'd lain. He rubbed his face, pleased by the familiar scratch of stubble beneath his fingers. He stood in a stark, shadowy cut between Neubonne's high towers. Daylight glimmered above; the sky was a rich robin's egg blue. The air stunk of garbage—a sour, fishy odor of decaying food and flesh.

The night was a blur. Many nights were lost to the caprices of the ink and his occasional and mostly unwelcome changes. It wasn't unusual to waken in an abandoned lot, a doorway, or park, or to discover himself cast off, postcoitally rolled onto the floor by his partner and forgotten. He thought nothing of beginning the day in confusion with no idea of his location, or his deeds or misdeeds of the night before.

"Ink," he said, his voice rattled by phlegm. Before morning coffee or bathing, or stopping to urinate behind a Dumpster, he would confront Jandi about that half-assed tattoo she'd given him. She'd known the ink was cut and she needled him anyway. Just because he was an addict didn't mean that he didn't have standards. Jandi wouldn't be pleased to see him, but she was more interested in earning than re-fusing cash. She was no better than him. She'd do anything for a wad of dosh and the opportunity to slide her needles in and out of some-one's skin. He wondered if she ever inked herself. The thought aroused him. He envisioned Jandi sprawled in her chair stenciling rose petals on the flesh of her belly, the ropes of her white dreadlocks swinging in time to the cadence of her electric needle. He smiled, one hand floating along his wasted flesh, looking for the scabbed sites of recent tattoos to rub.

There were holes in his recall but as he picked through the scraps, he began to patch together a haphazard timeline of the previous evening. A thin, dirty-faced girl had clung to his arm, shaking with need, twisting her thighs and fingers together as they waited to enter the club. They were denied entrance but once inside, when his ink and his stamina failed him, the girl deserted him for other prospects. Kirwan sniffed his hands and clothes; he smelled of the toilets and he flashed on the stinking men's room floor as he lay convulsing through the change.

Kirwan staggered along the alley's length, unconcerned with find-ing food to line his aching empty belly or warmth to ward away the frost. He thought only of Jandi, the whine of the needle vibrating beneath his skin, and the smell rising from inkpots newly opened, sharp with ash, salt, and resin.

Pop music blaring, a minibus whizzed by, suited commuters dan-gling from its open platform. He could catch a ride if he wanted but walking was cheaper. He knew this part of Neubonne and could be at Jandi's within the hour, to crouch in her doorway to await the turning of locks that would admit him into her den of vice.

Kirwan paused to lean against a ruined telephone booth, its glass cracked and broken. Another minibus rocketed by. Too late, he raised his hand. It lurched past trailing dancehall hits and lavender methane bubbles from its exhaust pipe. Once it had been easier, he lamented, scraping a wad of chewing gum from his shoe with a stick. He had had his own dosh and a fine house brimming with centuries of art and historical artifacts, each one insured by the most presti-gious auction house in Plein Eïre to back his fortune. Kirwan had been so well off that he could toss a trinket to any woman who shared his bed. A thirteenth-Dynasty bone china vase, more than seven hundred years old. A fertility idol carved from the bones of an extinct whale. A curved Magar blade, the battlefield prize of a fallen hero from another age, when armor was crafted from plates of leather and brass, and horses were kept safe from harm because they carried the fire of the gods in their eyes.

It went awry, as do most good things. He picked up the wrong girl and brought her home, the new tattooing fad so recent as to be un-heard of outside Neubonne's sin parlors and seediest of drug dens. She scuttled into his fanciful home, her gaze speeding over Kirwan's carefully cataloged collections. There was no charade of polite con-versation. She juggled her breasts two-handedly, like a grocer grips melons for the scale. The sex act was initiated and concluded so quickly, and with so little finesse, that it left Kirwan quite shaken.

"Is there something I can do for you?" He was alarmed by her swelling tongue and lips, the way she shook with tremors as she gy-rated inside her clothes.

"Spreading," she managed to say, biting her lips as a moan slid between them. Kirwan watched her thrash and convulse, her body manipulated by some demonic lover who gripped her with rough hands and bullied her against Kirwan's library wall. The girl spasmed wildly, her arms and legs jerking as she dropped to the floor, panting and heaving.

"I'm not even touching you," Kirwan breathed. He recognized a mind-blowing climax when he saw one. "How did you do that?"

Thus, for an exchange of gifts and promises of more when needed, she initiated Kirwan into the world of gray ghosts, where aggressive ecstasies played on raw and screaming nerves strung tight as a viola. Dreamy and delirious in a tattoo parlor's back room, the girl mind-lessly stroked her skin as the needle pierced Kirwan's flesh with tiny repeating stabs and the sewing machine's mechanic whine.

His chest took the first hit. Noviates received a triangular scroll of looped quill-pen curls that wound right to left across the pectorals and dropped into the V of the breastbone.

The change came, brought on by too much excitement and fear, too much wanting of this newly desired thing—an altered state to launch him into new heights of sensual satisfaction. Each fresh puncture was a fiery wasp stinger punched into his skin, the venom ground in against his will by an angry fist. Kirwan flickered between alter and primary, his Trader selves wrestling for the first taste of euphoria. His nipples reddened and swelled to bursting berries. He tucked his hand between his legs to pin his penis to his thigh and prevent its retraction. Accustomed to genital-grabbing, neither the tattoo artist, Kirwan's thieving and greedy ink rat companion, nor the few malingering loiterers paid him any attention.

The tattooist poked the final period into place and sat back, the ink gun dangling from his hand. He leered at Kirwan, flashing yellow teeth. With each new design, his culpability lessened. Meted out in diminishing portions and force-fed to the gaining masses, his personal allotment of sin was diluted to the point that he could easily and guiltlessly extract his payment in body cavities and cash, thus suffering no further stains upon his paltry, penurious soul.

The sin was a grievous thing laced by bloody stitches and fumy with the scorched rubber scent of disinfectant, made noisy by the ink rats' pallid arguments against their defeat and a ringing clatter of coarse blades and dull needles. The tattoo artist had once been a marine biologist, committed to saving cephalopods rather than milking their ink and injecting it into horny assholes. He would do penance in the next life for crimes committed in this one. The bearing of guilt grew easier when assuaged with money and lots of uninhibited sex with writhing women who wouldn't even recall his face the following morning. He sent them to their deaths with a smile.

"Here," he said to Kirwan, taking him by the hand and pushing him toward the mirror. "Take a look." *Read the warning. Make your peace with the death assured you.*

Kirwan ran a forearm over his pinking skin, smearing the blood that oozed around the handsome script stitched like yarn across his quilted chest. His eyes watered as he read. A terrible sense of fore-boding settled into his lungs, chilling his vitals and coating his an-ticipation with a killing frost. He wondered what he had done to himself when he felt it, the first thin tendril of smoke rising from a single spark. Each hair and skin cell vibrated to an urgent new tune, a hundredfold intensity to the panting openmouthed desire he sometimes felt as a woman when the monthly egg ripened and sent its come-hither signals to any sweaty he-man in close proximity. His entire body craved fertilization. Plunder, decimation, ruin. It was the worst feeling he could imagine. It made him want to rip the skin from his bones and fling it away and yet . . . his fingers reached to trace the words *grief, pleasure*. Touch activated the ink, sent him shooting higher and higher, desperate for the wave's crest but not reaching it. Kirwan could barely breathe as he scraped at the drip-ping blood and suffocated himself with lust. His eyes widened as he read the inscription:

Now you've done it. Made part of you the rare ink of an octameroon, half human, half cephalopod, an eight-legged monster of the singing sea, who dines on the flesh of the dead. Necrosis begins. Neural atrophy follows. Bliss feeds upon bliss and drains the well. Pleasure polishes the carcass bones. Grief will be the tuning fork and set the pitch for your decline. Let the depredation commence.

He smoothed each letter, sliding his fingers through the blood as he read the last sentence with a desperate, percussive gasp and a brief detour to unconsciousness. The change rampaged inside him, hun-gry for more. A female voice dirtied his ear, his alter possessed by the promise of achieving the acme of this ascent and its swift and breath-taking plunge: *Feed me, fuck me.*

"Jerusha protect me," Kirwan pleaded as the ringing in his ears obliterated the thud of his slack body, felled by ecstasy, slumping to the tattoo parlor floor.

How long had it taken to run through his wealth? Two years? Less? Waking destitute in an alleyway had become an everyday occurrence. It was not unseemly to him. After all, what better use of life than the enjoyment of its pleasures? His conviction was thin, however, and his assertions hollow. The ink had him in a death grip. Ink. Hardly worth the effort to trek across the Botanica to Jandi's if she would refuse him—and her ink was weak. Ink was ink but Jandi's was junk food and he wanted steak.

Kirwan took refuge inside the phone booth and fumbled in his pockets for a coin, but they were empty. Another might have been alarmed, thinking himself robbed, but Kirwan never carried anything of value and had neither wallet nor keys to protect. He traveled like a bit of newspaper on the breeze, unhampered by money or possessions. It amused him now to look back upon his former life, the constant parade of women and the antiques with which he paid them. Today he owned nothing but the clothes he wore, the vacant shell of a once-grand home, the ink-lust that consumed his mind, and the promise of nightfall. He needed naught else. Ink was the only thing of import, the only reason to rise and brave the daylight.

His fingers closed around a scrap of paper in his pocket. Kirwan had forgotten the number but now he recalled taking it from a swishy rent boy in pink glitter and cowboy chaps at the Dregs. He'd only glanced at the name then. The man was called the Star-Maker—a deft magician who transformed street slutlings into digireel superstars and catapulted Neubonne's sensation seekers into celestial vaults, flying on blue sugar cubes and syrupy red liqueurs tipped from gold vials into open, guzzling mouths.

There was one currently circulating through Neubonne's petite houses of pleasure and building up some lucky codfish's fortune. The reel played on an endless loop, filling the screens implanted in the walls and ceilings of the better tattoo parlors, close rooms with glossy, ebony-tiled walls and a shrugging, shiftless clientele of addicts in the making. Kirwan had caught glimpses of it over the shoulder of the ink rat who rode him, a toothless hag, half blind from having her eyeballs tattooed too many times.

Watching that Trader's change was like viewing a mugging in progress through the walls of her crystal coffin. Her fists beat the glass while hair sprouted on her chest and chin. A Trader woman (thin like himself but dark-haired and dark-eyed where fair Kirwan was blond and blue) shook off a shroud of smoke. Her eyes were wild as she patted the flat chest where her breasts used to be. Like him, she was of fluid, inconstant gender, capable of a total physical conversion from female to male, then back again. He'd wondered, fleetingly, if she suffered.

Think of the money, though, he consoled himself. *You can turn a pretty poxy penny, if you like.*

The receiver buzzed in Kirwan's ear as he dialed.

A terse voice answered, "Yeah?"

Kirwan clutched the phone as though it were the fringe of a magic carpet, waiting to whisk him off to the promised land. "I want to work for you."

A beat of silence and a smothered chuckle. "Right. Give us your locale and we'll pick you up."

When they came, pulling up to the curb in a stylish beige sedan, Kirwan doubted for a moment if he'd made the right choice, but gray ghosts danced beneath his skin and that demonic voice whispered again, *Feed me, fuck me.* They opened the car door, and he got in.

He hadn't ridden in a private car for ages. Neubonne was transformed by Kirwan's new perspective. Away from the grimy gutters and alleys, the city reveled in her fading beauty. He felt himself assuming a new importance as they pulled up the circular drive connecting the Morigi family towers rising 101 stories above the city center, fronting the Telec River junction. The black Onyx Tower was devoted to the Company's development division, its penthouses

owned by Matuk Morigi, the founder of monopolistic Tirai Industries, and his successor son, Chen. With flights of executive suites
and private flats, the white Quartz Tower was Neubonne's most lux-
urious residence. An enormous salt pillar, it rose layer upon glassy
layer, stunning the eye with its razor lines.

The little plaid-suited driver and his taller companion escorted
Kirwan through the Onyx Tower's pristine white lobby to the elevator.

"In you go," cackled the driver. "Up to your doom!"

The bell sounded with a genteel ping and Kirwan entered the
glass capsule clinging to the track scoring the building's exterior.
Early morning light pinked the sky. Faint clouds streaked the horizon—a storm moving in from the Southern Sea. Both North and
South Fork bridges gleamed, spans of steely spiderwebbing clinging
to the transverses linking Neubonne's island city center to the mainland. The shining silver coil of the Telec spilled into the ocean, a
channel of pulsing mercury cleaving a muddle of hazy tower blocks
and winding streets toward a harbor clogged with steamers and fish-
ers. To the south, the muddy Subor stagnated between mossy banks.

The elevator whooshed, and Kirwan's ears popped. He smoothed
his wrinkled shirt and bent to tie his shoe. The doors opened. A pair
of shiny black brogues planted themselves before him and a voice
fell on Kirwan like hot rain.

"My prize piggy." Chen's eyes rested on Kirwan's bony chest and
he smiled, showing pink teeth.

Kirwan rose to stare into the devil's face—a bearded chin, smirk-
ing red lips, wicked eyes, and lustrous black hair. The man from the
Hanging Garden introduced himself. "Chen Morigi."

Kirwan stood shivering in the cool room. He did not like this
man's superior manner, his intense, overpowering fragrance, or the
wealth that defined him and put Kirwan in his lowly place.

"Have you nothing to say?" Chen purred, as unctuous as a preda-
tory cat.

Kirwan shook his head, wary of the phalanx of men barring his escape. His legs weakened and inky ghosts swarmed beneath his skin.

"I'm pleased to see you. I knew you'd ring when you tired of that chimney sweep's ink. You want the real thing. Undiluted. Raw."

Resting a firm hand on Kirwan's shoulder, the man cocked his head. A thin line of strawberry saliva spilled from the corner of his mouth, and he flicked it away with a black kerchief. Kirwan knew how bony and insubstantial he must feel beneath the other man's hand.

"Have I aroused your interest, my friend?"

Kirwan's mouth watered. Blood traveled in small tight rings inside his trousers. The lure of ink enfolded him in its dark embrace and Kirwan's eyes began to glaze, anticipating its burn.

"Do you remember what I told you last night?" Chen pulled a small box from his vest pocket. Bright blue sugar cubes twinkled in the dim light. "Remember?" Chen rattled the box, making the cubes dance a jig. Obediently, Kirwan accepted one on his tongue. Kirwan would follow this man back to hell if he was telling the truth about ink freshly extracted from throbbing octameroon sacs, still hot and glistening with the rich honeyed brown of old, polished wood.

"Six films. I'll keep you in ink and doxies and rough trade, and whatever else you desire. You shall want for nothing." Chen caught Kirwan's head as it lolled on his neck, the bluing seeping into his brain and turning it temporarily to mush. Chen's men easily lifted Kirwan's skeletal frame and dumped him on a chaise.

Another smell, heavy perfume like a fox's musk, filled his nose. The redhead alighted by her lover's side, her cloak parting to reveal a lush dress of crushed green velvet.

"Chen," she whispered, rubbing her chest in a familiar gesture that only intensified Kirwan's ink-lust. Too well-known, that circular automated stroking. He closed his eyes, leaned closer as if to absorb the ink beneath her skin by osmosis, inhale its tart aroma, and activate the switches in his brain. Chen brushed her off. Snapping like a Christmas cracker, Chen's girlfriend stomped toward Kirwan.

He watched through blurry eyes as the redhead neared, her displeasure evident. Kirwan thought that she was not a very good girlfriend to be so dismissive of her partner's fancies. She crouched beside the chaise, inspecting his prone form with the manner of a beneficiary brushing flies from a corpse at a wake, and asked, "Who do you want?"

Her pointed nose and ginger hair were decidedly vixenish. Kirwan thought wildly of a fable, a raven tricked by a red fox and getting a comeuppance, but could recall no more than that.

"Come on! Who do you want for your tats? Who's your dealer?" She pinched a thin roll of Kirwan's flesh between her fingernails and twisted.

"You're the red fox," he slurred gravely.

"And that makes you the raven." She grinned, lips splitting to display white teeth as long and narrow as piano keys.

Kirwan shivered and groaned, crippled by bluing and the promise of money, sex, and ink, ink, ink. He'd never had it raw, only heard the stories of ecstasies unparalleled, a sensual delight so intense it caused stroke, paralysis, heart failure, and death.

They wanted him to change and perform vulgarities on film. After that, his fate would be tossed like dice in an alley. What would they do? Smother him, slit his throat, chop him into bits, or inject him full of belladonna and toss him into the Telec River to fatten the creatures slithering through the murk.

The woman pinched him again, bursting the capillaries in his skin between her fingers, like the bubbles on packing plastic. "Give me a name so I can rid my nose of your Trader stink."

Sweet Jandi, you won't forgive me for what I am going to do to you, Kirwan grieved, but his glee was greater and outshone his regret. "She has a shop in the Botanica. Her name is Jandi."

"Fine." The woman snapped his flesh as if breaking a bud from a twig. "Jandi it is."

10

BUTTERSCOTCH PLAID

JANDI UNLOCKED THE SECURITY GATE and winched it high, anchored the handle, and pulled the wooden boards from the storefront window. She stacked them beside her as she slid her key into the big padlock and released links of chain, wrapping them around her knuckles. She'd learned this lesson after a crazed ink rat had rushed her and forced his way into the shop, ripping bottles of ink from the shelves and scattering clean needles across the floor before she'd socked him and rolled him out the door. If anyone approached her now, she'd clout him on the head with a steel-wrapped fist.

She flicked her gaze down the street, noting the usual assortment of merchants setting up shop, bike messengers, and a few working-class stragglers waiting for a minibus. Two drunks huddled on the stoop of an abandoned office building slurping moonshine from a bottle reluctantly shared—each one eyed the other and waved his hands in complaint if a swallow was too long in coming. A pedicab driver cranked past, his face gray with fatigue. His bare, dirt-streaked calves were taut with muscle. Sweat dripped from his chin as he pushed three giddy club kids swilling fossil water up Gentian Street.

"Hey!" Jandi yelled. "Want a tattoo?"

The kids fell together, snorting and giggling. One of them stood up in the swaying cab and stuck out a tongue, frosted blue. Blue tongues; she'd seen an awful lot of those lately. A new class of drug circulated through the dance halls, and it was cutting into her trade. Her clientele was aging and the next generation was slow to pick up her tip. Ink was labor-intensive, hard to come by, expensive, hopelessly addictive, and the lusts for it all-consuming and soul-destroying. Bluing meant that you didn't need to find a partner or have to suffer the shame of hiding ink ghosts from friends and family. You didn't have to slink through back rooms or loiter in public toilets, looking for a quick screw to finish off your fix.

The Botanica was nothing but a big party zone; its predominant pharmacopoeia supplier would have access to endless customers. Jandi's trade was trivial in comparison to the lucrative fossil water market, but bluing and strawberry milk, a hallucinogenic herbal liqueur, created a rapidly spreading mania. Just when she'd finally surrendered to the Company's pressure and begun using the aphrodisiacal ink, a bigger wave crested to submerge her.

Jandi picked up her boards and entered the shop, locking the door behind her. *Appointment Only*, blazed a pink neon sign, but most of her clients showed up at any hour, tapping on the window and waving their dosh. These days, only tourists and teenagers made appointments, standing in line outside the shop checking their watches, wary of strangers but trying to look cool, as if they belonged in her neighborhood.

Keeping the door locked was another hard-learned lesson. Ink made people crazy. She'd begun seeing clients one at a time after another ink rat got impatient during an appointment, grabbed the needle gun from her hand, and tried to tattoo his own lips. That had been messy. She'd had to throw that gun away and it was one of her favorites, custom-made and irreplaceable. Jandi was pissed. Her irate client had punched the rat in the face, breaking his nose. She'd let the Neubonne police take care of him, though it had taken four hours for them to come collect him, during which time he thrashed in a corner, his hands and feet bound, a gag in his mouth to soak up the blood so he wouldn't stain her vintage linoleum.

As biased and unreliable as the Neubonne police force had proved itself, an officer or two did tend to show up when called and ask a few questions. Drug policies were not rigorously enforced. More frightening were morning rounds, when the city's paddy wagons prowled the Botanica, a gentrified municipality in Neubonne's third ward, collecting sleeping homeless from the doorways and tiny, fenced courtyards fronting blocks of luxury high-rises. Costumed in vinyl "splash suits," the police dragged the city's indigent (who had comfortably inhabited the abandoned and derelict buildings before TI demolished the whole lot in its pursuit of grand-scale economic reform) from the stoops of their former squats, tied their hands, and rolled them into paddy wagons bound for a dumping ground under the North Fork bridge. Blasting water and industrial disinfectants, a street sweeper trailed the wagons, sanitizing Peony Street, Iris, Foxglove, Magnolia, and more, making them as pretty as their namesakes before the current residents descended from high places to greet the day.

Jandi's shop straddled the border between the third and fourth wards. More than once, she'd roused a sleeper with a cup of hot coffee, the promise of buttered bread or sweet rolls studded with raisins. Enticed into her shop and grateful for her protection, the homeless extended their circle around her, pulled within the tenuous safety net of their fragile allegiance. After paddy and sweeper passed and Gentian Street gleamed in the rising fog of disinfectant, Jandi's guest would gather his or her belongings, poke a cautious head from the door, and wheel a laden cart into the morning, assured of another day collecting discarded fossil water bottles and performing the small tasks that served the city in invisible ways.

Today she had only two appointments on the book, but she could guess which of her regulars might appear. Markis was developing quite a habit though he partied only on the weekends; he'd likely drop by before closing for his Sunday night artwork. There were a few others who'd been away for a week or more but she could rely on the hub of her trade, Kirwan, to show. He came by nearly every day, his eyes ever more vacant, his skin blotchy and peppered with needle marks. She'd watched his slow decimation with concerned detachment. He'd been beautiful when they first met, sweet and golden as if carved from a honeycomb. With each tattoo, Jandi stole a bit of his nectar, sapping his vitality ounce by ounce until he became a gray ghost himself. Where he got the money, she didn't know, but he would find the means to pay her until there was nothing left to tattoo but his skeleton.

In fact, as she layered trays with a clean sheet of paper, a new needle, gauze, ointment, and bandages, she was considering banning him from the shop. He was too desperate and unreliable. She couldn't trust him to keep his head anymore. Although he was one of her best clients (he had the worst habit), she couldn't risk him bringing the wrong element to her door.

Jandi wrapped an elastic band around her prematurely white dreads. She scrubbed her hands, put the kettle on the electric fire ring, and lit a joss stick. This simple routine officially signaled the beginning of her workday. The books waited; she had to attend to them before week's end, when the rent man came calling for his monthly fee. Things were getting tight. Not enough regulars anymore and too many rats. She would have to parlay her talents in a new arena if she was to survive.

The glass door vibrated with a series of staccato knocks. Markis bounced on his toes, hammering the pane with his fist. "Let me in!" he mouthed.

He loped into the shop and gave Jandi a hard squeeze, crushing her to his chest. Jandi was a good-sized woman, curvy, tall, and strong, but in Markis's arms, she felt like a child.

"What's up, mama?" Markis released her and shrugged off his coat.

"Hey, little man," she smiled. It was their private joke. She was far too young to be his mama and he was built like a footballer with thick, meaty limbs, a broad chest, and the appetite of a bear.

"Get lucky last night?" Jandi's standard question. Her clients answered it each time as if it were the first, pleased by her interest in their conquests.

"You know it!" Markis settled into Jandi's old dentist chair and stripped off his shirt. A rank odor of musty sweat and liquor rose from his skin.

Jandi coughed and turned her head. "You smell like a brewery! Did you do it in a Dumpster?"

"Yeah. I didn't go home last night." Markis's momentary bravado failed him. "Not as easy as it used to be, yeah? I mean, I can still pull but the girls are rough as fuck."

Giving the foot pedal a couple of quick thrusts to wake the motor, Jandi primed the tattoo gun, letting it buzz while she pulled on her gloves and swabbed Markis's neck with alcohol. At this point in their lengthy acquaintance, Markis allowed Jandi to select the site of his next tattoo. She always chose well, rotated the sites often enough so that his subcutaneous fat did not become porous and atrophy. Jandi kept Markis's gray ghosts on the run from one another. She'd done the entirety of his ears two weeks ago, inking outer rims, pinnas, inner canals, and behind his small earlobes. As she did, she informed him that when the ink seeped into the dermis and muscle below it, it would spread to branches of the seventh cranial nerve leading directly to his brain. This neural pathway coordinated facial expressions, taste, and saliva production. His visions would be fantastic— sensations in his tongue and mouth would eclipse all other feeling. The whisperiest of kisses would crumple him into a wad of ecstasy and pitch him into the stratosphere to orbit among the planets.

It was an experiment (though Jandi did not tell Markis he was her guinea pig) that had not gone over very well. Markis had freaked out, frankly, and phoned Jandi to tell her he was too afraid of permanent damage to continue, but he came back anyway, just as she knew he would.

He turned to Jandi, the gummy whites of his eyes veined in red. He clumped a heavy paw on her arm as she poured distilled water into a tiny dish to mix his ink. Splattered droplets saturated the paper.

A bullet slammed through the metal door lock, ricocheted off the small cooling cabinet, and lodged itself in a smoking hole in the plaster behind Markis's head. Markis shrieked like a schoolgirl and leapt to his feet. Blood coursed from a wound on his shoulder and dribbled onto the flooring.

"What was that?" Markis screamed. "Jandi! What's going on?"

"There goes the lino," Jandi sighed, reaching under the dentist chair for the antique pistol stashed in a holster mounted beneath the seat. She cocked the gun, told Markis to shut up, and swiveled to face the door as two men kicked it in with unnecessary force.

"You've already blown the lock," Jandi said, keeping her pistol trained on the gunman, a short, wiry nutter in an orange and yellow plaid three-piece suit and bow tie. Jandi was too nervous to laugh, though she would later giggle at the memory of that ridiculous suit. His partner wore a black nylon tracksuit and gold sneakers. Both sported matching crew cuts, aviator glasses, and a stylized metal C pinned to their jackets.

"Shut yer fecking yawp, you goon!" The short one aimed his pistol at Markis, hunched quivering behind Jandi, clutching his shirt to his bare chest. "Cor! What's that nasty smell? S'like a baboon lives in here."

Jandi agreed; poor Markis. Still, it was rude to comment on it. Instinct told her to drop the pistol to minimize the tension but she held it level, even as the adrenaline hit and her arm began to shake. She stood slowly, ready to pump the plaid intruder full of rubber bullets. "What can I do for you gentlemen? Artwork is by appointment only. I suggest you take a card and call back."

"By the goddess, you're a pretty one." Square-jawed with sandy blond hair, the tracksuited thug pushed his sunglasses up on his head to get a better look.

"What do you want, lads?" Jandi would have to drop her gun soon or risk revealing her weakness. Five pounds of solid steel, she kept the antique gun only for show and emergencies. She'd never had to use this particular pistol, much less keep it leveled at a couple of clownish bullies. She failed to steady her arm and the gun barrel dipped drunkenly.

The taller one snickered and tucked his pistol into a jacket pocket, where its conspicuous bulge sagged the fabric.

Sloppy, Jandi thought. *Odd*. Her assailant's recklessness did not temper her fear, however. A badly handled gun was much more dangerous than one manipulated by a master. This fellow seemed too cavalier to convince her that he was well trained. She groaned. An amateur.

"You Jandi?" The short one planted his legs wide and folded his arms across his plaid chest in a deliberate, studied pose of menace.

Jandi frowned. She tucked her fingers firmly around her bobbing pistol, its cold weight a warm comfort. "Sorry, lads, you just missed her."

"Nice try, darling," said the short one. "You're going on a little holiday."

"Right. A holiday," echoed his partner, earning him a jab in the ribs from a plaid elbow.

"I'm not due for a vacation, lads, but thanks for the offer. You can show yourselves out." Jandi gestured to the door. She was glad for Markis's presence, even as he cowered behind the tattoo chair, his rancid odor permeating the room.

"Maybe you're not getting the picture. We've got plans for you. You're done here," said the tall, pasty northern boy.

Jandi cocked her head. The tracksuited thug had really nice skin for a hired goon. Smooth and buffed like an eggshell. He even smelled good, a bit gin-and-tonic-y.

"Thanks but I think I'll pass." Jandi pressed the barrel of her gun into his chest. His pale green eyes widened in a flicker of panic before he mastered his expression and summoned a sneer.

The plaid-suited pocket pal lunged at her. His temper was as short as his stature. "You don't get a choice. Now drop that toy gun and come along nicely." He was less pleasant and less attractive than his friend, although he smelled of the same cologne. He had a good haircut, Jandi noticed. She'd always imagined that hoodlums shaved their heads with straight razors or bowie knives, standing before a broken mirror beneath a swinging, naked lightbulb. Perhaps it was more au courant to appear less psychopathic than fashionably persuasive.

Aiming his gun at Jandi's nose, he reached up and grabbed her extended arm, twisting it away from his partner. Being shorter, he had to reach up at an odd angle. He grunted, mentally kicking himself. This was an unforeseen complication. He'd have to chat with his mate later and work out the details of successful henchmanning. The Plaid Lad leaned in, pressing his gun to Jandi's temple until her skin plumped around the barrel.

"Markis!" Jandi barked. A blubbering moan answered her and she cursed him.

"That's right, no need to be a hero," said the short one. "Now get your gear and get in the car. I ain't having no resistance or derring-do from you, madam. Understood?"

He fired a round into the ceiling. Shaking, Jandi set her gun on the seat of the dentist's chair.

"Right," echoed Tracksuit. "He ain't having it." He pronounced *ain't* with deliberate intention, as though defying his grammarian mother. "I ain't having it, and our boss ain't having it."

"Your boss?"

"Let's just say he's powerful enough to shut down your entire sector if you don't cooperate. Your choice."

Jandi nodded. *Just get them out of here. You can figure out the rest later.*

"Good." He dropped his gun. "Glad to see you got the message. Get your gear and let's go."

She fumbled through her kits, tucking ink pots, mixing bowls, needles, and gauze into a bag. While Jandi disassembled her tattoo gun and packed it in a small case, the menace in plaid poked around the shop, rifling through her files and commenting on her flash. The other one sat in the windowsill, watching her. His rapt attention should have made her nervous, but his face had a slack, innocent quality that disarmed her. She couldn't think. Markis trembled in the corner like a lapdog and she eyed him with disgust. "You're useless, you know that?"

Markis's lower lip wobbled. Jandi briefly repented. He was bleeding, after all.

"Say goodbye to your widdle puppy," sneered the short one. "You won't be seeing him again."

The lads each grabbed one of her arms and squeezed through the door with her. Aiming his key fob at the sleek new automobile parked in front, the plaid lad released the locks. The car beeped and the men shoved her in and closed the doors. She tried the locks but they refused to open for her. She shouted and banged on the window, trying to draw the attention of a messenger zooming past on his moto, but he didn't see her. She waited for them to get in and peel away but they just stood there, chattily consulting a list the little ringleader pulled from his pocket. They may as well have been perusing a take-away menu.

Inside the car, Jandi watched the goons' lips moving but she couldn't make out the words of their ridiculous discussion as they performed a thorough postgame analysis:

"Baboon? I believe a larger primate would have been more effective. A gorilla or orangutan. 'Fecking yawp' was excellent, though, coarse without being profane," said Tracksuit, aka Barret Scot, aka Butterscotch.

"Really? I didn't care for it. Too many episodes of *Cockney Bastards*. I must have absorbed it by osmosis. But 'by the goddess'? It's hoity-toity, over the top. Romance novely. Say 'sweet Jerusha' like everyone else, or 'godfucker,'" suggested his diminutive partner, Reginald Loren Woolley-Wallace, aka the Plaid Menace, who disliked his name intensely (though he much preferred Loren to Reginald, of which he was more disdainful, feeling the name too common). He had adopted the idea of dressing in plaid from a pulpy old spy novel, failing to see its intended irony.

"Surely you jest. Godfucker? Have I failed both primary and seminary school?" Scot said.

"We're killers, remember? Rock-hard and deadly. We've low IQ scores, violent pasts, and no regard for the law. It behooves you to exude toughness and reek of malice. Not 'hello, miss, you're very pretty, might I have your phone number?' This is real life, Scot, not a senior center musical theater production! Please!" He banged his fist on the car roof though he had to reach up to do it, thus exposing himself to Jandi's disdain.

"You'll have me out there on a limb, Plaiddie, spitting asinine curse words none can decipher," said Scot.

"Plaiddie? It's Mr. Plaid to you." Woolley-Wallace poked a blunt finger into Scot's chest.

"The Plaid Lad," Scot chuckled, batting away his hand.

"Your daily plaid and butter," riposted Woolley-Wallace. "Now, let's deliver this little tartlet and collect our cut." He lit a cigarette and tucked it into the corner of his mouth as he slid into the front seat, cranked the car wheel, and angled into Gentian Street's morning traffic, a raucous mix of pedestrians, pedicabs, cyclists, private automobiles, and fleets of minibuses. Scot scrunched against Jandi, his doughy face reddening.

"Must you smoke?" Scot groused. "It's such a callow affectation." The message light on his electronic notepad blipped.

"It's him." He frowned, scanning the lines of text and punching in his replies.

To: Buttrscotchkilla@siguemail.msg
From: C.Morigi@TI.ind
Sent: April 25, 11:19 a.m.

New orders: destroy the shop. Eradicate all traces.

From: Buttrscotchkilla@siguemail.msg
To: C.Morigi@TI.ind
Sent: April 25, 11:20 a.m.

Sir?

From: C.Morigi@TI.ind
To: Buttrscotchkilla@siguemail.msg
Sent: April 25, 11:22 a.m.

I'm sure you understand. Every needle, every ink spot and
pot, every foul gun and flash.

From: Buttrscotchkilla@siguemail.msg
To: C.Morigi@TI.ind
Sent: April 25, 11:23 a.m.

Any preference as to the method, sir?

From: C.Morigi@TI.ind
To: Buttrscotchkilla@siguemail.msg
Sent: April 25, 11:25 a.m.

If I find so much as a strand of gauze, I'll tie your balls up
with it until they wither and drop off.

From: Buttrscotchkilla@siguemail.ind
To: C.Morigi@TI.msg.com
Sent: April 25, 11:26 a.m.

Yes sir.

From: Buttrscotchkilla@siguemail.msg
To: theplaidmenace@siguemail.msg
Sent: April 25, 11:27 a.m.

Plaiddie, we're completely fucked.

From: theplaidmenace@siguemail.msg
To: Buttrscotchkilla@siguemail.msg
Sent: April 25, 11:29 a.m.

Cant msg whlst dribing

From: Buttrscotchkilla@siguemail.msg
To: theplaidmenace@siguemail.msg
Sent: April 25, 11:30 a.m.

What? Dribing?

"Driving, you prissy prep-school pederast! Can't message whilst driving!" railed Woolley-Wallace, swerving to avoid an elderly cyclist wobbling outside the boundary of the bike lane.

"Criminy. He wants the shop destroyed." Flummoxed, Scot scratched his head. "Reverse the car. We have to wrap up loose ends."

"Tie!" Woolley-Wallace raged in vein-popping agitation. "You tie loose ends!"

"Rein it in, mate. We've got company." Scot met Woolley-

Wallace's eyes in the rearview mirror and they both looked at Jandi, pressed against the passenger door in the backseat beside Scot. She rolled her eyes.

"Just for that," said Scot, narrowing his eyes until they watered, "you can strike the bloody match."

Woolley-Wallace flipped a quick U-turn at the next light and shot down the narrow lane. He jammed the brakes and skidded to a stop across the street from Jandi's shop.

"Get out." Scot dug the barrel of his gun into Jandi's ribs. "Slowly. I'm feeling clumsy today. My greasy finger might slip and pull the trigger. I don't want to kill you, of course, but accidents do happen."

Jandi stepped from the car as Woolley-Wallace popped the car trunk and extracted a red gas can. "Bleeding mother! Scot, you son of a poxy whore!" He flung the empty can at Scot's head.

Scot scanned Gentian Street. No petrol stations, though there was a minibus office at the end of the block.

"Minibuses don't use petrol!" Woolley-Wallace barked, storming through the shop's open door. "We'll just have to improvise. You took an improv course, didn't you, Scot? You mad Thespian bugger."

Jandi shook her head. Markis had fled, leaving everything wide open. Bugger him. He was off her client list for good this time.

Woolley-Wallace rifled through her cabinets. Finding nothing suitable, he fumbled with the small heater mounted on the wall above her sink, cranked the flame, and blew it out. Gas would stream reliably into the pipe, filling her shop with fumes, but it would take hours to accumulate into a deadly cloud with explosive potential.

Jandi's tormentor seemed to figure this out, for he flipped open a jackknife and hammered it into the cyndrilical gas reservoir until he created a bunghole stoppered by his blade. Rocking the knife back and forth, Woolley-Wallace cracked the tank. Visible fumes wavered in the air. A jet of gas streamed across his face, turning him an odd shade of green.

Scot dithered a moment before leaping forward to pull his mate toward the open door. "Good enough," he said, the stripes on his tracksuit going all wavy.

Jandi took a step backward, then two. The gas was getting to her as well, despite the fresh air billowing through the door. Those two bunglers giggled like maniacs, shoving shoulders and waving their guns about, saying "waaahh waaahh" and falling over in fits.

Now she could slip out the door, cross the street, start running, and be safely into the second ward within minutes. There, a couple of outlandishly dressed goofballs high on gas would be suspect among the gray suits and Jandi could lose herself in the warren of look-alike office buildings. She kept moving; a few more steps and she was outside. Several pots of aphrodisiacal ink, new needles, and her best tattoo gun were still in their case on the backseat of the car. Without her equipment, she couldn't work. What was the point in running away if she abandoned her livelihood as well?

A pedicab coasted to a stop beside her. "Need a lift?" The driver's wraparound sunglasses hid the shock widening his eyes as pain soaked his bones and he realized he'd been shot. Blood spurted from the wound in his chest and he pitched over, toppling from his seat to the street.

"Bastard!" Lips streaked with spit, Woolley-Wallace lowered his gun and lunged for Jandi, knocking her to the ground. "You're not going anywhere."

Her head hit the pavement but Jandi managed to stay conscious enough to see him pull off his bow tie, put a match to it, and flick the flaming cloth into the shop. The explosion knocked them off the curb. Cars lifted from the ground. The dead pedicab driver's bike flipped over on top of him.

Jandi shielded her eyes with sooty hands as Scot hauled himself up and limped over.

"All right?"

She shook her head, sick with defeat. It had been a very bad day.

His plaid in tatters, Woolley-Wallace limped to the car, dragging

Jandi along with him. Their ribald banter choked back, the men resumed their positions. Jandi meekly got into the car, holding her tattoo gun case to her chest like a baby. Ash grimed her window but she peered through gritty gaps to view the smoldering wreckage.

Woodenly, she turned to Scot. "Where are you taking me?"

He wore the stunned look of a ruminant confronted with his first lion and didn't reply as he pulled into traffic. Together they watched Gentian Street unroll behind them, a ruin crowded by gawkers. After a long moment, as if he'd rehearsed it, he said, "To meet the master."

Woolley-Wallace and Barret Scot, scholarship boy, pulled up the Onyx Tower's circular drive and valeted the car. Clearly, they were used to being there.

His plaid suit streaked and blackened by scorching, Woolley-Wallace commanded Jandi from the car. He was too free and easy with his gun for her comfort, swinging it around like a watch fob, using it like a pointer. Pedicab driver blood freckled his mean little face.

"I am not happy with you." Woolley-Wallace marched Jandi through the tower's double doors. I just had that suit made. It fit perfectly."

"A good fit can never take the place of good taste." Jandi was glad to see a muscle twitch within his tight jaw.

"You'll regret not being nicer to me." Woolley-Wallace forced Jandi through the opulent marble and granite lobby. Behind the front desk, a host of jacketed receptionists stared straight ahead, purposefully oblivious to Jandi's plight.

"I can't imagine that." Her tattoo case gave her strength. Though she had no shop to return to, at least she could start fresh, favorite tattoo gun in hand. A palette of colors and half a dozen bottles of octameroon ink would earn her enough to travel north. Neubonne was degenerating. While some sectors and citizens rose high, those in opposite stations sank further into impoverished despair. The chasm between affluence and destitution seemed to widen by the hour.

Ascending in the glass elevator, Jandi was unaware that beside her, Scot thrilled to the close warmth of her body. Hands tucked in his pants pocket, his nylon jacket drooping from the weight of his pistol, Scot was quiet. His earlier audacity was gone. He picked at a hole in his pants where a lump of hot metal had melted away the fabric, revealing two inches of pale, hairy thigh.

They exited on the 101st floor and followed a winding corridor to an unmarked door. Woolley-Wallace knocked twice and grinned, salacious and knowing. For the first time, Jandi's stomach flipped.

A man opened the door and waved them into an expensive suite, where a crowd of silent, black-garbed men waited. Woolley-Wallace tried to make small talk and was rebuffed. A second door opened, admitting a tall woman with aniline red hair. Her displeasure was obvious. Woolley-Wallace's flaking, burnt plaid deposited shreds of charred mustard-yellow thread on the white furniture.

"Dare I ask," she said.

Scot began to speak but Woolley-Wallace's raised fist quickly silenced him.

"Just following orders." Woolley-Wallace was disinclined to explain himself to his employer's harpy of a girlfriend. Though Chen would merely shrug and tell him to charge a new suit to the corporate accounts, Zarina was tightfisted and petty. She'd likely dock his pay for destroying TI property.

Zarina dispensed a slim envelope to Woolley-Wallace and he cackled, tucking it into his suit pocket. "For both of you," she admonished, enjoying his disappointment as he counted out the enclosed bills and gave half to Scot, while muttering under his breath.

"Pardon?" Zarina loomed over him, a full foot taller.

He shook his head, backing away from her wicked jack-o-lantern's grin.

"So, you're the tattooist." Zarina examined Jandi and decided that she did not like her. This meant that she would make things hard for her whenever possible and take delight in doing so.

"I have plenty of private clients," said Jandi. "There's no need for all the subterfuge."

Zarina behaved as though Jandi hadn't spoken.

"Really. I can keep a secret. You needn't shanghai me and toss my shop." Fists clenched, Jandi stared at Zarina, willing her to respond. "I'm talking to you. Hey!"

Refusing to meet Jandi's eye, Zarina snapped her fingers. "All right, boys." At Zarina's command, four men sprang to attention. "Take her to the studio and put her to work. We film at midnight."

Scot caught Jandi's eye as she left escorted by somber men in matching suits, each with a stylized metal C pinned to his lapel. She was certain that regret showed itself, and that he offered her a silent apology, but it could have been a trick of the light that made his green eyes water so.

Jandi was taken to another suite, this one largely empty save for two plainly made beds in opposite corners. There were spotlights on ceiling tracks, small cameras mounted on tripods, and a rack of clothing. Garish pink and red flocked wallpaper approximated some turn-of-the-century bordello. Gaudy gas lamps with fringed glass globes provided the only ambience. The beds and sets, she now realized, were messy, used. She began to struggle in the tightening grip of the goons who held her. Kidnapped to make digi-reels? It was illogical. Then she saw the table laden with the tools of her trade, arranged just as she would have done it herself. The paper towel, the dish of water and bottles of ink, the needles, salves, and gauze kept clean in glass containers.

She relaxed a bit, laughed aloud, and realized she was only there to tattoo. "This is it?" She shook off the men, heading for the table. She'd done film work before, mostly drawing fake tattoos on prisoner and gangster extras for serial dramas.

"Who wants inking? You?" Jandi pointed at the nearest man. He subtly shifted his eyes to the right, ignoring her. "How about you? You?" She got the same vexing response each time.

Responding to some silent summons, two men vanished while the remaining two settled themselves on a couch and stared at her.

Now what, she wondered. She was meant to tattoo someone, but who?

BUTTERSCOTCH WAS A BIT QUEASY. Distaste for the job sapped his resolve.

"You told me that we were just to collect the girl. I asked you specifically if there would be any physical violence involved and you assured me that there would be none." Butterscotch was snappish and tense. "'A quick and easy job,' he says, 'like nicking a loaf of bread from the bakery,' he says. Easy peasy pie."

Woolley-Wallace was annoyed. It was evident that Butterscotch had deceived him about his level of commitment. They'd entered into this arrangement knowing that it would require the performance of unsavory tasks and surpassing the stifling limitations imposed upon them by their parents and professors. Scot was less convinced that he should abandon what promised to be a lucrative career in the district solicitor's office for a law-shirking appointment as one of two hired thugs for the heir to Tirai Industries, an immeasurably wealthy landholdings monolith.

"Scot, you have always been and will continue to be a bother of the lowest order. You are a bloody madman now. You can carry a gun in broad daylight without fearing police penalties. We have our own flat in the Onyx Tower." Woolley-Wallace gestured to the opulent bathroom in which they stood, wiping away traces of the day's mistakes. "We are Company men, my lad, and everyone respects us for it."

"Not Jandi."

"Jandi," snarled Woolley-Wallace, mashing his fist into Scot's chest.

"Jandi," Butterscotch sighed, remembering her pretty face, her robust body.

"For the love of all that is holy!" The Plaid Lad smacked his mate's forehead with the back of his hand. "Snap out of it! Crikey,

you're such a girl!" Woolley-Wallace had been insulting Butterscotch's masculinity since primary school. He suffered from small
man's complex and always had to prove his male worth with showy
displays of arbitrary aggression.

"Plaiddie, you were reckless with your firearm today. The pedicab
driver . . ." Acid roiled in Scot's stomach. The image of that man
pitching into the street with his life spilling out of him saturated his
mind's eye and soaked his awareness in blood. "I mean, did you intend to kill him? And for what? Some minor etiquette infraction or
violation of your personal space?"

Woolley-Wallace stripped off the soiled suit jacket and vest,
bunching them into the trash chute. "Scot, I am a man of preemi-
nent moral character. Should I, in the execution of my paid duties,
decide that another person is threatening my person or my mates, I
am well within my rights to dispatch said person." He scrubbed at
the soot on his face, stepped out of his trousers, and tossed them after
the rest.

"Right, right, understood." Scot mangled a washcloth in his
hands, dripping water onto the bathroom floor. "Perchance you
hadn't considered that this lifestyle is meant to be farcical. It's a
panto, and some months hence, we'll be back at university."

"Pantomime? Farcical?" Veins popped out on Woolley-Wallace's
forehead. "This is real life, Scot. This is what being men means. Not
bloody pecking out theses and whingeing on at the pub about your
marks."

Though taller and a good fifty pounds heavier than Woolley-
Wallace, Scot was easily overpowered by his mate's Svengali-like
charisma. It had always been this way—Woolley-Wallace treading
with hobnailed boots on Scot's ambitions, crushing them into
crumbs. Scot was like a big bull with a ring through his nose, an animal needing to be led.

"He paid us, didn't he?" Woolley-Wallace stood before the sink in
his underwear, his short, ropey arms and legs oddly vulnerable beneath the contortions of his impish little face. If Scot, as emotionally

monochromatic as a cathedral's stone walls, was a house of virtue, then surely Woolley-Wallace was its crouching, filth-spewing gargoyle. Woolley-Wallace took roost on bland, nicely groomed Scot and proceeded to defile him with his excretions. Now cloaked in Woolley-Wallace's scat, Scot had come to resemble a gargoyle himself, hunched, bitter, and suspicious, with roving eyes and grasping claws, but beneath the deformity and excrement, the cathedral still stood.

"Do you know why I call you Butterscotch? It's cos you're so fucking sweet." Woolley-Wallace smacked grinning lips as Scot turned away, revulsion in his gut. Woolley-Wallace's body—his chicken-skinned limbs and the stiff nipples ringed in wiry brown hair, like little pencil erasers pasted on a mannequin—made Scot sick. He lurched from the doorway as if still loopy on gas fumes, thinking of the woman in the upstairs suite. She made him feel hopeful. She was different from anyone he'd ever met. For one thing, she'd stood up to the Plaid Menace, even if he bested her in the end with his graphic violence.

Woolley-Wallace thought he'd arrived, that employment with Tirai Industries was the pinnacle of success. They were Company men now, but a Company man Scot did not intend to remain.

A CLOCK CHIMED TWELVE BELLS and Jandi was suddenly alert, watching the men change shifts with robotic precision. There were armies of black-suited men at Zarina's disposal and she commanded them with the cool austerity of a sergeant. The Company regiment decamped en suite, arming themselves with cameras, barricading themselves behind floodlights and tripods.

"Get up," Zarina barked.

Jandi stood, wishing she hadn't eaten the food they'd given her earlier. It had spoiled in her tummy, leaving her wretched. She'd nearly become ill but choked back her vomit, then fearing that they had poisoned her, she had gagged herself and puked into the toilet. Now she was hungry again, and too wary to refuse Zarina's orders.

"Bring him in. Or her. Whatever *it* is."

Kirwan came in, blinking as if he'd lain too many days in darkness. Plastered over his forehead, his fringe had been roughly wetted and combed, but the back was a rat's nest. He was even thinner than before, his skin shadowed with scabs and the faded smudges of old tattoos. Shielding his eyes from the floodlights, he stumbled toward the bed. He wore a silky flowered kimono and his flexing bare toes, gripping bits of carpet between them, was the only sign of his nervousness.

"Kirwan!" Jandi called, but he seemed not to hear her. He took his place on the bed, loosening the sash of his robe and looking expectantly at Zarina.

Jandi pointed an accusatory finger. "You knew I was coming, didn't you?"

"Oh, hello, Jandi," he murmured, as if he'd just realized she was there. Kirwan's apologetic expression little disguised his eagerness and relief.

Anger replaced Jandi's surprise. "You got my shop blown up."

Suddenly intrigued by the carpet, Kirwan looked at the floor.

"You bastard," Jandi spat, her rage in full flower. "It took me bloody ages to pull that shop together!"

"Ooh." Zarina inserted herself between them, grinning wickedly. "A married's quarrel!" She laughed. "Stings a bit, doesn't it, what they'll do for their habits," she said, thinking of Chen. "How quickly they'll trade you for something better, someone else."

Kirwan shriveled further inside himself and Jandi's fists clenched. She would hit a woman. Having a uterus didn't offer any protection from her punches.

"You"—Zarina turned to Jandi, her eyes full of yellow fire—"need to cooperate." She jerked one of Jandi's white dreads, making her wince.

"Tattoo him." Zarina gestured to the tray of ink and needles. "And do it nicely. This is for film."

Jandi rubbed her sore scalp. She'd gladly tattoo Kirwan. Luckily, she knew exactly where to place the artwork to make him suffer the most. Already, the octameroon ink had begun to erode its bottle, pitting the glass. She twisted the lid, releasing oceanic odors of decay and fermentation. This ink was livid and alive. It reached for the lip of the bottle, eager to be free of its confines. As Jandi watched, gray ghosts came to life beneath Kirwan's skin. He arched and twisted, caught up in the coming rapture.

"That's right," Zarina hissed, "you'll get your dose. Just do your bit as you've been taught. And try to stay awake this time, so we can watch your eyes when you change."

Jandi had no idea what Zarina meant, but she did know that the ink before her was a much more potent version of the pigment she normally used. She couldn't risk a single needle prick. The scent alone made her palms flush red and blew across the sleeping embers of her own shelved desires.

"Please," Kirwan begged.

Zarina made noises of disgust.

Kirwan lay lank and wasted across the bed, his face sheened with want. "I'm sorry," he said, and as she had with Markis, Jandi forgave him. It lasted but a moment.

"Don't dilute it," he added. Scoffing, Jandi pulled the tray close and began to mix ink.

"COR, SHE IS REALLY TASTY," whispered Butterscotch, his breath fogging the glass of the one-way window behind which Jandi crouched, applying an especially intricate tattoo to the underside of Kirwan's scrotum.

"Jerusha, you're a nutter! She's got that fella's seed bag up her nose! You'd kiss that mouth, would you?" The Plaid Lad eschewed love and other warm human sentiments. Scot's growing infatuation with the tattooist irked him and made him even more surly and short-tempered than usual.

"I don't mind," Scot murmured, a blush on his pasty cheeks. "I really don't."

"You're a right twat, you are." Woolley-Wallace cuffed Scot on the back of the head for the benefit of Chen's wicked girlfriend, Zarina. She didn't look up from her book, so Woolley-Wallace smacked Scot again for wasting the first.

11

A GRIEF, A RIFT

FAROUJ AND SORYKAH CLAIMED the small galley as their own, huddling beside the propane stove while they ate. Sorykah lapsed into a brooding silence. Farouj refused to take her south to Ostara, rightly claiming that the spring currents circumventing the Sigue meant travel was possible only in a northerly direction, away from home. Unlike the reinforced double-hulled mail and supply ships that delivered goods to the Sigue twice monthly, the fishing trawler was too light to successfully navigate the floe fields, especially dangerous in spring, when rising waters and jagged ice calves made the channel doubly treacherous. Circling the Sigue's landmass to return to Ostara would take more than a week, by which time she could have already solved Farouj's little problem.

With mounting fury, Sorykah shoved the food around her plate. Though her stomach growled, she was too churlish to eat. Angry with Farouj for his willful con, and for pushing Soryk to accept a hero's burden. It was not Soryk's place, or hers, to rescue anyone.

Thoughts of Rava's kin—plucked and sucked and dumped back into the sea like spent feed, their drained husks littering the ocean floor—consumed her, but she blocked her ears against the call to duty. She had delivered the most painful injury herself, though; vague memories of some lovestruck alliance with Sidra's obsessive vengeance left a lump in her throat.

Farouj was silent, too, but not for lack of the words dammed behind his mouth—torrential pleading, remonstrations, and canny persuasions. Better that she not look at him than risk engaging in some disastrous conversation that would entice her farther from home.

Finally, the pressure was too great, and she burst. "I should not be here! There's no justification for your deception. This was not my decision. I'm in charge!" She pounded her chest with a fist, a decidedly masculine gesture that left Farouj wondering who was actually speaking, Sorykah or Soryk. "Not *him*. We speak with the same mouth but what I say when I'm changed is not to be trusted! You defer to *my* wishes, not his." She was shouting now and Farouj raised his hands, shushing her. Even as she said this, Sidra's chiding words echoed in her head, reminding her that Soryk's wishes were her own, those that she could not, or would not, voice.

"You'd prefer to go back to Ostara, pick up just where you left off? You'd turn your back on us?" He tapped his fork against the rim of his plate, an irate staccato.

"Maybe you explained it to Soryk, but *I* need to hear it again. You're just as capable of killing Morigis as I am. More so. You don't require my hand on the blade."

"I only ask that you come along to inspire my people, for they are moved by your tale. If one woman can rise up against tyranny, then surely we can do it, too. You think Chen Morigi's just a spoiled aristocrat, but Sorykah, you've no idea what he's unleashed upon the city." Farouj rubbed his brow as if smoothing away worries, and once again Sorykah sensed him grappling with a steely undercurrent of irritation.

"A blue plague? A storm of ruin comprised of digi-reels and drugs? Believe me, I understand perfectly well who he is." Sorykah raised her hands, helpless to defend herself. She couldn't see herself through Farouj's eyes, view the ring of light he envisioned encircling her head. "What do you want from me? It's too much!" Tears filled her eyes, further infuriating her.

Farouj set down his fork, gritting his teeth against the impotent fury that boiled inside him. What had he been thinking? That he would just present her to the Qa'a'nesh like a gift-wrapped savior in a box and all would be forgiven? That she would gladly abandon her entire life, so swayed by his cool charms that reason and personal imperatives would no longer matter?

Winches groaned and creaked on deck, and two crew members called to Farouj.

"Excuse me," he said coolly, avoiding Sorykah's eyes as he exited the galley.

A single tear dripped from her chin into her plate. How had it gone so wrong? She sensed Soryk's thwarted yearning to launch himself into the world and leave her life behind. Not for the first time, she wished that she could talk to another Trader, find out how s/he kept sanity intact through so many changes and shifts in perspective. She felt deeply broken, despite Sidra's healing ceremony. The queen had been certain that Sorykah's refusal to allow the change to come and go naturally, to segue between aspects of self, was a source of abiding misery. She had maintained a careful equilibrium and mostly managed to hold her shadow persona at bay, but it was wearying to keep the scales balanced—an act that required constant vigilance and well-controlled manipulation of her feelings. Never before had she drowned in pools of emotion. Never had the distant swirling tsunamis come ashore, obliterating her cautious façade of "self," until the loss of her children. Then she was an egg hurled against a wall, and everything—her illusion of control, her refusal to acquiesce to the man in her—shattered. Now she was left to collect the fragments, mop up the spill, and attempt some sort of clumsy reconstruction.

The noise outside ceased. Sorykah wiped her eyes and stood up to look out the window onto the deck, where the entire crew and Farouj had gathered. A fishing net pooled upon the deck. Everyone stood silent and staring.

Sorykah pulled her coat tighter and ventured from the galley. The small crowd parted for her, the deferential Aroulians gesturing her forward. The day's catch spilled from the net, a rain of glittering silver scales. Sorykah recognized pink subarctic char, translucent glassfish, nearly see-through but for the black orbs of their eyes, and snub-nosed cannibal cod patterned with green. Amid the catch beamed the startling glow of bloodless human skin and a length of mauve tentacle studded with white suckers and hooked with a keratinous claw. Sorykah gasped, covering her eyes with her hand. Childish to think that when she looked again, the horrible thing would be gone. Yes, it was still there, and she alone stepped through the mounds of catch, slipping on fish who stared at her with unseeing eyes. Sorykah grasped the humanoid arm, pulling at tissues gone rank with rot, the bones slippery within the flesh, extracting the limb and what followed from the pile. Sorykah dug and heaved, jerking free a pitted purplish tentacle.

The crew hung back, afraid to contaminate themselves with the touch of a mythical sea creature; as if by magic or command of the gods, they too might be transformed.

"Help me!" Sorykah brayed, incensed by the men's inactivity. Farouj responded, and then his mates, shifting fish and digging the remainder of the octameroon carcass from the pile. The creature was bald but for a few strands of glassine hair clinging to its scalp. Its nascent nostrils were sealed shut, and cartilaginous whorls of remnant ears pegged the sides of its head.

One of the fishing crew spoke rapidly, his voice escalating into hysteria. Farouj whirled and grabbed his shoulders, speaking in low, firm tones. The man backed away, heading for the ship's railing. Effluvia sprayed the rail as he emptied his stomach into the sea.

Sorykah dragged the corpse onto the deck. Most of the body was missing. Only one arm, two tentacles, and a portion of the human torso remained, its torn and ragged edges showing waterlogged layers of insulating blubber, thin colorless muscles, bones yellow and soft. Something had chewed up the tentacles with small, sharp blades; cuts scored the purple flesh, exposing the white beneath. Numerous tiny teeth marks indicated that the sea's scavengers had begun processing the body, following invisible guidelines as if marked out by a butcher intent on dismemberment.

Sorykah crouched beside the body, relief washing through her. It was not Rava. Not even her cousins Egil or Töti, she was certain. This corpse had been in the water for a long time, as indicated by its general state of decay. Though exsanguinated and partially frozen, it would soon start to stink as oxygen and bacteria hastened its decomposition. Sorykah poked at the body, numb to emotion. She shrouded her mind with science. She'd feel nothing, pushing her fingers into the split chest cavity, pulling apart the flesh to gaze upon the creature's dual hearts.

"Look at this," she marveled to Farouj. "Two hearts! A perfect symbiotic compromise between species."

Crouching beside her, Farouj masked his disgust at the sight of Sorykah's hands, buried to the wrists within the octameroon's carcass. "How so?"

"An octopus has three hearts. A human only one. Here is a being who is half of each, and nature has met itself in the middle." She ripped a bit, the spoiled flesh easily coming apart in her hands. "What is this? A bladder?" The membranous sac was thick and rubbery, ridged with scar tissues and old stitches. An acrid, bitter-smelling fluid oozed forth, dark and viscid as clotted blood.

"Don't touch it!" Farouj snatched Sorykah's arm away, and she yelped in pain. Bright red blood beaded the back of her hand. Farouj grimly extracted the small, rusted fishhook embedded in Sorykah's flesh. "I hope your vaccinations are up to date."

She nodded, milking blood from the wound. "Why did you do that?"

"The ink is caustic. Addictive. Rife with pathogens, I'm sure.

Should it enter your bloodstream, you'll catch any number of diseases, the least dangerous of which is tetanus. Getting octameroon ink into your blood is to walk through a one-way door. You'll never be free of its urges." Farouj sat back on his heels, watching ink pool on the deck. Gesturing to one of the crew, he said, "You'd better scrub it up, and carefully. It'll eat right through." He rose and pulled Sorykah to her feet. "Leave it."

Far from shore, the crash of ice sliding into the sea played muted, discordant notes, breaking the constant keen of Sigue song, like background music scoring a dramatic moment. Sorykah slid against Farouj as the trawler bobbed on the wake buffeting the boat.

"You see?" Farouj said, his arm tight around her as they staggered back to the galley and their unfinished plates of cold, congealed food. "Even the sea mourns the loss of one of her own."

Sorykah huddled at the table, wiping the stench from her hands. Bits of flesh lodged under her fingernails and she scraped them out with the tip of a knife.

Farouj shook his head. "The octameroons corralled Diabolo in ice. They are his jailers, his watchmen. One day soon he'll break free, and the world will be awash in water." Then he gave Sorykah an "I told you so" stare.

"You believe in fairy tales. Diabolo doesn't exist." Sorykah denounced Farouj's faith in the old gods, but her limp protests were unconvincing. "Anyway, the Devil's Playground is dormant. It hasn't erupted in more than a thousand years. Even if it blew, it's so far inland that the lava would freeze before it made it to the sea."

"The volcano won't purge itself in one go. There will be multiple eruptions, above and below sea. An undersea lava spill would be disastrous. The Sigue's landmass will melt and vanish. No more Ostara. No more Sigue song."

"Rava did tell me that the warming waters drove away her kin. Her family was going to patch the core holes."

"Not quickly enough. It won't matter if they fill in half the holes in the berg; it won't help. There simply aren't enough octameroons left to take to the task," said Farouj. "TI has created a market demand for ink, and for the fossil water whose production camouflages its true trade. They will wring every drop from the Sigue and toss it away when they're done. Just like the octameroons."

"Rava had scars when I met her, and newer ones when I saw her again." Sorykah pondered this, oblivious to the noise from deck, the ringing squeal of pulleys and the tumble of fish upon the boards. "Why would they capture her and let her go, if the others have died?"

"You said she's different," said Farouj. "Stronger than the others. She breathes air, she walks on land, and she speaks English. Rava is a carrion-eater, a child of the gods. Maybe she will be the one to finally break Diabolo's curse and bring her family back to land."

"But that's just a myth!" Sorykah said. "The old gods are remnants of a dead culture, nothing more. Those are just stories."

"True stories, apparently." Farouj smiled, but it was weary. "Or perhaps she just wants revenge."

"Against Tirai? Get in line!" Sorykah cried. "I killed the king and now must tackle the prince who sullies my name. Sidra has her own grievances for which she seeks recompense. Any relative of a somatic killed by Matuk or his thugs will want in on the action, too. The Morigis swim against a swelling tide, and I'm certain that they'll soon drown."

"Or we will." Farouj and Sorykah stared at each other until Farouj's sullen gaze softened and Sorykah began to blush. Not for the first time, she considered that she might be willing to accompany him on this chivalrous charade because she was attracted to him and compelled by his interest in her. She'd experienced none of it—the lust of a man who wanted her despite her fickle blood and transient organs, and she didn't quite know what to do about it.

Sorykah had a tiny room to herself, while Farouj bunked with his mates. His proximity on the ship—different from the *Nimbus*, when he had come and gone like some mechanical officiate issued from the submarine itself—left her off-kilter, listening for the sound of his voice, sending silent signals that he needed to work harder at convincing her.

While she slept, the trawler sailed past the entrance to the floe fields filling the channel between the mainland's southernmost point and the Sigue. Sorykah's awareness flickered between alter and primary, lost in that limbo between selves. Memories merged, overlapping images projected upon the screen of her subconscious mind. Captive in the House of Pleasure, her likeness wavered on silken sheets strung up from the walls, her vile, fledgling enjoyment and manifold humiliations broadcast for the minions' titillation. Chen's touch evoked a swarthy desire coated thick with revulsion. Even in sleep, she was cognizant of his power over her, a mesmerist's hold she was determined to break. If he were glass, she would shatter him. If salt or sugar, she would dilute and drink him down to wash the ghosts of future tattoos from her blood. If he were an insect, she would grind his carapace beneath her heel and crush him into dust.

Dream-Sorykah crawled from the bed, sliding and bumping down winding iron stairs to the Isle of Mourning's gardens, overgrown with clutching oenathe, whose tendrils snared her limbs as she moved with sluggish but terrible urgency toward the keening sea. She found the grotto, its cathedral ceiling soaring and illumined by sun-struck ice. The fathomless pool lay as smooth and still as a mirror. Sorykah placed her palm upon its gelid skin and broke through, reaching into that pitch-dark undersea night with a tentacle of her own, its purple claw slicing the sea, white suckers flexing and popping. Rava materialized from the depths in a cloud of deep red, her hair swirling like blood in the water, speaking in her own strange tongue. This time Sorykah could understand her—words like chips of sound, noiseless vibrato embedded in her brain, ringing and echoing, Ur's timeless ululation of grief—"Find the taken."

The *Nimbus*'s claw came for Sorykah. Metal clanged and blades flew, slitting open the sac of demon ink in her gut that spilled from the wound like fiery magma. Sorykah was the ink, a venomous infection spreading inside the skin, setting every nerve alight, bombing human senses and plundering human bodies with a demon's thwarted rage.

She woke, uncertain of her identity. Was she human or octameroon? Man or woman? She patted herself down, pulse slowing as she recognized her breasts and familiar smooth skin.

Tempest-tossed, the trawler pitched over the swells. Sorykah was unused to sailing atop choppy seas. Seasickness combined with surging hormonal floods left her weak and frightened. She thought of the spongy octameroon carcass the sailors had slid overboard, and sensed the ocean beneath them swarming with furtive life.

Sheets of water rose glistening and solid beyond her tiny window. A soup of ice and slush splashed the porthole. Water seeped into the room. It was just like all her nightmares, except that she was above the sea instead of below it in the *Nimbus*. She grabbed the railing of the narrow bed screwed into the floor, condemning Farouj and Soryk in one breath, and in the next, begging Jerusha to spare them and get her safely home to her babes. Ironic that she should have fought so hard to find her children and bring them home to a quiet life free from her enemy's grasp, yet the enemy within had willingly parted her from them. The trawler tipped and righted itself as the sea buckled beneath it. There was a weightless, free-fall moment and then the boat smacked the waves with a crashing crack. Soaked to the bone, water coursing from hair at long last mussed, Farouj burst into the room.

Sorykah flung herself at him, balling his sweater in her fists. "This can't be the end, not after everything that's happened to me!"

"It's fine," he soothed. "Just a little storm. Flynn's in charge and he'll steer us to dry land." He attempted to pry Sorykah's fingers from his clothes, but they seemed frozen in place.

"Don't go!" She shook her head and they moved as one toward the bed. "Please stay." She pulled him down beside her. "Stay."

Farouj took in the confining bed and the dank, wet room. He pushed the hair back on his forehead and wiped the water from his face and she watched, transfixed, as though she'd never seen one of his species before. He leaned forward and kissed her with a salty mouth.

Sorykah pressed her fingers to her lips as though he'd bitten them. She couldn't think anymore. There was only the catapulting sea, rivulets of water snaking across the floor, and Farouj, wanting her here.

The ship pitched and rolled as they fell backward onto the bed. As if a switch had been turned on inside her, arousal electrified her flesh. After many long years of chastity, her body clamored for sensation. Sidra, Chen, Nels, Elu, and Soryk/ah's conquests at the House of Pleasure—each of them had heaped fuel on the fire and now it leapt high and burned with fierce heat. She was suddenly so tired of pretending to feel nothing and need no one, to desire only solitude.

"More," she whispered. Farouj's mouth was full and cool, so unlike all the others. "I have to go home," she murmured. "Coming here was a mistake."

"Not a mistake," he said. "A choice."

"Soryk's choice!"

"Maybe, but he's part of you; it was your decision, too." Farouj slung Sorykah's thigh over his hips. "You can play the injured party but you're not innocent. Jerusha says we are responsible for each of our actions, especially the mistakes."

Sorykah gave him a wounded look. "I can't remember! It's not my fault."

"Excuses, excuses."

Her pleasure drained away. She closed her eyes. When she opened them again, Farouj was gone and so was Sorykah. Soryk was left with a strange, bleary sensation of frustration that left him turgid and angry. The thrashing sea quieted and beyond the porthole, Soryk recognized the Neubonne skyline, frosted with choking smog, and knew that his troubles were just beginning.

12

COLLUSION

"FAROUJ DAL TAJEET, SON OF Khourish dal Tajeet of the Aroulian Qa'a'nesh?"

Throat dry, he nodded, his gaze locked on Queen Sidra's pert face. Her bare breasts jutted at the edge of his vision, resembling the moon buns cantered around on fancy serving trays, their glazed, beige domes oozing dark honey. With her hair wound in tight coils, and a skirt fashioned from birch leaves, she was a stranger; he hadn't recognized her when she squeezed his elbow and guided him into a satin-draped nook at Chen Morigi's island House of Pleasure. It was only when he saw the knobs of bone on her skull that he knew her and bowed.

"How can I serve you, my lovely?" Farouj's mind reeled. He'd seen her climb the rickety iron stairs encircling the tall, tiered bed in the main hall and watched her press her body against the woman waiting there, evoking a startling transformation. He'd half thought the forest queen imaginary, some totem created by the Erun somatics to lend themselves credibility, but she stood confidently before him, determined to have her way.

"You're next in the line of ascension among your people, is that right? A son of the elders?"

"Yes, but . . ."

"So you will suit our purposes. You work for TI but I'm told your allegiance remains with the Qa'a'nesh. Your tribe trusts you."

"I wouldn't go that far. I'm *hamid-ghajin*, you know? Not full-blooded. Left the reserve years ago."

"But you travel within both circles. You have access to the fossil water plant and internal Company operations, so it won't look funny for you to go back."

"And why would I want to go back?" Farouj shifted, restless and intrigued. His skin itched beneath the coating of greasepaint. He felt ridiculous taking an audience with Sidra the Lovely while dressed as a leopard amid such debauchery.

"TI overflows with corruption. I will not stand for it anymore." Hands on her hips, her skin streaked silver and gray, she had issued her edict with the coolness of a snake. "My agents will reach the plant and gut it with spider-bombs at the full-night break before hay-day morn. From Neubonne, the smoke will resemble Haymaz bon-fires. They cannot, they *will* not," she emphasized, "delay the mission for any cause. Understood?"

"You can't do that! What about my tribe?"

"Get them out. I'm doing you a favor," she added. "I don't nor-mally deliver such directives myself, but it would be silly to waste the opportunity to do so, as we're both here." She grinned then, and tilted her head, mischievous as a little cat. "I won't ask your purposes in this house, just as you'll keep mum about mine. Agreed?" She ac-cepted Farouj's slight nod and left him there, dumbfounded.

That conversation was but two months old; Haymaz week began in three nights. Seven days of feasting and celebration launched to conclude when the Tide Moon was highest and the field grains made their first shy appearance, parting leafy curtains and stiff hulls to soak up more sun. Seven days to honor Jerusha's fertile blessings, each with its own rituals, dances, colors, and trinkets: saltday, vexday, grainday, hiveday, mazeday, vinday, and finally, hayday, when the sky would flash with gold fireworks, praise-songs drowned out the drone of quotidial complaints, and flaming, waxed-paper boats overwhelmed the gurgling Telec.

Sidra the Lovely had given Farouj until vinday to clear the Qa'a'nesh from the plant. It was not enough time. The days got away from him. The People were uncooperative and doubted him, laughing off his warnings and exhortations. He needed a miracle, a divine broker to shake the Qa'a'nesh from their lethargy. Someone to whom they would listen, someone powerful who had proven the Company's armor chinked and fallible. One who would cross the Glass Mountains, best Meertham, the Wood Beast, and the Gatekeeper just to slaughter the vile magnate of Tirai Industries—Sorykah.

By the time he formulated his plan, the Trader was long gone in pursuit of her babes. He kicked himself for being so slow to realize that he'd had the key in hand, and lost it. Waiting for Sorykah to surface again was agony. It had taken much manipulation of TI dockets to wrangle himself an assignment aboard the *Nimbus*, to arrange transport on the trawler and obtain the necessary equipment to extricate her from the submarine—all in the vague hope that he could successfully woo her into playing savior and inspiring the People to throw off their shackles.

Sorykah was not a woman easily converted. Soryk, however, had proven himself much more amenable. It would be easy to entice him into an adventure. Problem very nearly solved—what Farouj had not figured into his plans was the chemistry between them. Sorykah was prickly and recalcitrant, reluctant and secretive, and he could not resist her unspoken challenge.

CONFIDENT THAT SORYK WOULD soon be en route to the Erun city, Sidra retreated into the western tunnels to find her bombmakers.

A league of three, each bomber had one somatic deviation: a scaled ostrich leg and toes, a hairy, brown-nailed chimpanzee arm, and the ungulate's split hoof. Working together, they compensated for their shortcomings and pooled their collective venom and love for pyrotechnics to produce weaponry for the Erunites.

Older and mustier than the main tunnels, the western branch of the Erun city was its ghetto. Cramped, run-down, and smug with a disdain for those who preferred the safety of the patrolled and well-lit main branch, its packed soil ceiling was shored by wooden posts and pillars. A refuge for outlaws among the outcast, these somatics reluctantly accepted Sidra's rules. Carac and his recruits, Queen Sidra's brutish ragtag soldiers, kept dissenters in line with threats of expulsion and return to the surface world. For all their bravado, none would willingly exchange his safety for the threats from poachers and antisomatic extremists.

All three somatics blinked at Sidra when she entered their cave, their eyes wide behind magnifying lenses.

"Welcome, my lady." Tjaler was the ringleader. His chimp arm crossed his waist as he bowed and removed his goggles.

"How does the work progress?"

The somatics shuffled aside to allow Sidra a look at their creation, a mechanical spider bomb.

"As you asked—subterfuge on a string." Tjaler had an arresting face with diamond-cut cheeks and jaw, sunken eyes bright with intelligence, and a wide, puppetlike mouth. His greasy hair stank of unwash, but Sidra thought that he might clean up quite nicely. Were she not pregnant, she might invite him to her loft, a supplement for use during Carac's absence. She shook her head to divest herself of these thoughts, scrub away her longing for Soryk, and distract herself from her curiosity. The pregnancy left her feeling frail and breakable. Tjaler might be too aggressive. She sighed, a hand straying along the contours of a belly big enough to show through the heavy folds of her cloak. "A demonstration, please."

Udor of the cloven hoof deftly put the spider through its paces, showcasing its abilities. Operated by remote control, the spider could unlock doors and windows both standard and electronic, peg a guide wire into any hard surface, and descend some 1,500 feet. Sticky pads on its pinpoint legs allowed it to cling and crawl where commanded, and a time code signature would instruct the bomb as to the precise moment to ignite the charges packed within its body and explode.

"How can you be sure the force is great enough?" Sidra picked up the spider, flicking its metal legs with a finger. Only Tjaler did not react with a gasp and several backward steps.

"We've turned traitor. Taken charges from the docks in Neubonne, Blundt, and Ostara, using the Company's own technology against itself. Stolen blast points, to make our point." Tjaler smiled broadly, his face acquiring a simian leer as his human hand idly stroked the hairs along his chimp arm. "One cap is designed to split a glacier, create a crevice maybe one hundred feet deep. In an open room, in soft sand and rock, the effect will be much more expansive."

Sidra felt the baby wake. It seemed to strain to listen to the conversation through the muffling barrier of Sidra's belly. "Haymaz feast is nearly here. You must work quickly. How many spiders have you so far?"

Udor answered. "Fifteen, my queen. Each packed and ready for deploy at your command."

"Only fifteen." She sighed in dismay. "I do not want reparable damage. I want total annihilation! There is to be no coming back from this. TI shall not recover from our attack." Sidra grew heated, felt the blood rush to her skin, inflaming her temper.

Tjaler alone did not retreat from the queen, which impressed her as he'd intended. "Not to worry, my Lovely. We leave behind only ashes and crow feed." Tjaler stepped forward to take the spider from Sidra, his human and chimps arms working in tandem.

The brush of animal hair upon her skin sent shivers cascading through her. She may have to summon Tjaler sooner rather than later. After a thorough bath and debriefing, and requisite disease check and delousing. She smiled, the fire of revenge leaping in her eyes. "Go straight to the Aroulian fossil water plant past Desert Station Number Four. Once there, you will take advantage of the night to launch the spiders."

"Excuse me, my queen." Udor stepped forward, his nervous hoof beating a tattoo against the rock floor. "Would it not be better to strike while the sun is high and the workers are asleep? The guard will be less and—"

"Certainly, if you can salve your conscience after blowing up the laborers and their families who sleep during the day's hottest hours."

Udor crumpled and retreated. Sidra had a single brief flash of regret but quickly overcame it. Queens have hard hearts and military minds. She would not waffle and grow soft simply because hormones made the threat of tears imminent and turned her brain to porridge.

"They work from dusk till dawn, but the nights are growing short this time of year. There are only two chances to invade—during evening prayer and the full-night break, when they visit the surface. I've given a tribal agent until vinday to evacuate the plant, so the only ones inside should be Company admins and TI management. I don't mind them dying, as much," she said.

Tjaler bowed again. "As you wish, my liege."

Sidra scoffed. He took his courtliness too far, though she little minded his excesses.

"And after?" Pertana limped forward, hips painfully canted from the heavily muscled club of her ostrich leg. Pertana's exotic looks diverted attention from her awkward gait but not her scheming mind. Obsessed with money, blood, and spoils, she was the most avaricious of the western tunnel somatics.

"You are free to take from TI, but not the Qa'a'nesh. They'll need everything they have to rebuild a new society. We shouldn't make it harder for them than necessary."

Pertana dipped her head, albeit reluctantly.

Tjaler's chimp arm tremored in constant, unnerving movement. "My Lovely, will your advisor Carac be joining us in our mission?"

"No. I cannot risk his loss." Sidra gave Tjaler a hard stare. There was much unspoken, but he understood that they were expendable. "I should be very displeased if he is in any way endangered. Remember your somatic brethren both here at home and abroad. Though we are few and our connections sometimes tenuous, no one will harbor a deserter."

Tjaler bowed, raising his human hand in a gesture of prayerful submission. It was a good act, but Sidra was not deceived. The chimp arm disobeyed his will and grappled for control, clenching strong fingers.

Pertana and Udor turned back to the table of clockworks, fuses, and gears. Tjaler—he of the stark face and unwash—sidled close to Sidra as she departed. The tunnel's flickering lamplight threw grim shadows. Tjaler emitted an oily permutation, some physical manifestation of an inner slipperiness or ethical instability.

"My Lovely," and the way he said it—like a sugar cube of bluing—left a bitter aftertaste in Sidra's mouth after its sweetness had washed away. "You're in a delicate state." His eyes lingered on Sidra's rounded belly. "A woman shouldn't be left without protection in times like these . . ." He let the offer hang, a sour fruit, before he bowed and departed, leaving Sidra to run hot and cold with a calculating anger and latent fear of her own isolation. She should've slapped him, chastised him. Her thoughts flitted like circling swallows, pinching and pecking at seeds and strings. Threads that if pulled might unravel a larger conspiracy and expose mutinous kernels of doubt seeking soil and implantation. She should amass an army and ready her tunnel-dwelling bestiary for insurrection but she couldn't quite believe that Tjaler would have the gall to mount one. Sidra was beloved by her people. She instructed, nurtured, and guarded them. A single rogue element would not be powerful enough to overturn her years of purposeful and nourishing care.

She'd keep close tabs on Tjaler. If he managed to return from his mission, he'd find himself unwelcome here. The western tunnel was a thieves' den but an honorable one. Sidra was certain that the Erunites would close ranks around her if asked. By giving them an infant princess to adore, she'd rouse their protectiveness. Sidra's child would be the torch shining to guide her people into the new age, one free of Tirai Industries' stranglehold.

13

CONVERGENCE

NEUBONNE IS A CITY OF PAVED-OVER WRECKAGE, a concrete ocean of collided and settled half-sunken ships. Dense with particulate matter spewed by coal fires and smelting factories, humid and charged with odors of rotting algae, human filth, and refuse, Neubonne's smog is so thick one can bite into it, like cotton candy. This is the malignant cloud that reaches with long, diaphanous arms to tug boats to shore and muddle them along the quay. From the ramshackle fishing cabins, dilapidated ice houses, and rusting drydocks in the North Fork harbor, through the city's median, swollen with human commerce and activity, to the corporate park at its terminus, Neubonne's history hangs out for all to see, like washing from a line. Gray and relatively cheerless, its softening stone stained by soot and watermarks from the Telec River's seasonal overflows, the city is home to one million people. Settlers and searchers from every region of Plein Eïre crowd ranks of concrete apartment blocks, its shops, squares, and offices. They overflow the tent cities and wash like mud-tide from the northern hills, a smothering surge of need. A few somatics dwell here, too, though they are secretive and disinclined to public displays or trading and shove or slink or crawl through the congestion, trying to look normal but by their efforts, failing to do so.

Morigi affluence pools from the Tirai Industries towers, dribbling through Neubonne's wards toward the sea, and it stumbles in its attempt to transform the docklands, slums, and warehouse districts into pretty living places for strivers and up-and-comers on the make and take, the slick-suited commuters who traffic in finance and labor, paper pushers who use their briefcases and stylish handbags like weights to leverage their twice-daily leaps aboard the city's fleets of bubbling minibuses.

Two broad avenues bisect the city center from east to west. Plane and liquidambar trees line the central parkway, the only green growing things amid a quarry of cut stone and cement. Traffic courses in regular waves down their length—the ever-present minibuses, pedicabs, bicyclists, pedestrians, and shiny black town cars with tinted windows and hired drivers. High-rises subsume the crumbling monoliths, and they in turn lean against the pockmarked stone and rubbed-smooth wood of the piers. Young Neubonne advances on its elders, impertinent and pushy. From the sixth ward's houseboat-snarled waterways through its jumbled fifth ward, sidewalks gritty with brick dust and refuse, through the fourth ward and the Botanica's labyrinth of floral-named streets, to the third, glutted with boutiques and tiny sidewalk cafés where deals are sealed over leisurely luncheons, to the second, crisp with clean-lined bank towers and right angles of light and shadow, to the first and only, where Matuk the Collector built his iconic marble salt and pepper shakers. Twin towers the colors of snow and ink visible twelve miles inland from the shore exert an ineluctable force like the tines of a dowsing rod, seeking and drawing Sorykah, with magnetic intensity, into Tirai's puerile heart.

Four nights after dredging Sorykah and Farouj from the Sigue, the fishing trawler arrived in Neubonne. Easing into the North Fork harbor, where the slimy Telec dispersed into the sea, the small ship stopped briefly to allow Soryk and Farouj to disembark. The captain, a surly white man with the florid cheeks and bulbous nose of a chronic drinker, glared at their backs as they walked up the pier.

Soryk eyed the captain, who loomed in the window, looking cross. "Are you certain he won't reveal us?"

"Captain Flynn is no friend to the Company," said Farouj. "We share a mutual enemy. Flynn was captain of the Harbor Patrol before Tirai Industries bought a controlling interest in Neubonne's city government. TI privatized the patrol and dismissed Flynn without pay. He's never gotten over it."

Flynn hadn't gotten over it, but he wasn't a fool. He wouldn't nurse his grudge into the poorhouse.

As Farouj and Soryk disappeared among the people crowding the harbor, Flynn picked up the ship-to-shore transmission line and dialed. Flynn relayed his message and hung up, satisfied. The calls from TI's headquarters had gone out over the IER network. An ice miner and a Company admin had been reported missing in the aftermath of a coring explosion in the Sigue. *No need to detain*, warned the watch. *Advise of progress for the standard fee*. Flynn sent a report when he'd picked them up and was mildly disappointed that a guard rank from TI wasn't on shore to nab the two when they docked. TI might have shafted him in the beginning, but the Company was doing its part to make up for his losses by keeping him on as an informer. Flynn would anchor in one of TI's temporary slips for the night and go into Neubonne in the morning to confirm the growth of his bank account balance.

Awash in light and noise, the waterfront pulsed with life.

"We'll catch the first-light train north. Until then, we can kip at my place. Come on." Farouj slung their bags over his shoulder and led Soryk into the hectic metropolis. People and buildings jammed Neubonne's narrow isle. Dense and throbbing with noisy activity, the city flooded Soryk's senses. Vertigo engulfed him. He faltered for a moment, swayed by the overpowering instinct to flee, but steeled himself against it and pushed on, eyes smarting in the smog.

Farouj ducked between the planks of an overhead walkway and led Soryk into the shadowed marketplace beneath. He smacked the hand of a pickpocket reaching into his jacket pocket. The boy spat at Farouj, who snatched him up by his arms, shaking and berating him. The boy slithered from his grip and darted between creaking stalls to escape Farouj's admonitions.

"Now you see for yourself the legacy of the Morigis." Farouj brushed pickpocket grime from his clothes. "Matuk and his spawn have drained the wealth and culture of the entire continent, all the way from the Yashim border to the bottom of the Southern Sea."

"How many children does he have?"

"After Tirai, Matuk married Vierka, who birthed a daughter, Nuala. After he discarded Vierka, he took up with Lyshan. Matuk's third wife had three children. The first son died in infancy. Chen came next, followed by another son, crippled by a childhood fever. When he tired of her, there were others. No one knows how many claim his bloodline but only Nuala and Chen are currently recognized as official heirs to TI. There are several pending appeals to the lineage committee, but they may never be resolved."

Years had passed since Soryk's last visit to Neubonne and he was anxious to explore the city. The slow pace of their travel was maddening. "Can't we hire a cab or ride the minibus?" Soryk asked.

Farouj shook his head. "Eyes and ears are everywhere. Implanted a decade ago in every public square, shop, and transport. Matuk's method of preventing revolt. The city police will issue a dissenter's ticket if you're caught speaking out against the ruling family. Two tickets earns a stay in jail. Though Matuk is dead, his system limps along without him, a riderless horse. Would you hazard it?"

"I suppose not." Soryk longingly watched a minibus putter by, steamy windows dotted by the exhausted faces of industrial workers heading home.

High-rises soon appeared over the low, wet hills. Then, as if sprung from a pop-up book, skinny townhomes of rosy, speckled granite stacked the two-lane streets. Each one was draped in the forlorn elegance of an earlier era and fenced with flimsy gates of twisted iron—every arched window framed by columns and carvings of flowers, vines, and grapes closed its eye against the city's acrid haze. Though the storefronts had changed color and wore new slogans, Soryk knew them. All about him rang déjà vu's familiar bells. Every block was imbued with a memory. The heady perfumes of wealthy women, the clinging city soil and dust, the choking grit that swirled, stirring up currents of salt sea, fermenting garbage and grubby bodies formed a rich, intoxicating mélange.

There was food everywhere in the Dishy District, preemptive Haymaz feasting already in progress. Vendors barked enticements from behind wheeled carts as they rattled along the road, strings of brass bells swaying. "Two for one! Fresh and hot! Homemade!"

Burning spices popped against coal braziers and sizzling woks. Wooden dishy shacks dominated every street corner; blue flames hissed from propane tanks. Soryk's stomach rumbled at the sight of grease-splotched paper cones of roasted almonds and sugar-shelled pecans, peppered corn roasted in its husk, poutine—potatoes and curd doused in meat gravy, baked apples with cardamom custard, smoked meat sandwiches, fried fish and oysters. The smell of newly poured beer drifted from a tavern and Soryk could resist no longer.

Farouj followed Soryk into the pub and they guzzled pints of ale, sawed through the burnt casing of fennel sausages, and swabbed up plates of soupy pink beans with wads of chewy bread. Caught up in some private inner storm of emotion, light and shadow chased each other across Soryk's face. A flicker of memory intruded, a cold-lipped kiss, tasting of sea salt. Regret left his heart lead-heavy. It was a solid mass inside him, all his feelings for Sidra smashed down and compacted into this sour thing, aching within his chest. He knew he had no right to this life he so desperately grappled.

Soryk had a mad urge to get drunk and muffle all those nags in his head. He raised his hand for another pint.

Farouj took a deep swallow of ale and wiped froth from his mustache, leg jigging beneath the table. They had a schedule to keep. It would be so easy to get off track, to allow tempting diversions to sway Soryk from his goal. "Are you ready for this?"

"'Course I am!"

The pub's neon sign bathed the room in orange light as three young women pushed open the double doors, giggling and already tipsy, ankles wobbling atop precarious heels. Red and yellow blossoms wreathed their heads and bottles of colored salt hung from ribbons around their necks.

"But we should have ourselves a bit of fun, first." Soryk grinned.

Farouj's mild irritation showed itself. "Tomorrow is saltday. It's going to be a crazy week. We should get on the road as soon as possible."

"Everything on your timetable? What's the hurry? You push and prod me at a blinding pace." Soryk drained his pint and slammed the glass down. "You don't get it! I've had nothing of my own. Every little piece of happiness I find is stolen from me! Should I be here? No! She drags me about like a dog toy. I'm awake now, and I'm in charge. I may not be here tomorrow, so tonight"—he rose, running a hand through his short hair and eyeing the girls—"I plan to enjoy myself."

If Farouj upset Soryk, he might flee. He could not risk losing him. It had been such a laborious, delicate trial—the reeling in and capture of the Trader's interest. Sorykah had transformed since their first meeting at the House of Pleasure, become less malleable and agreeable. She must be handled with great care—this national treasure, this assassin of Morigis—if they were to succeed. He would defer and cater, and lead her like a bird following a trail of bread crumbs into the jaws of the beast.

Farouj suffered through Soryk's ham-handed flirtations and watched him struggle to learn the steps of the ritualistic courtship dance. He had no experience wooing women. But the girls accepted his company, and Soryk laughed when they poked gentle fun, teasing him about what they perceived as country naïveté. Farouj ground his jaws against his impatience, but Soryk was jolly after several beers. Eager to explore Neubonne's nocturnal amusements, Farouj was suddenly his best friend. Soryk wanted to head out right away, but Farouj cautioned against it, insisting it was better to sleep and prepare for an early departure. Soryk gave him a grim look. "We discussed this. Do we need to revisit the topic?"

Farouj gave in. "Okay, fine. Home first. We'll go from there."

Saltday began at the stroke of full-night and the streets were crisp with a dusting of salt flung by well-wishers. Most offices would be closed for the week or offer reduced hours, and this temporary reprieve lent Neubonne a festive air. Music spilled from the dance halls along New Market Street, amplified horns, bells, and drums in brazen competition with one another. Soryk reveled in the madness and noise of his first Haymaz. So this was what he'd been missing!

Hunched beneath a heavy cloak, a short, heavily bearded man ran up the pavement, panting and gasping. He smashed against Soryk as he passed in a blur of tactile panic and rank fear-sweat. Farouj caught a glimpse of reptilian green eyes, nearly fluorescent in their alien brightness, before the man disappeared into a dark alleyway.

Soryk and Farouj turned a corner and a wave of Jerushian marchers overwhelmed them. Bearing rough-made discs of polished bronze and nickel, the group hefted their symbols to the night sky and stomped a widening circuit, chanting, "Somatics out! Dégé Ko Jerusha!"

Farouj yanked Soryk through the throng, and wild-eyed marchers gawked at them. Farouj got a faceful of salt and threw blind punches as Soryk pulled him free. They burst from the crowd and sped down the street as the mob's demonstration escalated, smashing discs against unlucky passersby, knocking them down and tearing open their clothes, searching for signs of genetic deviation.

Soryk was shaking. "What was that?"

Farouj stopped in a doorway to rub stinging eyes. "An antisomatic demonstration. The Dégé Koans are a splinter sect of the Jerushian church. They think somatic participation in Haymaz and other holy days pollutes the goddesses' teachings. They want to reserve rights of worship for the intact."

"Are they dangerous?" No one made any effort to stop the mob. It continued down the street, spreading its message of violence and ruthlessly attacking an elderly woman hobbling along on crutches. "We have to do something!" Soryk cried.

"The Dégé Ko are funded by Morigi family donations. No one can touch them, so just forget it. You can't help her." Farouj led Soryk into the third ward, bordering the Botanica. The streets were named after Neubonne's many politicians, most of them defunct, impeached, or dead. Farouj unlocked the security door of a concrete apartment block with high, arched windows and rows of rebar jutting from sheared-off balconies. His flat was plain but clean, its whitewashed walls bare but for a pair of striped curtains adorning the windows. A battered punching bag dangled from a chain screwed into the ceiling. Blocky prefab furniture and stacks of yellowing books lined the room. Farouj emptied his rucksack on the bed, stripped off his shirt, and went to the sink to splash water on his face and neck.

The sight of Farouj's bare chest made Soryk's toes tingle and he whispered, "No! Not this time!"

"Are you talking to me?" Farouj called from the bathroom.

"Just thinking aloud," Soryk answered. He was certain that Sorykah would enjoy waking to find herself alone with Farouj. *Better you should sleep*, he thought. *I'm in control now.* His primary's voice was cooperatively silent.

While Farouj changed clothes, Soryk poked through his belongings: a neat row of bespoke gray suits hung in the closet. The open shelves held spare jerseys, linen tunics, scarves, socks, undergarments, a hairbrush, cologne, and pomade, all of it very mundane. Farouj also had a pistol wrapped in canvas, unloaded, Soryk hoped, for whom did he intend to use it against?

Soryk opened a red enamel box, expecting to find trinkets or cuff links perhaps, but blue cubes rattled like dice, emitting a faint odor of petrol and flowers. He stuck one of the candies in his mouth and grimaced. Sickly blue raspberry flavor.

Farouj emerged, rubbing a towel over his face.

Soryk flicked the enamel box at Farouj. "These candies are disgusting."

He caught it and groaned. "You ate these?"

"They're horrible!"

"Sweet Jerusha, Soryk. This isn't candy. It's bluing. Surely you know that much."

Soryk shook his head, smacking his lips against the bitterness that lingered on his tongue.

"Confiscated off an admin at the home office. This is the new scourge. Chen's invention."

"Not bloody likely," Soryk scorned. Chen was much too self-indulgent and lazy to spend time doing anything beyond drinking and rutting. Sorykah perked up a bit at the mention of Chen's name, a cellular response evoked by the memory of his hot skin and darkly arousing wickedness. Soryk smashed the feeling down.

"He didn't actually create the elemental composition, merely devised the application. Bluing is a solvent used in glass manufacturing. He gets the raw materials from Blundt, has a crew cook it up at a lab and add flavoring and a few organic agents to diminish its toxicity. Chen may seem foolish, but his wealth and power are immeasurable. Worse, he is entirely human. To him, somatics are toys, products. Animals for slaughter. That said"—Farouj placed a sugar cube upon his tongue; it sat intact for a second before dissolving in a pool of neon blue that sluiced across the whites of his eyes and disappeared—"you shouldn't trip alone."

Sorykah would never have voluntarily taken a drug. She was too paranoid about losing control or being swamped by strange reactions and feelings to experiment, but Soryk would not acknowledge the soft-focus fear that blurred his primary's vision.

"This stuff kicks in fast." Farouj gave a slow and lazy grin, offering Soryk his arm. "Here, smell."

The strangely personal odors of Farouj's unique chemical signature filled Soryk's head—the Aroulian desert's polished sands and astringent flowering cacti, unfamiliar spices, the tang of sea from his recent travels—the peculiar piquancy of one individual's blood composition. Soryk sniffed himself and got the strong odor of a woman—iron, milk, musk, and salt—smelled the feverish ether of the change dormant in his blood and weak hiss of testosterone leaching into his system as if from a leaky valve. He understood then how tenuous was his masculinity and how soon he would lose it. He said, "Give me one more night in the city. A little freedom . . ."

Inhaling faint drafts of Sorykah that floated like dust motes through the air, Farouj nodded. He could allow the alter a few moments to play. The primary would come back to him soon enough.

CROWDED WITH PEDESTRIANS, GENTIAN Street grew sluggish as the evening woke and stretched after its day of slumber. Neubonne's parkway was home to buskers, mystics, and magicians. Farther back, dealers and panderers lurked in the shadows and behind bushes, conducting their business with hushed efficiency. Dogs snapped and growled on the ends of leashes. Club kids woke from idleness to trot out their glittering finery.

Storefront shops defined the Botanica, an uninterrupted stream of trade extending to the city center. Farouj pointed out a sword swallower and a woman in red spangles and secondhand magnet boots, who balanced atop a ball and juggled flaming batons.

Soryk was dazzled by the crush of the human circus spectacle, marred only by a noticeable lack of somatics. It seemed strange to be among people again, to sense not a single genetic deviation from the standard design, so used was he to fur and feathers, claws and beaks. How was it possible that the Erun and its denizens were more real than this wall of human life smashed up against him? Yet Sidra, Dunya, Carac, and even the twins were but a dreamy fantasy, visions of smoke and vapor.

Farouj stopped in front of a boarded-up storefront. Soot blacked the walls and broken glass crunched underfoot. "Jandi's shop. She's gone." Farouj kicked a pile of rubble and peered through a crack between the boards. "This does not bode well."

"Who's Jandi?" Soryk was beginning to feel stupidly happy, even as tiny blades lanced his brain. Colors shone too bright and sharp amid the overpowering odors of bodies, each one a complex pattern of history, genetics, and illness or health.

"Jandi's a fence-sitter. She doesn't support Chen but she's not yet convinced that ink is a detrimental product. It's too lucrative for her to consider returning to traditional pigments. I've been trying for ages to get her to give up the trade. Now it looks like someone else has done the job for me."

Turning into a cul-de-sac, the street was a rippled riverbed of worn cobblestones and ankle-crackers—deep, broad gouges where stones had been pried up and never replaced. Gas lamps flickered behind warped, bubbled glass. Three-storied Reformation dollhouses tilted at precarious angles, each one faced with massive double doors that opened to expose its entire interior, just like a child's toy. Soft, splintering wood planks studded by iron brackets repelled entry to each house but one, opened to showcase a Jerushian church service. Peeling gold leaf reflected the creamy light of glowing candelabras. Choral hymns flowed over one another, hitting every minor note and drawing them out until each voice faded and another picked up the melody and continued it. Worshippers wore red velvet trimmed in gold braid, and two young girls on the balcony stopped singing to stare down at Soryk and Farouj.

Smoke rolled from burning pilgrim portals, and Farouj smudged himself with sweet myrrh and amber as they squeezed past the church into a fenced walkway.

"I thought the Qa'a'nesh followed the old gods." Soryk coughed and waved a hand before his face.

"Sometimes, but conversion is part of the deal. TI hired Jerushian missionaries to inculcate us after they took our land. Meekness suits them better than the old gods' vengeance." He stopped at a brick building embellished with diamond-paned windows and black iron gates encircling a small courtyard. Two people loitered in front, suspicious in their studied nonchalance. Soryk stared as they shifted and drew inward, each one subtly altering position as if protecting a wounded limb. The change was so slight as to be nearly imperceptible, but it spoke volumes to Soryk, who recognized somatics when he saw them. Yes, their clothes were oddly cut and baggy, their coats too heavy for the humid spring evening. Leather gloves and large, clumsy boots were coarse disguises camouflaging misshapen limbs. They were engaged in chatter but the woman, whose posture was thrown off-kilter by a spine deformity, regarded Soryk with a suspicious gaze. He yearned to talk to them. Were they from the Erun city? How fared the queen and Dunya the Dog-Faced Girl? But Farouj kept a tight grip and pushed him through a black door into a tattoo parlor with black velvet curtains and a black enamel floor. Rows of shining steel needles and silver-framed flash lined the matte black walls.

A few customers browsed racks of magazines and prepackaged digi-reels, but the real money came from the men and women streaming steadily to and from the back room, where a tattooist feverishly needled rudimentary designs into whatever bare body part was thrust before him. The routine never varied. Customers handed over their dosh. The tattooist dropped it into a lockbox mounted on the supply cart and the customer slid onto the chair, exposing an expanse of skin: breasts, belly, thighs, buttocks, or arms. Soryk was stunned to see a man drop trou and fall back in the chair, allowing the inker to part his buttocks with the casualness of a cattleman inspecting his breeding stock. Unflinching, the tattooist wiped his gun with a rag, shucked the old needle, and snapped on a new one, sweeping used mixing trays and toweling into a garbage bag. He sprayed a cloud of disinfectant over the exposed skin and went straight to work. The art wasn't pretty—mostly rings, spirals, lines, and a buckshot spray of dots—and the thin, stinging odors of diluted octameroon ink and rubbing alcohol filled the air. Freshly tattooed customers lined the corridor awaiting a sex partner. Those too eager to wait banged on closed doors, begging admittance to a party in progress. Manic groans and coarse language echoed from occupied stalls.

"Inside." Farouj nudged Soryk toward an open door, his body warm against the other man's back as they tumbled into an empty room. A shelf heaped with frayed and folded graying sheets and a torn plastic pallet spoke of bleak, loveless couplings, while a large digi-reel monitor suspended from the ceiling televised an orgy of images. On-screen, masked women and men performed perfunctory acts of love. Cut to a wild bacchanal—Soryk recognized the interior of the House of Pleasure and the rainbow lights that shot from Chen's favorite toy, the clavier à lumières. As the scene changed, rolling across sweating bodies and faces pinked by red drool, a nervous, anticipatory worry began to inflate inside Soryk's chest. He had thought it better not to witness Chen's wretched betrayal, but to remain ignorant and pretend none of it had happened when he so clearly profited from Sorykah's sorrow was a fool's choice.

Yes, there she was, thrashing through the hormonal glory of the change. Her eyes rolled back inside her head as she bucked and contorted, bright red, then ghostly pale, entering the stream where manipulative genetic tides waited to sweep her away and erase her woman's body. Hair sprouted on her male chest, like stop-motion photography, the growth of a plant filmed over several weeks as it bloomed. He couldn't watch himself clamber out of his primary's skin like a reanimant crawling from a grave. He wanted none of it. His guts in a knot, Soryk reached for the doorknob but the changing image on-screen caught his eye. Already, Sorykah was gone. In her place lay a reedy and washed-out blond. Soryk stared, his skin prickling. The woman was in a bad way. Lethargic and moving as if suspended in brine, each limb drifted through space, disconnected from her body. Stippled with dots and lines in varying shades of faded blue and black, her skin bore the battle scars of a lengthy ink war.

"Sweet Jerusha, I think I know her," Soryk whispered.

Farouj said, "Kirwan is a regular fixture in Neubonne's night-clubs."

Kirwan. The name was an alarm relentlessly pealing its call to action. Soryk turned to Farouj, stricken. He gestured to the screen bright with images of depravity and use. "Kirwan. The twins' father."

Farouj was incredulous. "Him? Are you sure?" An edge of disdain soured his voice.

Relief unfurled inside Soryk. Finally, he had discovered a way to liberate himself from his parental duty. Children should be with their natural father if the mother was absent. Surely he and Kirwan could come to some sort of agreement regarding the twins, and if Nels was willing to help Kirwan care for them, Soryk would be completely free.

"I can't leave Neubonne until I find him," he said. "Let's go." The new life he envisioned in the Erun tasted of sweet spring water, pure and new and entirely his. *Sidra, my lovely.* She would be so happy to have him home.

14

GRAY GHOSTS

RECLINING ON IDENTICAL CHAISES, Zarina and Chen lay supine beneath a hazy sun that little warmed their sun-starved, nocturnal skins. The smog was especially bad this year, a suffocating and acrid miasma that settled over Neubonne as if snared on the Morigi's high towers. Wisps of it draped the penthouse balcony and made Zarina's eyes sting. Chen's mistress had escaped the incestuous swamp of Chen's manor, la Maison de Plaisir, on the fingerling island that had been her home for two very difficult and unhappy years. It was much better now to be in the city, freed from jealousy and the slight guilt that occasionally tarnished her days. Better to be a concubine kept in a city penthouse than a serving girl in another house, equally fine. At least in Neubonne she had some authority and control over how she spent her days. It was easier taking orders from perpetually wasted Chen, whose only interest was the satisfaction of his animal urges, than the matron Marianna, who had encouraged her girls to live rather austerely, their only purpose to serve with a smile.

Chen's many caprices were too well indulged for him to off Zarina, as Matuk had his third wife, Lyshan. Knowing that your father had probably murdered your mother, along with the wives before and after her, might inspire one to a state of constant intoxication. While Chen had not expressly grieved after hearing rumors of Matuk's murder by the Trader Sorykah, he had indulged in a five-day bender of such lewd proportions that even Zarina was shocked. However much he enjoyed his family's wealth, Zarina guessed that Chen's character was too weak to separate from it and make his own way. Matuk's money bought only complacency.

Chen sat up and Zarina noted how thin he'd grown. Hunger for bluing replaced Chen's hunger for fine food, and too often of late, he'd rather suck sugar cubes than eat. Weakened by the strong acids used to manufacture bluing, Chen's teeth were beginning to show signs of rot. She preferred him on strawberry milk, a red tincture distilled from ayahuasca, dog-thistle berries, tabernanthe iboga, and galangal. Strawberry milk, Zarina thought, was like cranking the flames beneath your brain. Everything took on this lovely pink sheen—your whole body felt warm and deliciously alive. Tongues and fingers became highly sensitive, and everybody was your best friend. Strawberry milk made the House of Pleasure a play palace of throbbing, open, and willing bodies.

Zarina did not enjoy taking bluing though Chen forced it upon her and she frequently indulged him. Bluing skewed the senses. Zarina found that she could smell the blood inside other people's bodies, tell whether they were healthy or ill, pregnant or deranged, and Zarina desired none of this information. Highly addictive bluing also killed the sex drive; while strawberry milk made the flesh receptive and pink drool spill from smiling mouths, bluing was the poisonous seeping gas after the flame had died. It was in her best interest to keep Chen sane and healthy for as long as possible. He'd promised to buy her a house on the hills overlooking the North Fork bridge, but as yet, he had not delivered.

Chen jerked a hank of Zarina's hair. "You know, I've never been very fond of redheads. I should much prefer it if you were blond. See to it, won't you?" He left her there, naked on the roof of the world, glad that she could blame the tears in her eyes on the heavy smog and not her emotions.

When they descended from the penthouse later that night, Chen's mouth was a smear of vivid purple to complement his eggplant silk suit. Zarina sported freshly bleached hair. Her scalp was raw and scabbed from the harsh chemicals but in her tight gown, her yellow eyes warm against artificially flaxen hair, she was beautiful enough to satisfy Chen and keep him from wandering for another night.

It was exhausting, actually, she thought as she slid onto the pedicab seat beside him, to force this pretense of couplehood. She wanted only her house and freedom from this farcical love affair. She wondered idly whom she might have to kill to get it. As the pedicab driver cycled toward the third ward, Zarina decided on her next target, rather, her first and only target—that bitch Sorykah.

"My love," she purred in Chen's ear, "are you certain that the Trader is still alive? After all, we've heard only insinuations and rumors. It's possible that someone else has claimed her glory . . ."

Chen brushed her off. Flynn's message warmed his insides like a swallow of fine brandy and he wanted to savor its heat. "Don't trouble yourself over her. The proceeds from her digi-reels have already surpassed any other venture. I intend to repeat my success with Kirwan." His gaze locked on the crowds filling the streets as they neared the Hanging Garden. "See how my children flock to their father? Each one is a hungry baby bird, waiting to be fed. Blue snow, igbloo, sniffy-pops, blue goblins, frost, breath of death, the gripes, and my personal favorite, sugar kooky." Chen smiled. "Clever, aren't they? An homage to the sensory blessing that is bluing." Chen drew in the last curl of smoke from a hand-rolled tobacco bidi and lazily exhaled. "Zarina, my pretty little terror, it's time to mingle with the rabble." He shoved Zarina from the pedicab as it slowed to a stop. "I've got something else to attend to. You'll keep an eye on things for me, love, won't you?" He waggled a sheaf of bills at her. "Call those two bunglers of mine to see you home if I don't return for you. I may yet find what I am looking for tonight."

Zarina's pride stung as she stumbled from the pedicab. Like every other woman, Zarina was merely a diversion for Chen. Her emotional life was of little interest to one who preferred the elaborate mockery of lamenting Queen Sidra's abandonment of him to repairing his wounded heart. Though far from the Isle of Mourning and its telltale chiming bells that daily commemorated the moment of his heartbreak, Chen still paced the actor's stage.

Oman, the bouncer, grabbed Zarina's hand and yanked her to him. "Never you mind him, darlin'. He's not one for knowing a good thing when it bites his arse."

Zarina fought the urge to snatch her arm from Oman's sweaty, meaty grip. Best not to spoil her alliances yet. She pasted a saccharine smile upon her mouth and pressed herself into Oman's massive bicep. "You're so kind to me, Oman! It makes me feel"—she cut her eyes at the man, pleased to see that he hung on her words—"oh, I don't know!" She giggled mechanically. "Like a precious little kitten." She sickened herself. She squeezed the bouncer's fat fingers. "Let's go inside and see how they're doing at the bar. Chen asked me to keep tabs on his sales." She grinned as they entered the club, its hazy air a blur of pulsing lights, bass beats juddering her teeth. "In fact, he's put me in charge of collecting receipts. Even TI banks ask too many questions. Best to keep our partnership a bit more private, wouldn't you agree?"

"Indeed, miss, I do. Quite a good night so far. You'll be pleased to see how much you've already taken in." Oman led Zarina to the bar and instructed the bartender to tally up and hand her the takings.

Zarina smiled, temporarily forgetting the pain of her tortured scalp. "That was quite easy," she said to no one in particular, folding a fat wad of dosh into her pocket. "Candy, meet baby."

ZARINA WAS BEING WATCHED. Of the eyes that tracked her every movement, nuanced smile, and the actions of her theft, she was unaware. As well it should be, for Nuala Morigi was virtually invisible. Though physically striking, with her brassy ringlets, exotic beauty, and starched white clothing, she cultivated an aura of insignificance. She was a hallucinatory vision, a specter drifting through Neubonne society, whether high or low. Initially it had been Nuala's duty to spy for her father. She was naturally sneaky anyway, mistrustful, sleek, and catlike. Matuk had given her the job of bugging his entire industry with spy technology, an intricate netting of linked "eyes and ears" with which to spy upon his workers and executives, the million-headed informant wall fly.

Nuala's vast network of IERs was so firmly entrenched in Tirai Industries' infrastructure that the Company could no longer function without it. Her spying glass eyes were woven into the Company's very fabric to the point where the collapse of her network would smoothly disable TI's electronic brain. The minibuses, train stations, and public squares were wired, but the enormity and expense of implanting every single private and communal space with tiny electronic spies had proved too daunting. Even after years of diligent effort, she had not been able to successfully link an entire citywide system, necessitating occasional in-person forays to keep tabs on the Company's dealings.

She'd once sought escape from TI after a particularly nasty run-in with a thuggish glassworker and the disappearance of the young man she had hoped to train as her successor. She often thought of her lost love and wondered what had become of him. Soryk had been kind and gentle, alarmingly youthful and winningly naïve. Under her tutelage, he became an adept lover and a master artisan. When he vanished, the lighthearted innocence he had awakened within her diminished and died.

She was deeply dispirited by the world outside her father's high towers and fumbled unprotected beyond the walls of his stronghold. Without Matuk's money or the fortification of his name and reputation, she was lost. Now she understood that she would be forever yoked by blood and necessity to the onerous chore of preserving Matuk's vision of a company that operated without internal boundaries. More than a decade later, Nuala still slithered through the background like a freed shadow or an earthbound ghost.

Nuala wound through the bodies packed onto the Dregs' dance floor and clustered around the bar, her kohl-lined eyes searching for Soryk. She couldn't admit that she still sought him among the crowds, hoping to spot his sweet, handsome face among the riffraff, but he never appeared. If he was in Neubonne, he did not show himself.

Really, it was time to choose a new consort. The offers were numerous, the men she knew equally attractive, talented, and money-eyed, but their touch left her cold. She took up with a number of stylish young things and tried to find another his equal, but they were all wrong. They didn't possess that elusive, captivating quality of otherness her young man had so effortlessly borne.

A tall woman in yellow pushed herself on the bartender, her taut skin chalky beneath the revolving lights. Nuala slipped closer, watching. She recognized her brother's current bit of stuff, Zarina, and lifted an eyebrow. Chen's taste was inconsistent. He dragged any willing body into his bed and along on his escapades. Nuala supposed that having such a publicly broken heart conferred upon him some trite can't-be-bothered cachet, because no woman would ever measure up to his absent beloved. It was a very convenient strategy. Not for the first time, she wondered if all Morigis were romantically deficient, unable to accept or reciprocate love.

Tossing peroxide blond hair, Zarina flirted with the bartender. Nuala rolled her eyes at the woman's garishly cultivated innocence. She wore it badly, like a poorly made dress with fraying seams and off-cut lines. Nuala watched her accept a roll of dosh from the bartender. He grinned, beguiled by her robotic charms. Should Nuala interfere? It was only Chen's profits being stolen, not her own. She was uncompelled to rush to her brother's aid. Were the situation reversed, it was unlikely that he would return the favor.

In fact, the situation had turned, and Nuala now devoted her days to systematically dismantling the octameroon ink industry. Incapac-itated by ink-lust and guilt, it had taken ages for her to recover enough to atone for her sins. In the past year, she'd destroyed three tattoo parlors. One shot to bits with repeater guns, another blown to smithereens by Molotov cocktails, and the third rather clumsily de-molished in a conflagration caused by an exploding hot water heater. She wasn't quite sure how that happened, but the job was done, and she hadn't had to pay for it, either. Those two morons in Chen's em-ploy never questioned the orders that appeared on their message pads, orders that Nuala sent using her brother's hacked Company mail ID. Her actions affected her brother, but so what? She was guiltless. Chen had too much money to be broken by the cessation of a single trade. Their father had been like some mad scientist fo-cused only on the care and feeding of his wealth, a nightmarish crea-ture that was beginning to develop an agenda of its own. Too many projects and programs conducted in secret, and a surfeit of conspira-cies and backstabbing within the ranks of TI's upper management left Nuala doubtful that Chen even understood the extent of Matuk's treachery.

Nuala moved closer to the bar, disliking Zarina's parody of femi-ninity. She would offer, "Let me show you how it's done, sweet-heart," but that wouldn't be very ladylike, would it?

Zarina's presence in Chen's club—without Chen—struck an off chord. Nuala knew her brother had little loyalty, but he liked to sur-round himself with an entourage of sycophants who would stroke and massage his ego (*and any other body part he presented*, Nuala thought wryly) to feed the eternal flame of his requisite adoration. There was always some favored girl in tow, though their faces changed with astonishing frequency. Chen did not like to be alone. Rumor was that he'd been somehow responsible for their father's re-cent death though the truth was too deeply buried in insinuation and gossip for her to ferret it out.

Nuala's lack of remorse over Matuk's passing was a casual thing that she observed with an impartial eye. When she first heard the news, hope leapt up inside her, bright and shining. Surely the ink trade would end now. Too soon, she discovered that the trade, like everything within TI, was a multiheaded hydra. Terminating it would take a much more deliberate and final approach.

Zarina swirled away from the bar, aglow with triumph. Nuala shook herself out of her ruminations. She would trail the yellow comet of Zarina's hair, and perhaps, if the woman's activities threatened Nuala's livelihood, extinguish that cold star.

15

HAD I MY DRUTHERS

THE DREGS, PITVIPER, AND Tark & Ruby's—Soryk and Farouj visited them all, scanning faces hidden by shadow or lit by flashing strobes, searching for Kirwan. Soryk quizzed the tattooists and ink rats until he learned which clubs Kirwan was known to frequent. One ink rat recognized Soryk from the digi-reel, and told him that Kirwan's favorite spot was the Hanging Garden. Judging by the wounded look in her eyes and the venom in her voice, it was clear that she was another of Kirwan's conquests.

Evidence of TI's stranglehold on Neubonne's partying populace saturated the city. The debauchery escalated with the lateness of the hour. By 3 A.M., only the most hard-bitten addicts remained; tinted mouths had evolved from strawberry pink to violet to bright blue. Soryk and Farouj entered the Hanging Garden, certain that they would find Kirwan. It had just the right mix of decadence and danger to attract him. Soryk pushed through to the bar while Farouj made a quick detour to the gents', ignoring the pleas of ink rats eager to partner up. The bartender, a skinny woman with bulging eyes and spiky hair, gave him a quick look and moved down the bar. She paused and retraced her steps, her stare locked on Soryk. "Hey, I know you!"

Soryk balked. "No, you don't."

"Don't I? Because you look an awful lot like the Trader in those digi-reels." She leaned over the bar so that her perfume of cheap cosmetics, bidi smoke, and alcohol enveloped Soryk.

"I remember your face. Bloody hell, what are you doing here?"

Soryk backed away but the woman snatched his arm, calling to an evil-looking geezer with stringy hair and a crusty, braided beard.

"Adif! Come see! It's that Trader you like! From the films!" She turned to Soryk and grinned. "He's got a mad thing for ya, seen your reels a dozen times. He's even got your face inked on his arse!" She cackled, her fingernails cutting into Soryk's flesh.

Insisting that it was a mistake, Soryk shook his head, but the woman would not be dissuaded. Her witchy laughter and loud exclamations drew too much attention. Adif advanced, his sallow face lit with a mixture of longing and menace.

People pushed against Soryk, murmuring as they ran their eyes over him and made rude comments. Where was Farouj? Soryk could not see him through the throng of people surrounding him. He'd become briefly annoyed with Farouj's intrusive closeness, actually, and he'd been the one to slip from his side and lose himself in the mass of bodies. Now that Soryk needed his ally's cultured calm and authority, he was absent.

"Farouj!" His voice couldn't penetrate the din of pounding music and the excited ring of voices. Envisioning some sort of mob scene, he panicked. Adif closed in, but Soryk couldn't even hear the words coming from his mouth. Soryk had to control his fear. He could not risk transformation in such a wildly unsafe environment.

"Jorja," said a woman beside him. "Let's not agitate our guest." Soryk turned to see Zarina, one of the maids who had tended him at the House of Pleasure. Pretty in a pointy way, her skin was a plain canvas beneath heavy makeup and white-blond hair, and her demeanor was no longer servile.

Jorja reluctantly retreated and Zarina's icy stare stopped Adif from leaping over the bar to pursue them.

"Hey! Thanks." Soryk grinned. "That was weird. I thought they were going to drag me into a basement and poke me with hot forks or something to make me change."

"They wouldn't hurt you—they admire you. Jerusha knows why." Zarina gritted her teeth and patted Soryk's hand.

"Pardon?" Distracted by his search for Farouj, Soryk missed the tone of revulsion in Zarina's voice.

"Never mind." Practically choking with her need to squeeze the life out of Soryk and roll his limp body under the wheels of a passing minibus, Zarina steered him out of the club. "What are you doing here, anyway?"

"Looking for someone. Kirwan—do you know him?"

"Kirwan! What a coincidence. He's staying with us at the penthouse. Come on, I'll take you to him." Zarina could not believe her luck—proof that her work was ordained by the goddess herself.

"My friend will wonder where I've gone."

Though it dampened her anticipation, Zarina knew she must play her role carefully or risk Soryk's suspicion.

"Can you message him?" Zarina subtly pressed a few keys to disable her electronic notepad's transmission capability and offered it to Soryk.

"He doesn't like those. He prefers face-to-face contact. I'm sure he'll head back to the flat without me. I'll catch up to him later."

Zarina waved down a pedicab. Her head throbbed with sick desire. She might not be able to restrain herself long enough to delay her pleasure but would instead twist the stiletto she carried up her sleeve straight into Soryk's gut to watch his bile spill and stain the seats.

Soryk asked, "How's Carensa?"

Zarina would give the knife a few extra rotations just for that. Her fingers tightened into fists at the mention of her rival's name. "She's fine." It was mostly true. Carensa might eventually recover from the poison she'd "accidentally" ingested at least enough to grunt through her chemically burned throat.

The driver mounted the pedals, standing on legs as stocky as a bear's. He plunged down and the pedicab creaked and rolled. Only the shushing of the pedicab's rubber tires against the street and the driver's deep, measured breathing broke the calm. Shuttered shops, cafés, and TI administrative buildings lined the empty streets.

Soryk was relieved to be away from the club and cloaked in cool night air. Zarina would take care of him, just as she had before. "What are you doing in Neubonne? I thought it was impossible to leave Isle of Mourning."

"Chen wouldn't live there without an easy exit. He's too restless to remain long in any one place. He built a magnetic bridge between the islets that cross the channel. You throw a metal plate out over the first pole point and it hovers. You step on, toss out the next one, advance, and pick up the one you've left behind. You need only two plates to cross. But it's hush-hush. If people knew about the bridge, there would be no end to the parade of idiots coming to the isle, looking to satisfy their dirty fantasies. Chen prefers to keep his parties exclusive. He has a company to run now that his father is dead. He couldn't sequester himself on that pathetic little island."

"Chen's father?"

"Yes, he was founder of Tirai Industries. They own the bridges and roads, the glass and chemical factories, the banks . . ."

"The Merciful Father's Charity Hospital," Soryk added, recalling Sidra's lingering venom. "So, Matuk Morigi is dead."

Zarina cut yellow eyes at him. She realized that she couldn't kill Soryk without having to kill the driver, too, and having no particular vendetta against him, she decided it would be better to wait. Alone with her prey, she could better savor the Trader's death. "Chen's not certain but he's eager to take control of TI. There's been no word from Matuk for weeks. The old man was out of his mind. Anything could've happened . . ."

Soryk shuddered. His role in Matuk's death was still a secret, then.

He held Zarina's gaze—to look away would be an admission of guilt. He could only mask the image of Matuk's face contorted in pain and the rage reflected in his eyes as Soryk/ah javelined a fire iron into the old man's heart.

Zarina smiled at him but averted her eyes. Soryk could not read the intent in them and feared it dangerous, but then she squeezed his knee and said, "We're here. You'll see your friend soon." So Soryk convinced himself that he was being paranoid.

Tall tower blocks lined the one-way avenues bisecting Neubonne's heart. The skyscrapers seemed to sway in the night's breeze as if lulled like tides by the moon's gravitational force. At the avenue's end, white and black towers confronted each other—one reflecting faint blue moon and its shadow, grim and gray. The pedicab driver pulled into the half circle of light, took Zarina's money, and thanked her in Siguelandic. Zarina sneered at him but Soryk wished him well in his native tongue, the words coming with surprising ease, and the driver smiled before turning his vehicle into the night. A doorman swooped to welcome them but retreated at the sight of Zarina's stiff, expressionless face. Waves of déjà vu swept over Soryk. The Quartz Tower's starkly glittering façade was a ghostly echo of the white manor he had so recently fled. Unlike the interior of Matuk's manse, its bone-colored walls oozing moisture and cold, this was an opulent expanse of buffed ebony, black stone tiles, and fountains gushing jets of starless night. Memories lurked and prowled: the tower's raw insides, bare struts, beams, and scaffolding outlining its half-constructed skeleton; the Telec River viewed from high above, a toolbox filled with glass marbles sparkling with infinite numbers of tiny electrical sense receptors; faceless white books, white sheets, white-painted furniture, and white clothes, and the hazy outline of a woman's face haloed by brassy ringlets. The White Lady. These were the towers christened by their trysts. They had played among these endless rooms and stories. Certainly, the electronic eyes and ears within the walls still observed, calibrated, and transmitted their findings. It was just a matter of learning who was watching.

The elevator soared inside the tower's main artery and Soryk's ears popped. Bells pinged and doors opened on an expanse of space, black and unforgiving. A far bank of windows offered flashes of dim, foggy light, nothing more. Soryk turned but darkness met him as the elevator closed its doors, taking away its light.

Movement—a rustling to the left, then right. The sound of glass clinking, a metallic *tink*, a shearing noise that sounded like, but could not possibly be, a blade sliding from its sheath. Soryk moved toward the wall, fumbling for a light switch but not finding one. Should he head for the windows' faint light or look for the button to summon the elevator? Zarina had been perfectly nice at the House of Pleasure, *when watched by others*, instinct warned. Soryk had no knowledge of Zarina's personality or her behavior when alone. Anger smothered his fear. "Zarina!" He shouted and his call echoed in the cavernous room.

Zarina's cruel words rang in the empty, unlit flat. "I shot you down, yet you lived."

"Pardon?" Soryk said it automatically; he had heard just fine. Zarina's confession needed no repeating. Soryk's breath stilled, frozen in his lungs. Sudden flash of screams and flames, black smoke billowing, the broken balloon dipping and scudding over the sea, Elu's blood streaming and spraying.

Zarina shifted softly in the darkness. Soryk wished he had not been so foolish as to consign his trusted Magar blade to a place of honor above the fireplace in the Quonset. A single thread unspooled from his amygdala, the seat of his primitive brain, a sputtering fuse that made his skin ache and sent his belly into convulsions.

"Now I shall take great pleasure in finishing the job." Zarina slid around to Soryk's right. Though she remained out of sight, Soryk could feel the heat of her breath and hear the rustle of her layered gowns. Soryk lunged, his hands closing around air.

Zarina laughed. "I was astonished to see you at the bar. My aim is true. I shot down your balloon thinking you'd suffer more if I delivered your death in small doses. The terrifying fall, the sea plunge, the struggle toward shore, and your eventual drowning."

"Sweet Jerusha," Soryk breathed. "Why would you hurt us?"

"Elu," Zarina snarled, "should have chosen better. He said he loved me, that we would leave the isle together. We were going to buy a house on a hill, but when Carensa came he forgot his promise." Zarina's voice diminished, made rusty by grief.

Poor Carensa! Soryk's anger stirred and bubbled. Carensa had charmed him. Behind Zarina's bitter words, he sensed deadly action. "Why punish me for his doing?"

"Because I hate Traders. I hate *you*. I despise your disgusting wiles and foul odors. It's perverse."

"But . . . what about Kirwan?"

"When Chen's done with him, I'll be the one to tip him from the penthouse balcony. I've made it my mission, you see, to cleanse the world of your kind. How many can there be? Five? Ten? Not enough to present an obstacle."

Soryk's fingers skimmed the bare surfaces of things for something recognizable, a weapon or light switch. The flat was distressingly unfurnished.

"You won't find anything." Zarina laughed. "Stop looking. You've nothing to do now but turn your throat into my knife."

Soryk ran his hand along the wallpaper and trimmings in search of the elevator button and found a small control panel.

"You don't know the code. You'll never leave here!" Zarina cackled.

Could Zarina's yellow eyes see in the dark? How else could she know what Soryk did? It would have to be a fight, then, and an unfair one. Taken by surprise, Soryk would have to rely on wit and instinct to save himself. His vision blurred and his hands tingled, nearly numb. Waves of exhaustion rose and peaked. He wanted very badly to sleep.

"You're frightened. The change wants you, doesn't it?" Zarina gloated.

Soryk stumbled toward the windows' low pulse of light.

"I can smell your disease. Inside your skin, inside your blood. Sickness, treachery. I think it's what attracts him to you. He likes depravity, our Chen."

Soryk moaned; he was losing the fight.

"Chen," Zarina scoffed, "is mad for you. Really, I don't understand his obsession. His lust. I'm just a poor substitute. I can't change. It disappoints him. No matter what I do, it'll never match the thrill promised by your grotesque talent. Man into woman. How he regrets losing you!"

Soryk gurgled and sagged to the floor. He closed his eyes, felt Zarina's weight as she straddled him. Zarina's sharp knees dug into Soryk's arms, pinning them down.

Zarina pressed a stinging point into Soryk's chest. "Come on, let it go. Just at the moment you change, that's when I'll do it. By god, you stink." Zarina angled her stiletto blade between the ribs to the left of Soryk's sternum. She placed both hands firmly upon the knife hilt and pushed. The blade wouldn't descend. She wiggled it, felt it slide off a metal button, swivel into a gap of muscle, and scrape bone. Soryk bucked beneath Zarina, trying to throw her off. United against him, the change and Zarina together were too strong.

"This is the last time you will ever infect the world with your stench." Zarina took a deep breath and leaned on the knife.

16

REVELATION

LIGHT FLOODED THE ROOM. Zarina howled.

"Cripes, Zee, what are you doing?" Chen crossed the floor, followed by two men in black Company long-coats.

Startled, Zarina jumped up and quickly slid the knife into the sheath hidden inside her sleeve. Her mouth made indigo by repeated infusions of bluing that gave her a corpse-grin, she hiked the night-vision visor up on her forehead and gaped at him. "What are you doing here?"

"Who is that?" Chen peered down. "Holy mother. Sorykah!" Chen crouched, slapping Sorykah's cheeks. "Wake up, gorgeous! This vixen is about to suck you dry while you sleep!" He laughed and Zarina shot him a look of murderous fury.

"Tsk-tsk, Zee. You've been a naughty girl." Chen tossed her a handkerchief. "Wipe your mouth before you drool on my rugs."

Livid with shame and the lingering tension of *murder interruptus*, Zarina snatched the cloth and pressed it to her lips. The smell of

Sorykah's changing sleep clouded her brain. She wondered why it did not bother Chen. He seemed impervious to it while the odor drew ragged nails down the chalkboard of her nerves.

Sorykah stirred and struggled to open and focus her eyes. Chen yanked Zarina back and Sorykah groaned, rubbing the sore dents Zarina's knees had gouged into her forearms. Bloodstains darkened her shirt.

"Sit up, my friend! So good to see you." Chen clapped his hand to Sorykah's back, squeezed her shoulder, and yanked her to her feet. She stumbled, still groggy, rising fury damping her relief. Chen wrapped a possessive arm around Sorykah's waist and dragged her from the room, leaving his guests to Zarina's manic care.

"I heard you were in town, but this is a surprise. Couldn't keep away from me, could you?" Chen grinned, his hand clamped tight around her body. "Mmm," he murmured, kissing her neck. "You're definitely staying the night."

Limply, she shoved him off. Half an inch deep, Sorykah's knife wound throbbed. She could not clear her head and felt the floor swaying beneath her feet as they walked. "Where are we? How did I get here?" Sorykah peered out the window; rising river mist obscured the city.

"Heading for the Onyx Tower. Thought you'd like the white. All that immaculate snowiness ought to make you feel right at home." Suspended high above ground, the connecting walkway was a vertiginous link between the Morigi empire's twin poles. Silver clouds smothered the city, pressing a blanket of smog to the ground. "As for how you got here, you'd have to ask Zarina. She's the one who dragged you here by your neck scruff." He pulled her collar down. "You probably have teeth marks and scratches from that nasty kitty's claws."

"The Onyx Tower . . . this is Neubonne?" She sagged, resisting Chen's pull. She was meant to be on a boat heading back to the Sigue. Every time she tried to go home, she woke up even farther away. Had Soryk contacted Nels? Were the children safe at home in

Ostara? She remembered the dead octameroon, a stormy sea, and Farouj's kiss. After that, undersea-consciousness. Flickers of light, muted voices bubbling nonsense, vague sensations of movement. What had happened to Farouj? Sorykah was unsure of their parting. They'd last spoken aboard the fishing trawler, arguing over intent and rights of rescue.

From black to white, the rooms and corridors transformed themselves into photo negatives of the Quartz Tower. They entered a landscape of crisp snow and creamy ivory. Again came that sense of having-already-been, a repetitious overlay of events that left Sorykah more unbalanced and breathless than when crossing the tower walkway. Chen led her through a labyrinth of corridors and doors requiring pass codes and keycards to enter. Morning sun, filtered through starched linen panels and glass blocks, slanted across the constant white and made Sorykah squint.

At last, a resting place. A plush suite, its expensive furnishings promising respite high above the weary world's troubled streets. She was tired, as if she'd been up all night traipsing through an urban jungle. Her empty belly rumbled. She yearned for sleep—true, unchanging sleep. The white sofa enveloped her like a puff of chantilly cream.

"Tell me about your journey from my isle. You remember, don't you, leaving my house?" Chen gave her a syrupy grin, his gaze traversing Sorykah's body in naked appraisal.

She remembered that gaze—this man who behaved like a friend, but who, she knew, was much less. Nodding and sensing herself enticed into a trap, she asked, "Why are you here?"

"You don't think I could stay away forever, do you? Someone has to run things in my father's absence."

A little bucket of icy adrenaline tipped itself within her chest, splashing fear everywhere. She trembled, her pain forgotten. Did he know? She would play the ingénue, naïve, wide-eyed. If only she knew what had transpired between wakings! Her greedy alter gobbled up more and more of her life. Soryk had spoken there in the wood when she was most lost. He'd whispered to her, his voice almost indistinguishable from her own thoughts, but he said nothing here, had not implanted a directive in her brain to guide her.

Chen sat beside Sorykah, his hand heavy on her shoulder, fingers brushing the swell of her breast. He grinned, blue stains edging his gums. She could see the wear upon his skin, aging creases and shadows, the wicked spark in his eyes a no-longer-leaping flame. "So good to see you."

"And you as well," Sorykah conceded. She wanted to hate him, for her sake and Sidra's, but Chen's was a familiar face if naught else. He smelled of smoky plum and betrayal. She recalled the taste of his tongue stinging with mint oil, the scent of crushed lavender, the invasion of his sweat-labored skin, as hot as a fire poker. The insouciant mask he wore slipped, revealing something austere and unlikable.

"Meertham has not been in contact with me. I sent a messenger to my aunt's house, the only one of my father's siblings still in contact with him, and she's not there. Mind you, she's lived alone beside that volcano for decades. Her continued existence is miraculous in itself but her hovel is empty, her plants and books gone and the beasts she kept slaughtered in the yard."

"Perhaps it is only Meertham who is ill, or worse."

"My father was not well and his sickness forced him to do many reprehensible things, but he was no fool. Majority control of TI passes to his successor only upon proof of his death. Undeniable, incontrovertible evidence of his demise." Chen grinned, rising to open the polished silver case resting atop the sideboard. He raised the lid, revealing a bare skull nestled in a bed of white velvet. "Note the pitting, indicative of *general paresis of the insane*. The syphilitic old satyr! At least I won't inherit his madness. I take my pills like a good boy."

He juggled it like a ball and pitched it to Sorykah, who fumbled the catch, her finger hooking an empty eye socket. Revolted, she dropped it to the ground and watched it tumble away.

"So tell me, my gullible friend, how did the assassination of my father proceed?"

"Assignation?" Sorykah choked, not trusting her hearing.

"You heard right the first time. *Assassination*. I could not have planned it better myself, with you to play the rube. How to finish him off was always the question, Meertham being beyond bribery. You can imagine the difficulty of hiring someone stealthy and courageous enough to confront my deformed sister while avoiding detection from Sidra and her gang of thugs! Long did I ponder and wait, certain that a solution would present itself. A terrible price was paid, I suppose. Radhe suffered, but she was a mindless monster. She emptied the Erun and tarnished my family name in the meantime. Even so, it was worth the delay. He is gone"—some unsettling and chilling expression slithered across Chen's face—"and Tirai is mine."

"I might have failed," cried Sorykah, shaking.

"But you did not!" Chen crowed. "Love drove you on! Revenge goaded your every cursed Trader step. No one else would have made it. You could not possibly remember all the things I whispered in your impressionable ears. The liqueurs, the herbs, the hallucinogenic toxins with which I effected your conversion from female to male, all played their role in prying open that little nut of a brain and sucking up all the suggestions I planted."

Sorykah paled. Yes, thrashing in that glass coffin while Chen blew smoke into the box. She saw herself imprisoned within Soryk's heaving frame, swimming inside and sinking below the mille-feuille layers of their shared awareness. Shock weakened Sorykah's reason, leaving her dense and uncertain. He stroked her short hair, and she knew that this was how he would settle a chicken before breaking its neck for the soup pot. If he kissed her, she might crumble into bits. "You wanted him dead?"

"If only to mount the throne. Isn't that how these things go? The son overthrows the father and claims through strategy or brutishness what will one day be rightly his anyway—he just pushes the clock hands ahead. Even better," Chen continued, "was the product of my enforced delay. What was I to do with so much time on my hands? What would be my particular contribution to the Morigi legacy? My father dominated Plein Eïre. Under TI's influence, he resurrected the capitol, lifted this once great city from poverty, and tripled its population. So many bored young minds!"

The blue tongues, the sugar cubes, and insidious ink market had not sprung from the ground like corpse mushrooms: They had been nurtured. Fed and groomed — a deliberate affront to Sidra and those she protected.

"What other nastiness have you perpetrated upon us?"

"I'm quite proud of the bluing. It's much more effective and more addictive than my pink tonics. Herbs have a wishy-washy take-it-or-leave-it quality, but one hundred percent synthetic bluing is merciless."

"Why?" Soryk thought desperately of the somatics who had succumbed to Chen's spell and the octameroon bodies heaping the floor of their saltwater catacombs.

"I need to make a name for myself." He popped open a small tin and tucked a blue sugar cube into his cheek. "What shall I do with an entire country at my disposal?" A corner of his mouth lifted in a grimace or a smile. "Make more money."

Chen pulled slim vials of colored liquids from a cooling cabinet beneath the bar. He dropped a blue sugar cube into a glass and added a dash of red syrup. The swizzle stick clinked. Magenta liquid bubbled. Chen crouched before her, one hand gripping her thigh. Swirling the foam around the glass, he offered it to Sorykah, who refused.

"You're so virtuous. It's nauseating," Chen said. "Just a taste. We'll have such fun."

She shook her head, defiantly pressing her lips together. The pleasure of defiling Soryk/ah's Trader flesh had proven too great a temptation. She was nothing more than a fetish, a conquest to add to his menagerie. Outrage filled her stomach with acid.

Chen said, "I know how to do it now. I've been practicing, you see, and the other has shown me there's no great trick to it. A bit of upset, that's all. Would you prefer that I make you cry first or will you comply?"

Sorykah's irritation and fear coalesced into a single urge to punch

Chen. Vibrating with hostility, she shoved his hand away. "You think it so easy?"

"Easy and profitable."

Sorykah struggled to escape and he let her go, amused by her stumble for the door.

"You make me a wealthy man, my dear. Don't be so quick to leave me. I think you owe me a debt. My ring, to start. Tirai's heart, that precious ruby, is no longer upon your finger. Did you sell it? Lose it? Give it to the Gatekeeper to save your skin?"

"Your ring? That's all you want?"

"That and much more. But we have plenty of time to discuss the details of our new agreement."

Sorykah rattled the crystal doorknob. "Let me out!"

Chen grinned. "You can jump out the window if you like. Only a hundred stories down. Who knows? You might survive just long enough to regret your decision."

The locked door had precisely the effect that Chen had anticipated. Sorykah panicked.

"Your pupils dilate. It's happening now. Splendid! A private show!"

Sorykah fought madly to stay afloat on the rising river of fear threatening to close over her head. Even if she fought Chen and knocked him unconscious, it would not facilitate her escape. The heavy bolted door was solid steel. The change buckled and writhed, spilling through her cells, assuring conversion and destruction. Chen sprang and was upon her, his tongue convulsing within his mouth. He caught Sorykah just as her legs slid out from beneath her. Chen swirled the glass and foam overran its rim. "Now, drink this up. It will make you happy. There's my good girl!"

Sorykah moaned and her mouth fell open, slack and waiting. Chen tipped the drink into her mouth, licking up the spill that dribbled down her chin. He nosed the skin of Sorykah's neck and behind her ears, seeking that elusive Trader fragrance, distressingly faint to senses dulled by too much bidi smoke.

"You are so luscious, I can hardly stand it." Chen slurred, pawing at Sorykah.

Waves of disgust and desire pitched inside her, threatening to cap-
size her reason on a tumultuous sea. Why did he captivate her so,
even as every shred of sanity and self-preservation urged her to flee?
Sorykah struggled beneath Chen as he plastered her with blue
kisses. She smarted against her body's primal reaction to the memory
of his fevered skin and the animal way he'd coaxed the shudders
from her skin. *Shit, shit, shit,* she groused. *Do not enjoy this! It's completely inappropriate. You must get a grip on yourself.*

"Come to bed," Chen insisted, dragging Sorykah into his bedroom. Unlike the snowy purity of the front rooms, these furnishings
and surfaces were cut from shadows and nightmares—even the
morning light seeping from the wide windows lost its luster and
paled within that sinister den.

Sliding between skin and fabric, his hot-fingered hand dabbled
against the wound between her breasts. Toying in her clotting blood,
he said, "I want to be in you, on you . . . all over you when you
change."

She groaned. What was it Sidra had said about Chen? Ah, yes.
"It's like I'm on a diet and he's the cake." *He's the cake.* A satiny,
butter-drenched, artery-clogging wedge of molten chocolate cake—
delicious and deadly. Sorykah shoved him away but the strawberry
milk, and whatever else he'd put down her throat, manipulated her
senses and left her languid. She smelled charcoal in him, something
that made her think of bloody flesh cooking on a brazier and the
stench of rotted bodies on fire.

Chen's long hair tickled her face as he pressed her onto the black
furs. "I have grand plans for you, my darling." His fingers were steel
cuffs upon her wrists. "If one Trader is this popular, just imagine
what riches two will net! We'd be treated to a spectacle the likes of
which this city has never seen. Kirwan does whatever I ask. Not that
I do," he laughed.

Kirwan. She hadn't seen him since their one-night stand and
didn't want to. Anger shining in her eyes, she said, "What's all this for
then, the fawning and drooling and clutching me like you'll never
let me go if you've already got another?"

Mollified—for her show of emotion pleased him—Chen said, "Dear heart, calm yourself. That ink rat could never replace you in my affections. *You* are my one and only, my very favorite Trader. Would I have made all those exceptions—guaranteed your place aboard the *Nimbus*, excused your lengthy leave from your position—had I not cared about you? For you, I bent the rules. I let you keep your home and your job as a reward for dispatching the final obstacle preventing me from taking control of TI. For you"—he nuzzled her cheek—"I arranged a very generous settlement to be delivered to your nanny. She can keep the house, and she's set for life. She'll care for your babes just as if they were her own, I'm sure. It's in the agreement she signed."

Hysteria clawed at Sorykah. "What agreement? Nels cannot keep my children!"

"I had to make sure that you wouldn't worry over them in your absence. After all, when I heard you disappeared during a coring blast, I couldn't quite believe that you'd been so foolish. So I expedited an arrangement to help you, whatever the outcome of the accident. We are meant to be together, don't you see?" A rash of sweat beaded Chen's forehead. His mouth scalded her skin.

"You love Sidra," she squawked, her mind in turmoil.

"Sidra," he said darkly, "does not love me. Should I mourn her forever, when I have a new amusement in my bed? Now, we have a tattooist on staff but I've tinkered with the art and I think I'm becoming quite skilled." Chen pulled a broad-barreled hypodermic from his nightstand drawer and uncapped its two-inch needle. Octameroon ink had already begun to warp the plastic. "Since the other Trader is hopelessly addicted to the stuff, it's not much fun to work with him. He hardly responds anymore. It takes gobs of raw, undiluted ink to get a rise out of him these days." He giggled at his own joke. "But you, my darling, will have quite a different reaction. Jerusha, it's going to be spectacular."

Sorykah blanched as he waggled the needle.

He shucked her trousers, exposing her buttocks. "This method's a bit more time-consuming than using a tattoo gun, but the longer needle injects the ink into a deeper layer of the dermis. It takes more time to activate, but the effects wear off less quickly. I've been practicing on myself so I've got a steady hand, which I'm sure you'll appreciate."

Dizzy with fear, she struggled to keep her transformation at bay. It was such a blight—this disease that turned her mind to jam and sapped her strength every time she needed it. For years she'd maintained careful control, avoiding any situation that might alarm, frighten, or arouse her in an attempt to control her body's fickle fix on a single gender. She'd led a very cautious and uninteresting life. Until Matuk had stolen her children, she'd been convinced of her mastery over the change and the forgetfulness that accompanied it. Now she realized that she'd gone about it all wrong. She should have forced herself into difficult, emotionally challenging situations, tested her power and will by pushing herself through the change as often as possible. Then it would not creep or pounce upon her in moments of desperation, leaving her helpless and weak. She might have a chance to rescue herself and would not be prey to fortune hunters, sadists, fetishists, and fatal jealousies. Perhaps if she succumbed, Soryk would wake and fend off Chen. Surely her male primary would be irate at the intrusions and assumptions of Matuk's son, and resist tattooing.

The needle bit her flesh and she screamed. Ink stung and burned. Hypnotic drift borne on the rhythm of pulsing bioluminescence— Rava's message echoed again, a skinny string of subconscious words, "Find the taken."

Chen stabbed her again and again, the needle dulling with each jab. Soon he rose and said, "Touch it and I'll have to tie up your hands."

The ink throbbed within her skin, leaden and fiery. Its fierce urgency subsided and the change melted away. Sorykah lay beneath Chen, exploring the ink's unexpected effect. The sensation of absolute calm was a novel one, as strange and shocking as her first orgasm. The kaleidoscope of worries that spun incessantly through her head stilled and came slowly into focus. The world acquired a brilliant clarity. Her heartbeat's rapid pulse decelerated, and suddenly, she could *see*. Her persistent, fuzzy disorientation receded. Sorykah had fought for space within the cloisters of a shared body; now she filled all the corners of those inner rooms. Fingers that had floated within too-large gloves now enjoyed a perfect fit. Energy, power, and single-minded vision were hers. No more overlap of dual consciousness, no more echoing voices and urgent *otherness*, barking for her attention. It was a very seductive feeling.

Sorykah calmly turned over, wrapped her fingers around Chen's neck, and pressed, just enough to discomfort him. Surprise flickered in his eyes, quickly replaced by a salacious glint.

"That's right, get all your anger out. I can take it. Your hands feel like butterflies on my throat."

Sorykah squeezed with both hands, suppressed fury rising to the fore. Chen grinned maniacally, even as his lips turned purple. Disgusted, she released him and crawled away while he lay coughing behind her.

"See?" Chen rasped. "You're incapable of hurting me. Admit it. You like me. Like what we do together."

"You blackmailed me. Took horrible advantage. Every inch your father's son," Sorykah snapped, jerking up her pants.

"He was a small man," Chen laughed. "I like to think I have a few more inches than he!"

"You are vile!"

"Maybe so," he said, getting to his feet. "But you love it, and myself being so incredibly rich and essentially above the law, there's nothing you can do about it. Play along, darling, if you want things to go well for you." Chen lit one of his ever-present vanilla bidis and blew smoke in her face. "Sit tight. You can box with me after we finish filming."

Chen pulled out his message pad and typed a few words. Immediately three identical men in long-coats entered the room and took up positions blocking the door.

"Just in case you get any funny ideas about trying to leave before you've committed your change to digi-reel." Chen wiped his mouth on his sleeve. The bluing's effects faded, and an irritating regret took their place. Damn grief, come to trouble him again. He forced a grin. "We have a good twelve hours to play before the ink wears off. Be a good girl while I'm gone." And then he was.

Sorykah stared at the men in the room. They looked like Siguelanders.

"*Tikk ōs Siguelandic?*" she asked. One man's eyebrow twitched, but they resolutely ignored her. If any of them spoke his native tongue, he was too loyal to Chen to be enticed into conversation. Sorykah thought that she might be able to subdue one man on her own, but not all three. She thought longingly of Farouj and wondered if he searched for her. If he believed she'd deserted him to return to Ostara, would he search for her or just let her go and continue on his way alone?

She slumped against the window. The Telec spewed filth into the ocean and turned the blue-gray waters a lurid, chemical green. Far from here, Nels was alone with Sorykah's children. Emotions jostled within her, but this time the change did not waken and emit its stinging signals. She remained resolutely female, and without Soryk's familiar if annoying presence, entirely alone.

17

WAKING THE DEMON

SWEET AND GENTLE GOWYR was a good boy easily led astray. He was naïve and trusting, two traits that did not serve him well in the Sigue's avaricious environment. He'd done all right for himself until he reached the Sigue—had navigated the well-disguised routes and trails leading him from the Erun city, taken the train from Fair Fallows to the harbor, and bought passage aboard a supply ship. Grim and dirty Colchester, lacking Ostara's subtle village charm, proved too much for him. Mainland vices had seeped down the coast from Neubonne, ferried by traveling sailors and fishermen. Bluing infiltrated Colchester's seedy bars. Ink rats on the run from addiction loitered on its mean street corners, crouching in doorways and recruiting the uninitiated, peddling blue sugar cubes and tainted, reconstituted strawberry milk.

He was so innocent, that boy! Just sixteen, though tall and hefty, and already built like a man. It's just as well that Sidra would never discover his end for it would have broken her heart. Perhaps if Sidra had realized how young he was, she would have selected another in his stead. Certainly, his mother bade him farewell with tears and a hard look in her eye. Resentment simmered. Queen Sidra took her boy from her; Yetive could not refuse to let him go.

Gowyr planned to stop in to surprise his da' and spend a few nights with the father who was not expecting him. He wanted to tell him about life in the Erun city, show him the sketchbook crammed with clever drawings of the city's residents, and proudly announce his new role as queen's messenger. Though his da' chose to remain in the world of men, he was kind to somatics and understood his son's need to explore his roots by living in the Erun with his mother.

He arrived in Colchester, brimming with self-importance. When an ink rat slipped her arm through his and led him to the squat she shared with ten others, he considered it a grand adventure. When she slipped her cold hand inside his fly and her blue tongue inside his ear, he considered himself extraordinarily lucky. Sidra's purse of coins was soon emptied and the all-important message, telling Soryk of Sidra's pregnancy and requesting his return, was forgotten. Yetive would curse Sidra and vow revenge when her son did not come home. Whether he'd chosen to stay with his father or become lost, she did not know. Gowyr's father would not discover the boy's absence for months. When he finally found his son asleep in a gutter with frost caking his beard, Gowyr had lost twenty pounds and several teeth and had acquired the stony, frozen expression of a statue. He took his boy home, cut the lice from his hair, and at last mailed the wrinkled, water-stained letter he found in Gowyr's pack. Sidra the Lovely's message was once again en route to Soryk, but by then the queen was already dead and Yetive complicit in her demise.

NELS KNEW NONE OF THIS that bright vexday morning, her high-heeled boots skidding over lumps of melting ice, unspoken prayers intonating in her head. Kindly Oona, owner of Ostara's only wash-house, practically jumped up and clicked her ancient heels together when Nels asked if she would watch the twins. Like Oona's sporadic English, Nels's Siguelandic was limited to the basics, but they understood each other. Fanning away heat from the fires that blazed beneath the washtubs, Nels tapped her watch and held up one finger. The old woman eagerly nodded, lifting Ayeda to her lap as she directed one of her young grandsons to hold Leander.

Nels strode into town. The *Nimbus* had pulled into port not a week after Sorykah's departure and sent a Company man to the Quonset to report that she had vanished during a blast. They'd combed the sea, deployed diving modules, scanned the berg and seafloor for signs of her body, but the locator on her diving suit was silent and the sea, "As you well know, miss," said the Company man, a tall, plain-faced corporate drone in the requisite thermal suit, long-coat, and oiled hair, "is dark and impenetrable to even the most sophisticated technology."

He pressed a sheaf of documents into Nels's hand. "Sign these and you can quietly get on with your life."

Nels frowned, speed-reading pages of fine print.

"There's a substantial settlement, of course. You won't feel the loss . . ."

Nels gawked at him.

"Financially," he added hastily.

That had been a bad day. The admin handed her a slim file containing a completed death certificate, the date of Sorykah's demise the same as the one on her message to Nels. She'd refused to sign them, of course, but did keep the papers. She had to think but couldn't do it clearly when she was still reeling from the horrid error of sleeping with Soryk and the sudden realization that she was now totally responsible for Sorykah's children.

A report on the short wave radio (a pirate frequency used by somatics and English-speaking Siguelanders) spoke of a body found on the southern shore near the ice caves. Wash-ups were an unusual, but not unknown, occurrence. Maimed and killed by sport hunters, somatics occasionally drifted ashore, battered by ice in the floe fields or defiled by rot and fishes in the equatorial currents flowing from the Bay of Sorrows. The frozen corpses of travelers ill-prepared for the Sigue's harsh weather littered its interior, but this latest grisly arrival sparked curiosity. The Siguelanders wanted to conduct their own investigation before the Company got involved. As soon as she heard the report, Nels loaded the children into the sled and headed for Oona's. She had to see for herself.

Nels trekked through the Sigue's back streets to avoid the admins who clogged Ostara's main vein, Port Street. The *Nimbus* remained anchored in the harbor and she did not want to risk diversion by some obsessive, falsely well-meaning Company man.

It took just half an hour to reach the ice caves. A clutch of people—*Somatics? Siguelanders?* she wondered—packed the coast. Worry churned. If the body were Sorykah's, what would she do?

Nels elbowed her way into the center of the crowd. Mottled by bruises, an arm lay on the icy beach. Ragged flesh dangled from the severed shoulder joint. A Siguelander reached out to splay the hand's tapered fingers, linked with translucent webbing. Nels exhaled sharply. *Not Sorykah.* She staggered back, her eyes watering. A woman skirting the shore cried out, raising overhead a pale pink tentacle some seven feet long and staggering under its weight.

Nels turned toward town, its low buildings glinting in the morning sun. She felt the day's coming heat, the volcano's steaming breath that would thin the icicles and further weaken the landmass along the harbor. She tugged off her scarf and opened the neck of her coat. The babies were safe for now. She would take a minute to find a quiet place, lit by the white sun and ringed in gray sea slowly bluing in the strange, sudden warmth. She would ask the holy mother to return her mistress to her. When deep in prayer, Nels did not sense the absence of Sorykah's spirit in the world. She must still live. Nels would wait, then.

The sky was a fierce and vivid azure. It seemed that every resident of Ostara was out of doors relishing the extraordinary spring, marveling at the lack of need for coats and the Sigue's dull whine, diminished to a hum. Vexday smudgepots—split, coal-mounded barrels heaped with lumps of amber and sweet myrrh resin—sent spirals of mustard-colored smoke winding high into the air. Locals smudged themselves as they passed each pot, taking in a deep lungful, then coughing and barking up phlegm, expelling their vexations and returning them to the fire for banishment. Newly freed of regrets and grievances, light-hearted Siguelanders thronged the streets. Merchants peddled gravy-dripping, newspaper-swaddled handpies and ladled brown beer from battered tin vats into communal cups. Nels found a few coins in her pocket and bought a spiced fish handpie and a pint of ale. Someone had dragged a couple of bar stools onto Port Street, and this served as a perfect people-watching station. Nels ate her pie, marveling at the novelty of eating hot food that was not half frozen by the time she raised it from the wrapper to her mouth. The good beer was creamy and mildly bitter. Bells clanged as a fishing boat tied up and several Siguelanders jumped ashore, shouting and grinning. They turned out their nets on the docks, and Nels saw one man swing the carcass of some monstrous, prehistoric fish toward the gathering crowd.

She ran a hand along her bare arm pricked with gooseflesh and tingles of arousal sprang up at her touch. She could not cleanse her mind of her indiscretion or evade the pressing memory of Soryk's slender body, his familiar dark eyes, her employer's gestures diluted by her alter. She told herself that sleeping with Soryk was incomparable to sleeping with Sorykah. She forced herself to see them as two separate beings, not one in the same, though the body was the same, its fleshy bits of putty rolled, smoothed, and newly shaped. Days later, the night sweat of Soryk/ah's change seemed to permeate Nels's skin and the sound of Soryk's voice, a shifting and disturbing emulation of Sorykah's, wended through her thoughts like an accusation. The dalliance with her employer, an egregious error, coupled with Sorykah's disappearance combined required immediate action. She would tackle it with her usual strategy of ardent prayer and unshakable faith. Something good must come out of this mess, mustn't it? But as the sweltering sun beat down, it seemed to Nels that Jerusha had temporarily forsaken her. She must ask for temperance, understanding, and patience. Though she'd grown to love Ayeda and Leander, Nels was keenly aware that she was the help; Sorykah could terminate her employment at any time and for any reason. Would she consider sleeping with her alter a breach of trust? Nels wondered. If and when Sorykah returned, the deed would lurk between them, threatening to reveal itself with bitter, begging tears. She would be safe from further folly as long as Sorykah remained herself. Should Soryk wake, he would gaze upon her with knowing in his eyes, remembering the taste of her body, the feel of it in his hands.

Maybe the beer made Nels's thoughts fuzzy, or the unwieldy, needy affection that swamped her common sense. She longed for a second chance to make Soryk forget Sidra and see that Nels would be a better mother to his children than a lusty queen with a delicate constitution and an inflated sense of her own importance. Nels was bright and steady, cheerful and kind. She was a good cook, kept a tidy house, and the sink free of dirty dishes. A loyal, devoted girl, well practiced in the application of romance, Nels would make a fine wife to an ice miner. Unlike Sidra—so selfishly concerned with the gratification of her lusts that she would keep Sorykah forever smothered within her alter—Nels was certain that she could bear the changes with cheerful ease. As long as they came to some sort of understanding, Nels thought things could work out very well for all of them. Sorykah liked her well enough—hadn't she rescued her from Matuk's evil clutches? Soryk would grow to love her in time when he saw how well she kept his house and his babes.

There were few other options available to her. Nels had come to regret her decision to specialize in sacred texts during such a libertine age, when the popular study of the holy mother's words was on the wane. It was either the Sigue or the nunnery for her. Another domestic position perhaps, but if the father was handsome, or the son too close to Nels's own age, well . . . she shivered at the premonition of a life spent moving from one broken household to another, her prospects diminishing along with her looks.

She shuddered. *What a disaster.* Perhaps it would not be so bad if Soryk were free to give himself to her, but Sidra had stitched her name across his heart and stamped "Mine" in indelible ink upon his unlined forehead. The queen's grubby fingers gripped Soryk's free will and squeezed.

Nels polished off her pie and drained the glass. She returned it to the vendor, who promptly dipped it into his vat, beer dripping from his calloused fingers, and handed it to another customer. Nels slipped out of her coat and wiped the moisture from her brow. The surreal day was oppressive, smothering. The Sigue groaned, ice singing in peevish complaint. Smudged clouds billowed inland, darkening the sky above the waste. Seismic thunder barreled underground and a wave of beer sloshed up from the vat. Everyone froze, gaping at the sky as the Devil's Playground bucked and rippled. Belching smoke and lava, the volcano drew in deep, gasping breaths and exploded. Flaming ash rained around the distant volcano like falling stars.

An anguished cry rang out, and a taut *crack* whipped through the air as the stone retaining walls snapped and ripped, buckling the wooden pier and dumping chunks of ice into the sea. Slush jetted skyward. Glacial planks split from Ostara's harbor and crashed into the waves, toppling frantic bystanders who thrashed and shouted in the frigid waters. Foaming seawater arched up to net a teetering body and pull it into the sea. People crowded the harbor's ragged edge, shouting and leaping as the ice sheared away from the beach. A miner toppled into the sloshing waves and was crushed between floating ice blocks. Drowning people climbed over him, pushing the bloody body underwater in their desperation to free themselves of the sea's icy grasp. Men dove in and heaved themselves out again. Bodies thrashed on a jagged ridge of ice. Bodies lay soaked and still. Fishing boats crammed the bay, tossing ropes and dropping skiffs into the water to help fish out corpses already grown stiff.

Admins tried to wrest control from the milling locals, who seemed capable of only hysteria and blocking efforts to clear the harbor. A woman ululated, loudly lamenting the demon's return. Prayers and epithets uttered by miners and Company admins filled the air while the Sigue bellowed in outrage, or jubilation. Nels turned away from the commotion as Company men began to lay corpses in a row along the ice for identification. She ran back to the washhouse and the children, skidding through mud puddles as ash blotted out the sun and sky. Oona's grandson was nailing closed the tin shutters, his curls shaking with every frantic beat of the hammer. Oona crouched swaying in the doorway, chanting as she blacked the snow with powdered volcanic rock. She drew a half circle marked with two symbols, cut her palm, and shook drops of her ancient blood onto the ground.

A mobile of magpie wing bones and skulls spun from the eaves, clattering in the sulfurous wind. Oona raised a gnarled, quavering finger. Blood trickled down her palm into the channels of her wrinkled skin. *"Rivas Diabolo. Su dimas es revenat."*

Nels turned to the boy for translation. He trembled, the hammer bouncing from hand to hand as he repeated his grandmother's words. "Diabolo wakes. The demon is coming."

18

INSIDE SKIN

THE WHITE LADY APPROACHED *Soryk one evening as he sat in the empty window frame of a high-rise. Soryk liked to recline on the thirtieth-floor ledge, which had the best view of the Telec River, a scummy, toxic watercourse that drew sewage from Neubonne's chemical processing plants into the Southern Sea. Foul though it was, when the setting sun lit up like a bonfire, the river's glossy oilskin and floating refuse reflected vivid pinks and oranges so bright they almost seared the eye. Soryk watched the river's glow intensify, gleam, and fade before night settled over the city and lights appeared on the smoky horizon, winking like jarred fireflies.*

Soryk reached for his flint striker to kindle the oil lamp's wick when a hand stayed his own and a woman's low voice murmured, "Don't."

Invisible but for the glow of her snowy tunic and gleaming bronze curls, the White Lady gazed adoringly at her city, an ugly place made beautiful by the obscuring evening.

"This is my favorite time of day, too." Her voice was as smooth as

caramelized sugar. "I usually watch from the penthouse, though I see now that I've been missing the best view. From up there, the Telec is more worm than snake."

"It's venomous either way," Soryk replied, startled but pleased to have a companion.

"You wouldn't believe how far this company's reach extends and into what nefarious pockets it has poked its dirty fingers." She pointed to a vile streak of luminous green tinting the water. "That runoff is from Tirai's smelting plant. The organization created to spearhead the Telec's cleanup is headed by a Tirai man. The agency that oversees the cleanup organization is on Tirai's payroll and on it goes. We're gnats caught in an immense web. Tug one string and the whole thing moves. Look, I need something from you."

"From me?" Soryk was stunned. He had never considered that he might be in the position to offer anything of value to another.

"I've seen the work that you do. You've gotten far but the glaziers won't allow you to achieve anything that will threaten their hierarchy. You're an outsider, a paid laborer. You've done this well only because you're talented and they like you more than they are threatened by you. That will change."

Soryk didn't appreciate hearing his own fears so succinctly voiced. How long could he remain a journeyman, and how high could he climb the ranks before the envious glaziers tore him down? With few other options available to him, he had little choice but to follow this path toward its natural conclusion.

"What do you want with me?" He glanced at the White Lady, awed by her proximity.

"I'm working on a project in the Southern Cross and one of my suppliers has become unreliable. I no longer wish to work with him but no one can provide what I need. Except you." She faced him, her eyes shining like a panther's. A breeze blew over the river and caused him to shiver, or was it the effect of the White Lady's gaze that so thoroughly chilled him?

Reaching into her jacket, she extracted a white pocket square tucked around several small, heavy objects that she placed in his hand. Five glass marbles tumbled from the linen into his hands. Fractal light patterns sparkled like mica dust deep within the marbles' cores.

"What are these?" The tiny orbs sat heavy and solid in Soryk's hand, warming to skin temperature as he rolled them in his palm.

"They're IERs—Intelligent Energy Receptors, the Tirai giant's eyes and ears. They sense hidden intentions and can detect minute variations in sound waves that might indicate subterfuge, confusion, plotting, and intrigue. They also transmit a radial pattern of body temperature fluctuation that appear as a series of numbers. During negotiations, the numbers pop up on a flashpoint. . . ."

Soryk looked lost and the White Lady sighed. "It's a transparent light display that can be read only by someone in a specific position. From any other angle, you see nothing. They're used in every boardroom and office. The executives at Tirai use them to signal each other during messy meetings. The flashpoint numbers register the veracity of each participant. Essentially, they're little lie detectors."

Soryk now understood why he'd so often had the disquieting sense of being on display when working in the empty Tirai offices.

"Where are they hidden?" He scanned the reaches of the dark room for scattered glints of light.

"They're everywhere—melted into the walls and furniture, plastered overhead, buried in the floors. Completely undetectable by infrared, X-ray, metal detection, ultrasound, Geiger counters, stud finders, or magnets. The Tirai giant sees and hears all, but presents itself to the world as a deaf mute."

The White Lady squatted beside him to avoid touching her immaculate blankness to the dirty floor. She hugged herself and shivered, wrinkling her nose to announce, "The river smells of sulfur." She offered a calculated smile. "Have we got a deal?"

Soryk rolled the warm marbles between his fingers. They felt like ball bearings, gumballs, or candies—things innocuous and harmless, when they were anything but. He raised his eyes to the White Lady's grin, luminous in the dull light reflected by the stinking toxic river and *the livid polluted sky. He would say yes because he was eighteen and craved adventure, because she was beautiful, untouchable, and a little terrifying, and because he liked a challenge and needed to prove to himself just how good he really was.*

Later, when it was done, they would stand in this very window, illuminated by Neubonne's red chemical haze. He might feel her hands upon his back and the ground rushing up to meet him before oblivion claimed him, and it seemed to him then that it would not matter how their alliance ended, just that it should.

NUALA MORIGI, THE WHITE Lady, rarely watched what transpired in her brother's private apartments. His lewdness and frequent intoxication revolted her. However, she'd been intrigued by the appearance of his blond doxy and the aggression she displayed at the Hanging Garden, demanding her ransom from the bartender like a gangster collecting protection money. It sparked Nuala's interest, if only to see her brother forced to swallow a mouthful of his own harsh brew. Zarina departed the bar on the arm of the man Nuala recognized with a jolt of shock. Years had passed, but Soryk was nearly unchanged. His black hair was shorter and his build slightly fuller, but his soft-jawed face and mud-colored eyes were the same. She remembered the feel of his skin, the noises he uttered when teaching him her body's secrets, and his willingness to abandon himself to her teachings. How wonderful to see him again, even if from afar!

As the pedicab driver cranked slowly along the avenue, Nuala followed on her white moto, weaving between trees and parked automobiles, bumping over curbs and darting betwixt bubbling minibuses. She'd made such a habit of her evasive maneuvers it was no longer possible for her to walk or drive in a straight line. Nuala was as slippery as a serpent easing from the riverbank into the current, eyes locked on its distant victim.

Distracted by the arrival of two Company men, Nuala had eavesdropped on a meeting with the shifty Nunn and the odious Bodkin.

They spoke of profit margins and trade routes, ink extraction, fossil water distribution, and train schedules. Nuala ran her fingers along the dials of her IER reader, tuning in to Chen's frequency to analyze his reaction to the discussion. He was excited, but whether from pleasure, fear, or anger, she couldn't tell. His reading was high, while Bodkin's hardly fluctuated from its baseline. Eager to please and ridiculously overconfident, Nunn's fluttering heart betrayed his nervousness even as he attempted to match Bodkin's steely calm.

Nunn was an insignificant fly flitting among Bodkin, the bear, and Chen, the honey pot. Nuala could tell that he knew himself superfluous but Bodkin was their father's man, his history tightly entwined with Matuk's. Chen would naturally have dealings with him, though Nuala was certain that Chen didn't quite comprehend the nature of the bloodsucker he'd invited through the door. She didn't understand their talk of trains, but it was clear that Chen did and was disinterested in further discussion.

"Do what you must." Chen brushed off Bodkin's questions and immersed himself in his snuff boxes. Dosed and suddenly garrulous, Chen escorted the men to the apartment where Zarina straddled Soryk, her knife poised to plunge.

Slipping up the secret stairwell, Nuala was again glad for her advantage. Matuk had never properly mentored or groomed Chen, whereas Nuala, several years older than her brother, had the advantage of her father's expertise and a greater measure of his sanity during the years he'd trained her. She alone knew each of the hidden passages folded between the tower walls, and only Nuala had access to the IER cabinets, just as Matuk intended, for there was no one more trustworthy than his own daughter, especially one over whom he dangled a spectacularly dreadful threat.

Crouched within the small spy cabinet tucked in the gap between elevator and stairwell, Nuala watched Soryk disappear within the skin of his primary. Had Nuala not witnessed the transformation herself, she'd never have believed it possible. The concealed door and soundproof walls ensured that her exclamations would go unheard, for she had loosed a stream of speech upon seeing the juddering flashpoints on her IER reader. Calibrating Soryk's respiration, temperature, heart rate, and carbon dioxide output, numbers leaped erratically—17, 24, 3, 9, 40—in a way she'd never seen before. IER technology was consistent, reliable. The numbers should not stutter along the scale without reason, as they did now. They ought to proceed in steady order; a jump of a single digit, two at most, was permissible under extreme duress.

Chen pressed too closely to Sorykah. IERs leapt. Nuala watched her half brother pour a beaker of fluid into the woman's mouth. Chen, that glib seducer, kissed the mouth beneath his even as the body in his arms wilted and drooped across his lap. Hands rose and pushed, however weakly, against his chest. She struggled to rise, but her gestures were flaccid. Grown pointed and flushed with strange rosy heat, her face seemed to shift and slide beneath its skin as she struggled to escape Chen's weight bearing down upon her, the blue stain transferred from Nuala's brother's mouth to Sorykah's. The scream shook Nuala from her trance. Men did not scream like that, with high, warbling wails of betrayal. Staggering from the lingering effects of the changing sleep, the man Nuala had known as Soryk argued with Chen, gesticulating with slender, female hands.

Nuala hadn't been paying attention to the gossip that flew through Neubonne, a swarm of tittering locusts descending to consume the digi-reels of a Trader's change and sate its gluttonous appetite for sexual novelty. She'd thought the reels another of Chen's sordid diversions—some hedonistic moneymaking chicanery he'd unleashed upon the populace. Nuala didn't believe that Traders really existed; they were the antiheroes of myth, fabrications of the popular imagination, but Nuala had also once believed the old gods false before she proved otherwise and loosed a terrible destruction upon them. She'd done enough damage. She wouldn't let her brother inflict a serious injury on one she had once loved. Nuala took up arms and came out of hiding.

SORYKAH SMELLED THE ETHERINE before she saw the woman wielding the aerosol can. With the noiseless certainty of a stalking cat, the woman advanced into Chen's bedroom, her white clothing an assault against the room's oppressive darkness. One man fell beneath the etherine spray as the other two leapt into action, pulling guns from their pockets. Bullets hissed and guns beeped, the fight unfolding in odd silence. Clouds of sickly sweet vapor hovered in the air. The woman in white slashed one man's throat with the half-moon blade hidden in her palm. The last man knocked her to the ground but made the mistake of going for the blade first. She shot a jet of etherine into his face. He moaned and fell back, unconscious.

The woman leapt to her feet, holding out her arms as if contaminated while she scanned her clothing for smears of blood or dirt. The cut man lay twitching on the floor, blood spurting between the fingers he'd clamped to his neck. She eyed him with revulsion. He had the sleepy gaze of one disturbed during a dream. Then her expression shifted and she said, "I didn't mean to do that." Lifting the hem of her trousers to avoid the mist of blood, she sprayed etherine straight up his nostrils. He passed out immediately.

Dazed by fumes and shock, Sorykah cowered in the corner. Striking and odd, the woman in white crouched beside her, a gesture that struck Sorykah as familiar.

"I'd never have believed it if I hadn't seen it myself." The woman's olive skin was flushed.

Sorykah had the sensory memory of winding those brassy curls around her fingers.

"Soryk." Nuala inched closer, her gaze roaming over Sorykah's face and clothes. "Are you there?"

"Who are you?"

"Don't you know me?" The woman in white laid a hand upon her heart. "Nuala. We were lovers."

Sorykah stared at her. "I don't remember."

One of the men coughed and Nuala grabbed Sorykah's arm. "They're waking up. It's time to leave now. Come on!"

"Wait a minute!" Sorykah snatched the skull box from Chen's dresser and tucked it beneath her arm. *Incontrovertible proof, be gone.*

They dashed through the black suite into a tiny service closet where Nuala pried up the carpet to reveal a narrow trapdoor. She pointed at the opening. "Hop in. Get down on your hands and knees and crawl to the left."

Sorykah did as instructed, knowing that whatever Nuala had in mind couldn't be any worse than staying behind to endure Chen committing her changes to digi-reel.

Nuala followed Sorykah through the crawl space until they reached an intersection. She directed Sorykah up a ladder and out into another service closet.

"It's safe here," she announced as they stepped from the closet into an unoccupied office. The lights flickered on, illuminating a small, windowless room. Layers of dust coated the bare desk and bookshelves.

Sorykah marveled that she'd stayed present through all the excitement. She had grown used to trading gender whenever her emotional equilibrium was disturbed. Thanks to the octameroon ink, she'd finally discovered a way to rein in her body's whims. Farouj's warning rang in her head, *"You'll never be free of its urges."* Ink-lust might ruin her, too, leave her desperate to attain the only tool she'd ever found capable of halting her transformations. Sorykah wanted only to flee the tower, find Farouj, and get back home—but Ostara wasn't the safe haven she imagined, was it? Chen kept tabs on her. He held the purse strings and would easily strangle her with them if she displeased him. She'd have to disappear with her children and find a new job, a new home. The prospect was daunting.

Miffed by the damage done to her pristine garments, Nuala said, "My clothes are dirty. I have to change."

"I don't see anything," Sorykah said. "You're fine."

"No, it's there. I *feel* it. I have to change." The White Lady stood on the chair, shoved aside a ceiling tile, retrieved a stack of folded white clothing, and quickly stripped down to her underwear. Sorykah averted her eyes but there was nothing else to look at in that barren room, and her attention soon returned to Nuala, whose navel wore a flap of skin, like the drooping lid of a dozy eye.

"You used to say I watched you even when I slept." Nuala zipped up her trousers. Her bare belly disappeared beneath a white pullover, and the fleeting remembrance of the sight of her body had coaxed from Soryk/ah's memory faded.

"Tell me about us. I don't remember you, but I think you speak the truth."

"I was training you to make Intelligent Energy Receptors." Nuala tucked her soiled clothes into the ceiling and replaced the tile. "We lived here while my father was building the Quartz Tower."

"Matuk is your father? That makes Chen your brother . . ."

Bleakly, Nuala said, "Half brother. We had different mothers. We weren't raised together."

Sorykah felt ill. She'd been rescued from the quicksand by a viper. She would never escape this family's clutches. "You support him."

"Never! I am only here to do my job—to be Tirai's eyes and ears."

"What do you do with the information you gather? Report back to your father? Chen?"

"Does it matter?"

"Yes, it matters!"

"I do my duty, as I must." Nuala lowered her voice, as if betraying a confidence. "Matuk deceived me. He knew my secrets and used them against me. Still, I do what he demands, because there's no other option for me. I chose to make a sacrifice. . . ."

"I don't understand. What power could they hold over you?"

Nuala blew dust from the desk before she perched on the edge and told Sorykah her story. With a listless voice, she spoke of returning to Neubonne to discover that Matuk had already sent the *Nimbus* on a mission to capture octameroons. The men were too enthralled by their liaisons with Matuk's daughter to resist gossiping about them. When Matuk realized the ink's potential, he had to capitalize upon it. Nuala described a nightmare without end. Matuk built the fossil water factory far from the Sigue as a guise for the octameroon farm hidden in its depths. He captured and kept Ur's children, milked their ink, then bottled and sold it to tattoo artists he'd recruited and trained. He took the lion's share of profits. No one objected. They were all getting rich. It wasn't until Matuk refused Chen's offer to distribute bluing and strawberry milk at the tattoo shops that relations between competing Morigis grew sticky.

"Matuk didn't want anything to detract from his earnings. Why should he let his son muscle into his market and woo clients away from his very lucrative trade?" Nuala said. "So Chen decided to launch a coup de main the quickest way possible—by killing him."

Mission accomplished, Sorykah thought ruefully.

"Everyone continues as before, but there are disruptions and strange alliances brewing. Chen and Bodkin have some nasty gimmick up their sleeves. There's too much tension within TI. Too many hands in too many pockets. It's getting ugly."

"And you," Sorykah asked. "Who are you loyal to?" *Besides the memory of our long-ago affair?* Sorykah could not imagine that her alter had been intimate with this stoic, rather intimidating woman. Nuala had rescued her but she was Morigi, and thus as unreliable as summer storm clouds.

"Loyalty means nothing here. I do what I can to stem the trade by destroying the Botanica's tattoo parlors. Chen's thugs are too dumb to confirm that he's the one actually issuing orders. It's easy to deceive them by sending instructions in the guise of my brother. Chen's too wrapped up in his own world to care about what looks like a rash of petty crimes. At least I can do that much. You should go now. They'll be looking for you."

Chen said Kirwan was an ink rat. Was it true? Had he really pawned himself for a few tattoos? She couldn't leave him behind. "They mentioned another like me . . ."

Nuala pulled her IER reader from her pocket and fiddled with the tuning mechanism. "There is someone in the penthouse suite who's been there for several days. His readings are strange, just like yours. Others come and go, but he does not."

Sorykah's heart leapt. "Can you take me to him?"

"Yes, but then you have to leave. My brother's like a dog. Once he gets his teeth in something, he never wants to let it go. He'll scour the city for you. Get out of Neubonne as soon as you can. Go far away and don't ever come back."

KIRWAN WAS DYING. The ink was too strong. Uncut and unfiltered, swarming with pathogens that consumed muscle and fat, leaving him a ragged skeleton with the chitinous stare of a blind octameroon. As gelatinous as congealed blood, the ink that Chen provided was tangy and acidic. It ate through the ceramic mixing dishes; Jandi's complaints soon yielded scooped-out beach stones carted up from the Sigue and dense enough to repel the ink's corrosive nature. Stinking of decay, it hissed when she applied water—a liquid demon.

The doorbell chimed and Zarina waved a finger, directing the Plaid Lad to admit a clutch of paid slags: a female ink rat not yet too far gone; a couple of fancy boys with fake fur jackets, tight jeans, and crests of stiff, pomaded hair; and one young and rather frightened-looking girl. Woolley-Wallace pinched the girl's bottom and sucked a toothpick, settling comfortably on the couch to watch the filming. Zarina yawned immensely while Jandi sat nervously wafting one hand as if cooling a burn. Spotlights and cameras clicked on and Kirwan stumbled into place like a robot, his limbs shaking and movements jerky. The fancy boys went to work immediately, not even bothering to remove the gum from their mouths. Kirwan arched and thrashed, eyes rolling, saliva bubbling from his lips.

Jandi looked away. She hated to see Kirwan so entirely enslaved, and despised her own role in his humiliation. Kirwan spasmed

broadly, much to the dismay of the ink rat sitting beside him who ignored his twitches with pointed and evident disdain.

Scot sidled over to Jandi.

"Have you hurt yourself, love?" His voice was softer, a bit more
cultured now, and Jandi noticed.

"So it's all an act. I knew something wasn't right about you!"

Scot took Jandi's wrist in hand and inspected her palm. Bravado
surged from some hidden source, emboldening him. "I don't see
anything."

"There! I pricked myself with the needle. It's never happened before. My hands were cramping with the odd angle."

Indeed, a single black dot marred her pretty skin. She stayed his
hand, urgent in her warning. "Don't touch it! You'll activate it."

Warmed by the new, growing sensation of protective desire and illuminated by his sudden awakening to emotion—for Jandi saw the
lights come on inside him and transform his plain, pasty face into
something receptive and interesting—Barret Scot, scholarship boy,
sent a whisper of breath over Jandi's skin. It electrified the dot of ink
beneath her dermis and something like the blooming of a poppy—
what she could only describe as "red"—flowered from a single
fingertip.

Behind them Kirwan took it six ways, spittle bubbling from his
open lips as the rent boys abused him like some wad of play dough.

"I should like very much to remove you from this place," Scot
murmured, shaking off the pretense of street tough.

Eager to grasp any lifeline offered, Jandi grabbed at the chance.
"I'd like that as well."

"This is the last film." Scot's neck crawled with the intensity of the
Plaid Lad's narrow eyes upon them. "I offer you no false hope. Your
executions are already planned."

Jandi pressed the ink dot, hoping to alleviate some of the terror
that crawled over her like a beetle. "What can we do?"

"I shall lead you to the killing floor. Dispose of you myself. Despite his aggression, my mate there has a weak stomach when it

comes to actually spilling blood by hand. He'll be happy to turn the task to me." Scot carefully wiped his aviator glasses on his shirt, a gesture at odds with the nylon ferocity of his slicked-back appearance. "All right, love? I know these are odd circumstances to request that you trust me, but you have few options at this point."

Jandi nodded, the room around them—its noisy copulations, the whirring of digi-reel cameras, the almost audible irritation emanating from Zarina and the Plaid Lad, and the wet sucking sounds of moist flesh—faded into the distant, steady static of a radio tuner hovering between stations. Butterscotch had pale green eyes the color of lake water, and they glowed with subtle warmth when he gazed at her. Even Jandi's former husband hadn't looked at her with such obvious adoration on their wedding day. *Who are you? Why are you here? Where will we go? What comes next?* Questions filled the air between them. In those brief seconds, Scot, transformed by a deeply profound, instantaneous attachment, conveyed that whatever happened, they would be all right. "Simply follow all instructions with the confidence that I shall get you out of this." He stood, pulling down the guise of hired thug like a mask. He looked at her coldly for Woolley-Wallace's benefit, and hid his lake water eyes behind the aviator glasses.

During each day of her service, a gaggle of silent goons guarded Jandi and Kirwan at every moment. When Kirwan wrapped the last digi-reel, Zarina finally got up from the couch and paid the slags in cash and trade: tiny bottles of ink and cardboard ring boxes packed with crumbling blue sugar cubes. She sneered at Jandi, made disgusted noises at Kirwan, and departed, leaving them alone among the debris of his degradation.

Nearly comatose from excess, Kirwan sprawled naked on the bed, twitching with the aftershocks of the change, his body shifting between male and female. The Plaid Lad stood riveted by Kirwan's changing spectacle, like a dog nosing a particularly fragrant turd. Jandi threw a blanket over Kirwan's body, breaking the spell. The Plaid Lad snorted, tugged his crotch, and retreated.

Scot entered wearing a shower cap, rubber gloves and boots, and a butcher's apron. Jandi nearly threw up at the sight of him, menacing and cloaked for a clean kill. He apologized in advance for killing Kirwan and said quietly, "I'm sorry, you know, I just thought it would be easiest if it was me. Rather than the alternative." His fingers flexed around a pistol handle. "I really have to shoot you. They'd believe that I bungled one but not both terminations." He spoke as though reading lines by rote, detached from the meaning of the words themselves. "They watch us, you see."

"Here's how it happens," Scot said quietly, advancing on Kirwan's prone form. "I'm meant to shoot you both, one bullet to the brain, after which I shall string you up in the bath, slit your throats, and let you bleed out like pigs."

Ah ha, Jandi thought, now realizing the purpose of those sturdy hooks mounted in the ceiling over the large, deep bathtub. She hadn't been able to suss it out before, the sheets of polished silver that lined the walls in place of tiles and absorbent, bloodthirsty grout.

"Then I simply wrap you in plastic and tip your bodies down the rubbish chute, straight into the incinerator. Bloodless bodies burn faster and with less odor than those full of liquid. But this is our best chance to escape. They let the bodies hang for hours before tossing them out. Once you're strung up, they lose all interest and won't check on you for ages." Scot stood over Kirwan and aimed his pistol at the Trader's head. A muscle twitched on Scot's cheek, some nervous tic that assured Jandi he did not relish this moment. He fired the pistol. A low-toned electronic beep was the only noise to indicate that the gun had launched a bullet deep into the smoking hole a millimeter from Kirwan's skull. Blood seeped from the surface wound and soaked the pillow. Kirwan did not stir.

"For effect," he mouthed, turning on her. Jandi shrank into sofa cushions, her mind catapulting from one extreme emotion to another. He would save her. No, this had all been foreplay to him, a ruse to leave her supple and compliant. He stood over her and she smelled latex and blood. Jandi was wildly distracted by the polka-dotted shower cap on Scot's head and the gleaming hunting knife jammed through a back belt loop. For one terrible moment, she thought that he really meant to kill her, then he raised his sunglasses and she saw his serene eyes. "Trust me, Jandi," he said, so softly that she was certain she had imagined it.

"This is going to sting a bit," he announced, pressing the pistol barrel to Jandi's skull. For the second time, she heard that low electronic beep and then nothing more.

"Wake up, love! It's over." Scot shook Jandi's shoulders. Her eyes popped open. "Really, that was most convincing! I'd have thought you dead had I not known you were merely pretending. Come on, my darling, on your feet."

Jandi tumbled from the plastic sheet Scot had trussed her up in. Sweat pasted her clothing to her skin. Blood clotted the wound on her head and she was a bit frantic, but otherwise, very happy to be alive. "I wasn't sure there, for a minute. You had a crazy look in your eye."

"Acting!" Scot chirped. "It would have been my concentration at university had *mater* and *pater* not put their feet down. Let's make a move."

The deserted basement had a creepy vibe that rattled Scot's nerves. There were too many spiders, shadowy corners, and strange clanking noises. The incinerator wheezed and roared as it devoured the sheeting and Scot's apron, knife, and shower cap.

"Up you go! That's right, love, straight through the coal door." Scot put his hands on Jandi's bum, pushing her through the small opening.

"Hey! Watch yourself!"

Scot scrambled across heaps of coal, where the deliveryman dumped his weekly load. The door locked from the inside and only the coal man had a key to the other side. He couldn't fasten it behind them. A head start was their best defense against discovery.

"Apologies, my darling. Just anxious to be out and away." Scot grinned, thinking that he'd never again wash his hands. His message pad trilled, indicating a new alert.

"My mate's on his way to the penthouse to tidy up for the next film. Faster, girl! Haul yourself through!" Bile filled Scot's mouth as he imagined Woolley-Wallace's reaction when he discovered his birds flown the coop. He'd purple with rage, his stiff little limbs vibrating with the urge to pummel and bully Scot.

Scot and Jandi landed on their feet in the alley. Triumph elated Barret Scot. He'd gotten the girl. He was free. The feeling that had weighed him down slid off his shoulders, leaving him exhilarated. If only he'd had the courage to stand up to Woolley-Wallace years ago, but then, he'd not have met Jandi.

Scot marveled at the insane risk he'd taken by faking two executions. He meant to kill Kirwan; he just couldn't do it in front of Jandi. He wanted her to think highly of him. Soon enough, someone would discover Kirwan in the penthouse bathroom just as Scot had left him—semiconscious and bleeding. He'd been alive when Scot hung him up on the draining hook, and that was good enough. That poor sod would be better off if Woolley-Wallace finished him. Ink rats led short, miserable lives. There was nothing for Kirwan to look forward to but death. Scot took a deep lungful of morning air. However acrid and unpleasant, it was the beginning of a new day and a new era.

"What now?" Jandi could take off alone, but Scot had proven himself trustworthy and affable. She had no shop to return to and her best client hung from a hook a hundred stories above them. Chen and the Plaid Menace might come after her, or Zarina with her ranks of speechless TI zombies. Best to stick with Butterscotch for the time being. When he smiled at her, he was actually quite nice looking. She could do much worse, and had.

Scott brushed coal dust from Jandi's white dreads. His fingers trembled when he pulled them away and he eyed them in surprise. They stared at each other, marveling in the baffling intensity of a sudden attraction.

Scot plucked the metal C from his lapel and tossed it on the ground. The future belonged to them. "Wherever we go," he told Jandi, "we shall go together."

19

PUSH THE NEEDLE

HUNG BY HIS ANKLES, Kirwan dangled above the bathtub. Blood dripped from his pale hair onto the white porcelain, its stain barely long enough to spill a few precious drops into the drain.

Sorykah gagged at the sight of him. Instinct suppressed her fear and she climbed into the tub, lifting his head on her arms. "Help me take him down!" she cried.

Nuala balanced on the tub's rim while she and Sorykah easily lifted Kirwan's slight frame enough to loosen the bindings from the hook. He folded into their outstretched arms, a paper doll with cardboard bones. Sorykah had not seen him since the night of the children's conception, nearly two years earlier. Wasted and brutally thin, Kirwan's deep complexion had turned sallow. Gray ghosts and bruises spattered his skin. Carelessly hacked off, his hair jutted from his skull in tufts. His silver eyes, so like their daughter Ayeda's, rotated slowly in sunken sockets and fixed on her, unseeing.

Theirs had been a fleeting fancy because Sorykah finally admitted to herself that she could not exist in a vacuum—her body craved touch. Kirwan, probably taking her only to satisfy the ink-itch that must have been newer and stronger then, had been handsome, charming, and kind as one is kind to those to whom there is no obligation or promise.

Sorykah remembered the tattoo he'd sported that night: an enormous liquid-suspended mermaid that rode his belly, her hair entwined with the faded lettering on his chest—"let the depredation commence"—the mermaid's tail descending beneath the waistband of his trousers to slap his privates with her fishy fins.

Sorykah laid a hand on his, bony and rough beneath her own soft skin. "Do you remember me?"

Kirwan stared, his mouth slack. Purple phlegm slimed over his lip and across his chin. Tears blurred Sorykah's vision. He was destroyed. There was no point in telling him about the babies, not that she'd intended to anyway. She might have offered it to him as a deathbed gift, but now she saw that he had already fled into the shades and left this collapsing wreck behind.

"Remember? You gave me your Magar blade." She wished she had it with her, could press it into his hand and convey its killing strength to him. Nuala was distracted by displays on her IER reader, so Sorykah whispered, "It was the blade that slew Matuk the Collector. I killed him with it, *your* blade." *And with it,* she thought, *unleashed his son's deadly wrath, which he has turned upon you and which will devour you.*

"Kirwan," she repeated. "Do you know me?"

He nodded vaguely, his head floppy upon a weak neck.

"Can you walk?" She could not leave him here. He was the father of her children. It was her duty to save him, or at least to try. However casually, he'd given her the two best things in her life. If, some future day, the twins inquired what had become of their father, at least she would have this story to tell, some brief vision of him to offer: "He was very ill. He died loving you." She planned the lie guiltlessly. It was nothing—a trick-tongue or pesky fly to shoo away.

Traders came into being only through a genetic fluke so rare that perhaps only a handful existed among the world's inhabitants at one time. The second method of creating Traders, well, she had experienced that firsthand after a fruitful one-night stand. Discovering the twins' ability to change had come as a dreadful shock. Frequently had she chastised herself for not sensing Kirwan's difference that night. How could she have been so blind, so self-absorbed? Two Traders together—the odds were so small, she wished she'd been able to place a bet on it and set herself up for life. Sorykah slithered beneath Kirwan's arm, hoisted it onto her shoulder, and levered his weight onto her back. Nuala draped a bedsheet over Kirwan's naked body.

Tucking the sheet between them, Sorykah asked, "Which way?"

"Follow me." Careful to keep her distance from Kirwan and his soiling leakage of blood, Nuala slid aside a marble wall panel, allowing the three to enter a network of low corridors just wide enough to traverse by walking sideways. Like a mouse within the walls, Nuala scurried through twists and turns, guiding Sorykah toward a hidden service elevator. Though Kirwan was light, Sorykah's muscles ached under the strain of carrying him. It was a relief to deposit him on the floor of the lift, less so to realize that Nuala was abandoning them.

"Go down to level B, and follow the staircase to the green doors," Nuala said. "One leads to the Quartz Tower, the other to the incinerator and garbage rooms. Keep your feet on the seam in the floor— there's a blind spot where you won't be seen. There's a coal chute behind the incinerator. It's your safest exit."

"You're not coming with me?" Daunted by the prospect of disposing of Kirwan and finding her way back to Farouj, Sorykah wanted an ally.

"It wouldn't serve either of us. My place is here. Whatever devotion I had to Soryk remains with him. I've done all that I can. I'm sorry." Nuala pushed the elevator button and closed the gate.

"Wait! Take this." Sorykah thrust the box at Nuala. "Matuk's skull. Chen had it."

Nuala's expression was grim, but she accepted the box and pushed the elevator button.

"He said that the board required physical proof of Matuk's death to transfer majority control of TI." Sorykah shouted, "Better you than him, right?" As the elevator descended into the shadows, Sorykah hoped she hadn't made a terrible mistake.

Kirwan twitched as consciousness returned. At least his legs seemed to work, for he shuffled mechanically beside her, groaning like a ghost.

I know what ghosts sound like. Sorykah thought of Matuk's murdered wife Tirai, a terrifying vision in the Collector's chamber room and a blot upon her eye. "You sound as if you're calling long-distance," she said to Kirwan, kicking open the unlocked coal door and pushing him out into the muggy morning air.

Warily scanning the alley for the presence of Chen and his flunkies, Sorykah was relieved to find it deserted. She imagined that thwarted Zarina paced the penthouse floors, gnashing her teeth and nursing fatal fantasies of revenge.

"I'm taking you home. Where do you live?" She could see Kirwan's house in her mind, a boxy, modern building perched on a cliff overlooking Neubonne and the Telec River, but she could not recall the address. "What street? Come on, tell me."

Kirwan mumbled something and began to shake. Sorykah propped him against a power box jutting from the pavement. *Useless,* she thought. It would be easier to discard him on the curb like the sack of refuse he resembled. Kirwan would soon return to his desperate, shabby existence while Sorykah left Neubonne, with or without Farouj. They'd never see each other again. He barely even remembered her. She eyed him, wondering how she'd feel if she simply walked away from him. But she saw shades of her daughter in his face, in the silver of his eyes and the yellow feathers of his matted hair. *Shit shit shit,* she grumbled, hoisting him to his feet.

Sorykah hailed a pedicab and shoved Kirwan into the seat. She suspected that if Kirwan was a serious ink junkie, his club circuit would be familiar to Neubonne's regular pedicab and minibus drivers. He'd get his tattoos, head to the Dregs or the Garden first, and failing to score there, venture from the Botanica to the seedier bars like the Pitviper, Spawn, or Club Quartier to dredge the barrel bottom. He'd had money at the start; likely that he was known, brought his girls home, and sent them back again when he was done. She gripped Kirwan's jaw between her fingers and angled his face toward the driver. "Look at him. Do you know him?"

The driver, a black-haired man with the high cheekbones of a Sigue native, scanned Kirwan's face and shrugged.

"*Siguelander, arc es ma'khin?*" Sorykah asked again in his own tongue.

He stared at her.

"*Arc es ma'khin?* Do you know him?" she demanded.

The driver nodded.

"*Es pors dué a son samela.* Take us to his house." She hoped that she had correctly conjugated her verbs. Otherwise, she'd just asked this man to build her son a house. Since he began pedaling without comment, she guessed that she'd gotten it right.

It was grainday and the whole city smelled of baking bread. Fanciful Haymaz loaves, glazed braids, and stuffed buns filled bakery windows, promising sustenance in the new year. The pedicab creaked and swayed as they bumped over the joints of the North Fork bridge and slalomed through traffic.

Kirwan's house was high on a hill but the driver did not tire or complain, even when they were moving so slowly that Sorykah could've gotten out and walked and beaten him home. There were few dwellings here, mostly old wooden houses built before the last war, drafty and shifting on their foundations amid stretches of tall, fragrant grass. It was peaceful. Traffic died down along this private road. The morning sprawled thick and humid with the competing odors of spring wildflowers and the fetid Telec, reeking of spilled petroleum and rotting garbage.

Sorykah urged the driver through the broken gates of a house she recognized, disembarked, and watched him pedal away, the noise of his tires against the gravel diminishing to a faint and sandy hush. Was someone watching them? The broad courtyard was empty; its planters spilled over with decayed vegetation. There was no sound but for the occasional chirping of a bird and the creak of rusted wind chimes. Sorykah searched the yard and road, saw no glint of metal or human movement, deemed it safe, and turned her back.

"Come on, you." Sorykah hooked her arms beneath Kirwan's and dragged him toward the door. She was surprised to discover it open, but once inside, it was clear that there was nothing of value left for thieves to steal.

Kirwan's cavernous rooms rang with their footsteps. Sorykah's heavy breathing echoed as she dumped Kirwan on a lumpy, bare mattress pushed into a corner. This had once been the receiving room for visitors. Beyond the double doors at its end lay a private parlor, its niched walls beset with treasures, the home of her Magar blade. Sorykah investigated the ransacked rooms, each one sadly barren. Dirt and leaves lined the floor, blown in from the yard through a shattered windowpane. The story of Kirwan's decline was etched on the walls. Blank spaces remained where he had ripped away artwork to pawn. The empty shelves were a testament to his desperation, and splinters along the wooden floor planking revealed gaps and gashes where Kirwan had pried up furnishings and carpets to sell.

Deep gouges marked the plaster; it was as if a wolf had been kept caged there. A frieze of decorative moldings lined the wall several inches from the floor, and there too were signs of abuse. Sorykah bent to examine the chipped and splintered wood.

"Are those teeth marks?" she marveled. Yes—she traced a perfect bite mark snipped from the enameled wood, like a half-eaten cookie.

She rubbed her sore back, the site of Chen's tattoo. The ink didn't seem to do much for her; admittedly it was both a relief and a disappointment. Where was her blinding, screaming ecstasy? Why wasn't she scratching troughs in the plaster with her fingernails, biting great chunks of wood from the walls, and capsizing on orgiastic seas?

Though they had nothing in common but the babies and their one night together, Kirwan captivated Sorykah. Finally, she was with one of her own. She was in no great rush to say goodbye to the only other person she knew who understood the tragic complications of a Trader's life.

Kirwan groaned. Sweat dripped from him like water from a spout. His square jaw had softened and grown smooth. Sorykah knelt beside him, opening the sheet to reveal pointed miniature mounts topped by pink snow that radically altered the topography of his former shape. She couldn't resist. She squeezed one and murmured, "Hmm." *They're real, all right. Fascinating.* Is this how people felt when they looked at her after a change, as if she were a specimen in a zoo? Everyone always gave in to their urges to press and prod her flesh, reassuring themselves that Soryk/ah, in either incarnation, was still human and real, not the inhabitant of a dream.

Kirwan's changing-smell was a too-strong perfume, rich and cloying. She feared that it would pull her under its spell and put her body in flux, but the deeply injected octameroon ink seemed to have the marvelous and astonishing effect of paralyzing the change. Once it wore off, she'd again be susceptible to rapid permutations of gender. She had to get away.

She stumbled back, tripped over a broken water pitcher, and landed hard on her back. It hurt, but the force of the fall irritated the ink inside her skin. Maybe the stuff needed more elbow grease to become active? Chen did say it took a while to work. A small wave burbled hopefully, but did not crest. She felt some insubstantial thrill, unlike any natural human sensation. It felt like the first staticky burn when anesthesia begins to wear off and feeling returns.

"You've had a look." Kirwana sat up, robe gaping open, the room's coolness making her thin chest quiver. She still looked like an ink rat—one that had escaped an ugly brawl.

"If you hadn't woken, I'd have taken everything off. Consider

yourself lucky." Sorykah smiled crookedly. The ink was making her
loopy, randy. Kirwan did not care about his bared breasts. *She*,
Sorykah corrected, perplexed that she should still grapple with gender pronouns when her own identity was so flexible.

Kirwana skimmed Sorykah's figure, taking in the patchwork of
blood on her shirt. "How long have you had art?" which meant also,
Will you share your vice with me? Kirwana wished for some sort of
dipstick with which to measure Sorykah's depravity.

"This is my first. I'm not sure I like it." Sorykah lifted her shirt to
display the tattoo. Three stippled lines marked her swollen flesh.

"Your ink is too deep. It won't activate there. Why did you inject
it so far below the skin?" Kirwan's female alter had a slow, husky
voice.

"I didn't. Someone else's idea." *Chen.* The name sat heavy on
Sorykah's tongue.

Ink manipulated her flesh and obfuscated her thoughts. It was all
she could do to keep from freaking out. The simple image Chen injected beneath her skin seemed to writhe beneath her fingers.

"I swear, I feel it moving," she murmured, transfixed.

"Only because it's still new to you. Your senses haven't been
dulled by it yet." Kirwana groaned, struggling to piece together the
journey from the Onyx Tower suite to the empty house. "Did you
bring me here?"

"Yes. Don't you remember?" Did Kirwan also share Sorykah's rare
affliction, the Perilous Curse, a disease of memory?

"Sort of. I feel like crap, actually." Kirwan's alter stared at Sorykah,
trying to place her. "I remember you. Come back for another go?
You can see there's nothing left."

"I'm not here for that. I just couldn't leave you with those monsters. They left you to die. They were going to incinerate your body.
How would I tell my children that I'd let their father come to such a
cruel end?" Sorykah clapped a hand to her mouth. She hadn't
meant to blurt it out like that.

"Children?" There was a long pause while Kirwana digested this information. "There was just the one time. One time, one child, at most. Are you sure it's mine?"

"They're twins," Sorykah said. "You look like a woman but you sound just like a man. I hope I'm not as callous as you when I'm male." Another slip. She was distracted by the heat that seemed to radiate from the tattoo cranking up the dial on her internal thermostat.

"When you're male," Kirwana said with a low laugh. "Don't you know that it's not nice to tease? You're nothing like me. I've been with you. You're an ordinary woman. People pay for my services. What do they give you for yours?"

She annoyed her. "I'm valuable enough for Zarina to have tried to kill me twice, and for Chen to sell digi-reels of my change. Yours, too. We're on the same reel."

Kirwana barely lifted an eyebrow in surprise. "Well, one does what one must. If that's true, you should have changed by now. We're contagious to each other, don't you know? We avoid each other like the plague. Who wants to shape-shift all night long? It's a nightmare."

"Then why haven't you changed back?"

Kirwana was surprised by this. "I don't know. It's like a yawn, I guess. As long as you don't do it, I should be okay. You stayed in character that night."

"My control was better then," she remarked ruefully. "I have to get out of here. Bad feelings all around." She peeked from the unadorned window, searching the barren courtyard, but there was no one there. "I thought I heard something."

"Whatever." Kirwana shrugged. "The sooner you're gone, the sooner I can get back to being myself."

"Just like that, with no preliminary. Isn't some sort of instigating factor required? Mine kicks in at times of high emotion. It's nearly impossible to manage," Sorykah said.

"You can train yourself to change when you want to. It's a talent that comes in handy. You just concentrate on it. Imagine the parts you want puffing up or disappearing beneath your hands."

"Do you lose memories? Wake up not knowing where you've been?"

"Only if I've been drinking. And that, sweetheart, is what we in the business call a blackout." Kirwana gave a lazy half smile and rubbed the gray ghosts dancing beneath the skin at the site of her most recent tattoo. "If you were hoping for some sort of happy family reunion, it's not gonna happen. Babies aren't my thing. I'd be a lousy father . . . or mother," she amended, eyeing her breasts.

Sorykah was nervous. She really ought to leave now but sunshine assaulted the empty courtyard and would spotlight her every move. Then there was that miles-long slog down the hill, over the bridge, and back to town, all on foot. She was hungry, thirsty, and tired. The stained mattress was beginning to have a certain appeal.

Agitated, Kirwana rubbed her skin, digging in with the palm of her hand. Pathetically scrofulous Kirwana didn't care how unappealing she was. "Since you're here, why not help me scratch this itch?"

Sorykah shuddered at the thought of sex with this dirty, blood-caked wretch. Kirwana was nothing like the man she'd been the night they'd conceived the children. She sought some lingering connection, some memory or fond reminiscence, but, barring Sorykah's sense of duty toward Kirwan/a, nothing united them.

"Prefer me as a man? I can do that. Watch." Kirwana closed her eyes in concentration. Moaning and rocking her bony frame, she convulsed and shook. The changing smell flooded the room and made Sorykah nauseous. She could taste Kirwan's androgen on her tongue. Sleep crested inside her, filling her with transformative urges. The ink was a levee holding back the hormonal flood.

Kirwan shifted and opened his eyes. *He* smiled weakly. Sorykah fell to her knees beside him. The mattress was wet with sweat. She ran a finger along his jaw, over the lump of Adam's apple now prominent in his throat. Even his eyebrows were thicker and more unruly than just a few moments before. She saw herself in him, a lost and lonely person desperately clinging to some elusive fantasy of normalcy.

"I've never—" her voice caught in her throat. "—never known another. It's almost impossible to think that you are real."

"Not real," he murmured. "No one ever sees me. They see only my freakishness, something they want to hold in their hands and bite into like an apple. The change is who I am. It's the only thing I have left to give the world."

The scent that had repulsed her just a few minutes earlier was now strangely enticing. Only the deep tattoo stymied her conversion. How would she feel knowing that Kirwan knew how to prevent the change and withheld the secret from her?

Pity and compassion were too entangled for Sorykah to understand which one motivated her to ask Kirwan, "Do you have any ink here? And a hypodermic needle or a razor blade? I want to show you something."

"Me with ink?" Kirwan's laugh was a dry rattle. "That's like asking a dead man if he's got any life left in 'im. If I had ink—" he raised himself on an elbow and met her gaze with pinpoint pupils—"I wouldn't share it with you. Tourist!"

"Forget it then." Sorykah purpled beneath a mortified rush of embarrassment, shame, and regret. She hadn't known him when they made the babies, but then, she hadn't known they were making babies.

Something—a memory stirred, the expression on her face— made him cuff her lightly on the arm and mumble an apology. "Sorry, I forgot my manners. It's been a long time since I had any company." He licked his lips and grinned conspiratorially. "There's a drop I keep for emergencies. Nicked it off a rat in the Garden last week."

"But don't you want to save it?"

"Lady, I have an emergency damn near every day!" This time, his laughter was genuine. "Have to keep replenishing my stash. There's a kit taped to the underside of the kitchen sink. When you get back, you can show me this marvelous trick of yours and tell me about these so-called babies."

A SLEEK BLACK AUTOMOBILE CREPT uphill. Gravel crunched beneath its wheels, just as it had beneath the wheels of the pedicab that passed them on its way down. It was unusual to see a pedicab so far outside the city—few drivers were capable of such long journeys. Zarina clapped her hands as she watched him pass, certain that she closed in on her quarry.

A sensation akin to sexual arousal warmed her skin. She would not fail this time. The pleasure of a kill delayed taunted her, teasing with infinitely feathery strokes. She wanted nothing but the thrill of taking Sorykah's life. She tapped the shoulder of the man driving the car, and he swiveled around to face her. "Park outside the gates. Yes, stop here."

"Right you are, miss." Woolley-Wallace eased the private car into a sloping ditch beneath the low branches of a massive oak tree. He studied the house's chalky red façade, its broken gates, and the high weeds pushing apart squares of sidewalk. "You sure this is it? Looks deserted to me."

"I'm positive. The rent boys said they'd attended ink parties here. Kirwan's lived in this house for years. He's known in every tattoo parlor, pawnshop, and bar in Neubonne. What can I say?" Zarina exited the car, squinting in the noonday sun. "Bad habits leave a trail."

Woolley-Wallace had a new suit of green and purple tartan. He considered stashing his jacket and beanie in the car for safekeeping but changed his mind at the last minute, figuring that it was better to don full regalia in a battle than run at it half-cocked in shirtsleeves.

Zarina waved him over to the side of the house to stand guard while she explored the property. Its faded glory shone through every chipped tile and curl of peeling paint. There were three modular levels, each with its own expansive balcony and rows of beveled windows, most of them shuttered. Gentle hills rolled around the house, and she imagined that the upper levels offered a panoramic view of the Telec, Neubonne, hills, and ocean. Though mildew stained the wooden window frames and ivy gnawed at the stucco, the house had marvelous character. With a lot of labor, it could regain its former magnificence. She wondered if Kirwan had considered selling, but then where would he go? The house was the only thing of value that he owned besides his own skin, and both of those decrepit shells declined in value daily. Still, if Kirwan were out of the picture, no one would stop her from moving in. Chen could easily approve the property transfer and this magnificent house would be hers. It was fair payment for her services.

Zarina hated somatics and Traders, but she hated Sorykah even more. Zarina blamed Sorykah for everything bad that had happened to her in the past year. Sorykah was responsible for Elu's death, for if she had not captivated him so, Zarina would not have had to shoot down their hot-air balloon and send Elu plunging to his bloody end. Sorykah was responsible for Carensa's poisoning, too, because Zarina simply couldn't stand listening to the girl's constant eulogizing of Elu, or her fantasies about Trader life and Soryk. It was Sorykah's fault that Chen had gone mental after the death of his father, pitched from guilt to gladness at Matuk's demise. Had Sorykah not bumbled back into their lives, Zarina would be decorating her own house by now, not monitoring the penthouse captives. Most of all, Zarina hated seeing that gleam of intrigue in Chen's eye. Nauseating.

Woolley-Wallace jiggled in agitation, impatient to start cracking skulls. He snapped his fingers, and Zarina hurled a chunk of broken concrete at him. Woolley-Wallace ceased snapping. Sorykah appeared in the window, squinting and anxious. Zarina signaled the Plaid Lad to enter the front door and restrain Kirwan, as planned. She freed the clasp on the knife hilt and her stiletto slid down her sleeve into her hand. She'd let Woolley-Wallace kill Kirwan, or better yet, she'd do it herself. Kirwan would be a nice little dessert to add to her murderous menu. *Sweets to the sweet*, she thought, and followed Woolley-Wallace into the house.

"YOU MUST HAVE SOMETHING HERE. You have to eat once in a while," Sorykah called from the kitchen. The ink was there, in a mildewed bag beneath the sink. She put the tiny vial of octameroon ink into her pocket. There was nothing else, though, not even a cracker crumb or tea bag. She turned the tap, which spat and hissed, empty of water.

Voices sounded from the front room. Terror zinged along Sorykah's spine. *Zarina.* She froze, paralyzed by panic. Zarina padded from room to room, searching for her. Sorykah had only a moment to act. She would not allow Zarina to deprive the twins of both parents. One of them had to survive, and it couldn't be Kirwan. Sorykah darted for the mudroom door. The slide lock resisted and then gave with a squeal. Shaking, Sorykah pulled the door closed behind her. The patio behind the house was an empty expanse of hot tile. Steps led down to a drained pool with a foot of green muck at its bottom. Beyond that, an iron fence barricaded the property. She would have to run around the front and chance being spotted by Zarina and the Plaid Lad. There was a gap in the fence where a rusted post had broken away. Sorykah hurled herself toward it and away from the scream that sounded behind her, a harpy's vengeful cry. *Don't look!* she commanded, resisting the desire to turn around and catch Zarina's eye. She squeezed through the gap, her breasts painfully crushed between the fence rails. She was stuck.

"You can train yourself to change," Kirwan had said. She saw now that it was indeed a handy talent to have. Had twelve years passed? The intra-muscular tattoo still ached. She'd have to work against the ink. *Concentrate,* she urged. She focused all her energy into a single beam and burrowed inside herself, looking for Soryk. She imagined her breasts receding and growing smaller as she eddied among the coming transformation, forcing her eyes open, turning away from its seductive lure. Sleep sucked at her, but her breasts diminished and she slipped free. The ragged edge of the broken fence caught her hair and ripped it from her scalp. Sorykah ran downhill, skidding through scrub and thistles. Frantic and exhausted, she headed for a sheltering copse of oak. The road curved ahead, and already, a black car descended the hill, blond hair fluttering from its open window.

Sorykah could not run across the road to the other side without being seen, but she could slip into the open drainage tunnel that channeled runoff from the hill. Sorykah scooted into the pipe, grimy with debris. She couldn't see light at the far end, but fear pushed her forward into the cloaking darkness. The pipe rumbled as the black car passed overhead, searching for her. Certain that she had left Kirwan to die, Sorykah crawled sobbing toward Neubonne.

20

SHIFTING SANDS

SORYKAH WALKED THROUGH THE NIGHT, leaping at every shadow, dodging every black car, and seeing Zarina in every blond woman's face, hoping all the time that Farouj had not left her behind. Crossing the North Fork bridge, she crossed the walkway through strings of mummers and beekeepers pushing hives and toting glass jars of honeycombs. Haymaz feast was the most important holiday of the year yet she had rarely ever celebrated it. Three days in Neubonne and she was already thrice-blessed: saltday, to demarcate future days from those past; vexday, to rid oneself of gripes; and grainday, to nourish the body for the conquests and trials of coming seasons. Today was hiveday, and beekeepers stood at the city posts handing warm cuts of waxy honeycomb to all who entered the city, sharing the bees' blessing and promising sweetness in the new year. Sorykah took hers gratefully, biting into the wax and sucking honey from each cell.

Had she been in a vehicle, Sorykah would have kept to the main road high above the refuse-heaped vacant lots and tent cities that sprawled flapping and crowded beneath the bridge, but the footpath emptied out into the Telec ghettos. Mummers and beekeepers kept to a single path and did not venture deeper into the slums, but Sorykah wandered here and there, absorbing the sight of homeless somatics squatting in tin and cardboard sheds. Ink rats clustered together, rubbing one another's skin with enough friction to draw blood. She pushed away guilty thoughts of Kirwan but her hand slipped down to cup the tiny vial of octameroon ink she'd taken from his house. A long needle, a deep injection, and she could stay.

A black-market butcher slapped bloody wares onto a rickety folding table. Bloodstained, fingerless gloves gripped a rock-sharpened cleaver that chewed through cheap chops and racks of gristle. Neubonne's poor lined up to buy their allotment with sacks of coin and thick stacks of old food vouchers, worn soft as silk. The butcher wrapped his cuts in torn garbage bags and laid into a long tentacle, the same mauve and orange as Rava's skin. Sliced into rubbery filets, the meat was chewed raw by a few dicey-looking, blunt-faced somatics, the scraps thrown to mangy dogs.

Poor Rava! Her exhortations to find her missing kin still lingered like a rebuke. Sorykah fled the ghetto, searching for any known street or building. She had no objective but to find Farouj. No resources and no allies except those dodgy Morigis. *Soryk*, she addressed her alter sternly. *If you want out of this mess, you have to help me. You and me*, she thought. *Not me. When did I become so divided within myself?* She assumed she'd begun referring to alter and primary separately after her first change as a teenager, but looking back, she knew the split had always been there, otherness lodged like a splinter in her heart. So much of the past year was wrapped up in her control issues: how much to allow, how much to suppress. She's been intent on segregation, not integration, and now wondered if she'd erred in her thinking. Sidra had encouraged Sorykah to explore self-incorporation if only to selfishly gain easier access to Soryk.

If he is me, and we are I, then I know where I'm going. Remember finding the Erun's secret door? She stopped questioning the path her feet followed and simply walked. She'd eaten nothing but that bit of honey and was starting to feel loopy when she spotted the exposed rebar on Farouj's building and staggered toward it. Buzzing court-yard lights cast a fluorescent glow; all the windows were dark but one. Farouj answered her feeble knock. He looked awful—ashen with worry, his eyes shadowed by sleepless nights. Neither one spoke. Farouj simply pulled her into the room and pressed her to him. She let him strip off her filthy clothes and tut-tut over her blistered feet. He tucked her into the pocket of heat beneath the bedcovers and co-cooned himself around her.

When she'd had to travel across the Sigue and Erun to reclaim her children, fury blazed like an inner fire. That fire had since died, leaving her cold and empty inside. Walking back to Neubonne, her rib cage was a darkened lantern sheltering the cold wick of her heart. She would soak up Farouj's life force, let it smolder inside her like a swig of moonshine. Perhaps he could make her feel warm and alive again. Pressing her hands to his chest to gather strength from his *t'naq*, she closed her eyes and slept like the dead.

When she woke, Farouj was sitting on the bed opposite, reading. His bag was packed and the room tidied. He smiled at her but the tenderness was gone. "There are fresh clothes for you in the bath-room. Clean yourself up. Time to leave Neubonne."

Ostara was Sorykah's only destination. She'd dreamed she was making pancakes for the children, and the taste of maple syrup still lingered in her head, but like roaches after the detonation of a chem-ical bomb, the bad thoughts came slinking back. Kirwan, whom she'd abandoned to die; Rava's people, captured and drained like sturgeon for roe; the Aroulians toiling underground like blind moles; Chen's many abuses of privilege. Zarina could still turn up at their door, kill Farouj just to spite her, and plunge her blade into Sorykah's neck.

Despite the duty that nagged, the pledges wrung from her, she in-sisted, "Take me home."

Farouj's face grew hard but he nodded, reluctantly, and snapped on the radio to break the tension. A woman's carefully pitched voice delivered the news. When she heard the Sigue mentioned, Sorykah came to sit on the bed beside Farouj.

". . . among the fatalities, three officers from the submarine *Nimbus*, two administration workers, and eight residents of Ostara. The harbor collapse was apparently caused by a natural fault line in the landmass, but a preliminary investigation has revealed that the ice was weakened by unusually warm currents from the seasonal thaws. Five people are still missing and presumed dead. A spokesman for Tirai Industries offers his condolences to those affected by the accident. Speaking from the site of the accident, Mr. Nunn promised full recompense to the families of the deceased officers and miners. No word yet on whether that will also extend to the Siguelanders and residents of Ostara who were also injured and killed." There was shouting in the background, sounds of unrest amid sharp bursts of Siguelandic. "Mr. Nunn!" The reporter was heard pushing into the crowd, plunging through crackling parkas. "How do you respond to these accusations that the collapse is the result of Tirai Industries' activity in Ostara?"

"That's not proven." Nunn's voice was harried, his brogue expanding under stress.

"Is it true that the Company ignored warnings from the Siguelandic tribal elders? This woman claims to have seen lava spills inside the—"

Nunn cut her off with a terse "No comment!" Electronic equipment buzzed in concert with the hiss and squeal of feedback in the microphones before the report ended and the station anchor cut the transmission.

Furious, Farouj snapped off the radio. "You see? TI is a parasite digging ever deeper into the marrow of this land, yet you'd go back to work for them. Strap on your gear and jump into the sea to mine ice, like nothing happened."

He was right. Even after everything she'd seen, she would go back to her job and her life, because it was all she had. Sorykah didn't have the luxury of job-hopping or quitting out of principle. She had a family to support and no one to help her do it.

"I'm handing the solution to you, gift-boxed and tied with a ribbon." His voice grew soft and coaxing. "Free the People. End the slaughter of octameroons. Carry on the work you've begun." He cupped her face in his hands and she blushed, thinking he might kiss her again. "Come with me to the desert. If we crush the pillars that uphold TI's foundation, it *will* topple."

She wavered, imagined Soryk leading the battle charge, flag in hand, a blaring horn at his lips. *For valor, for honor . . .* she thought she heard him say. *For Sidra.*

"I want to go home," she whispered.

Farouj sighed heavily and rose from the bed. Sorykah felt trapped. She wanted only her freedom. If she went home, she'd return a second time from a mysterious disappearance to work with a crew grown even more surly and resentful of her liberties and the Company's favoritism. She'd mine ice, knowing that octameroons netted from the sea filled the hold. She'd be culpable in the destruction of the old gods and the Sigue itself. Remaining in Neubonne would leave her mired in a swamp of tortured lusts and longings, where the remedy to those ills was too readily available. Chen would find his way to her again and tuck her neatly into his pocket. The Erun was Sidra's domain and though safe and welcoming, the greatest reception would be reserved for Soryk. Sorykah couldn't willingly give herself away like that. She'd always feared that the more time she spent as her alter, the harder it would be to reclaim her life. *Her* life. *My life,* she thought, despairing of certainty and strong conviction. Sorykah couldn't quite believe that she'd become responsible for so many people's happiness. Their safety and well-being rode her shoulders like a yoke. As she quickly bathed and dressed, the events of the past few days replayed in her mind. The edge of her Magar blade split open a whole new world and all the creepy-crawlies came streaming out. Plein Eïre was riddled with Morigi vermin. She must stamp them out. Chen would never leave her alone. Ayeda and Leander would be in danger as long as the Morigis ruled. If she ran from her duty, she would live the rest of her days in fear. The threat of another abduction or some slick coercion would forever lurk. Would she risk raising them in a corrupt and uncertain world, where they would suffer all of their mother's pain? It was her duty to offer them a better life. She could only be certain of that chance by knowing that all impediments to their security were removed. Sorykah did not want her precious children growing up alongside ink rats and digi-reel makers. If she could do but one thing to ensure Ayeda and Leander's future, what would it be?

Once more into the fray, said an inner voice—her own. "I met someone while I was away . . ."

Farouj struggled to mask his disappointment.

Sorykah quickly added, "Another Trader. Kirwan."

"You found him! That's wonderful."

Sorykah frowned and continued, "Not so wonderful. Chen has him. He's in bad shape."

"Well, did you get what you wanted from him?"

Sorykah considered the tiny bottle of ink in her pocket. "Yes. I got what I need." She paused, reluctant to share her second gain—that the change was an unwieldy talent she might possibly learn to control.

"And now?" Farouj asked.

"Now we go to the desert."

NOXIOUS FUMES AND SMOG pooled between Neubonne's low hills, a pungent, dangerous wine fermenting within an inland bowl. The country of Plein Eïre was neatly packaged, an assemblage of microcosms laid out in sharp alignment. Moving north from the pole, travelers encountered tundra, taiga, unilateral bands of forest, sloping hills and sloshing bays, prairies, and finally, a vast desert of superfine silicate where dust devils swarmed and travelers sometimes disappeared in powdery quicksand bogs.

As Sorykah and Farouj left the hiveday festivities behind them, the plains rolled out, a broad welcome mat of high grass, wildflowers, and weeds, sun-bleached and sparse. The northbound train chugged and steamed mindlessly. The open prairie washed Sorykah's gaze in yellow. Farouj grew pensive as they neared the desert. He had too much hope invested in Sorykah's ability to save the Aroulians. She was the most dubious and unreliable of rescuers. He had believed the myths, products of whisper, rumor, and need, but now, misgivings diluted his faith in her. Sitting across from her, Farouj narrowed his eyes and pretended to sleep while he watched her. Not that it mattered; she was too deep into her own thoughts to feel his hooded stare.

He'd begun to doubt his plan and her ability to carry it out. She would falter and hang back, change her mind, resist the call. Her *t'naq* would be cool and weak. There was little investment for her, a bit of glory, a taste of vanity. The dilution of her guilt.

Could his vision be trusted? He had ventured into the *wet world*, as the Aroulians termed the land surrounding their desert, a fearful place inhabited by sullen sea demons and irritable rain gods, where water ran from the sky in great splashing tears to drown the nonbelievers. On his return, the tribal sage had asked the ancestors to speak through the flames and advise this wandering son. Farouj communed with Ur, the primordial spirit of death and mourning. He stared into the heart of a blue fire and saw Sorykah there, a tempestuous water spirit, a sword-bearer with a blade of ice. Ur's lament rang in his ears as visions danced before his eyes. Ur showed him a woman with four arms and two heads, one bearded, one smooth. The left side of her body was dark and the right bright with light. She parted the sands, cleaving the dunes like anthills beneath her blade, and let stream the Aroulians, freed at last from bondage.

The woman sitting across from him—the one he'd tracked and courted and protected—bore little resemblance to the Fury of his vision. Farouj thought that perhaps the old gods were just characters in a fancy story that explained fate's vagaries, but still, he treated his vision as truth. He would carry Sorykah like an effigy of the old gods, Ur and Asta, the arbiter of their divine will.

Humming, eating peanuts, and blissfully ignorant of Farouj's fantasy, Sorykah watched the scenery stream by. She couldn't quite believe that she was traveling away from home instead of toward it. Foolishly, she was putting herself out of a job. Some useful part of her brain seemed to have frozen and ceased functioning following her flight from Kirwan's house. When she'd finally found the end of the drainage pipe and crawled into the sun, dazed and thirsting, she knew that she'd left some essential part of her behind. Her humanity perhaps, for she had made the inhumane decision to abandon Kirwan to certain execution.

"Do it for your queen," Farouj had cajoled.

Not for Sidra, she thought, *but for my babes. My darlings, I do this for you.* She imagined the plant—some rust-streaked steel monolith—deflating and caving in upon itself and Chen's anguished cry when he learned what she had done to him. Deeply satisfied, she smiled.

What began as a film across the train windows smeared itself across Sorykah's vision, an indefinite beige.

"Smog?" She pointed out the window.

Farouj stirred from his contemplations to look. Concern creased his brow. "Sandstorm. The train will have to sit it out." He checked his watch, as if their assault could not be delayed. "We could be here for hours." Collapsing against the hard bench, he sighed.

Sand spiraled within sand, an inner vortex spinning counterclockwise. Transfixed by the funnel sweeping back and forth, drawing in and thrusting forward in rapid cycles, they watched the enormous column of sand pattern the glass, a scratching, tinkling noise camouflaging the more sinister sounds beneath. Farouj jumped up, oddly uncomposed, his mouth gaping. "Parallel tracks, here. The storm will be used as cover." Panic dried his tongue.

"What is it?" Sorykah scanned the faces of the other passengers, glib and conversational, obviously ill at ease but not yet frightened.

Farouj wiped beading sweat from his nose. "The night train! Sweet Jerusha, we'll be murdered."

The night train. That vehicle of death—guns blasting, bodies falling. The crunch of bones beneath Sorykah's shoes, blood reeking on the saturated meadow.

Farouj gripped Sorykah's hand. "We must leave before it arrives. It will pull up alongside and then . . ."

"Bang, bang," finished Sorykah.

Sand clouds consumed the train.

Farouj yelled, "We have to jump! The rails are going to hurt, but don't stop. Cross the tracks, walk thirty paces, and drop. Cover your head with your coat and wait until I find you."

Glass shattered in the adjacent car. The railcar tipped malevolently; screams sounded, followed by silence.

Farouj shoved Sorykah through the connecting door. Flying sand needled her skin, ground into her eyes, and clogged her mouth. The night train slid silently toward them, its hot yellow eye dust-dimmed. They leapt. Steel rails bludgeoned Sorykah's limbs as she fell, lurching across the gap and squinting against the whipping wind. Farouj tumbled into the storm and away, disappearing like a tiny sailboat tossed on high swells and plummeted into deadly vales. Sorykah staggered forward. She'd forgotten to count her paces but began now, starting at ten. Behind her sang the constant shriek of steam. Shunts of gunfire glowed white. Silence. Except for the squealing brakes of the northbound train, there was no sound.

She tasted her own blood. Grit caked her nose and ears. The sand was as warm as a blanket left to dry beside a fire. Sand snaked inside her clothes, forcing itself between her lips, pressed tight. Farouj was somewhere in that storm, his mouth full of sand. Sorykah tugged her long-coat over her head as the rustling sand mounted her back, as heavy as wet concrete. She would wait, and he would find her. She was the savior of the Qa'a'nesh, slayer of Matuk the Collector. He would not let her die. Still, she couldn't help but imagine rising to shake off pounds of sand and finding the train's shattered carcass broken across the tracks. She'd been foolish to leave her haven of home and family, for this glory. She rocked inside her mound of sand, listening, hoping, and waiting.

Farouj's voice rang out over the dunes. Sorykah shifted, her wind-lashed skin rubbed raw by stinging grains. Sand sucked the moisture from her body and left her parched. Her dust-caked throat could only squawk. Farouj's voice veered away. She peered through the crusted slits of her eyes as she wrestled free of the Aroulian desert. Sunlight struck her body like some evil, remorseless thing. Cream-colored dunes undulated beneath a throbbing blue sky that stretched forever into the distance. Farouj was a shimmering blur on the horizon. Sorykah wished that they were still tethered, so that she could simply pull him toward her instead of willing him to turn and see her.

She managed a croaking call, spat sand, and called again. This time he turned and waved. Not until he gathered her to him, offering sudden strange comfort, did she recall the trains. Farouj tightened his embrace, commanding her to withhold her screams and bear down on her anguish, expelling sorrow stillborn.

"Wait here. I'll fetch water from . . ." — he could not bring himself to say "the wreckage" — "the dining car. Then we continue on foot."

Sorykah forced herself to turn and view the slaughter, heaped upon the dunes among a rain of shattered glass. Red-dripping bodies dangled from broken windows. The train had settled on rails sifted with sand and human litter. The far night train slithered south, shielded by dust clouds.

Farouj returned carrying a water jug and two satchels. He slung one bag over her shoulder. "Here. It's all I could find. Didn't want to stay there too long . . ."

Sorykah noted a smear of blood on his hand and Farouj dipped his hands into the dune, washing them as if in water. A hot, errant wind dashed the sand.

"Very warm today, even for the desert. We must keep moving," he said.

Sorykah nodded—at least, she imagined that she felt her head moving atop her neck. Her agreement was evidenced by the double set of footprints they left as they marched perpendicular to the tracks.

Water eased the path for her words. "Why are we going this way? Won't we get lost?"

"As if we aren't already," Farouj replied.

"Don't say that. I'm to have confidence in you. You promised my safe return."

"Move in behind that rise. We won't want to be seen, just in case . . ."

They walked steadily. Perspiration dripped down Sorykah's forehead. "I've seen this before. Two months ago, in the Erun Forest. It was night then, and that train weasel-stealthy, just as this one. Many dead. Shot by air guns, I think."

"The night train travels the forest paths now?" asked Farouj. "I was unaware of a line there."

"A single track, unused but for a weekly cross-country train. We were to board it, but Carac . . ." Sorykah hesitated, feeling as though she betrayed the par-wolf's confidence. "Sidra's man"—here, a quiver of envy—"was to see us aboard. He lit the signal lamp and we watched the black flame burn. A train materialized from the mist, and it too had a glaring yellow eye."

"I'm fairly certain that the night train is connected to Tirai Industries," Farouj said. "But I can't figure out why TI would carry out such a public campaign of annihilation. It has stealthier means of eliminating its enemies."

Sorykah said, "Everyone killed in the Erun was somatic. Maybe there were a few people there, too. Sidra said that some of the forest dwellers had fled poverty or threats in the cities. They found it easier to live off the land than deal with the bureaucracies and petty politics that censured them in the cities."

"The people aboard our train were just travelers, though. Families, tourists, migrants. How could they pose a threat to TI?"

"I overheard some people talking about an event in Bokhara. It was a festival of some kind, or a conference, maybe."

Farouj stopped and looked at Sorykah, his mind churning. "The Gathering of Tribes! It happens every ten years. Aroulians, Siguelanders, Bokharans, and all descendants of the Qa'a'nesh attend."

"That's you! Aren't you going to go?"

"I'm not really welcome."

"What did you do?" Sorykah couldn't imagine dapper Farouj causing enough trouble to have been ostracized from his own tribe. "And why go to so much trouble to rescue those who turned their backs on you?"

"My mother was a Qa'a'nesh matriarch; my father was a *gahjin* outsider. They met during a trading expedition. She brought him into the tribe to live as her husband. It had been done before. But my father was ill, and my mother didn't find out until it was too late and she started blistering and bleeding. Three other women also became sick. Two of them were daughters of the tribal elders. My father took four women and two unborn children into the grave with him.

"The elders wanted to send me to live with my father's family. My grandfather thought I would continue to infect the tribe. We didn't get along." He flashed Sorykah a wan smile. "My grandmother refused to let me go. After she died, I left the reserve and now I'm considered a deserter."

"So yours is a quest for redemption."

"Among other things. I promised my grandmother that I would help the People."

"What does the gathering have to do with the night train?"

"I'm not sure, but almost all the tribes work for TI in one capacity or another, even if they don't know it. TI has so many divisions and sister corporations, it would be very easy to think yourself working for the competition only to fill Tirai's coffers with the fruit of your labors."

"Sidra encourages somatics to subvert TI in whatever manner possible," said Sorykah. "Perhaps the somatics and tribes were planning to work together against the Company."

"There's no better way to preempt a revolution than by killing its insurgents," said Farouj. "These deaths ensure compliance from the living and silence from the dead."

"Then we must be sure to stay alive."

THAT NIGHT, SILENCE FILLED the space between them. Back to back, they lay sandwiched between blankets pilfered from the train. Velvety darkness crested the dunes. Sorykah recalled the Erun and totted up the differences between Sidra's cool, immense forest of quiet and creaking trees and Farouj's desert, its only sound the broom of the wind sweeping the sand from dune to dune.

Farouj's proximity made Sorykah pensive. Sidra was Soryk's love. Soryk was Nuala's love. He could even have Nels, if he wanted her. Chen was Sidra's love, and Sorykah's betrayer. *And I have none,* she thought, *no love at all.*

Myriad heartaches and regrets surfaced. She had seen too much death. She'd lived her entire life in a placid state of quiet terror, unharried by passion or pain, until a single night with Kirwan embarked her upon a lengthy and exhausting journey, which had yet to end.

Farouj's breath came evenly—he did not snore. Even in sleep, he retained his dignity. She wished that he would waken and touch her. Sorykah turned over and slipped an arm about his waist, comforted by his solidity and closeness. He stirred and placed his hand across hers, holding it firm. Sweat ran between her breasts and the breeze tossed a handful of sand into the air. Together on the cooling dune, they slept.

Morning brought punishing heat. Farouj and Sorykah trekked across the pale desert. There were no plants to enliven the unvarying view of sand heaped upon more sand, only the gleaming silver rails running along beside them.

Sorykah's skin was cracked and red, despite her best efforts to shield herself from the sun. The oppressive heat was a feverish malignancy drawing itself over the land. Two degrees warmer and she'd begin to hallucinate.

"There, you see?" Farouj pointed at a distant shimmer on the horizon. "Desert Station Number Four."

Because Desert Stations Two and Three had been nothing but rickety aluminum sunshades with solitary, green-painted benches, Sorykah groaned.

"This one has a café."

"*Café!* What a wonderful word!" Sorykah perked right up. She imagined beakers of iced lemonade, water beading the exterior of the glass, cheese and tomato sandwiches, and cool quarter-moons of melon.

Her hopes sagged as they neared the station, a cluster of dusty tents fashioned from heavy rugs. Tassels and banners flapped in the wind. Dromedaries huddled on the sand, slitting their eyes against the glare. Snippets of sporadic conversation peppered the air.

Farouj wiped his face with his sleeve and pulled Sorykah inside. She blinked as her eyes adjusted to the dimness. Three men in linen tunics sat cross-legged on the carpeted ground, sipping tea. Tall glasses at least, but no lemonade or ice in sight. A teenage girl in modern dress, her dark brown hair looped into a careless bun, greeted them.

Everyone looked at Farouj, and the girl spoke first to him, a slippery trickle of words.

Farouj translated. "This is Mehemija. She works in the café."

Mehemija gestured to a shelf laden with bottles of fossil water and pointed to Sorykah. Farouj spoke quietly, his native language like a mountain stream's melodic babble.

"She thinks you want fossil water, because you are foreign." He pursed his lips. "You don't, do you?"

Sorykah shook her head.

Mehemija seated them with the others and brought tepid mint tea, flat bread, and a spicy lentil paste. Farouj ate quickly, but Sorykah was too sunbaked to do much more than gulp tea as a muted conversation blew around her like shifting sand.

Mehemija dawdled nearby. It was clear she wished to join the discussion. Her bright black eyes gleamed with interest, but she refrained from joining them.

Farouj turned to Sorykah, his face grave. "The night train passed four times this month. There have been two pogroms—"

"That we know of," Sorykah said.

"Yes, perhaps more. These men are Aroulian nomads." Farouj gestured to the rumpled and wrinkled three, their cropped beards in various stages of graying, their short hair dusty from many days of travel. "When Tirai Industries bought our land, a few resisted and TI expelled them for being corporate dissenters. We call them the wanderers."

The oldest man skirted the plates to pat Sorykah's hand and smile. Farouj gazed at her with a sheepish, contrite expression.

"He thinks you are my wife." Farouj smiled awkwardly.

The man's palsied hand shook as it held Sorykah's. He said something incomprehensible, and she looked to Farouj for translation. Shadows obscured his face, but she was certain that he colored in embarrassment.

"He wants to know if you will stay woman long enough to bear me sons and daughters." Farouj cleared his throat. "He's joking, of course."

Now it was Sorykah who trembled. "How does he know?"

Farouj shrugged and looked away. The old nomad squeezed her hand and relinquished it.

"He saw the digi-reels?"

Farouj shook his head and resumed eating.

"Come on," she pleaded. "You can't keep this from me. How does he know?"

Mehemija took this as an invitation to insert herself into the circle. "The name Farouj means *consort of Asta*. It is an old legend." She smiled, eager to display her knowledge and her English. "He thinks this because of the way that you look, because you are *gahjin* from the wet world."

"What's wrong with the way I look?"

"Black hair, any-color eyes. Like Asta, who feared the coming of foreign gods. War gods from the dark half of the world. They rode horses made of fire and carried lightning bolts snatched from the sky. They wanted to destroy Asta's house and enslave the gods, Sun, Sky, Ocean, and all the rest."

"To what end?" Sorykah was rapt, even as a sick feeling percolated inside her and Farouj refused to meet her eye.

Thrilled to have captured the woman's attention, Mehemija launched into her careful recitation. "To claim the bright side of the world! In those days, the earth did not spin as it does now. One side was forever dark and the other light. Asta and her gods lived in the sun and grew the most luscious fruits, swam in a warm sea. You know, they lived a good life." Emboldened, Mehemija reached for the bread and stuffed her mouth. Excitement was rare at Desert Station Number Four, just like the company of women. Only the old nomads traveled here, occasionally, accompanied by their wives and children, but they were so shy and fearful, Mehemija was never able to befriend them. Her father was often absent, leaving his teenage daughter perpetually deprived of companionship.

"The shadow gods planned their attack. Asta had to rest for five days each month to prepare her body to birth new gods, mountains, birds, and beasts. They would wait until Asta's long sleep, then storm the palace, kill the gods, and take their places.

"Asta had a pet magpie. Magpies are black and white because in those days, they flew between the dark and light sides of the world. Sometimes the stars would wander from the shadow side to the sunny side. Stars are silly; they do not pay attention. If a star visits the daytime sky, no one can see it, and it will become lost. There are some lopsided constellations today because of lost stars. Asta's magpie had the job of watching the stars in the shadowlands and retrieving any that strayed. That is why a magpie likes shiny things, even today. Asta's magpie saw the shadow gods advancing and flew to tell her. But the sleep was coming and she could not resist it."

Sorykah had stopped breathing. A sleep one could not resist. The coming of the shadow gods too eerily echoed her own struggle to remain dominant against Soryk's onslaught and demand for consciousness.

Mehemija continued. "The shadow gods were like ghosts—they lacked skin and bones. Their attack was swift and deadly. The sun gods were so used to their easy life, they could not defend themselves. They had no weapons or training and no desire to fight. They offered to build the shadow gods a new palace, and to help plant orchards to feed them and carve rivers to water them, but the shadow gods wanted only what they were not meant to have."

Farouj and the nomads sat at attention, like children clustered around a storyteller. Even if they could not understand the meaning of Mehemija's words, the nomads savored the rhythms of her voice and the suspense that filled the tent.

Profoundly uncomfortable, Sorykah said, "I do not see myself in this tale. Perhaps it's better if we don't finish it."

"No, no!" Mehemija clung to Sorykah's arm, and threw Farouj a pleading look. "You have to hear the end. Don't leave yet!"

Farouj nodded, and Mehemija spun the tale toward its grim conclusion. "Before she sank into sleep, Asta hid in a handmaid's room, very plain and far from her beautiful chambers. She knew that if the shadow gods found her, they would cut off her head and loose the power of the universe, creating eternal chaos. Determined not to be found, Asta split herself in two. A boy and a girl lay together on the bed, so closely entwined you could not tell whose limbs were whose. As their eyes closed, the shadows stormed the house of the gods," Mehemija recited.

"Yes, there was carnage and death, and the destruction of the old gods. The shadow gods wore their skins like cloaks. When Asta awoke, her boy and girl selves went to survey the damage. Strangely, everything appeared in order. The gardens were blooming and the ponds and rivers clear. The sun shone bright and hot but all was not well. Though the gods walked in the light and plucked fruit from low boughs to gorge themselves, they cast no shadows. They had lived so long in darkness, they forgot that they were supposed to have them and so did not conjure them. Devoured by grief and fearing the axe against her neck, Asta decided that she must remain split. If the shadow gods found her, all would be lost."

Perhaps it was the smothering heat or the close air in the heavy tent, but Sorykah felt claustrophobic and lightheaded. She asked, "You memorized that whole story?"

"Yes." Mehemija beamed smugly. "I've heard it many times. My father told it to me."

"I did not know that you were listening so intently as to repeat the entire thing word for word," said Farouj.

"She's your daughter?" Sorykah was aghast. "You didn't tell me you had a child. You left her here alone? By herself, with the night train prowling and strange men? Think what might have happened!"

"She is quite all right," said Farouj. "Better here than owned by TI. She would have been ruined. She needs the sun and sand—her freedom."

"Farouj!" Sorykah was irate. "You cannot abandon a girl to this life."

Stunned by Sorykah's outburst, Mehemija stared at her. Never once had she thought her life or her upbringing strange or improper.

Electricity bounced between Sorykah and Farouj. The nomads smiled as the barbs volleyed back and forth, thoroughly entertained by the spat.

Farouj's face had lost its light. "This is the best life I can offer her."

"Surely she needs more than this! What about school? What if something happened to her? How would you know?"

"I chose to keep her aboveground. Consequently, she cannot live any other way. I will not consign this child to a life of darkness."

Outside, the camels snorted and chuffed. One of the nomads went to investigate and shouted to the others. Farouj panicked. Sorykah's anxiety infected him. His pretty daughter was too vulnerable here without his protection. He'd been foolish before.

"Mehemija, stay close," said Farouj.

She scampered to her father's side, delighted by his alarm. The nomads collected their things and roused the camels.

Sorykah ran outside. Her eyes ached in the brightness as she searched the empty desert. An unmarked train skimmed the tracks, a silver-gray millipede. She was about to raise a hand and hail the driver, but the sunlight's gleam in the single yellow lamp on the train's nose triggered unwelcome memories. Returning from its mission, the night train traveled in daylight, as bold as brawn.

A scuffle ensued inside the tent. The nomads left and climbed onto camels that lurched upright, shaking sand from long shaggy necks. Farouj squeezed his daughter's wrist and argued with the men.

"Sorykah!" Farouj waved wildly, careful to stand in the shade of the tent where he would not be seen by the night train's riders or crew. "You must leave. These men say that the night train shoots *gahjin*. We will be safe here but you should go now."

"What about you? Your daughter? I won't abandon you!"

Farouj released Mehemija and stomped across the sands. He shook Sorykah angrily, his composed façade broken at last. "Why do you argue? I'm trying to save you! You are safer with them than me. I can't protect you here. Go! *Go!*"

The old nomad's camel dropped to its knees beside her. Farouj shoved her onto the beast's hairy hump, hot between her legs. Sorykah sneezed and gripped the old man's waist as the camel stood and sauntered into the desert.

"Farouj!" Sorykah cried. He waved her on, frantic as the train approached.

"Get to the plant. I'll find you!" Farouj shouted.

Sorykah's camel broke into a jostling run and Desert Station Number Four was soon behind them.

FROM HIS OFFICE IN his private train car, Bodkin viewed the activity at Desert Station Number Four with disinterest. He wouldn't waste bullets on a few scraggly nomads. He watched them mount camels and ride across the sands like mice fleeing a cat. Satisfaction warmed him as his power grew. He felt like a magician, snatching the cloth from beneath Chen Morigi's well-set table, deftly claiming control of the Company without rattling so much as a single china teacup.

The intercom buzzed.

"Yes?"

"The next northbound passenger train has been delayed until the tracks are clear, sir. What would you like to do?"

"Carry on. We'll take them from the rear this time. I don't want any of those tribal grunts reaching the gathering. Understood?"

"Yes, sir." The conductor disconnected and Bodkin messaged his contact at the plant to confirm their arrival time. The octameroons were to be sedated and packaged for travel, their tentacles coiled and bound, their bodies slathered with glycerin and wrapped tightly in plastic. A slow IV drip of oenathe jelly and fossil water would sustain them for two days until they reached their new home at the Neubonne Aquarium.

Everything was proceeding as planned. He'd arrive at the plant to collect precious cargo just before Queen Sidra's agents blew it up concealing his theft while diminishing the Morigi fortune. His Erun spy had confirmed that the bombmakers were already en route. Pertana messaged him from Desert Station Number One when she picked up the sand bikes and supplies Bodkin had left for them. Pertana lied easily and well. Bodkin trusted that the others—a vile chimp-handed man and a clumsy oaf with a giant goat hoof—believed her claim that Sidra had procured the bikes for them. Why should they doubt her? She was paid to be convincing.

21

HAPPINESS AND ITS SOMBER COUSIN

SIDRA'S NIGHTMARES WERE TANGIBLE, terrible things. They were closet monsters, these horror-show spectaculars. Sometimes she thought she was losing her mind, not enough to go all-out crazy, but enough to make her feel as though she slid across slick wet ice, that her footing in reality was unstable.

Gowyr never returned from delivering Sidra's message to Sorykah, and as the weeks dragged on, Yetive became increasingly abrasive. Banning her from the city simply to avoid her rage would prove divisive and counterproductive. Yetive must stay, but Sidra would not further jeopardize her own health by continuing to seek treatment from one with an obvious and growing grudge against her. Nor could she fully entrust her care to the Erun's somatic nurse, a fanatical woman with the wheezy, pushed-in face of a pug and a distrust of prayerless medicine. When she wasn't muttering incantations to the Blessed Mother over Sidra's belly, she peppered her speech with so many "praise Jerushas" that every conversation automatically doubled in length.

The queen should not keep her own care. That was foolhardy. Sound judgment was lately a sparse commodity in Sidra's world; she was just as apt to request a stick of dynamite and start blowing up tree houses just to hear the big bang and resultant shower of falling de-bris as she was likely to spend an entire week in her room, sobbing, brooding, and sleeping.

"This isn't healthy," she advised her mirror image, arms folded across the top of her belly. "Can't be normal." She'd never been pregnant before; what did she know? The mothers she'd nursed at the Merciful Father's Charity Hospital were often beyond reason, too distraught or too neglected or ill to take pleasure in the usual simpering displays. Instead they turned up their noses at cooing over infants they would soon relinquish.

The brittle smell of Carac's wolfish tang had become too much for Sidra and she had banished him from her rooms. She preferred instead to roll in the sheets she had never changed, hunting for rem-nants of Soryk's odor and sighing over old stains. Sidra paused to press her nose to the pillow and catch the last vestige of Soryk's scent. Drowsiness would cloud Soryk's expression, leaving him momentar-ily unresponsive as he fought the sleep and Sorykah's desire to push through and command his body. Soryk/ah had never been able to lie still and keep quiet in their shared bed. Sidra was a magnet and Soryk the iron filings trapped behind the thin glass of Sorykah's will.

For the first time in many years, Sidra wished that she had a tele-phone. Technologically, the Erun was a century behind the main-land cities. Neubonne had infrared phone systems, electricity, pixel screens, and digi-reels. The Erun had wood fires, bells on strings, cis-terns, and gravitational water pipes. Calls were made in person, letters delivered by hand.

Lacking elevators, minibuses, IERs, electronic message pads, and tracking pens, Sidra was forced to capture her emotions with ink and paper. Or was there something better? Even if Gowyr had suc-ceeded in handing over Sidra's missive, her words had elicited no response from Soryk/ah. What else could she send? She ransacked her home, searching for an object that would make a bold statement. A baby bootie? A cradle? A vial of her blood or lock of her hair stuck through with briars?

What would speak to Soryk as he slept within the shell of his primary? She wished that she could package the whole Erun, fold it up, wrap it in paper, and dispatch an entire forest to him. She pawed through her bags and pouches of herbs, seeds, and other forest findings with the intention of crafting some deeply meaningful structure or mobile, sculpting her love in feathers, ribbons, and fern, but nothing seemed to suit the occasion of an announcement of paternity. Then the glossy ovoid seed of an ice tree slipped into her palm. Sidra pulled it from the cloth bag. It was the size of a quail's egg and burnished brown striations marbled its hard shell. Like the fetus within her womb, it was a tender green shoot curled in wait.

Sidra polished the seed with cold fingers, rubbing it to a hard shine. She'd wrap it in red silk, with instructions to soak the seed overnight in water. Morning would draw the water through waking cells, split the hard casing, and rouse the dormant tree. Ice trees grew faster than beanstalks and just as tall and strong. Their silvery white bark peeled in tiny, papery snowflakes, and stalactites of oozing sap hung and trembled like icicles from their branches. The rare ice tree was the most profound and sentimental of valentines, as each one nurtured Asta's divine essence within its pith.

Sidra's pen summoned her, "Come and claim me," just as a lover would. Sidra rubbed her belly, firm as a summer pear, and sat at her desk. There was much to do—wars to monger, dissent to stir.

A voice called from below. That's right; she'd summoned Hans, how long ago?

"Wait there, I'll be down shortly," she hollered. Without Carac around to run interference, she had to handle everything herself.

Quickly now, the message. The pen felt impossibly light in her hand, as if the quill might take flight. The gravity was in her words, and she consigned their weight to paper.

> *In this there is only one truth—*
> *the bloodline must be severed*

the bud protected, its future ensured.
Death waits to take me to the shadowlands.
She feeds upon me as I wither,
my every breath exchanged for hers.
Care for her when I cannot,
this bright child of mine.
If I loved you too quickly,
it was only because I had not the luxury of time.

There! She rolled the paper tightly and secured it with string. Perfectly succinct. She returned her antler crown to her head, tied up the note and seed in a silk pocket square, and took the stairs slowly, her hips aching with each step. She passed the note to faithful Hans my Hedgehog for dispensation to a messenger bound for the pole. His quills rattled as he took her package into his small hand. Nose twitching, beady black eyes squinting and darting, Hans fretted over Sidra's health.

"My lovely, you look peaked. Again, I urge you to consider your frailty."

"Frail? Never!" She shook a fist in the air. "Pregnancy won't get the best of me, you'll see." But even as she spoke, she sensed the infinitesimal fractures that spiderwebbed her bones growing wider and deeper. Always conscious of the subtle sounds of breakage resounding within her body, Sidra knew her time was running out.

"Hans, this must be delivered to Ostara. There is no room for failure. Soryk's absence suggests that my message hasn't yet been received. Choose someone more capable this time, less vulnerable to suggestion and seduction, for we cannot risk a loss of time or people."

The manic look in her eyes frightened Hans and he trembled and rattled beside her. "We'd care for her, my queen. Your princess won't be abandoned."

She clutched his arm, ignoring the quills that pierced her flesh and drew blood. "No one will love this child! She'll grow up wild and alone. Who will take her? You, who cannot carry a baby for fear of stabbing her? Dunya, a madman's housemaid? Carac?"

It was little consolation to Sidra, knowing that she'd called destruction down on their heads by scheming to undermine the Morigis' empire. Someone would want retaliation, if not Chen then the higher-ups on the board at TI. They tolerated the ascendant son's whims but would override his decisions if something threatened their superiority or interfered with the flow of wealth. She simply needed Soryk; then she could face things. Even if crippled by a laborious birth that fractured her pelvis and left her stunned from pain, she was certain that she could still rule the Erun and care for their daughter with him by her side.

"Hans, when the package is delivered, you must instruct the messenger to watch her open it and follow all instructions. Make sure that you do this."

"Yes, my lovely. As you wish."

Distracted by other concerns, Sidra waved him away. Hans headed home, his heart heavy. He'd enjoyed but a few years of security in the Erun city and now it all threatened to fall apart. His duty was a burden he'd not discharge lightly. He must choose carefully. Among the Erun's somatics, however, there were few who could easily pass through the human world without drawing suspicion. Most of the Erun residents had been badly mistreated by the intact. Fear was their watchword. Who would willingly risk his neck to ferry mash notes to the queen's boyfriend? This was not an urgent royal matter, he thought, but oh, he did so want to see his queen happy! Without her protection, Hans could easily imagine himself living in permanent isolation, forced to go back to eating bugs to survive.

He racked his brain, pulling out a few quills in his nervousness as he sorted through the list of Erun residents. Who was most trustworthy? Who could get the job done?

Something rustled in the tunnel ahead of him. There were sounds of digging, usual in an underground city. Barking, however, was uncommon. Kika, Sorykah's red-and-cream furred sled dog, pranced and leapt, pawing the earthen floor. A grubbit burrowed through the tunnel wall, and Kika scratched after it, eager for a meal.

She paused at Hans's approach, eyed the empty grubbit hole, and trotted over to Hans.

"Hello, Kika." Hans carefully scratched the big dog's ears. She enjoyed his company but required careful watching, so that she'd not rub against his quills and scrape her skin. She nuzzled his hand, her electric green eyes curious.

Kika, Hans thought, an idea shaping itself in his brain, was a good dog. A responsible dog and very faithful to her mistress, or master, as the case may be. Kika adored Soryk/ah and would follow her everywhere. Kika had already proven her nose, memory, and sense of direction keen. She had free rein to wander through the Erun, and did so with confident ease. Hans knew that she had accompanied Dunya when she returned to the burned shell of the marble manor to collect yellow salt from its meadow. Kika always found her way home. Would she be capable of finding her way back to the Sigue and Sorykah?

The journey was fraught with peril. Harsh weather, poachers, animals, or the sea could claim her. How long would it take a dog to cross the tip of Plein Eïre and cross the floe fields to the Sigue? Hans snapped his fingers and Kika sprang to attention, head cocked, her tail wagging fiercely. Hans led her to Dunya's house, knowing that the dog-faced girl was with Yetive, training in midwifery. Kika was reluctant to ascend the carved narrow stairs lining the tree house wall but did so with coaxing. Hans tugged her into the small storeroom. Ayeda and Leander's discarded toys lay in a basket, along with the small spoons, tea towels, and other accessories left over from their brief residence in the Erun. Hans held the basket out to Kika.

"You want to see your mistress again, yes?" Kika sniffed the babies' things and wagged her tail harder. "Can you find your way home, dog? You're a good girl to stay here with us, but your mistress needs you more than we do."

Hans took a tea towel and sniffed it. There was a ghostly scent of baby: milk, urine, sweetness, and something peculiar to Traders alone. That should be enough to guide her home, he thought. Among all people, only Sorykah and her kind emitted the peculiar aroma evident to only the most keen-nosed of somatics. Kika ought to be able to smell them from miles away.

"Let's go, girl! Time to go home." Kika followed Hans through the Erun city. Hans avoided the main tunnels, where he feared running into Sidra or Dunya. The tea towel hung in his hand like a bloody knife, evidence of his crime. Sidra told him to find the most trustworthy messenger; she hadn't specified whether the courier be human, somatic, or animal.

It was just a love letter, after all. He imagined that if he opened it, it would merely beg, "Come back to bed."

Sidra's red silk was warm in his hand. Soon the sweat from his small brown palm would stain it. His hands shook as he stroked the ice tree seed—a beautiful stone he was almost tempted to keep— and read the queen's note.

Because Sidra had never expressly announced to Hans, "I am pregnant with Soryk's child," he hadn't yet pieced together the clues: Sidra's swelling belly, her lethargy and moodiness, the strange and sudden whims that sent him scurrying through the tunnels at all hours. Like his namesake the hedgehog, Hans's small eyes focused only on what was right in front of him. He wasn't prone to great leaps of imagination, but now, mulling over her note, the truth blazed before him. Danced around and evaded with morbid flowery words, but a truth nonetheless. He expected that Soryk was as thick as himself; Sidra's meaning would fly right over his head. Better he should write it out plainly. Carefully, for gripping a pen was difficult, he added his own laborious postscript.

Kika stood patiently while he wrapped the message in burlap and knotted it firmly beneath her neck. He worried for a moment that Sidra would be angry when she learned that Kika, her last link to Soryk/ah, was gone. Dunya would surely be dismayed to lose her companion, but she had Hans now. If Kika brought Soryk/ah back with her, no one could complain that he hadn't done his job.

Hans unbarred the door leading from the tunnel to the forest. He rubbed the tea towel over Kika's muzzle. "Go home, girl. Go to Sorykah!"

Kika's tail wagged ferociously at the sound of Sorykah's name, her body vibrating with energy. Hans opened the door and Kika sprang up the steps and into the warm air. She sniffed the ground to orient herself, gave Hans one final glance, and took off running.

DUNYA HUMMED A DITTY and pursed her flapping lips in an attempt to whistle. The sound, rather like a teakettle screeching from inside an asthmatic dragon's throat, lifted itself into the air. "Ahhhoooo-woooo! Aroooroooo!" Dunya sang, her voice lifting itself into the air like a balloon, thrilling her with its sound. She'd not tried adding words yet—she was still growing used to being able to make noise and to waking each day without constant dread filling her belly or a loneliness so sharp-edged and savage that it took her breath away.

She inserted a whistle between the notes, a whuffy sort of wheeze that was the result of many weeks' practice. Her lips simply could not purse for a proper whistle but she kept trying, her entire being buoyant with a helium joy that kept her floating two feet off the ground. Sidra had given her an empty tree house in the eastern tunnels where many families dwelled. The eastern tunnels shared a common room—an underground cave with a high ceiling of split rock open to the sky—several paths to the surface, and much traffic, talk, and hustle. At first it was overwhelming. Dunya refused to leave her new home, remaining tucked into a corner beneath a knobby ledge on the wooden wall while she quavered and panted with fear as her body excised a lifetime of tragedy. She neither slept nor ate, and barely moved but to lap up a little water and finally to answer a knock upon her door.

Hans my Hedgehog, a short, beady-eyed man, his back clothed in short quills as sharp as stinging nettles, had taken charge. Like Dunya, he had suffered much and found the Erun city a wonderful reprieve from surface-world pain. He was small and gentle, old enough to have loved, lost, and resigned himself to permanent loneliness due to the peculiarities of his appearance. At Sidra's insistence, he came to Dunya's door holding a basket of fruit buns and boiled eggs in hand, a few clean towels in various states of wear, and a sprig of dry lavender, tied with a string.

Sidra told Hans, "Dear Dunya is gentle and loyal. She'll need a good friend and I can think of none better suited to welcome her than you."

Hans had blushed and stammered, folding his hands over each other, quills rustling with a delightful sound of paper crumpling. In fact, Sidra so loved that odd sound, with its hint of river reeds in a brisk wind, the tumble of pick-up sticks spilled upon the floor, and tens of other wonderful noises, that she sometimes riled him on purpose just to hear it.

Lucky for Hans, Dunya admitted him and accepted his gifts. They'd spoken little during that first meeting, but Hans returned to escort her around the city. He was pink with pride as she crowed and cooed and howled at every fantastic thing—the rain cistern, the hydroponic gardens strung up the sides of the cave walls where sunlight illuminated them like a hundred glowing lights, and a healing steam room, vented from a mineral spring far below in the rock bed.

"Beauties and glories aplenty," Dunya said with a smile. At least Hans had hoped it was a smile, and not a grimace, for it did seem that she was about to reach over and nip off his head with those long teeth of hers.

Dunya had never had a friend before. Only Meertham, whose rough and tardy kinship came at the end of his life. Still, it had been sweet for a moment. Dunya's eyes grew shiny at the memory of his kiss—her first. She wondered what it would be like to be kissed again, and then wondered what came after that. Her fantasy quickly ran aground; Dunya lacked the knowledge to launch it further. She was satisfied with kissing. Her forced breeding, another of Matuk's abominable experiments, was so far removed from that brief moment of tenderness she'd experienced with Meertham, she couldn't even begin to connect what was done between her legs to the little spark of excitement that came with a kiss. Getting another had quickly become her life's mission.

Now, thinking of Hans and the forest expedition to gather wild mushrooms and garlic planned for later that afternoon, Dunya sang again. It was a new sensation, this joyful noise. Not loud enough though. She opened her throat and howled, practically prancing with effervescence as her voice filled every available inch of space inside her tree house and spilled into the corridor. She was so intent on singing that she did not hear her door open or the aggrieved footfalls of one large and rather exasperated par-wolf striding into her chamber. His scent—musky, pungent, and alluring—submerged her in its richness. Dunya froze, nostrils twitching. She did not even turn to face the scent-carrier, so enraptured was she by his odors. Her lids drooped over eyes gone glassy and slightly crossed, her body slackened as her tongue unrolled and fell from her open mouth. She let the smell curl up inside her head, fill her senses, and overwhelm them.

Carac paused, stunned by Dunya's sudden transformation. She leaned into the air, transfixed by some private rapture. Her nostrils visibly flexed, she lapped slowly at the air, gulped and lapped again. Carac began to think he oughtn't watch this. Dunya's actions were so intimate, he believed them better conducted in private. His consternation slightly altered the chemical composition of his odor. Dunya sensed this and whined softly.

A muscle in Carac's lip convulsed as he watched a large bead of saliva drop from Dunya's hanging tongue to the floor. He cleared his throat, a deliberate human gesture of warning, and waited for Dunya to acknowledge him.

Slowly the fog cleared. Dunya pulled in her tongue and turned to face him, her eyes focusing on Carac. She said nothing, merely stared, chest heaving. Overwhelmed by his closeness, the piquancy of his smell, Dunya whined again, an unconscious seepage of noise.

Carac apologized for interrupting. "Miss Dunya," Carac repeated, serving her with a side of annoyance, "would you please?"

Dunya stopped. Carac, Queen Sidra's par-wolf advisor (and something else, she knew, but was too naïve to decipher just what), despised whistling.

"It's just that my ears are so sensitive," he explained.

The expression of personal happiness was new to Dunya, and she was brokenhearted to have had her first seedlings of spontaneous glee so quickly trod upon.

He'd come to tell her not to sing so loudly—in fact, he ought to tell her not to sing at all—but seeing her now, so small and obviously helpless to defend herself against sensual intrusion, his reproof fizzled out.

Ever mindful of the male need for purpose and the hedge that responsibility provided against mischief, Sidra had charged Carac with Dunya's protection. Dunya had been Matuk's housekeeper. Though bought like a pound puppy and made to serve him those long years, she was tainted by her association with him. Some of the more politically minded somatics might take it in hand to punish her for her master's misdeeds, so Sidra placed Dunya with the families and children, gave her a small home easily defended, a trusted companion to lend her credibility, and a guardian, all of which dazzled poor Dunya, whose resultant expression of delight made Carac's ears bleed.

He groaned inwardly. "Just checking, miss, to see that you have everything you need."

Dunya snapped out of her trance, alive with energy. "'Course I do! Couldn't ask for more, me. 'Tis only . . ." She paused, unsure of herself. ". . . only that yer smell makes me 'airs rise and me legs go wobbly."

Carac stiffened in embarrassment.

"Probably best that ye not come round quite so much. If ye don't mind. I've got 'ans now, ye see."

Hans my Hedgehog! Bad enough Sidra had gone all soft and pie-eyed for that girl-boy Soryk. Now the damned dog-faced girl rejected him for some pinch-faced little needle-nose!

Carac scowled, ire brimming black within him. "That's the way it is, then." He retreated, hackles bristling as Dunya's song resumed.

Too dignified to stomp, Carac retreated to Sidra's house in a grumbling funk. Though they had long shared living quarters, Carac was suddenly inspired to find his own space. Soryk and Dunya conspired to muscle him out of Sidra's life. And the baby! Not a word spoken about it, no confidence from his queen, she who could barely keep even the most mundane procreative secret and celebrated the news of every birth with sparklies and handfuls of home-made confetti. (At least, Carac mused, he'd not have to spend an evening cutting said confetti.) How could she think he'd not smell the presence of another person growing inside her? Was it his child or Soryk's? The thought made him gag. Sorykah was much more agreeable than that milk-bred stripling with his scraggly, adolescent beard!

"Rrargh!" Carac raged, his vision blurring with anger and the sudden intense desire to sink his teeth deep into live muscle pulsating with rivers of hot blood. The taste of raw meat would calm him, and the hunt soothe his nerves. Rarely did he resort to wolfery, but as anger condensed his humanity and smothered it beneath bloodlust, he knew that the only way to tame the beast in him was to give it free rein, or at least a very long leash.

Since Matuk's death and the passing of the Wood Beast, the Erun was alive with creepy-crawlies, flying featheries, and burrowing and digging things, all of them delicious and easily caught. Carac stripped off his shirt and boots. His mouth watered as a shiver ripped along his spine. Blood would soon quench his anger. He took a little-used tunnel, claustrophobic and dusty but a quick exit to the surface. Outside, the sky was a pale, watercolor blue above enormous swaying trees littered with flocks of dun sparrows and other squawkers. The wind carried many scents, things blithe and ignorant of the end awaiting them, as Carac inhaled deeply, chose his direction, and began to run.

As he crashed through the forest, planning only to run as fast and far as possible, he was unaware that Dunya and Hans hunted mushrooms near Carac's chosen hunting grounds. Poor loyal Carac! Every little glimmer of friendship or companionship was a taunting and fickle flame, offering warmth and acceptance, but just as quickly extinguished. It wasn't until he discovered Dunya canoodling with Hans that he realized why she annoyed him so.

HANS MY HEDGEHOG, SHORT-STATURED, gentle, and shy, was the perfect consort for Dunya, who had suffered grievously at Matuk's hands. Circumstance prevented Dunya from enjoying any normalcy in the only romantic experience she'd ever had: kissing Meertham, Matuk the Collector's devious, massive, half-walrus henchman, as he lay abed dying at the manor. Meertham was Dunya's only friend, and that rather reluctant truce had developed at the end of Meertham's life. They'd shared a single kiss, Dunya moored on the great bulwark of Meertham's body, relishing the close warmth of a touch offered with kindness.

Hans led Dunya into a fragrant forest grove, sun-dappled and dew-damp. Dunya thrilled to find tiny wild strawberries, the first she'd ever seen. There were so many new things to discover in the real world, and her delight at even the most mundane occurrence lifted Hans's mood.

Dunya sniffed out the wild sage and a few spring onions that Hans promised to serve in an omelet. Thrilled, Dunya just managed to refrain from licking his face, converting her ardor into a rather open-mouthed buss that left Hans shocked with pleasure and astonishment. He responded by taking Dunya's furred hand in his own and the two grew equally amorous, petting and stroking fur and quills. They would never go any further, but the novel sensation of arousal and acceptance, two feelings that had never before coexisted in either of them, sent them both into a frenzy of affection.

Carac bounded from the wood, focused on a fleeing wild hare. The hare was freakishly large. The newborn Erun had an abundance of food, and in the absence of predators, the hares proliferated. This was his second catch. The first warmed his belly, the taste of its meat metallic in his mouth. He killed more for sport and tension relief than hunger, so it little angered him when the hare bounded beneath a clump of briars and vanished.

Carac stopped short, his gaze locked on Hans and Dunya, entangled in some laughable parody of lovemaking. Startled, they pulled apart and stared at him. He was rank and bloody, his odor thick with arousal and hormonal pique. It wormed into Dunya's nose and rattled her senses. She'd warned him to stay away from her. She didn't like the way his scent, his presence converted her hard-won normalcy into rough animalia, reminding her that she could never be anything more than a dog-faced girl.

A growl expanded in her throat. Hans quivered beside her, his protests diminishing in her ears as her vision narrowed to a point. The blood pushed her over the edge. The sight and smell of spilled life, Carac's limbs and mouth coated in death. Dunya had seen too much of it. Matuk covered in organ slime and congealing crimson paint, bodies ground down into mulch and sludge on his autopsy table, their remains discarded by the bucketload. Buckets Dunya had carried down those marble tower stairs, over and over again, buckets she had dumped into the charnel house pit—a slurry of bile, blood, and tissue, where maggots steered boats of bone through a chunky red sea.

Hans couldn't possibly care for someone like her! Dunya gawked at him, new horror in her sad eyes. Dunya pushed Hans away as she struggled to free herself from the powerful bonds of Carac's odors and Hans's affection.

Though timid and prone to melancholy, Hans was not easily put off his goals. He'd set himself a new task: bringing out the best in Dunya. He saw only the good in her and knew that there was a deep reservoir of affection and gentleness to draw from. He'd not let coarse, angry Carac destroy Dunya's flimsy ego.

"Leave me be, 'ans! Ye've got no sense to be messing wit' the likes o' me!" Dunya resisted the grip of Hans's small hands, but he held firm.

Hans turned on Carac with surprising ferocity. "Get on with you! You've no business here!"

Hans's high voice was strangely compelling. Carac wavered, his head swimming. Until that moment, he hadn't admitted to himself that he fancied Dunya. Fealty to his queen impaired his inner vision. Loving another would surely be a betrayal of Sidra, so he pretended to feel nothing. Dunya irritated him only because she was irritating, not because he wanted her. Shamed, Carac hunched his bare back and retreated into the trees.

"You're safe now," Hans said, smoothing Dunya's furry cheek. "Remember that."

KABOOM

PARALYTIC WITH WORRY, SORYKAH stayed with the nomads for a night and a day. The relentless heat and constant agitation of camel flesh rubbing against her buttocks aggravated her gray ghosts. Sorykah's longing for ink waned and intensified in swinging arcs of lust and repulsion. *Steady on*, she admonished, focused only on that little vial in her pocket. Thoughts of Farouj lingered in her head. Farouj, the mysterious. He'd lured her into this misadventure and with every play, its twists and turns grew more kinked and treacherous.

Night came, lit by a moon that seemed to roll along the tops of the dunes. A light flickered some miles distant, yellow and white, on-off like a blinking star. Trucks lined a packed earth road beside a tin sign with peeling paint: "Property of Tirai Industries and the Unified Tribes of Qa'a'nesh. Trespassing forbidden." Vats of cheap red wine sat in the back of a truck, awaiting vinday celebrations. Though it shoved Jerusha down the throats of the Qa'a'nesh, TI spared every expense to do so.

Trespassers will be shot, she thought. *Shoot first, ask questions later.*

Nearing a circle of white clay domes, Sorykah's fellow made his camel kneel and shooed her off. She hung back, tempted to run after them. At least they were familiar and a link to Farouj, safety, and the way home.

Located at the bottom of a deep desert crater, the fossil water plant conducted all operations underground. The hole was sixty feet wide and dropped three stories below. Balconies ringed each level. What came next—a leap into the trench? Sorykah rappelling into the canyon with her blade between her teeth, popping off hand grenades as she swung from ledge to ledge?

Sorykah wished she'd been less distracted by her lust for lemonade and had paid better attention to Farouj's strategizing. She'd enter the plant and see for herself just what could be done. If Farouj was there, they'd find each other. If he didn't turn up, she supposed she could ask one of the admins to contact Chen for her. Despite her recent strangulation of him, she suspected he'd be pleased to hear from her and forgive her trespass, though the idea of asking Chen to rescue her turned her stomach.

Electric light flooded the desert, throwing stark shadows between the dunes. Sorykah dropped to her belly, hovering behind a rise to watch the workers climb from the pit to enjoy their full-night break. People conducted the mundanities of daily living. Children played ball. Adults gathered to smoke and talk in low voices.

Two tones reverberated from the loudspeakers. Like ants answering their queen's alarm call, the Qa'a'nesh moved mindlessly toward the gaping hole's ladders and lifts. Clanging bells and the groaning clatter of machinery echoed in the night air.

Just as Sorykah stood, determined to investigate the plant, three people appeared at the edge of light. People? She squinted. One dragged his foot; the others moved strangely, crookedly. They were far from home. Somatics roamed the entire country but tended to group in safe havens like the Sigue and the Erun, better protected by the strength of their collective presence than anything else.

The somatics conferred and dropped a box they carried. Sorykah watched them root around in the box, seemingly oblivious to capture, or else certain of their safety. They pulled out bits of equipment, stringing two tripod transmitters and lashing harnesses to their belts. One man strapped a pair of goggles over his eyes and scuttled toward the hole. He signaled the others and they descended. This did not bode well. Had Farouj recruited somatics to assist him in his campaign of destruction, or something more sinister?

"LOOK, THERE'S SOMEONE ELSE here." Udor of the cloven-hoof pointed a knobby human finger at Sorykah's distant figure, and the camels trotting off over the dunes. They watched her near, and knew that she saw them. Unbeknownst to Tjaler's crew, Sorykah's destination lay several levels below the bottling plant, where nefarious men in small, dank rooms did bad things to the children of the gods.

Although Tjaler hadn't recognized his queen's Trader lover when she first appeared, something about her hesitant, nervous gestures jogged his memory. They had met once in the Erun city. Clearly, she couldn't distinguish him outside the familiar surroundings. "Queen Sidra's pet. I doubt that she is capable of real harm."

Pertana scratched her head. "Do we abort the mission?"

"Leave her be. She's not worth anything to us." Crossing the desert on three-wheeled sand bikes, Tjaler had been surprised to see Sorykah and her companion escape the night train's slaughter. He toyed with the idea of telling Sidra about Sorykah's budding romance in hopes that she'd finally stop brooding and make space for him in her bed. Then he realized that returning her to their queen would earn him much favor. His heartbreaking tale of rescue would impress her. Moved by his gallant efforts to protect the Trader against the night train's onslaught, she might decide that Tjaler was a better guardian and advisor than that moronic par-wolf. "Now that I consider it, if you see her, hold her. We'll bring her back to the

Erun with us. Queen Sidra will be mighty pleased to have her Trader back."

The others exchanged glances and Pertana rolled her eyes behind Tjaler's back. His growing crush on their pregnant queen was tiresome.

Tjaler's chimp arm reached for the bag of explosives and fumbled with the zip. He palmed one of the powder-packed clay pots as if he meant to start lobbing bombs into the night. Pertana shuddered. Sometimes it seemed that Tjaler's arm had its own agenda and consciousness, and it worried her. She knew no other somatic whose change was so poorly integrated into his human self.

Hunkered on the sand, sharing bidis and drinking warm beer from a canteen, the bombmakers waited. Soon the lights clicked off, and darkness descended on the dunes. They hoisted bags onto their shoulders and set off across the sands. Together they edged up to the enormous underground chamber and descended the service ladders, seeing little through the steam. The upper levels were deserted. The workers toiled far below, where sand and clay insulated the fossil water processing rooms from the sun's heat.

Tjaler and the others were absorbed into the factory. It was as if their skin turned transparent, their breathing ceased, and their shadows deserted them. They rounded each floor level by level, hooking spider bombs beneath the railings edging the pit. They moved slowly, trusting their senses to alert them to danger. Vapor clouds hid them from view, but it also meant they would not see an attacker until it was too late. Tjaler's chimp arm swung and flexed strong fingers, poised for the kill. The somatics tucked clay bombs impregnated with remote ignition devices into crevices, cabinets, and drawers as the Qa'a'nesh changed shifts, filing quietly up and down stairs and service ladders, fresh faces replacing weary ones. Tjaler and Udor crouched and waited while Pertana slipped through the doors to access the inner rooms. Tjaler contemplated placing bombs in the nursery where the children studied, played, and napped. Although formal education was discouraged, the Aroulians maintained cultural lessons in language, art, and story. Mathematics and writing were forbidden. TI wanted its workers ignorant so they would have no alternative but to remain at the plant.

Udor sensed Tjaler's hesitation. "Would you leave this room untouched?"

Sidra would be angry with Tjaler if the plant were left intact enough to be rebuilt and resume its processes. They had a hundred spider bombs—enough to annihilate the entire compound. The plant was a sprawling labyrinth of corridors and chambers. Machinery crunched and clanked in the bottling room. Empties cycled past, paused, and guzzled water from gushing spouts. Full bottles shuttled along a conveyor belt, were stamped with labels, capped, and heatsealed. Despite the vinday festivities taking place throughout the rest of Plein Eïre, white-capped Qa'a'nesh workers sat behind glass windows, their attention focused on the lunches they unwrapped, complained over, and consumed.

Checking his watch, Tjaler gestured Udor behind the enormous vats of fossil water. The spiders wouldn't detonate before Tjaler activated their fuses. Pertana had instructions to meet him on the surface thirty minutes before the full-night break, giving them enough time to clear the blast zone. Comprised of multiple cells, the bombed rooms and supports would implode beneath the sand's weight. Casualties couldn't be avoided. A handful of Qa'a'nesh lives in exchange for the rest of the tribe's freedom from Tirai would be worth the sacrifice. Unless he bumbled into Sorykah by accident, Tjaler wouldn't find her among the warren of rooms and corridors. Should he delay completing his mission until Sorykah was proven safe? He'd win either way.

Heat began to overpower the cold, evaporating the steam. Tjaler and Udor flattened themselves beneath a sorting table when two company admins entered the bottling room. Truncheons dangled from their belts alongside EMPs and aerosol cans of etherine. Their conversation was mundane. They seemed rather ordinary and much less villainous than Sidra made them out to be. They wore Company suits and insignias and roamed freely, while the Qa'a'nesh were cooped up like chickens.

Udor looked at Tjaler with a question in his eyes. Again, Tjaler hesitated. He was a bomber. He murdered quickly and from a distance. Not in person and not just for the pleasure of it. He liked the excitement of explosions, a thrilling sensation that left all his senses happily humming. Tjaler less liked the way incipient excitement aggravated his capricious control of his lone somatic appendage. It had always been disobedient and reluctant to be leashed.

Udor's hoof pinged against the cooling vat, drawing the admins' attention. There was nowhere for them to run without exposing their hiding place. The admins came closer. Tjaler's chimp arm twitched in agitation. It danced at the end of his shoulder, fingers grabbing and squeezing air. He commanded the arm to relax; it responded by knocking into the sorting table leg, making the crates heaped on the tabletop shake and clink. Fearing discovery, Tjaler bit his chimp arm. He tasted blood but felt nothing.

The admins were almost close enough to touch. Tjaler had a quick and terrible vision, his right hand acting alone and with deadly intent. Then he could touch them and did, springing from his hiding place, chimp arm outstretched. The admins responded quickly, brandishing electrified truncheons. Fifty thousand volts of power burned through Tjaler's body, singeing chimp hair. Tjaler tossed crates of fossil water bottles like alphabet blocks. Severed from his control, the arm rampaged. Tjaler was dragged along after it, hurling bottles at the admins. Agitated by the ruckus, Udor beat the admins. His cloven hoof kicked and stamped, caving in bellies and bodies. Terrified, the Qa'a'nesh cowered behind glass.

Tjaler grabbed a truncheon and made short work of one admin. Brains oozed from the man's crushed skull like a yolk seeping from a cracked egg. The other cowered beneath Udor's hoof, raising his hands to block a fatal blow. Udor stomped and the second admin slumped against the floor.

Panting, Tjaler turned to face the workers. In the low lights of the bottling room, it appeared to the Qa'a'nesh that Tjaler and Udor cast no shadows. Indeed, these were invading gods from the dark side of the world. The Qa'a'nesh had nothing left of their culture but stories, carefully preserved and hoarded. Tirai Industries' assimilation campaign had scrubbed away every trace of nomadic independence, but it could not erase the stories that shaped their souls. The workers wiped mayonnaise from their mustaches and scrambled for the emergency pull on the wall behind them. Alarm horns shrieked. Orange warning lights flashed.

Tjaler heaved and grunted. His chimp arm throbbed. He leapt over the sorting table and rattled the door to the office. The Qa'a'nesh had wisely locked themselves in, and they gaped at him as he hollered and ran from the room, Udor close behind him.

THE SKY LIGHTENED FROM BLACK to gray and the desert began to broil as if an oven switched on and fanned its fire across the sands. There was no sign of Farouj. Sorykah could not wait through the heat of the day for him. Taking advantage of the murky morning, she sidled across the sand, checking the road and domes for signs of life, but all was empty and still. She followed the Aroulians' path to a freight elevator but, fearing its noise, elected to descend via the iron ladders connecting each level.

Electricity surged through the plant's wiring, making it crackle with artificial life. Aside from that constant buzzing, the compound was like a ghost town. Heat throbbed from the sunbaked sands and rolled across the dune to spill into the hole. Cold air and humid vapor rose to meet it, creating an opaque fog framed by shimmering heat waves. The steam grew thicker as Sorykah fumbled along the platform of level one, groping for the railing. Safety lights were fireflies trapped in gauze. The vapor, a chilling combination of extreme heat and subterranean cold, made her feel ill. Sorykah clung to the rail, blinded and lost. A horn blared and near doors whooshed open and closed, making the vapor swirl and dance.

There were voices speaking a language that sounded like a record album being played backward. Her infernal twin, not Soryk but panic, came to meet her. Wherever she went, whatever she did, it was there, lurking like a thief and conspiring to steal her brief joys. Fear of discovery and capture, fear of running and being lost, fear of drowning within herself—Sorykah could not conquer it. Ink could not quench it, nor love lighten its load. She wished for her Magar blade to cut it from her soul, amputate that demon limb, a second head that forever second-guessed her and whispered sour some-things in her ear.

Even the change was preferable to this helpless feeling. Did Soryk share her fear or was it a product of her unique body chemistry and experience? She would change now just to avoid it—so what if it meant the forgetfulness of the Perilous Curse? She'd manage to get herself out alive. Sorykah turned her focus inward, searching behind her racing heart for Soryk's hand, with which to pull him to full awareness. She'd take his place in sleep and leave it all behind.

The changing sleep came more easily when she went looking for it. Soryk stirred within the body of his primary. He would have woken fully had the touch of a man's hand not sent its signal through Sorykah's pores and deep inside her cells. The man, Farouj, calling her back to him as if charming a serpent into submission. She an-swered, and Soryk's all-too-short moment of awareness faded. He de-scended again into limbo and slept.

"It's you!" Sorykah hugged Farouj hard, relief washing over her. His touch was as welcome as a blinking buoy on a strange sea. If not an island of safety, he was at least a sandbar offering a temporary beach.

"Yes, I found you. TI technology is good for some things." He held up an IER reader similar to Nuala's. "The jersey you're wearing is embedded with magnetic threads. Not enough eyes and ears to gen-erate number readings, but enough to let me find you."

Sorykah beamed. This was one occasion when she was happy to have been spied upon. "Why didn't you tell me before?"

"You might have objected. I didn't want to risk you running around naked . . ." Sorykah couldn't see him but she heard the teasing in his voice.

"I'll take you to see the ink labs in a moment. First, we see to the children."

They groped along the walls until Farouj found and opened a door. The utilitarian room was full of children, seated upon the worn carpet on paper bag pillows. They gawked at Sorykah, a stranger from the wet world.

A woman, who could've been Farouj's sister for the similarity of their features, got to her feet and embraced Farouj. They spoke softly and she ran a finger along Farouj's cheek, an intimate gesture that sparked envy in Sorykah. Someone cared for him. That was a good thing. It meant that he was lovable, and worth loving.

"My aunt has been waiting for this moment. She too wants our people freed, our children returned to the sun. She will take them topside while you and I find the others and begin the exodus of my people," Farouj said.

His aunt, Sorykah sighed. *Only a pretty and quite young-looking auntie, nothing more.* She was surprised by how glad she was. "Am I supposed to change?"

"My aunt trusts me and the children trust her. Just hold out your hands." Farouj smiled. "Let your *t'naq* blaze."

The children rose awkwardly on bent, rickety legs. Soft and weak, their diseased bones could barely support their weight. Marshalling the children into orderly lines, Farouj's aunt opened the door. As she passed Sorykah, she tipped her head in respect and drew a finger across her throat. Had it been meant for Sorykah, it would have been terrifying, but she knew the slit throat was intended for the admins of Tirai. It was too late for these children, deformed by rickets, but future generations would grown strong and straight. Sorykah was glad to help them. Trailing the woman out the door, each child dipped his or her forehead to one of Sorykah's outstretched hands. Some gripped her fingers with their own warm, grubby ones and stole glances at her with sparkling brown eyes. She was charmed and imagined her *t'naq* as a bold fire that caught the sleeping cinders of the Qa'a'nesh rebellion.

"That's done." Farouj was relieved and invigorated. A mutinous gleam shone in his eye. "Now we find the tribal elders. Stick close."

An inner door led to a series of corridors. A few Qa'a'nesh roamed between rooms and levels, attending to their duties. Some recognized Farouj right away, while others did not. Those who didn't let their dull gazes slide away, disinterested in another Aroulian and the *gahjin* stranger at his side. Farouj bade each one pause and formally greeted them, placing his right hand behind their heads and pulling them close until their foreheads met. He whispered something in his native tongue, and Sorykah squirmed a bit as each pair of eyes met hers, laden with the same convolution of suspicion and hope. He said in English, "Today we evict the shadow gods from our world. Sorykah Minuit is the slayer of Morigis! Welcome her, for she has come from the land of Ur to liberate us from the tyranny of Tirai. The revolution begins today!"

She was mortified by Farouj's melodramatic introduction. The workers reacted almost identically to the pronouncement of rebellion. They stared and shook their heads, gesturing to Sorykah.

"Gather the elders," Farouj repeated. "Join us in the communal room to witness the rise of our ancient goddess! Touch her, and let her *t'naq* be the hammer to smash your shackles!" Farouj's infectious enthusiasm spread, like windborne wildfire sparks, igniting all whom it touched.

Farouj took Sorykah's hand, and she wondered if he too drew strength from her *t'naq*. "I told them this day would come but they are too enslaved by oppression to have hoped for its arrival. Now they'll see. We will rise triumphant and throw off this burden."

Deeper they descended, waking sleepers in the living quarters. Farouj located a grizzled, prune-faced elder, a cranky and agitated old man who resisted the call to arms. Farouj argued with him, pointing at Sorykah, who felt that she should swing a blade or utter a war cry. The agitation escalated. The elder shrieked at Farouj; though Sorykah couldn't understand his words, it was clear that Farouj received a nasty dressing-down. Farouj was so angry he looked ready to assault the old man.

Sorykah jerked his arm, pulling him from the room. "What was that about?"

"My grandfather," Farouj spat. "He sold his soul to the Tirai devil and doesn't want to leave. He'll turn us in to the admins who work here. We have to move fast. The admins are vicious in the enforcement of their rules. We outnumber them but they're armed. Quick, let's get to the communal room. Your change must be swift. Are you ready?"

Sorykah quailed. She never thought she would deliberately court the change. She'd spent her whole life running from it, and now, she thought wryly, Soryk had her by the balls. Or was it the other way around?

Farouj stopped and pressed his mouth to hers. "You can do this."

She nodded as they pushed open metal double doors and entered the communal room. There were already about twenty Qa'a'nesh waiting, many of them elderly and frail. Their chalky skin had a bluish undertone, and their black eyes were haunted as they searched Sorykah for some sign of the divinity they'd been promised.

Deep in the plant's bowels, machinery hummed and clanked. Drafts of vapor seeped under the door. With great tenderness, Farouj led Sorykah into the center of the circle. "I'm right here beside you," he whispered. "Just a flash—a bit of beard or flat chest—and then we'll go. Don't be afraid. You can do it."

Sorykah met the expectant stares of the gathered elders. She didn't find the skepticism she anticipated seeing there. Instead a respectful hush settled over the room and several of the elders clasped hands, craning forth kinked necks and straightening humped backs to better view the miracle.

Sorykah thought furtively of the deep tattoo's arresting power and understood that this might be the last time she need ever change.

Time to make friends with the enemy, she thought. "Just concentrate on it," Kirwana had advised. "Imagine the parts you want puffing up or disappearing beneath your hands."

She didn't know if it was easier to make her female self vanish or to rouse her male alter. The Qa'a'nesh began to whisper softly, an intonation that sounded like a prayer. She closed her eyes and lost herself in the rhythm of their voices. *Soryk, wake up. I need you.*

Nothing happened. A burst of panic stung her chest, and then, deep within, a heavy male energy stirred in slow, sleepy response to her summons. The tingles came, an army of red fire ants on the march through her fingers and toes. *Come on!* She dared him to rise and felt Soryk's gaining consciousness floating up to meet her own. Hot hormonal undulations ran through her tissues. She juggled two images—her diminishing breasts and shrinking womb, and the flow of power through her muscles, the weight of Soryk's penis and testes hanging between her thighs. His thighs. It felt so real. *Soryk?*

I'm here. His voice was familiar now, steady if not exactly reassuring.

Her face itched and she reached up to scratch it, eyes popping open at the scruff of stubble beneath her fingers. She saw the room as if through a lens, the edges of it curved around like a soap bubble, became aware of the pressure of Farouj's hand around her own. The elders raised blood-scored palms and flicked droplets on her as Farouj extended her hands to them.

Was it the power of her *t'naq* that filled her head with a steady vibrating hum? No, the elders made that noise far back in their throats, a purring rattle, as they clustered around her, gripping their bloody hands around hers, running gnarled fingers along Sorykah's arms to soak up the victory of the Collector's death.

Slowly, Soryk slipped away and her vision cleared. Blood smeared her arms and dotted her clothes, but the elders had seen Asta's reflection in her and were transformed by it.

"Come on." Farouj smoothed her hair, her soft female cheek. Back in the open corridor, they shielded their eyes against painfully bright sun. Searing heat poured into the pit and evaporated the vapor.

Farouj hugged her. "You did good. Thank you. They'll spread the word now and move everyone topside. We should follow them."

She found her voice again, still a bit stunned by her success. "I told Rava I would find her kin."

"You can't help them, you know."

"Maybe, but I have to see the octameroon processing area, at least to tell her what I've seen."

Farouj sighed, his gaze taking in the levels of the plant where Qa'a'nesh roved, noiselessly climbing the metal ladders to the surface. Qa'a'nesh crowded the elevators carrying boxes and balled-up blankets. Sorykah trailed Farouj to a tall ladder fastened to a steel support beam linking the balconies. They descended, Farouj first, hanging over the open pit. So far their presence had gone undetected by the admins and she was emboldened by this.

Somewhere far above them, a muffled "boom" sounded. The earthen walls vibrated and spit chunks of clay. Alarms blared. Admins swarmed from their offices, truncheons in hand. Farouj swung around the ladder and leapt to the lowest level. Sorykah followed him, clumsily falling the last few feet and scraping her hands and knees. Admins advanced to the ladders, truncheons swinging from their wrist straps. Contorted with fury, their faces were doubly devilish in the flashing orange light. The lift opened, spewing admins onto the floor.

Farouj rattled a locked door. A shadow darkened the peephole, the door sprang open, and a Qa'a'nesh woman waved them in. Farouj shoved Sorykah through and slammed the door behind them. The admins need only wave their passkeys to get in, but the woman used her shoe to hammer a triangular doorstop into the jamb. It would slow the admins but a moment. Long enough for Farouj and Sorykah to hide.

Farouj crouched, panting, when they heard admins animated voices. He waved Sorykah ahead as footsteps sounded in the corridor behind them. The alarm blared, numbing Sorykah to its urgency.

Farouj shoved Sorykah into a cold room with scratched stainless steel walls, a tiled floor inset with drains like a communal bath, and wide porcelain tables. An unholy cross between a morgue and an abattoir, every grisly surface showed signs of wear: repeated dirtying and cleaning. The salt smell of the ocean and an intensely unpleasant odor of spoiled fish filled the air. A conveyor belt trundled steadily along one wall, transporting small steel boxes from this room through a hole in the wall to another beyond it. The tables were scored with cuts but dry, all equipment neatly stacked and set aside. Surgical knives carved from Sigue stone—that particularly corrosion-resistant mineral—lay heaped in a shallow sink basin. Water tanks quietly percolated; air filters gasped and burped. The cell was lined with aquariums, six feet by eight feet high. Each tank glowed with murky blue light. Water seeped from a cracked seal and dripped down, soaking the floor. The saltwater tanks had been recently emptied. Calcification crusted the waterline, marking its rate of evaporation.

Another explosion rocked the plant. The walls rippled and bulged. Sorykah screamed. A lone admin staggered into the chamber, panic-stricken and gasping. Fresh blood dribbled from a burst eardrum.

Farouj grabbed a stone knife and raised it high. "Where are they?" he demanded.

The admin lunged toward Sorykah, yanking on her arm and tugging the neck of her jersey, exposing her bare shoulder. She shrieked and pushed him off but he clung like a barnacle. "Get off!" she screamed. "Let me go!"

The admin's voice was overloud, broken by hysteria. "I have to get out!" He shook Sorykah, wrenching her neck. "How do we get out?"

Sorykah stomped on the man's foot, breaking fragile bones. He surrendered her and turned to Farouj, almost as an afterthought.

"Where are the children of Ur?" Farouj shouted. "The old gods! What have you done to them?"

A series of deafening explosions rattled the aquariums. Cracks spread across the glass like winter frost. A fog of sand, steam, and debris made it difficult to breathe. The admin howled in frustration, too addled to concentrate as Sorykah and Farouj clung together.

"What's happening?" Sorykah shouted. "Is this your doing, Farouj?"

"Not part of my plan!" He yelled over the noise. "The ceiling's caving in. We have to leave!"

One by one, the tanks shattered. The door was firmly wedged in its bent frame and impossible to open. The conveyor belt continued to slide along its path. The tiny gap wasn't big enough to squeeze through. Cold, slimy water gushed around their thighs but this only made it easier to climb over the broken glass into a tank, where Farouj hefted Sorykah onto his shoulders. She ripped the filter from the wall and discarded its fan and hoses. Stepping on Farouj's shoulders, Sorykah wiggled though the hole, plunking headfirst into the corridor on the other side. There was a small metal hatch, and she opened it for Farouj.

"Good thinking! Come on." Farouj took Sorykah's hand and began to move toward a far gate ablaze with safety lights. Sorykah swayed on her feet, eyelids drooping. She reached up and touched her head. Blood coated her fingers. "I hit my head," she murmured, dazed.

Farouj caught her as she sagged to the floor. He shouted at her, but Sorykah heard only his voice from far away. Her head swam with octameroon visions. Farouj shook Sorykah, rousing her from a vivid nightmare. He saw the faint ebb and return, slapped her again, and forced her to keep moving. "Ur's children are gone, but I will not lose you, too. Wake up now, and walk."

THREE LEVELS ABOVE THEM, two somatics scurried up ladders, emerging from the smoking pit into the relentless light of day. Spider bombs popped and banged below the sand. Pertana and Tjaler staggered across the dunes, their eyes tearing in the smoke and sunlight.

Udor was lost somewhere in the pit, taken from them by furious, frightened admins.

Company and Qa'a'nesh battled each other on the sand, the admins fighting ferociously, though outnumbered. They had electrified truncheons on their side, but the Qa'a'nesh were fueled by rage, confusion, and a collective desire for revenge. Admins fell beneath pummeling, bare fists. Qa'a'nesh streamed from the pit crowing and crying, their hair spiked with dust. Nomads lined the horizon, camels snorting and shaking shaggy heads. A ripple split the sand. The pit buckled, sucking bodies into its depths. Tjaler ran and Pertana followed. The outbuildings vanished into the collapsing sand. Chaos reigned. People ran shouting and screaming.

Tjaler stood atop a dune, grinning. His chimp arm jerked and swung in agitation. Pertana stood a distance away, sweat dripping into her eyes. She wiped away the sting and discreetly pressed her hand to a pocket on her canvas soldier's pants. Four stone bottles of octameroon ink filled her palm, cool even through the fabric of her trousers. She already had a buyer lined up, a tattooist who used to have a shop in the Botanica. Pertana didn't think it would be difficult to locate Jandi and make the sale.

Tjaler said, "Get the bikes. We're done here."

"What about Udor?" Pertana asked. "You'd leave him here, not even look for him?"

Tjaler shrugged with one bulky shoulder and one wiry one. "Perils of the task, love. He knew what he was in for. Now get the bikes. I mean to enjoy this show a while longer."

"Aye aye, captain." Pertana saluted Tjaler and headed for the sand bikes, parked behind a dune a half mile distant. Tjaler would wait an hour for her return before making the trek to the bikes himself. There he would discover Pertana's bike gone and his own disabled, oil staining the sands below cut lines. Enraged, Tjaler would let his chimp arm smash and rip apart the bike. A vector of wrath, the chimp arm would propel him across the sands. It would foolishly hail the night train when it slid past. Tjaler would fall beneath a barrage of noiseless bullets. His half-human body would fry and shrivel on the fiery sands, and no one would ever miss him.

    ·

THE SUN WAS PALE GOLD. Dusk reclined on the dunes. Mehemija's story of Asta and the invaders lingered like a song within Sorykah's brain. To drive the shadows back into darkness, she must reclaim the house of the gods. Then Asta would again be whole and mend the split within her.

Sand floated high above the desert as the pit continued its inward collapse. Most of the Qa'a'nesh had accepted the refuge offered by the nomads assembled on the sand beyond the perimeter of the property. The nomads were few and their camels slow but they had come to help the tribe shake off its shackles. Jubilant workers whooped and ran across the sands. Some staggered, dazed and moaning, tears striping dirty cheeks. A group of children huddled on a far dune to watch the pit widen. Defeat was evident in the admins' somber faces. Some ransacked the outbuildings to steal equipment while others made a dutiful, if robotic, effort to corral the Qa'a'nesh and reassert the Company's dominance.

Farouj said, "My daughter wants to attend the Gathering of Tribes. She asked me to accompany her."

Sorykah offered a weak smile. The lump in her throat made it hard to swallow. The surge of emotion embarrassed her.

"But I could go with you, instead . . ." Farouj shouted above the noise of falling sand, raised voices, and nuzzling camels.

"Wouldn't you rather go to the gathering?" Sorykah gestured to the clustered Qa'a'nesh. Farouj's grandfather folded his arms across his chest, refusing to move even when others pushed him toward a camel.

"Not really. Mehemija is used to getting along without me. She'll be better off with her aunts for a while."

"Don't be silly. You belong here. I'll be fine on my own." She fumbled with her clothing, wondering how in hell she was to get back to the Sigue without him. She was trying to be gallant and self-sufficient but it came across like a rejection. It wasn't the journey that worried her; it was being without him. She'd never spent so much time in one person's company, aside from Soryk's tryst with Sidra, which she little remembered. She did recall the feeling of going to sleep in the arms of one she cherished and knew how cold the bed could be without that body beside her.

Farouj clapped an arm around Sorykah's shoulders and gave her a friendly squeeze. After the intimacy of their night on the dunes, it was a strangely laconic statement. She couldn't help but feel thrown away, and she said so.

Farouj raised black eyebrows. "I'd never toss you away. Why would you think such a thing?"

She had no answer. Farouj spoke but it took a moment for her to comprehend the significance of his words.

". . . an escort to the Sigue. Did you hear me?" He had to shout as he dragged her a from the mêlée.

"What would you do in Ostara? Neither of us can work for Tirai. I'll have to give up my house." The weight of it pulled her into despair. She was out in the wide world again, starting over with nothing.

"We'll figure it out. Take me home with you." Farouj's kiss was sandy but sweet. Sorykah laughed but his warm embrace could not drive away the chill that settled within her. She had killed Matuk the Collector, destroyed the most insidious of his enterprises, and liberated an entire people. She could not begin to imagine the swift and terrible retribution Chen would launch upon her. The *Nimbus* still orbited the Sigue in search of Ur's children and digi-reels polluted Neubonne's pixel screens. A relentless vehicle of death, the night train crossed plains, mountains, and meadows in search of somatics to slaughter. Sorykah had only crippled the Tirai giant, not felled it. The Erunites were in danger of dying at TI's hands, butchered like sheep after lambing season and left to decay in their little tunnel city. Sorykah might tire but she could not rest or cease her onslaught against Matuk's kin.

Distant Haymaz fireworks popped and fizzed, showering gold

scintilla over the cities of Plein Eïre. In Neubonne, revelers waved crackling orange sparklers and blew cheap tin horns. Jerushians inked their wishes on strips of colored rice paper, heaped them in the pilgrims' grates to burn on mounds of red-pigmented coal, and gathered to sing hymns of rising and welcome. Dégé Koans pummeled every somatic they could find while the city police abdicated duty and crowded the third ward publicans, clinking pints and smashing the empty glasses against the tiled floors. Scurrying ink rats indulged their lusts, scratching and rubbing and dodging gray ghosts. The clocks struck full night and chimes pealed in every crumbling brick tower, deep and resonant, as the new year began.

23

ENDGAME

CRUSTED WITH SMEARS OF dried body fluids and violet saliva, Chen withdrew from the women in his bed, its black silk sheets crumpled and damp. Dirty plates, empty champagne and shot glasses, and clothes littered the floor, the remnants of Haymaz feast. The two women, whose names he could not recall, sighed and curled into a sleepy embrace. Black candles flickered, their feeble light faintly brightening the dark room. It wasn't yet dusk, but Neubonne's perpetual smog dimmed the setting sun and made the room dreary. Chen's brain was fuzzed by herbal liqueurs. He'd not thought it possible to overdose on strawberry milk, but he'd discovered the hard way that it was. His head throbbed. The succubae in his bed had drained him of all fluids, hope, and life. Copulation—Chen's usual cure for depression, anxiety, guilt, or boredom—wasn't doing the trick today. He still felt horrible—worse than before, because now he was parched and needed a bath.

He couldn't quite understand when things had begun to change.

Was Matuk's death the instigator or had the shift commenced its evolution in prior years, when Chen's father became trapped in his summer palace of white marble? The foundation of the Morigi empire had cracked and everything dependent on that strong base rocked and trembled in the shock waves. Earlier that morning, Bodkin had come to the penthouse to report the destruction of the fossil water plant in the Aroulian desert. Chen had merely shrugged, ordering the girl with him to keep her hands to herself for a moment so he could concentrate. Something about Bodkin's manner disturbed him. Perhaps it was the way he imparted information with the icy formality of a royal butler, or the hint of satisfaction that twisted the man's mouth into an imitation of a smile. Whatever it was, Chen didn't care for it.

He'd considered dismissing Bodkin from his position with Tirai Industries, but the finance administrator had been with the Morigis for most of his life. Bodkin was Matuk's right-hand man; more than once, his experience had proved invaluable to Chen. Still, his glib superiority was annoying at such an early hour. Also unwelcome was the news that the fossil water plant and the related industries that formed the current bulk of Morigi investments and holdings had been blown to dust.

"How did this happen?" Chen was peeved by the inconvenience of the entire incident.

"Mr. Morigi, it's unclear whether it was an act of vandalism committed against the Company or simply the result of faulty equipment within the plant. The worst aspect of the disaster was the defection of workers."

"Defection? The Qa'a'nesh own the land that the factory sits upon." Chen frowned. "Don't they?"

"Their claim is a tenuous one and our recognition of it is a goodwill gesture more than anything else. Their rights to the land are as easily dispensed with as the sign marking the land's boundaries or the factory itself. You see how quickly they abandoned their stake." Bodkin leered again, servile yet smug as he departed.

Chen shuddered. He'd been remiss in his duties as scion of Tirai Industries. Bodkin had too much control and Chen must reclaim it.

The women snored beside him. At least Zarina had been a silent sleeper. Where had she got to? Chen went to the window to survey his city. She could be anywhere. Perhaps she'd become the victim of some deviant's crime, but Zarina was more devious than any man Chen had ever met and more single-minded in her pursuits. If anyone was in danger, it was the citizens of Neubonne, not Zee.

Chen's bedmates would stay or leave as he wished, but it was less fun commanding his own personal harem than it once was. If he were a miner like Sorykah, a worker at the fossil water plant, a sailor, or one of the many underlings in his employ, he'd have to expend the effort to win over women with his charm and graces. Bah! It was a waste of time to do that dance. He'd noticed silver strands in his beard and a new weariness in his eyes. Chen envied the simplicity of Sorykah's attachments to home and family. He had no such ties himself. The House of Pleasure was but one port of call among many. The Erun city was closed to him, his father gone and his siblings dispersed across Plein Eïre. Matuk's many unions assured disconnection and unfamiliarity among offspring. Chen had little contact with his family. He couldn't voice it, but he'd grown lonely. Only drugs and the endless vanilla bidis he smoked helped to numb the ache. Sentiment was a by-product of age. It had no meaning or purpose in a life like his.

There was no chance of rebuilding his relationship with Sidra, the only woman he had ever loved. She had too much contempt for him. How many doxies had he filled up and tossed aside, how many lovers had paraded through his life? Enough to wear down the pile on the carpet. It tired him to begin anew each time, to play the rube and rascal. He needed someone who would stay and be loyal, even if she did not love him. Someone fairly intelligent and ambitious, one whose sangfroid suited her like freckles on a redhead—Zarina. There was a woman who knew the score and kept her expectations realistic. Too scheming to express her irritation, Zarina hung on while Chen dragged her across the country, being a good girl in hopes of earning the promised house. Had she finally tired of the wait and abandoned him? Zarina was loyal when it suited her goals. If Chen purchased a grand manse on the hills for her, it could entice her to return to him. It was easy enough to lure her back into the fold. The house would be his because he'd hold the title, but Zarina could transform any pretty, empty shell into a home for them both. After all, a paid courtesan was better than none at all. Chen picked up his EMP and contacted his solicitor.

SINCE INSTALLING HERSELF AS a resident of Kirwan's house, Zarina had worked slavishly to clean, polish, and restore the mansion's faded beauty. Now every scrubbed room and surface sparkled. She'd acquired a few choice pieces of furniture; Woolley-Wallace proved adept at locating salvageable goods from trash lots and curbs. He'd brought her an antique dining table with a rickety leg, two matched chairs, a bed frame, assorted crockery, china, and bent flatware, rescued from the bin behind the restaurant supply store.

Zarina discovered a treasure trove of linens in an upstairs cupboard. Stained by some unmentionable liquid that had stiffened them into cardboard, a soapy hot water wash transformed them into curtains and a tablecloth. Next she planned to scrape the gunk from the bottom of the swimming pool and brush green moss from its decorative tiles.

Donning a battered pair of Kirwan's dungarees, Zarina heated water in a bucket on the fire pit in the courtyard. The scrub brush felt solid in her hand; the citrusy smell of detergent made her happy. She was glad to know that she'd been right about having her own home. It did wonders for her attitude.

Back inside among the cool shadows, Zarina opened the windows to air the rooms. That body in the library was really starting to stink.

"You promised to get us a shovel today!" she called up the broad stairs. "That smell is unbearable. They can probably see a fog of death hovering over the house all the way from Neubonne."

"You'll have to drive me. I'm knackered. I can't make the walk on my own." Invalid-frail, Kirwan limped downstairs clutching the rail.

"And you know that I can't take the car into town and risk being seen. Chen will be looking for me and I'm not ready to be found."

"We could prop the Plaid Lad up in the driver's seat. Tie his hands to the wheel and make it look like he's driving." Kirwan grinned at the image.

"He's rotten! He'll leak all over the leather. I'm not spoiling my car with that little monster's excretions."

"Maybe you'd rather he was still alive?"

Zarina vigorously shook her head. "Never! I did what I had to do."

"I still don't understand why you helped me," Kirwan murmured.

The warmth that temporarily softened Zarina's hard features cooled. Had it really been only four days since the Plaid Lad lay down for his dirt nap? Woolley-Wallace had hung about Kirwan's house, running errands and making himself useful only because he couldn't think of anything else to do while Zarina searched for So-rykah. When Zarina returned from Neubonne, fuming and thwarted, she had discovered Woolley-Wallace making himself cozy with the unconscious Kirwana. The Plaid Lad had badly sprained the Trader's leg in the attempt. Zarina vaguely recalled stripping off her blouse, twisting it into a rope, and strangling the Plaid Lad with a homemade garrote. She was more sickened by Woolley-Wallace's desire for the Trader than motivated by heroism and irked by his pursuit of second best. The little plaid monster had had the nerve to flirt with her, thinking himself fit for the mistress of Tirai's heir. She'd smirked, withering him with poisonous words and a murderous stare. Delighted to see him retreat, his pride punctured, Zarina had dined on the pleasure of rejecting him. Superiority was a tasty dish soured by the realization that she'd pushed him too far. Half naked and bug-eyed, he lay where he'd fallen, a bloated purple sausage in a tartan casing.

When Kirwan woke from the change, he didn't question the body beside him or the platinum-haired woman in his house. It seemed somehow appropriate that his guardian from the Onyx Tower should follow him home, that his digi-reel director would continue to plot and pace his actions for him. Just as a cat will refuse to play with a dead mouse, his apathy dulled Zarina's hatred. He seemed to expect his own death and was almost disappointed when it didn't follow. No longer in the mood to murder, she exchanged Kirwan's life for a claim on his house. As the days passed and Zarina's outlook improved, the lingering impulse to kill him faded. They cohabited with a strange and sudden intimacy like two caged tigers allied against the keepers and trainers of their particular zoo.

Woolley-Wallace's seepage was beginning to stain the floor.

"We really don't need a swimming pool, you know," Kirwan mused. "We could fill it with dirt and plant fruit trees."

"Apples, apricots, pears," Zarina said.

"Persimmons, plums, and pomegranates. They'd thrive with the right fertilizer."

Zarina giggled, a strange sound like the bark of a red fox. "Do you think the apples will come in with plaid skins?"

BODKIN PACED HIS OFFICE, his black boots scuffing the white tiles. Woolley-Wallace and that other idiot had gone AWOL from TI. Bodkin resented Chen's imperative to locate those two shirkers. Zarina had vanished, too, and although that meant less interference in Company business, it left Chen without a handler. Zarina was an efficient and useful buffer. Without her, Chen's shoddy business skills were more troublingly apparent. He cared about all the wrong things. The missing town car, Woolley-Wallace's expensive suits, and earnings taken straight from the Hanging Garden's till dogged Bodkin's meticulous bookkeeping but barely concerned Chen. Typical of Matuk's children, Chen had limited understanding of just how much money he had, where it came from, how to get more, and what to do when it was gone.

"That's your job, Boddy old boy. It's always been your job. You make the money and I spend it. We're in a blissful marriage of equals." Chen laughed away Bodkin's concern. "If you have something of import to relay to me, do so. Flighty women or brainless hooligans and their unpaid tailoring tabs are of no consequence to me."

Incapable of ending any conversation without imparting a final jab, Chen had added, "You squeeze every nickel until it bleeds and screams for leniency. It's no wonder you never wed."

Bodkin begrudged the toadying role he was forced to play, but soon enough, his adroit machinations would bear fruit. When he'd caught every last octameroon in the Sigue, Bodkin alone would control the flow of aphrodisiacal ink, forcing TI to purchase from Plein Eïre's sole supplier at whatever inflated price Bodkin set. That, at least, was the practical part of the plan. But having those demon spawn in his care set his mind reeling. The older he got, the more disgusted and disenchanted he had become with the general decline of social mores. Plein Eïre's southern cities had degraded with the introduction of bluing and an influx of mutated genes. Once a hidden cultural subset, the somatics, united under the leadership of that dirty forest queen, were gaining in strength and number, and their increasing political power threatened Bodkin's vision of fully segregated societies. They pushed their way in where they had no place. They practically flaunted their deformities, an open affront to Jerusha's divine ordinance.

The archpriest of the Dégé Ko Jerusha church forecast a coming somatic uprising. In need of wealthy allies, Ton-Andrev facilitated Bodkin's private study of the True Texts, pointing out the passages that condemned Asta's descendants as progeny of the dark deceivers, the shadow gods. If somatics further mixed their bloodline with the intact, warned the archpriest, Jerusha would condemn them *all* to the shadow world. Ton-Andrev showed Bodkin a series of scrolls detailing the deceivers' elaborate tortures—graphic woodcut prints of strange, limbless creatures, their huge mouths inset with rows upon rows of tiger teeth, biting, sucking, and draining the life force from the fallen. Bodkin could evade this sentence by devoting himself to the Dégé Ko mission of somatic suppression.

Ton-Andrev encouraged Bodkin to continue Matuk's work and cleanse Plein Eïre of its somatic infestation. The Collector's goal had been misguided, even if the application of his personal philosophy achieved the church's aims. Bodkin might set a new example with which to inspire the laity. It was Ton-Andrev who assembled a crew to run the night train. Ton-Andrev who interpreted the runes that declared the Gathering of Tribes a deceiver's coven and ordered its attendees diverted, detained, or destroyed. Bodkin procured the train, funneled donations—much of it diverted from TI's income streams—into the church's coffers and hosted "love feasts" to honor the goddess.

Tithes collected at the feasts would help to pay for construction of the new holding tanks at the Neubonne Aquarium. Taking the otameroons was easy. The admins at the plant didn't question his orders. The beasts' handlers shocked and subdued them at Bodkin's command.

Bodkin's message pad trilled.

From: G.Nunn@OST_CO.ind
To: Mr.Bodkin@TI.ind
Sent: May 4, 4:47 p.m.

Cargo safely relocated. Operations will resume within the week. Plans for expansion to continue? Undersea conditions impede specimen collection.

From: Mr.Bodkin@TI.ind
To: G.Nunn@OST_CO.ind
Sent: May 4, 4:50 p.m.

No matter. Take them all—alive, this time. Organize a withdrawal from the Sigue. Transfer ops to new locale. Production to resume ASAP per agreed upon revisions. You are my man now, not Chen's. Devotion earns its own reward.

IT WAS A HARD INDUSTRY, this toil of ancients. Rava and her cousins swam as if the devil were on their tails, for indeed he was. Diabolo's waking fury grew hotter by the hour. Volcanic vents split wide and boiled the sea. It was too hot for the octameroons to approach the vents directly. Every chunk of ice melted before it could stop the flow. Rava hauled shipwreck debris from the land shelf below the floe fields: snapped masts, rusted panels, busted crockery, and bent propellers. Ur's children packed ice core holes with sand, bones, and handfuls of seafloor debris, bandaging the Sigue with garbage.

The octameroons had few forces to rally in their defense. Sighted Rava served as the guardian of her kin, patrolling the berg to sound the subsonic alarm should the "boomer" appear. Flight was their sole recourse against its sonar pulses—those who lingered too long within the blast range would soon find themselves dragged into the *Nimbus*'s hungry hold. Rava was desperate to end their slaughter but her family had swum through the same waves, tended the same tunicate fields and ancient berg since time immemorial. They would not be moved despite their decimation and Rava's pleas.

Two were lost during a stealth raid. With darkened lights, the submarine idled on the seafloor, hidden within a bed of glass tulips, translucent white stems writhing around its hull. When the octameroons came to tend their fields, the *Nimbus* launched sonar blasts that shattered the sea.

Rava sought Sorykah in Ostara but could not locate the only human to whom she felt connected now that Pavel was gone. Desperation lured Rava away from the Stuck Tongue's hookah pipe. Urgency urged her back into the sea in search of a solution. She began to spy upon the *Nimbus*. It was a mission of extreme danger, for the boomer's claw hung ever ready to strike and pluck its catch from the sea. Rava had evolution on her side in the war against the *Nimbus*'s technological advantages. The *Nimbus*'s radiant heat was a blotch against the Southern Sea's black canvas. The sight that made Rava a freak among her own kind allowed her to watch the submarine's crew repair their hull. Wielding a wand of fire, they melted the *Nimbus*'s metal frame. Rava did not delay. She struck, a ferocious blur of hooked tentacles, ghostly human flesh, and beetroot hair. The two crewmen were easily dispatched. Rava curled a tentacle around the tubes on their backs and ripped. Air bubbles gushed from the broken oxygen lines. The men flailed and fell, heavy as stones into the deep black water. She gripped the wand in her human hand, tinkering with its dials and triggers until it spit white-hot fire and the sea boiled around the jet. To disable a shark, one must sever its fins. Rava had done this once before and she determined that the boomer was also a shark, rapacious and deadly. She would cut off its fins, too. The light from the wand scalded her yellow eyes but she held it firm, watching the fire eat through the propeller shaft, severing it from the *Nimbus*'s body. The amputated blades joined the bodies on the ocean floor.

Rava heard the boomer churn and struggle but she could not watch it sink, for her eyes were full of white fire, the afterimage of a welding torch forever burned onto her retinas. She had stared too long at her saving sun, but she could not mourn the loss of something that distinguished her as a freak among freaks. When the boomer hit bottom, Rava relished its soft thud and the cloud of sand that billowed into the sea.

Far below the surface, Rava was certain she could hear the singing Sigue Sea. That crooning hymn, played by an orchestra of shifting, singing ice, rang out over Ostara, and Ur's immortal voice lilted in pleasure as the forgotten goddess relished her distant daughter's retaliation.

KIKA FOLLOWED HER NOSE, fully trusting it to lead her home. She recognized the odors of the meadows and marshes that linked the Erun Forest to the rocky shore reaching inland from the floe fields. She remembered the Sigue song, a sweet lullaby that sang her home across bobbing islands of ice to the white waste's endless span. Kika knew the volcano by its odor of sulfur. She nosed the door of the deserted house she found there, smelled the faded aromas of her mistress Sorykah. She delighted in the faintest whiff of a sealskin samilkâ that Sorykah had once worn. The smell of her dead team, her beloved Kite, and the others she'd known since puppyhood haunted the empty rooms. Volcanic soot layered the floor like black snow. There was nothing there for Kika and so she kept on, her empty stomach growling. Juicy grubbits didn't inhabit the waste. Hope of food pushed her on through sleety winds. The strange spring heat softened the waste's otherwise bitter frigidity. Without this incidental kindness, Kika would have frozen to death.

Mud pushed through melting snow. Strange green things burst from the ground like stray hairs from lumpy moles. Quonsets and wooden hay houses grew before her eyes. Muted Sigue song hummed in Kika's ears, drowned out by human voices. No one paid any attention to a scrawny sled dog, her white fur made gray with grime. Nose twitching, Kika wove through the people. She could smell the babies now, their peculiar scent signature setting them apart from Siguelandic children who smelt of fish, kerosene, and the ocean. Sorykah's babies rivaled the sweet perfume of fresh-sliced apples.

Strongest at the door of a small silver Quonset hut, the scent confirmed her home. Kika whuffed and sneezed, prancing happily and wagging her tail. Yellow light filled the window but the door did not open for her. Kika barked and scratched. She heard footsteps. The handle squeaked and turned. Nels gasped. Kika leapt and licked, the scent of Traders thick in her nostrils, communicating welcome messages of home.

Nels chopped meat fine and dished it up for Kika and the babies. They ate bits of boiled potato and Kika begged for more. Nels stuffed the dog with food until her belly bulged between thin ribs and she staggered to a corner of the kitchen to sleep. Chattering and squirming, the babies endured the imposition of Nels's washcloth as she wiped food from their hair and faces. She made the motions of bedtime rituals, sleepwalking through baths, diaperings, and good-night kisses, thinking all the while of that red silk square on the kitchen table. Red like a valentine, red like kissed lips and blushes. Someone had tied that silk to Kika's neck and she had borne it for miles. Who would trust a dog to deliver a message, for what else could it be, a stained and filthy bit of silk cocooning a hard nugget like a bad memory entombed within a shell? She dare not speculate lest she break her own heart.

Kika snored in the corner, legs twitching. Nels sat at the table, cupping her hands around her coffee mug to warm them. The crimson cloth burned like a bright flame. The silk tore apart in her fingers. A black stone tumbled free. A bird's egg? A square of fragile onionskin opened paper petals, smeared ink seeping across the page as it exposed its tender sentiments to Nels's scrutiny. The words jumped up to sting her.

> Care for her when I cannot,
> this bright child of mine.
> If I loved you too quickly,
> it was only because I had not the luxury of time.

Not Soryk/ah's writing, but Queen Sidra's, her name and royal seal stamped across the paper. Her throat tightened. *Silly girl*, Nels rebuked. *What a foolish child you are to think this meant for you! Yours was not a grand romance.*

Along the bottom edge, in a cramped, careful hand, someone had added a postscript.

> sir/madam
> our queens health declines as the baby grows bigger.
> She wont come right out and ask for you direckly—shes
> too prowd. but she needs you by her side now and al-
> ways. if she dies, every thing will be caos. all her plans
> & such wasted with no one to charge the erun. the child
> will be an orfan. she will disappear like the stars in day
> light. hurry back.

Anesthetized to emotion, she followed the note's instructions. The ice tree seed sat in a bowl of water, a photo negative of an egg yolk swimming in white.

"Care for her, when I cannot." Nels mulled over the message, dwelling on those many nights in the Erun when Sidra had drawn Soryk upstairs after her as if he were a dog on a lead. Nels knew that look on Soryk's face when besotted by his wily forest queen. Soryk would have gone to fetch the new child and resume his life in the Erun. Would he really have left Nels with the twins, expecting her to make everything all right? Sorykah would go ballistic. She wouldn't have abandoned them. Worry made Nels toss and turn all night. Finally, as dawn broke over the Sigue, she slept.

Kika's bark roused Nels. Groggy with a stifling emotion too pallid to be called sorrow yet too deep to be anything else, Nels descended the stairs into a storm. Dendrites of ice tree skin drifted through the air, a baker's lazy powdered sugar dusting. A fine shedding of papery bark dotted the floor. The kitchen table groaned, sagged, and cracked beneath the weight of the ice tree growing on its back. Roots and branches slithered around table legs and curled between the slats of wooden chairs.

It took Nels most of the morning to dismantle the table and drag the ever-growing ice tree through the Quonset to the outside. The terrifying tree was almost brawny enough to rise up on its taproots and walk through the door of its own accord. Iridescent leaves shimmering in the noonday sun, Sidra's gift pushed adventitious fingers into the permafrost as Nels watched. Mud shoveled itself up from the ground in heaps. Water plumped the tree's cambium and strained its peeling bark. Sap beaded and dripped, making sticky-sweet icicles that hung two feet down.

What can it mean? She couldn't fathom the intent behind Sidra's strange poem or the ghastly tree sprawling across the road and shedding its dandruff everywhere. *If I were a queen whose man ran away, what would I do or say to get him back? I'd give him some essential bit of myself in lieu of my heart, something to speak for me when my words were too frail or clumsy to do the job properly.*

Sorykah's neighbors left their homes to gawk at the fecund, fast-growing tree. Even old Oona trundled down the road from the wash house to view the miracle. She hooked a wrinkled arm around Nels's elbow and peered up through shaggy gray bangs.

"Ice tree! He love you."

"Loves me! Why do you say that?" Nels blushed.

"Sign of Asta. Very rare. *Fas por amanat es enet mori gran sason e cadus*," Oona quoted, shaking a gnarled finger.

"One who loves from within the grave bestows the gift of the seasons." A gaunt man with a protuberant beak of a nose closed in on Nels. "Are you acquainted with the poets of the realm? Saint Catherine is too mawkish for my taste but the romantics love her. Ha!" He guffawed. "Pun intended. Is that a pun?"

Nels raised blond brows, her expression pained. "Not really."

Ravenlike in appearance, the man cocked his head and gazed at Nels with keen eyes. "Not a gift from your sweetheart, I presume, for if you realized the preciousness of this gift, there'd be a smile upon that pretty face."

"No. It's not meant for me."

"Pity!" He scooped a handful of bark snowflakes in his hand and sprinkled them into the breeze. "Most extraordinary! Like a phoenix born of ashes! I haven't seen one of these since I was a boy. The ice tree is only created when the seeds of the holimak tree are exposed to high heat and then frozen, a pairing of events that occurs very infrequently in nature. Ice trees are cultivated like pearls but I thought it a forgotten art." He leaned close to Nels as if imparting state secrets. "Someone has kept this in their pocket for a very long time, saving up for a rainy day, I suspect."

Oona broke off an icicle of sweet sap, stretching and snapping it like saltwater taffy. She stuck it in her mouth and grinned widely, exposing several missing teeth.

Oona patted Nels's hand. "Babies?"

"Inside. They'd love to see you," said Nels.

Oona trotted off, springy-stepped with anticipation.

Clearly the man was in no hurry to depart. "Are you versed in the story of the holimak tree?"

Nels shook her head, humoring him. He exuded an aura of deliberate solitariness but he seemed happy to abandon the affectation to chat with Sorykah's buxom nurse.

"In the distant days of the old gods, there was a war. Shadow spirits from the dark half of the world overthrew the house of Asta. To escape them, Asta split herself into two. As a woman and a man, she was able to evade their detection, for the shadows wanted to kill her and be troubled no more. The shadow spirits did not suspect Asta's male incarnation but the maiden's disguise she wore could not smother the light in her. Unable to find her, the shadow spirits slaughtered all goddesses, maidens, mothers, and crones." He sighed with regret as if remembering a scene recently witnessed. "Asta's male half buried the female half beneath a holimak tree. The heat from the goddess's decomposing body created the first ice tree. When seeds fell and sprouted, the ice trees wrought a false winter. Ice tree bark flew so furiously that it clouded the sunlight that had first attracted the shadow gods. Without sunlight, the shadow gods found the bright side of the world grown bleak as their own, and retreated.

"Spring and winter intermingle within the ice tree. It signals death and the continuation of life. It is half a heart, seeking reunification with its missing portion. Are you half or whole?"

"Sadly, every bit of me is right here." Nels forced a smile in the face of Sidra's magnificent declaration of love for Soryk. "But I know someone who'll be happy to see it."

24

HEARTS, REPAIRED AND BROKEN HERE

FAROUJ TOOK CARE OF EVERYTHING; Sorykah didn't even have to think. As they left behind the rubble of the caved-in fossil water factory, he was so solicitous that she almost expected him to carry her on his back to keep her tender feet from the hot sand. They walked aimlessly, putting distance between themselves and destruction, but Farouj soon moved with purpose toward a far-off object, a sparkle in his eye.

The fretwork of tracks cross-hatching the sand told them there had been others there who were now long gone. Blood trailed from the body of a dead somatic, his face twisted in agony. Tattered pants revealed a misshapen leg finished with a broad hoof. A three-wheeled sand bike sat abandoned beside him.

"I haven't ridden one of these in ages! Cripes, it's hot!" Farouj shook his hand and gingerly examined the bike. "Fuel tank's half full. That's enough to get us back, if we're lucky."

Its vinyl seat gummy in the intense heat, the battered chrome of its pipes and handlebars like fire irons, the bike was as magically incongruous as a flying carpet. They waited until dusk for it to cool down enough to mount without singeing off their nethers or branding their legs. Sorykah sat behind Farouj, her thighs gripping his, her arms around his waist. He smelled of sweat, dust, and smoke—sort of manly and dirty in a good way. When he opened the throttle and made the bike growl and jump beneath them, she threw back her head and laughed. Sorykah nestled close to Farouj as the bike roared over the dunes. She'd never ridden a sand bike before, or moved so fast. She felt miraculously free. Stars raced overhead as they sped south. It was still dark when Farouj pulled up to Desert Station Number One and turned off the engine.

"Wake up, sugar cake." He pried Sorykah's arms from his waist, and stretched, groaning with pleasure. "That was a long ride! My bum has gone numb."

Sorykah laughed sleepily and followed Farouj into a small shop built of corrugated tin and concrete blocks. Iron bars latticed the windows. Three hard benches on the train platform offered meager comfort to travelers.

Two old women ran the station, neither one much taller than the counter they stood behind. Her scraggly hair apparently dyed with shoe blacking, the less wizened of the pair hopped up on a stool to greet them in a cracked voice. Farouj ordered two breakfasts with tea. He added sugar and lemon to both cups, spread a napkin on Sorykah's lap, and handed her a fork. She giggled at his every chivalrous gesture. His kindness was a strange and mysterious joke, and in her exhaustion, she found it endlessly amusing. He wetted a napkin with cool water and pressed it to the back of her neck. Sorykah easily submitted. She felt like a rare and exotic animal handled by an expert and even-tempered handler. Would he bathe her and brush her hair? Choose her clothes and serve her breakfasts in bed? Farouj would probably feed her from his fingertips if she allowed him to, and she wondered if and when she might tire of his attention.

Romance and soft words were alien to Sorykah, but she gulped them down like ambrosia. Her training at the House of Pleasure, though effective, left her ignorant of the usual preliminaries. The sensations Chen and Elu had wrung from her body were soured by a taint of coercion. She had no such associations with Farouj, who should have parted from her at the factory. To the newly liberated Qa'a'nesh, Sorykah was a fallen figurehead. They had no more need of effigies or rescuers. Instead Farouj elected to escort Sorykah home.

A mournful whistle sang in the distance, tardily followed by the clackety-clack rhythm of the overland train puttering through the lonely evening. Farouj squeezed her tight and assured her that the dinged and dented steam engine bearing down on them was the southbound train, not an agent of Death. When he turned her mouth to his and kissed her, she melted into it. Aboard the clattering once-daily train to Neubonne, Farouj paid for a private sleeping cabin, led Sorykah into the tiny room, and locked the door. Her heart hammered in double time as he closed the blinds of their compartment. She would not let herself think of anything but *this*. Giddy arousal flowered in her belly as she lay back on the sunken, mushy bed. Farouj's eyelashes butterfly-kissed her cheek. They made out like teenagers, smooching until their mouths were bruised and their tongues ached, until Sorykah's neck was splotched with hickeys and beard burn. As Sorykah lifted her jersey overhead and shimmied out of her trousers, she decided that when they got home, she might just ask him to stay.

SORYKAH RETURNED FROM THE DESERT exhilarated but weary. "I never want to leave home again!" She sank into the chair cushions, squashing squirming babies to her chest.

Tears stung Nels's eyes, remembering her reaction to the handsome, polite man who accompanied Sorykah home. When Nels opened the door to find him standing behind Sorykah, she'd nearly vomited from the shock. He could've been anyone, but he and

Sorykah rubbed against each other like cats, practically purring aloud. They brushed ice tree bark from their clothes and Sorykah sent the man to her room to settle in while she cuddled her babies. Nels watched her feeble plans die. Sorykah's attention was saved for her children and man. Sorykah's hugs felt wooden and insincere. Sorykah's questions, her gratitude and praise of Nels, were the hollow products of duty, nothing more. Even the story of Kika's miraculous return elicited only polite interest.

Sorykah said nothing to Nels to indicate that she remembered Soryk's naughty misdeed. It felt like an insult to remind her of their tryst, and to what aim? To alleviate Nels's guilt, to encourage a repeat performance, or perhaps to punish Soryk/ah for her sloppy personal control over what Nels could think of only as a disease?

Sorykah could not know of the nights Nels had lain awake in her employer's bed, wishing fervently for an easy way to insert herself into this ready-made life. Home, man, and babies all prepped and ready. Their trio needed its fourth to become a quartet, balanced on all sides, but Sorykah and Farouj had eyes only for each other. Nels hated the way that Farouj strode into the Quonset and upset her order, acting as though he already lived there and shifting things around. The cups didn't belong in that cabinet! Sorykah preferred milk in her tea, not lemon. He even wanted Kika to sleep outside tethered to a pipe in front of the Quonset. Nels was shaking by the time she climbed into bed. Was she being childish and irrational? Sorykah was happy. Her smile was an anomaly on a face usually fearful or grim. Farouj was nice, too nice, and just the tiniest bit dull. Even-keeled and mannerly, polite and conscientious. How ordinary! Nels disliked him on principle alone.

Worst of all was Sorykah's lackluster response to the ice tree. She wasn't dazzled by the enormous sprawling tree that had grown to overshadow the Quonset in a matter of days. When Nels handed her Sidra's note, Sorykah feigned cheerfulness though a shadow crossed her face.

"It's from Queen Sidra!" Nels cried.

"So you said," Sorykah replied, a touch of that old coolness creeping back. "I'll look at it later."

"It could be important! Kika came all the way from the Erun by herself to bring it to you."

"An amazing feat, no doubt, but why would Sidra trust a dog to carry a message to me if it was urgent? Kika must have been traveling for weeks. Whatever the trouble was, I'm sure it's resolved itself by now."

"Soryk wouldn't be so cold." Animosity swelled and spilled.

"What do you know about what Soryk would do?" Sorykah's new and fragile happiness was tested and found wanting. Some furtive longing swerved and shifted. A memory flashed—Nels naked on her back, her hands tight on Soryk's hips. Sorykah resisted its invasion, knowing as she did so that Soryk had done a shameful thing. What portion of a primary's consciousness was liable for its alter's behavior and vice versa? Did the Perilous Curse, that disease of forgetting, absolve Soryk/ah of accountability? She liked to believe that primary and alter operated as independent selves. Conjoined personas shared heart, liver, lungs, and stomach, but separate brains conferred autonomy. Sorykah could ignore the doings of her left hand or play deaf to the words spilling from her alter's mouth but was horrified when Soryk's memory of his night with Nels became hers. Sorykah gasped and covered her mouth. Poor Nels!

Dinner was miserable and awkward for Nels. Sorykah wore her couplehood like a halo that shone its light into every corner and warmed the room. During the night, the babies cried and before Nels could put on her wrapper to tend them, she heard Sorykah's voice shushing them, followed by the man's voice, hushed and playful, and his light footsteps descending the stairs to the kitchen. Pots rattled and clanked. Water ran. Sorykah and Farouj spoke softly, their words a muddle through the barrier of Nels's door. She put her pillow over her head and prayed.

Farouj loitered in the house like a street corner thug looking for trouble. At least that's how Nels saw him. She fervently wished that he and Sorykah would fight and break up or that he'd grow bored and take off, but he stuck around, as stubborn as a barnacle. Sorykah encouraged Nels to cash the check that arrived, compensation for loss at sea. Some clerical glitch or bookkeeping error (orders from the Onyx Tower penthouse, Sorykah surmised) overlooked the fact that Sorykah was quite alive. The Company ignored her and she them. Diabolo slept and the Devil's Playground was quiet again. Siguelanders built a new harbor anchored in the thawing black soil. Sorykah had tried and failed to find Rava's kin. The ink trade had staggered to a stop then start, as procurers and suppliers adjusted and eventually recovered from the demolition of the fossil water factory. Ink still flowed in Neubonne and trickled down the coast to the pole like a dribble of pus from a purulent sore.

It didn't feel like anything had changed, though gears deep within TI's machinery lost teeth, caught, and jammed. The night train rolled through empty fields, searching for somatics in hiding. Freed Qa'a'nesh reached the Gathering of Tribes and reclaimed their stolen spirits. Chen's empire rocked precariously while the source of its upheaval contentedly played house with her new lover and noodled about with waterless wash pad formulas and molecular dishwashing cabinets.

Soryk woke up a few times, making brief, disruptive appearances. He never stayed long—one glance at Nels sent him scurrying back into hiding.

Snow fell. Tiny crystals stinging with cold signaled the end of the strange summer. Holding hands at dinner one evening, Sorykah shyly announced that Farouj had asked her to marry him. Nels smiled woodenly, chastising herself for selfishness, and offered congratulations only because it was expected. The next morning, the nanny stood at the bottom of the stairs, bags in hand. Sorykah and Farouj came down, each holding a baby. Nels marveled at the ease with which Farouj handled the children. Ayeda especially seemed to adore his calming presence. Sorykah handed Leander to Farouj and sent him into the kitchen. After the door closed, perspicacious

Farouj giving them a moment of privacy, Nels handed Sorykah a
letter.

"What's this?" Sorykah unfolded the paper and read Nels's simple
notice of resignation. "You're not leaving us, are you?"

Nels nodded. She was already buttoned up in coat and hat, her
fingers tight around the bone handles of her bags. "Something I've
been considering for quite a while now. In college, I studied sacred
texts. Though they didn't have a place for me at the time, the Temple of the Blessed Jerusha has written to say they want me. I've been
assigned to a project." She shifted on her heels, impatient to leave
before the tears came.

"That's wonderful." Sorykah was careful with her words. "It
sounds like an extraordinary opportunity."

"Oh, it is! I'm going to repair illuminated manuscripts." Nels offered a lukewarm smile. "Just my thing, poring over manky old
books."

"Is it?" Sorykah wanted to comfort the girl, assure her of her place
in the household, but she refrained, fearful that close contact or high
emotion would spark the change. "In that case, I'll be happy for you.
Sure you won't consider staying on? The children will miss you."

"No, thank you. I've got to get moving or I'll miss my boat."

"But what about your pay?"

"The temple sent travel vouchers with my acceptance packet. I've
given you the address, so you can send it to me there."

"Nels, are you certain? This is a big decision."

"I got the letter months ago. You were gone, so . . ." Nels fidgeted
and bit back tears. "I wasn't going to go but I might not get another
shot."

Much went unsaid. Neither woman wanted to mention Soryk's
misbehavior.

"You'll write to us, won't you? Tell us how it goes?"

Nels nodded, wiping away tears.

"You can always come back to us if it doesn't work out."

"To us," Nels noticed, not "to me." Soryk had nothing to say to her. She ran a sleeve across her cheeks, mopping up tears. "Best get going."

Sorykah grabbed Nels and hugged her tight. Despite knowing what Soryk had done, it felt like a breach of protocol to embrace her children's nanny. Sorykah smelled tuberose on Nels's clothes. Her voice deepened when she said, "I'm sorry."

Nels wrenched away and was gone.

THE NINE VEIL GATES—ramparts of chiseled limestone mortised into place by the Blessed Mother's laymen some four hundred years earlier—rose up to block out the white sun. Temple flags snapped in the wind, and spinning prayer wheels of hammered tin hummed like cicadas. Burnt offerings clogged the grate of the pilgrim's fire.

Nels stood in the shadows, where morning dew soaked her shoes. This was not how she'd envisioned Jerusha's temple. She imagined flower fields where the Blessed Mother's daughters and acolytes clustered in loose circlets, their voices light and good-humored, but this was a place of chilly gray skies where ominous walls cut the sky in two. Dormant fields lay combed into neat brown rows. The roads remained empty. Not a single cow, lark, or bluebell broke the monotony. Heavy clouds rolled overhead and a distant burst of thunder rumbled. Raindrops splattered the dirt.

There was little life outside the temple—a few compacted wattle and daub houses, the train depot, and a lone shop selling weak tea and travel goods to the road-weary. Nels had imagined pilgrims camped outside the gates, their gaily colored tents flapping in an incense breeze; laughter and the sounds of contemplative living: dialogue, questioning, and the rhythmic intonation of prayer-songs. A woman exited one of the mirthless houses, wrapped her shawl tightly around her shoulders, and bustled to the teahouse without once glancing Nels's way. She offered no neighborly wave or greeting, and this left Nels suddenly overcome with regret.

Nels turned toward the main temple gate and pulled the bell.

Several minutes passed before the door opened, and a homely girl with freckled olive skin and wiry brown hair appeared.

Nels held up her letter of assignment. The girl gave it a cursory glance.

"Oh yeah, I heard 'bout ya. You're in my dormitory." She waved Nels in and Nels gave what was now the outside world a parting look.

The girl held the door wide and bellowed, "Last chance! Better make a run for it!" She slapped her knee and guffawed. "Shoulda seen the look on your mug! Ooh, that was fun. Always gotta make the new ones sweat a little bit. Come on!"

Knees knocking, Nels dragged her heavy bag into the foyer as the door slammed shut behind her. She gripped her prayer medallion and breathed, *Blessed Mother, please let this not be a mistake.*

SORYK STOOD BEFORE THE MIRROR, fingering his jaw and wondering if he should let his beard grow in. It was easier to distract himself with random thoughts than return to the bedroom to face Farouj. Pray that he still slept, giving Soryk time to work out what to say. He couldn't hide in the bathroom forever. Farouj knew what he was getting into, didn't he? Sorykah couldn't keep a secret like hers for too long. Soryk picked through the scraps of his primary's most recent memories. Coming through after the change was like walking into a room the morning after a raucous party. There were leftovers everywhere. Sorykah's emotions littered his mind. Most of it looked like garbage to him but sometimes he discovered something useful on the floor. This is how he learned Nels had gone before he'd even entered her room and found the dragon's eye pendant lying discarded on her dresser.

Soryk tiptoed past Farouj, soundly asleep in Sorykah's bed. Soryk wrinkled his nose; Farouj was shirtless. Thank Jerusha he hadn't woken up in the man's arms. It would've been awkward. One of them would have to relocate to the couch if Soryk stuck around. Soryk grabbed his clothes and dressed quickly. He didn't want to leave Farouj in charge of the twins, but if he hurried, he could get in a walk before they woke. Time alone was all he needed, half an hour to put the latest developments into perspective. Kika wagged her tail wildly and followed Soryk outside.

The sun was just coming up, illuminating the ice tree bark that swirled around the Quonset and heaped in powdery drifts against the neighboring buildings. Bulging holimak roots forced the house up from the ground. Sap dripped everywhere, leaving syrupy puddles the size of coins.

Soryk squatted by the tree and scratched Kika's ears. "I wish you could talk! What's this tree mean, hmm? Must be awfully important if you brought it all this way just for me."

He needed Carac to interpret Kika's snuffles and tail wags for him. Then again, if Carac were there, Soryk could just ask him what it meant. Or go straight to the source and ask Sidra, if she was speaking to him, that is. She'd been so reticent and withdrawn during their last days together. He deeply regretted the way he'd left her, dragged away in the middle of the night by his primary. So much was left unsaid and the summer months passed in silence with nary a word spent between them. If only he could talk to her again! He'd write a letter. It wasn't much, but at least she would know that he missed her. Until Soryk/ah's selves came to an agreement about how to manage their disparate lives, alter and primary would suffer each other's whims.

Soryk sat down at Sorykah's desk. Although he'd never used it before, he opened the right drawers to locate writing paper, pens, and envelopes. He smoothed the blotter flat but a rise persisted. Soryk lifted the blotter and removed two folded leaves of paper. He read the first, "Instruction for an Ice Tree," and the second, lined with Sidra's precise printing:

> There is a light in this place
> A red spark beneath the hill
> A hummingbird's heartbeat
> Divinity
> A change, feeding like a fire

> *Amidst a mound of ashes*
> *A change to break the coming world*
> *And paste it back together.*

What does it mean? Elusive and tantalizing, the truth in Sidra's pretty words flitted just beyond his grasp. He was still pondering it when he heard the weekly mail thump into the bin and the postie's courtesy knock. Tucked among the usual assortment of local flyers and policy notices from the Company was a torn, much-abused envelope stamped with a pair of antler horns. Shaking, he gingerly unfolded the letter. Wrinkled, ink-blotched paper flaked apart in his hands. *"Death waits to take me to the shadowlands . . . Care for her when I cannot, this bright child of mine. If I loved you too quickly, it was only because I had not the luxury of time."*

Then he knew that smell of schoolroom paste on Sidra's breath, the easy tears, and swollen breasts she'd asked him to handle more tenderly. Just like Sorykah when she carried the twins. Soryk had been deeply asleep during their gestation, but his body shared the experience. His primary's womb must be dormant inside him, just as his organs hibernated within her, awaiting rejuvenation.

Sidra was pregnant. Like cheap glass, she would shatter under the strain of carrying. Hadn't she once warned him of the manifold dangers to her existence? If assassination or accident did not take her, the synthetic marrow in her bones was its own death sentence. The doctor who performed her radical treatment insisted that her skeleton couldn't bear the stress of childbirth without fracturing into a hundred brittle pieces. She'd been careful, or lucky, before him. While Sorykah gallivanted around the desert playing Farouj's messianic games, Soryk's beloved languished. He would go to her as quickly as possible. Soryk bounded up the stairs and into the twins' room to pack their things. He didn't plan to return.

"Do all Traders make such a habit of running out on their lovers?" Farouj blocked the door. Thank Jerusha he was wearing pajama bottoms.

"Don't know. I'm not running out on anyone. I'm running to someone. Sidra needs me."

"What if I need you? And what about Sorykah's needs?"

"I'm so tired of everyone thinking they can kiss or frighten me just to get the person they want," Soryk snapped. "Really fed up with being jerked to and fro, awake, asleep, never knowing where I am or what day it is. *She* brought you here, I didn't. *My* life is in the Erun and Sidra wants *me*, Soryk."

"Look, we need to learn how to get along. I'm not going anywhere. You'll have to get used to me just as I'll have to accommodate you."

"Accommodate me? You can't be serious."

"How is anyone going to have a relationship with you if you take off the moment you change? Even if you stay in the Erun, Sorykah will want to come back to me. You should make peace with at least one of your lives."

Farouj was right, though Soryk didn't want to admit it. He couldn't keep racing between two completely divergent worlds and two very different lovers. It would be disastrous for his mental health, and confusing and disruptive for the twins. Soryk brushed past him into the nursery. Ayeda and Leander stood in their crib, flashing gap-toothed grins. Soryk jammed clothing and diapers into a travel bag, his mind reeling. No one had ever offered to stick around through the changes. Everyone in Soryk/ah's acquaintance was interested in either alter or primary, not both, or the simple satisfaction of their curiosity, not embracing Soryk/ah as a whole person. Even Sidra, who claimed to adore Soryk/ah's every inch, wheedled for Soryk's return when he slept within Sorykah.

Farouj trailed Soryk into the nursery and his voice was kind when he said, "Go and do what you must. Then come back to me and we'll see what happens."

25

TIME MEASURED IN BONES

Daughter,
(*I'm so certain that you are a she I can't think of you as any other.*)

This is my legacy: a hollow tree, a city of jesters with animal faces, a canyon land—never bridged—between what has been and what could be, half a man who adores me, and half a woman who will learn to love you.

You could have a sister and brother, a house with running taps and heat, and a mother and father packed into a single box. You could spend your entire life among people and never know the truth of what this world offers and withholds. This possible existence is a pretty one, clean and complication-free. You have a right to this life.

I pushed the seeds of my soul deep into your little body. Just like an acorn awaiting its future birth, you'll

carry me within until there is water enough to germi-
nate those seeds and bring me back. Not my body—
this flimsy and forgettable shell won't serve me long
enough to instruct you myself. Not my words, for those
too will diminish, just as the order I created will dissolve into anarchy. Not a memory of me, for you won't
have known me long enough to retain any piece of me.
What then? What will you do when the world crumbles
about your ears and the sea reclaims all harbors? The
shadow gods will come again to carve their names
into our backs. It will be a bloody trial that you must not
fail.

Just as Asta gained new life through the splitting of
her soul and the creation of the ice tree, just as Jerusha
canopies the faithful with blessings, I foresee a blessed
second life for you. The first will be short, its prequel a
bad memory that your father will strive to forget. Your
first life—schooling, play, minor heartbreaks—will be
over before you know it. The second will begin at the moment of your choosing. You are destined for greatness,
my brilliant daughter. It is in your genes.

Beware—powerful forces work together in darkened
rooms like vermin nesting in secrets and filth, fattening
the citizens of Plein Eïre on regurgitated propaganda.
These forces wield platitudes like swords to keep questions at bay. They consign the impoverished, deformed,
and dangerous to shantytowns and exile. They pump a
steady stream of narcotics, hallucinogens, and erotoma-
niacs into our cities. Their existence is a rat plague that
must be drowned. You'll play the pipe and lead a merry
insurrection.

To you, I bequeath my queendom. Yours is my crown
of antler horn. Wear it with pride. Be fearless, for you'll
have no other option. Be kind—words always sound

sweeter when honeyed. Be forgiving, but firm. Take pity
on those who deserve it. Stomp on those who do not.

Love your father and honor your mother, because
they are one in the same.

A last word of advice: Poetry soothes all stings.

Your mum, Queen Sidra the Lovely

Sidra folded the letter and stamped it with her seal. She tucked the
letter between the leaves of a volume of Saint Catherine's poetry, her
favorite. Gritting her teeth against a contraction, Sidra continued
packing the baby's cedar trunk. It was the size of an infant's coffin—
the Erun's resident woodcarver and gravedigger had presented it to
Sidra for an unspecified use. "For the baby," he'd said, ignorant of his
dire prophecy.

"A keepsake box," Sidra said.

"If you like." The morose gravedigger departed, leaving Sidra dis-
comfited.

The box was almost full. Sidra had spent the past month tucking
away bits of things she found useful, necessary, informative, or sentimental: feathers, beads, knives and flint strikers, seeds and herbs,
each packaged with a descriptive note detailing usage, dosage, and
guidelines for planting and preservation. There were wee sweaters
knitted of soft white lamb's wool, and kid leather boots the size of
plums, and a fancy quilt pieced together by the somatic mums'
sewing circle. Sidra placed her poetry book and letter inside, then
unpacked and repacked the trunk. Something was missing. Photo-
graphs. She examined her room, wishing that she could preserve it
on film. Her daughter wouldn't understand anything about Sidra's
life. It would all be hearsay and faulty recollections grown warped
with age.

Another contraction squeezed Sidra's womb. She tried to breathe
through it but found it hard to stay calm. Every single one of her
bones ached. Peeping and preening, a little yellow bird hopped from
perch to perch in her cage of twigs. Hans had the genius idea to train

the bird to fly to Yetive when released, and the midwife knew that its arrival was an urgent summons from her queen. Like the gravedigger's keepsake box, the yellow bird had unpleasant implications. Sidra feared it a coal mine canary presaging her doom. She tried to be practical and dismiss her doubts, but one cannot unring a tolling bell.

Soryk should appear any moment. Didn't he know how much she needed him? Sidra peered out the small round window of her loft, searching the forest for him. She wished desperately for a whistle that would carry all the way to Ostara and sound its alarm. Sidra cramped and groaned. She regretted not heeding Yetive's advice to check into the Merciful Father's Charity Hospital in Neubonne. At least her midwife there would not begrudge the patient, but she chose to stay in her forest, draped in greenery. Neubonne was a pit. She'd not birth her baby in that iniquitous den. She didn't voice her biggest fear, that Chen would find her in hospital and provoke another petty confrontation. He always made such a display of his heartbreak, desperate to wring further guilt from Sidra.

Sidra squatted, panting. Her breath wobbled out as her uterus tightened and clamped down. Each gripping contraction came on harder. She held her breath as if making a wish. The contraction released. Water trickled down Sidra's thighs as another contraction peaked, thrusting her into a stormy swell. Wave after wave crested and receded. She feared the lightless vortex, streaming into darkness with no end in sight.

Her pregnancy was a journey that must be endured to its conclusion. There was no abandoning ship mid-crossing. Queen Sidra the Lovely raised the cage door. "Fly away, little bird. Tell Yetive I am ready."

YETIVE HAD NOT FORGIVEN SIDRA for stealing her son, Gowyr. The midwife could not refuse to treat the queen and risk expulsion from the city. That didn't mean that she would do it gladly. Yetive's touch had grown coarse, her expression dour. She gave Sidra only the minimum of consideration. Gone were the lingering visits and talks over tea. Sidra would have forgone the appointments altogether had pain not driven her mad and robbed her of peace, sleep, and joy.

Yetive ground up her remedies, swirled the herbs into a glass of tonic, and thrust it at Sidra. "Drink, my lady."

Sidra recognized the sense of unwelcome duty permeating the midwife's gesture. Sidra had also cared for patients she disliked at Merciful Father's Charity Hospital, women whose carelessness threatened their pregnancies, women who disdained the child in their belly. Sidra refused to judge them simply because she was averse to their flippancy. She hoped Yetive did the same.

"How goes the pain?" Yetive rubbed her palms together to warm them before placing her hands on Sidra's exposed belly. The herbs were intended to relax her, ease the pain and free her mind from dwelling on it, but Yetive doubted their efficacy. Sidra's constant cheer was dimmed, her once-smiling face drawn tight with strain.

Sidra grimaced against the invasion. Her skin was so tight and sensitive, she could feel each individual callus, ridge, and line of Yetive's palms. It was agonizing to sense those fingers slipping between layers of skin and fat to the taut muscle of her hard, red womb. Sidra squeezed her eyes shut, screwed up her mouth, and bore it.

Her uterus contracted in Yetive's hands. Sidra hadn't wanted to admit that labor had begun. Foolishly, she hoped that by ignoring it, it would go away. Now she was sorry to have summoned the midwife to her room, for it meant that birth was under way. There was no delaying the baby's arrival.

"Sweet Jerusha, that was a good one!" The contraction surprised Yetive. The queen wasn't due yet for a few weeks. "How long have you been having contractions?"

Sidra didn't want to speak and name this thing that was happening to her. It was worse than being torn from shore by a tidal wave and dumped into the wild and thrashing sea. She stuck her fingers in her ears to block the snap-crackle of her creaking, brittle bones but that only amplified the sound.

Yetive brusquely cleared the table beside Sidra's bed, pushing aside the box of ginger, the notepad of poems furiously scratched out and rewritten, the weird assortment of small things she kept in bags—beaks, bones, claws, twigs, feathers, and balls of hair and fur. Yetive wasn't prepared for this early birth. There were no blankets or sheets at the ready, no clean water for washing. The unsterilized piss pot lurked in the corner, broadcasting pee-stained malevolence. Dunya had gone to gather yellow salt from the manor meadow and wouldn't be back for hours. This wasn't Yetive's first solo delivery but she didn't like to do it alone with such a difficult pregnancy as this. She'd need a helper with strong hands and a strong heart—in case decisions had to be made—and a strong stomach to withstand the blood and ripping flesh.

Sidra's man Carac was the only one Yetive would allow to attend. Hans was too nervous and his quills too dangerous. "My lady, Dunya has gone on her errands and I need an assist. Where is Carac? How do we summon him?"

Sidra moaned and balled herself up, enduring another contraction. "I don't want him. I want Soryk. Where is he? Why hasn't he answered my messages?"

Yetive said nothing. A man who'd left a woman wasn't likely to be lured back by the arrival of a baby. "Carac, ma'am. Is he near? Can you call him?"

Sidra petulantly flapped a hand at the wooden whistle hanging from the bedpost.

Yetive stood at the top of the stairs and blew once, then again. "It doesn't work! Not a sound. Must be blocked." She shook the whistle, hoping to dislodge whatever she imagined blocked its pipe, and blew again, hard and long. Notes too high for human hearing pierced the Erun air. Somatics cringed and covered ears. Nearly a mile distant, Carac jolted as if electrocuted. The deep forest was his refuge, but the leafy trees and dense bracken could not hide him well enough to escape Sidra's emergency call. For a moment, he considered ignoring her summons. She would be angry when he finally responded, but by then he hoped that she'd have solved the problem on her own. As much as the man in him resisted, his loyal wolf-heart would not allow him to abandon her.

Yetive returned to Sidra's side. "This whistle is broken."

"He heard it. He'll come."

Carac soon appeared in Sidra's doorway, tongue flopping from a foamy mouth. Yetive shuddered, again considering the rumor that Carac was Sidra's consort. It was possible that the baby Yetive delivered would arrive with salt-and-pepper fur, a pointed muzzle, and lycanthropic milk teeth. Sidra assured Yetive that her child was Soryk's progeny, but Yetive had birthed many children who arrived wearing the feathers, quills, or scales that their fathers lacked. She'd wait and see, and stifle her surprise.

Yetive quickly directed Carac. "Wash yourself and boil water. Find clean linens and something to wrap the baby in when she comes. Bring new oil and some broth or fruit for the queen."

Carac did as told, worry dulling his senses. It was a self-protective measure. Had they been fully attuned, surely he would have smelled death lurking in Sidra's room.

It was a long labor. More than once, Yetive wished for respite but she didn't dare leave Sidra alone in Carac's care. He served her unflinchingly, just as Yetive hoped. Exhausted by her slow progress, Sidra drifted between sleep and wakefulness, calling Soryk's name. She asked for Father Halloran, Sorykah, and even Chen. Carac withstood it all, seeming not to mind that his name was absent from her list.

When the baby's head crowned, Yetive cried out but Sidra was silent. Slimed in red, the baby slid into the midwife's hands. Though small enough to curl in just one of Yetive's palms, she was perfection in miniature, as plump and well formed as a full-term babe.

"My lady, your daughter is here! See how pretty and fine she is!" The momentary rush of a successful birth temporarily muted Yetive's grudge. Joy enlivened her weary face as she stroked Sidra's arms, attempting to rouse the queen from her stupor. Carac loitered nearby, his mouth open to strain the scent of Sidra's blood through his sinuses. Sidra did not respond when Carac surrendered to impulse and licked her face. Yetive assessed and bundled the baby. She placed her on the queen's chest, but Sidra did not embrace her child. Yetive grabbed the queen's arms and pressed them around the baby; though Sidra barely moved, she held the pose.

The placenta was slow in coming. Cayenne and lobelia tinctures failed to speed its expulsion. Sidra was too out of it to nurse her baby, an easy remedy to help the uterus spit out the afterbirth. Anxious for its delivery, Yetive kneaded Sidra's belly to force the placenta from its moorings. Yetive's massage was unproductive; the placenta resisted her efforts. Yetive had no choice but to slide her hand into the queen's birth canal, maneuvering past dangling membranes into the gaping womb. Fluid filled the uterine cavity, making her job a slippery one. Yetive ran her fingers along the placental edge, prying it loose. As thick and hot as a fresh liver, the organ peeled free with a slurp, a filmy purple thing layered in veins. Yetive, at last, cut the umbilical cord.

"Take this to the kitchen and put it into a clean pot." Yetive gave the placenta to Carac and he departed with it carefully balanced in his hands. Somatics could be a bit dodgy when the smell of blood was in the air or just-slaughtered meat available for the taking. "Keep your mouth off of it!" She yelled down the stairs. "We'll need it later!"

Carac grunted in response. Yetive turned at the sound of the queen's voice, a soft whisper into the ear of the baby on her belly.

"My lady! How do you feel?"

"Worse than you can imagine." She grimaced, struggling to rise a bit. "The pain . . . it's too much. Something has gone wrong."

Yetive blanched, expecting a gush of crimson blood. None came, though Sidra could barely manage to shift her weight in bed, crying out as she did so.

"You were unconscious. I had to remove the placenta by hand. That must be what you feel. Now look at that gorgeous girl at your side." Yetive didn't want the queen to dwell on the specifics of manual removal. "I'll give you something to help you sleep but you should try to nurse her first."

Sidra seemed not to hear. She tipped her head as if listening to distant music. "He's coming. I hear footsteps in the forest."

A shiver traveled Yetive's spine as she peered out the window. "There's no one there."

"He's too far away," Sidra murmured. "Too far. All legs creeping, the green widow sleeping."

"My lady? Are you all right?" Yetive gathered the new baby to her, the tiny thing that hadn't even had a chance to suckle.

"Beneath the eaves, below the leaves, creeping creeping on feet of pins, pricking picking with hands of tin. Quickly child, lift the latch, walk in, walk in."

Strange poetry, not Saint Catherine's. Sidra's pupils eclipsed the bright iris around them. Yetive swaddled the baby and placed her in a dresser drawer upon the floor. What would be the repercussion for killing the queen, even by accident? Might Carac, in his grief, rip out her throat? The somatics would have cause for revolt, bickering over royal rule and ascension.

Yetive poured a strong measure of Sidra's palliative homebrew and tipped it down the queen's throat. She slipped easily into sleep. Her amputated horns parted her hair, a gruesome accessory to her outfit of bloodstained bedsheets and postpartum mania. There was nothing to do but make the queen comfortable and wait. In the meantime, Yetive had to prepare the oxygen- and iron-rich placenta. She believed that feeding it to Sidra would help replenish lost blood volume and prevent the anxiety and depression that often accompanied troubled births.

Carac returned and camped out on the floor beside the bed. Yetive left him with strict instructions to call her if Sidra worsened. In the kitchen, Yetive rinsed the placenta and drained its surplus blood, barely enough for a pudding. Best prepared while it still retained the mother's body heat, the placenta would work well cooked in a hearty stew. Yetive quickly sautéed cubes of potato, tomato, peppers, and parsley in butter, then added chunks of placenta. Realizing that it hadn't been fed for many hours, the smell of food made her stomach rumble in complaint. She poured stew over a round of flat bread and carried it upstairs. Carac shot Yetive a doleful look when she entered.

"My lady, it's time to eat." Yetive shook Sidra's arm. Her bones felt crumbly inside her skin, like a sack of broken biscuits. A raw sort of sickness crawled up through Yetive's guts. Once, she and Sidra had quickly and quietly discussed the outcome of such a complication. Sidra knew that she could not save herself from difficulty, alone in a wood, alienated from people. She'd made the decision, understanding that she might also be issuing her own death warrant. Yetive would be made culpable. If Sidra died in Yetive's care, the midwife would have to slip away and leave the Erun city. Fearing Gowyr's return to his mother's empty house, she was reluctant to do so.

Yetive cut a small bite of food and pushed it on Sidra, who swallowed without complaint. Next, Yetive ordered Carac to find Hans and Dunya while she prepared fever tonics and packed Sidra's womb with clean gauze soaked in antiseptic. Someone would have to milk the city's dairy goats or find a wet nurse for Sidra's wee girl. They would have to sit with the queen in shifts. Yetive would warn Sidra's most trusted friends of the treacherous turns on the road back to health: an accelerated pulse rate of 140–160 beats per minute; extreme abdominal pain and swelling; fever and shivering fits; loss of reason; apoplectic fear; and worst of all, an inexplicable, sudden improvement in health masking a fatally gangrenous womb.

Sidra stirred and called for Yetive. "Bring her to me, would you? And my notebook and pen. I'm inspired and want to catch it before it's gone."

"You should rest," Yetive said. "There will plenty of time for that later."

"Time? We don't have need of lies. I don't have time . . ." Her sobs startled her.

Then Hans was there, with Carac and Dunya. Soryk was not.

"No word yet, Hans?" Sidra's weak voice was tinged with panic.

"I'm sorry, my lovely." His quills rustled, making that sound she so loved. "Soon. He's practically at your doorstep, don't you think?"

Dunya vigorously agreed. "One of 'em will answer yer call. Be a fool not to." Her furry hands reached for the new baby, no bigger than a teapot. "Oh, yer a fine and lovely lassie, just like yer own sweet mum!"

Sidra pointed to her notebook, its leaves crisp with her handwriting. "Give that to her father when he comes."

Carac broke his mournful trance. "Her father?"

"Soryk. Her father." Sidra didn't mean to sound cruel and injure her faithful, adoring par-wolf. She was distracted by the heat that billowed in waves from her spongy womb. It would be her belly, not her bones, that took her. She was surprised.

"Hans," Sidra said. "He's coming, isn't he?"

"Yes, my lovely. He'll come." Hans smiled through his tears. "Just you wait."

26

MEMENTO MORI

ONCE THE ERUN VAULT had been a place of wordless terror and such deep and limitless silence that the black primordial sea bottom could not rival it, for even there, little creatures paddled through the ink bearing their own lights, and fed or fasted according to their skill. Now caterpillars and ants trundled beneath the Erun's soldierly trees. Birds tittered and cawed; leaves crackled and rustled. Insect jaws tapped out an industrious rhythm as they feasted on years of accumulated decay. Chirping songbirds quieted and nestled under wing as massive speckled owls preened for the hunt.

Soryk carried Ayeda and Leander, one in each arm as he traced the now-familiar paths to the Erun city. Already the forest wore an overgrown air of neglect. The tiger trap entrance was shoddily disguised. Leafless branches had been tossed carelessly over the pit, leaving the door visible. Soryk staggered on until he found another entrance, this one hidden beneath a patch of thorny nettles. He set the babies down, relieved to be free of his burden. He needed Nels.

Again, he regretted spoiling their relationship. *Stupid penis*, he thought. *Why can't you mind your own business?*

Soryk propped open the wooden door while he gathered the twins and crawled into the Erun city tunnel. It stunk of mildew and spoiled food. Sidra's rules and her influence were already waning. Lamps that had once burned with a steady light smoked and sputtered. A few wicks winked, sucking up the last drops of oil. The tunnels were quiet except for the baby babble announcing their arrival.

Tree house doors hung open, the occupants having fled their homes. Soryk's throat tightened. This was all a bad dream. He found Sidra's house, hoping that she would call from the high ledge, rush down to welcome him with tight hugs and ardent kisses, cooing over babies grown plump and giggly. Emptiness greeted him. The lamps were doused, the tree house chilly. Carac did not materialize to glower and threaten Soryk with glimpses of his cruel teeth.

Soryk badly wanted to rest, to climb the winding stairs to the cozy room where he'd spent so many hours beneath the bramble of Sidra's hair. He longed for that creaking treetop love nest scented by ginger, beeswax, and herbs. If only he could sleep in their bed and dream of her again. There was no time for nostalgia. The twins were hungry and he was exhausted. Dunya would help, kind Dunya, with her sad brown eyes and need to please. She'd be delighted to see the babies again.

He found her in her little house. Though gloomy, her mood improved when she opened the door to Soryk and those bonny twin stars. Leander reached for her and Ayeda followed his lead. Soon they were happily gnawing biscuits and Soryk was drinking the tea Dunya forced on him.

"Ye've left it to the last minute, mind ye. We thought ye'd never get 'ere!"

"I came as quickly as I could. It's just me on my own. It's not easy getting through this forest lugging these chubsters. My arms are about to break off!" Soryk set the children on the floor.

Dunya peered into the tunnel behind him. "Where's yer baby minder? Gone off on 'er own?"

"Nels didn't come." Soryk hesitated. Dunya seemed incapable of understanding the complex nuances of a dalliance gone awry. Anyway, it was none of her concern. He was guilty enough about his indiscretion without having to explain it to the dog-faced girl. "She's gone to join the sisters at the Temple of the Blessed Jerusha. You know how she is." Soryk folded his hands, mocking Nels at prayer.

Dunya gathered Leander to her, admiring his delicious fatness. She wished she could keep him for herself, but she was not his blood, nay, not even of his kind. Sorykah had crossed the waste alone, braving both Wood Beast and Collector to find her babes before Matuk could work his evil and leach their savory drippings to formulate his repulsive potions. Dunya saw the red ring of a death narrowly escaped encircling twin necks like a slinky chain. She fretted that they remembered the chilling bite of the marble manse where Matuk had dwelled, stewing in his insanity. Did the past haunt them? Were those two babes spoilt inside by their abduction, the lack of milk, the cold and dreary danger that had hovered, week after agonizing week, as they awaited rescue?

She turned the baby like a handpie in a hot oven, searching for signs of lasting damage. Soryk's watchful eyes were two polished beach stones from the shores along the Bay of Sorrows, black and gray, and muddy green. He nursed his own private anguish, Dunya thought, and perhaps still grieved his wild catapult into the world of somatics and madmen.

"Where's Sidra?" A meaningless question that fulfilled Soryk's role in this gross simulation of normalcy, as if he could stretch out the minutes and delay the inevitable.

Dunya growled faintly. "Me lovely wanted ye so badly. Always callin' for ye, like 'er 'eart was breaking. Thought it was them bones that did 'er in. They crumbled like yellow salt but it was the fever that took 'er, rantin' and ravin' till the end. Poor lady!"

"The end." Time stopped. Dunya spoke but Soryk heard only the slow, dull thud of his heartbeat and blood-rush in his ears. Dunya blathered on, the loose skin over her muzzle flapping, grossly comedic. Too late was what he was. Too late to tell Sidra the Lovely of Sorykah's triumph in the desert, and far too late to touch her warm living flesh and beg forgiveness for leaving her. She had been dead less than a week and already, exodus and dissolution had tumbled her marvelous house of cards. Dunya rattled on about somatics fleeing the Erun and fires in the tunnels, fevers and blood, suppurative organs and the baby—Sidra's little heartache.

A kitten mewed somewhere and Dunya cocked her head. "Och, ye 'ear that? The princess is awake." She returned Leander, bustled into a nook and made shushing sounds, alarming in their wet ferocity. An infant fussed and quieted. Soryk's blood drained from him, leaving him pale and shaking. He didn't want to see this snippet of Sidra, fashioned from her cells and tissue like some remedial science project. She'd killed his beloved queen with her insistence on becoming and her refusal to fade quietly into the darkness that spawned her. Like Carac, Soryk brooded over Sidra's fidelity and dismissed any paternal claim to her child. She couldn't be his, could she? He didn't want the responsibility of his own child. He suffered enough managing Sorykah's twins.

Dunya returned with a wad of fabric. "Shush, me dove." Dunya nuzzled the white blanket, audibly sniffing the baby. "She smells like 'er mum, all woodsy and clean." Dunya thrust the bundle toward Soryk. "Take a whiff, it's lovely."

Soryk shrunk back as if from a poisonous viper. "No! I don't want her!"

Insulted on the baby's behalf, Ayeda began to cry. A model of solidarity, Leander offered his own lusty bellows. To complement the duo, Sidra's child added her own thin cry to the chorus. Soryk blocked his ears against the infants' indignant wails. He couldn't bear those cries; they pierced and deflated him, left him ragged. Lurching toward the door, Soryk thrust himself into the sanctity of the tunnel. Somatics grouped at the junction ahead. Soryk longed to speak to them and learn how the city had so quickly degraded, but his eyes swam with tears and he did not want to be seen. He ran into the western tunnel where sounds of mourning echoed. A woman sobbed and an animal whined in pain. There was too much sorrow here. Soryk collapsed against a snarl of bared tree roots. Whose heartache did he carry? There was no halving of emotion, no sleepy subliminal distress pushing and tugging at him. Sidra integrated Soryk/ah with pleasure and again with pain.

"*She wanted ye so badly at the end.*" The end, the end. The termination of Sidra's short and wonderfully sweet life. It was not right that she should leave him just when the bloom of romance spread full petals, opening itself to lushness. How many years had he lost while submerged within his primary? His own experience was a frayed and wavering line lost among heavy, meandering scrawls. The gnawing unfairness of it worried him like a bone between a puppy's sharp teeth. Her loss was an unintended injury. Though innocent, the teeth still cut.

Where is my little elfin queen? Lost, lost.

Her voice leaden within their shared awareness, Sorykah warned, *She's left you behind to sort out her mess. You cannot have her back. You've only the memory of her skin and her giggle to tide you over throughout the ordeal of this unbearable, quick-change life. Those things will wane and you'll forget soon enough. One distant day, she'll be nothing but a faded stain upon your recollection of this era. But run and she'll come creeping after you, a phantom on your heels. You cannot leave this place behind.*

Sidra's cure had become a curse—alter and primary at last thinking with one brain, speaking with one voice. Soryk would howl like a wolf to show his grief but no amount of anguish would make time dance a retreat, subtract the fatal semen from Sidra's womb and cast the baby back into the foam.

Every moment existed within its own fragile suspension. Balance was easily lost, regret all-consuming. When Carac staggered down the tunnel toward Soryk, the par-wolf's eyes red and bleary, his gait clumsy from an excess of drink, it upset Soryk's frail equilibrium. Pitched into a terrible fury, Soryk lunged at Carac. Carac went down easily, a scarecrow knocked from his perch. His gaze was cowed and pathetic, his once handsome salt-and-pepper fur turned grimy and foul. He reeked of Sidra's herbal liqueur.

Soryk attacked the par-wolf, pummeling his slack muzzle, the lurid flopping tongue that had surely been put to use in a hundred crass ways. Too drunk to land a punch, Carac fought back clumsily. Soryk soon abandoned the sport. He could feel Sidra's hot disapproving stare and hear the reproach in her voice.

Soryk crawled off, panting. Carac staggered to his feet, swung at Soryk, and missed.

"Your fault!" Carac howled. "All your fault! We were fine till you showed up." Carac swigged homebrew from a wineskin and sobbed, falling against the tunnel wall and gouging out chunks of earth.

Soryk turned and ran back to Dunya's. The dog-faced girl and the twins wore matching blue smocks. She'd smoothed Ayeda and Leander's hair down with grease until it looked painted on. He wanted to laugh at the shiny incongruity of their patent-leather heads and dour smocks, but he could not.

"Mourning clothes. Made 'em meself. Did a pretty good job, too."

Soryk murmured dull agreement. He couldn't believe that Sidra was dead. Questions sat like stones sewn into his gut.

"There's one for ye as well, if ye like. Ye can grieve in peace as long as yer smocked. No one'll laugh at ye if ye cry."

Soryk's mouth was too chalky to speak. He took the proffered smock but didn't put it on.

"Mourners comin'. I tell ye, ye couldn't 'ave got 'ere a minute later. Get in line; we're gone to ring the bells and light the pyre."

Big bronze bells clanged with shrill clappers and palms beat a tattoo upon skin drums. Shaking ring-rattles of tiny bones, the funeral parade passed outside Dunya's door, all the Erun's somatics smocked and wailing, two vertical lines of blue pigment marking their faces from forehead to cheeks. The somatics had become a warring tribe, decorated for their battle with death.

"Grab yerself a baby and let's go. The 'ole city's been waitin' for ye." Dunya took the girls and joined the procession.

Soryk and Leander fell into line. A few Erunites nodded a greeting; others gave him hard stares and some ignored him completely. The mourners wended through long tunnels to a distant exit and filed up stone steps into the forest. They came into a clearing, where jagged peaks of slate sheared like guillotine blades from the mountainside and trees grappled for root space in boulder-pocked soil. These were the ruins—what remained of Matuk's long-defunct construction project on the southern side of the Glass Mountains. The corridor he'd used to transport marble to his manor had collapsed years ago, and the site abandoned, leaving behind a junkyard of white marble blocks split by time and weather.

The ruins were the only place in the forest open enough to bear a fire and accommodate the somatics who traveled from as far north as Dirinda, Bokhara, and Auburn to pay respects to their deceased queen. There were three brothers from the Merciful Father's Charity Hospital and several men Soryk did not recognize and did not want to know. For three days, blue-smocked mourners poured into the forest, their faces pinched by anguish. Though it seemed that their population was strong, its numbers had diminished, victim to the night train's campaign of slaughter. They arrived weeping and forlorn; the death of their queen was the death of hope. They sought only a taste of ashes, the chance to press their thumbs into her gray remains and transfer a bit of her to their tongues after the pyre cooled.

Swathed in bleached linen, Sidra the Lovely lay in state atop a pyre of white birch branches. Someone had brushed her hair satin-smooth, wiped the dirt from her face, and laid a crown of white blossoms upon her brow. The scab-capped tips of her tumorous horns were greased with cerulean mourning pigment. She didn't look like herself at all. Not just marble-smooth and hard, but scrubbed clean and transformed into someone else's vision of a queen. Not his Sidra, crouching to whisk up some earthy concoction of seeds and leaves, a grin pinned to her mouth. Not his grubby darling, her bright eyes sparkling with mischievous desire. This person was a stranger.

Soryk pulled at the linen. Sidra's hand was blue-nailed and iced with frost. Whatever frail suture keeping him together worked loose, a zipper unzipping to dump his guts on the ground. He was turned inside out, wearing his skin backward, all his nerves and vessels exposed to the air. Someone took his elbow and pulled him away, propelling him into the swelling crowd. Hands tugged Leander from his grip and he surrendered the boy to a somatic woman, who patted his back in clumsy sympathy.

Services commenced with the lighting of fireflies. Young Pieter was first to lay his posy of oak and acorns on Sidra's chest. His pink eyes crinkled and swerved, striving to manifest some last vision of his guardian. One after another, mourners filed past Sidra's bier to pay their respects. Many pressed kisses to her dead hand. Others heaped flowers or small gifts on her chest until the mound overflowed, obscuring her face and tumbling to the dirt.

Hans my Hedgehog's hands shook so badly that their pointed black nails clicked together. Nervous shivers shook his quills, making that clattering reedlike rustle Sidra had so loved. An autumn breeze cut through the trees and made the leaves clap and dance. All of these things served to muffle Hans's voice so that his eulogy was but a whisper, a suggestion in the minds of the somatics gathered to entomb their queen.

Dunya took comfort from the children, cordoning herself against sorrow with their squidgy bodies. She displayed amazing strength until drunken Carac broke ranks, fell to his knees, and loosed a real wolf cry, piercing and grief-stricken. Carac's outburst signaled the others to vent their anguish. The rather orderly congregation went wild. Braying, barking, and moaning, their hysteria startled the birds from the trees. Ravens swarmed skyward, a whirling storm of inky feathers. Dunya keened like a professional, as much in sympathy for Carac as Sidra. Infested by ghosts, the Erun grew grim and cold beneath darkening clouds. The babies began to cry. Carac loped around the pyre, teeth gnashing and foaming before he broke for the trees and vanished.

Hans put a flask in Pieter's hand, and the boy followed Carac's circuit, lashing oil at the pyre, staining Queen Sidra's linens with accelerant. Hans took a flint fire starter and lit the first taper of rolled beeswax. Somatics shuffled forward, candles extended to catch a flame. Without Sidra to call the burning, they dallied, uncertain flames wavering. Prayers and rites did not sing themselves—they squirmed unseen like the maggots in Sidra's mouth. Hans my Hedgehog took the lead, his quivering lips parted to sing his queen into the next world as dripping wicks found drops of oil, consumed them, and began to burn.

THUNDER RATTLED THE SKY and rain showered down. It was just the sort of storm Sidra would have delighted in, a lightning-crack deluge that turned the paths to mud and amplified all colors and sharp green scents. Sidra's final jest, putting out her own funeral pyre. Tasked with keeping the fire lit despite the rain, the brothers from the charity hospital walked around the pyre, putting their torches to the birch and turning the flames into waiting gaps of air. Wood, then flesh, blazed. Despite the freshening rain, the air stunk of burnt hair.

"Ain't ye going to say a fare-thee-well to yer lady?" Dunya sidled up to Soryk, Sidra's child in her arms. The baby was no bigger than a loaf of bread. Her little face, as red and damp as a newborn's, scrunched itself into puppy wrinkles. Locked in the throes of dreams, the child writhed and moaned.

She must know that her mum is gone, thought Soryk. *She dreads what awaits her, as do we all.*

Dunya thrust the baby at Soryk, but her hands would not relinquish her. She clutched that baby, her fingers knotted in swaddling, tears dribbling down her cheeks and wetting her fur. Afraid that Dunya might drop her, Soryk took the infant. He did not realize that she was losing another child. She thought that this baby would be hers to keep, given that no one else seemed fit to care for her after

Sidra's death, but tacked to the head of the baby's cradle was a square parchment envelope cut and glued by hand, Soryk's name scrawled across its face. The ink was blue-black now instead of mahogany, but retained its fragrance of ash and resin, acerbic and strong. Sorykah would later run her tongue over the letters of her alter's name, resisting the urge to cut the paper into small squares and soak them in extracting alcohol to distill Sidra's last words and needle them forever beneath her skin.

The child curled against Soryk's chest, a tiny furled bud. Distress furrowed her brow, and her dark hair stuck straight up from her head. Sorrow shrouded Soryk's heart; he could barely breathe. The eyes of all the somatics fixed upon him, glazed with grief. His throat ached. His eyes stung and he blinked to clear them. Sidra's words resounded with gruesome new clarity: *"Feeding like a fire, Amidst a mound of ashes, A change to break the coming world."*

Together Soryk and Sidra's child stood at the brink of a precipice with the wind at their backs, eager to tumble them over its edge. What would happen to the Erun city without its ruler? How would the somatics defend themselves against the night train's assaults and the growing chaos in Neubonne and the cities of the Sigue?

There are dark days ahead. Pray that there is a light to repel the gloom. Oh my darling, Soryk thought, *why did you abandon us?*

The pyre raged behind him. White smoke streamed skyward. Rain wet his face as the somatics began a chant, bending to sweep their knuckles along the ground and rising in a wide swinging arc to fling leaves into the air, voices like fists to pummel the gods for taking back their daughter.

The baby nuzzled against him, seeking milk. This hungry little orphaned grub was Sidra's legacy, not his. She stared at him, her gaze startlingly cogent, rosy lips open in an O of astonishment. Soryk sensed her dismay at this new predicament that bound them, an unlikely team of left-behinds. He wanted to hand her off to Dunya and run like Carac, his feet pounding the loam as he left this tragedy behind, but he owed it to Sidra to protect her daughter. Soryk pressed the baby to his chest and sensed her drawing comfort from the strong, steady beating of his heart. It was all he could offer her.

Soryk lifted Sidra's final missive from the baby's blanket and unwrapped it one-handedly. There was just enough light to make out the words:

> *I am too much alone. This strange wild life I have chosen is a fickle companion. I tire of it and the sometimes-silence that flits around me like a bird. So I kept her, thinking not that illness would take me and leave her here, a babe in woods, but that she would rise and grow like a sunflower to wash away the gray. Between us, she was the divine spark, the culmination of our two energies, fierce and electric. Her name is Teszla, and she is yours.*

Acknowledgments

Selections taken from the poem "The Goblin Market" by Christina Rossetti (1865).

Thank you to my wonderful husband, Anthony, for cheering me on, giving me time to work in peace, and graciously supporting my chai habit. Much appreciation goes to the brilliant women of the Page a Day Writer's Group—Ondine Kuraoka, Deborah Ayers, Claire Yezbak Fadden, Trish Wilkinson, and Sharon Cooper—for sharing this marvelous journey with me, and for their insightful feedback and support up until the stroke of midnight on deadline day. (http://pageadaywriters.wordpress.com) Many thanks to my dear friend Gayle Feallock, for counseling me on the necessity of hope and somewhat-happy endings. Thanks again to Skyler Mills, my technical expert for all things submarine.

Visit me online at www.IceSong.com, or follow my Twitter feed @kirstenikasai.

KIRSTEN IMANI KASAI writes dark fantasy, horror, and erotic fiction. She lives in Southern California with her husband, children, a dog, and a frog, and yes, she's been inked. Visit her at IceSong.com or at Facebook.com/Kirstenimanikasai.

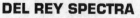